House
o f
N o th

A **M**YTH OVER **M**IDDLE-MERE

by Philip Wortmann

Contents:

*There is
only one way into the contents of this
book,
I'm afraid.*

The door is the

 *page.*

Turn it,

*and a little world shall open in your
palm.*

Part I:

of the Return

to the End

Chapter One
A Long Shadow Cast

The dark timbers of the house cracked in the cool of nightfall. The flames of the brazier snapped in rhythm with the creaking of an aged chair on which sat an elder man. Atop his head was perched, at a skew angle, a felt cap. His wife had made it for him last autumn, and already it looked ten years old. His fur-lined cloak was wrapped tight about his weary form and he, smiling contentedly at the last red of sundown, stretched weathered hands leathery toward the flames. He sat atop his hill. The stoop of his house, raised slightly by stilted legs, fell steeply away with the grey of the crags beneath.

Before him the hard turf was a sea of red and faded green, spilled dun by the twilight. The hill whence his gaze went out looked into the west, where, across the river, the foothills began to climb into the snow-clothed mountains beyond. Amongst the nearest of the foothills, stood Glimwæth, the wooden city of Imnir. It sat astride its fell like Imnir himself might have straddled his loyal bear in the days of a faraway past.

"Oh how that great man's beard must have flown like a banner in the west-wind! How his mane must have caught the breath of the mountains!" said the elder huddled by the brazier on his stoop.

"What's that dear?" came the loyal voice of his beloved from the golden warmth within his humble home.

"Oh, I was just thinking of our forebears again, heart. There's nothing that needs worry you!" replied the elder man.

"The dinner's ready, dear, if you'll come inside," said she then.

"In just a moment, heart. The sun is almost dark," replied the elder man.

When the last of the iron heavens had lost their bluing hue, the elder watcher on the hill arose from the chair with a creak (this time the creaking of his bones), and began to shuffle toward the doorway, when another thing caught his eye.

"Now what is this that weathered wends its way towards us?" he muttered to himself.

Below a shadowy shape had emerged from the woods and was winding up the cairn-marked path towards him.

"The dinner's ready, dear!" his wife's voice issued from comfortable behind once more.

"Is there enough for three?" asked the elder watchman, resting his hands on his hips and narrowing his eyes.

"What now, dear?" came the loyal voice.

The elder watchman descended the stairs and crossed the small yard to their bleached gate. It was set in the chalk of neat-cut stone which walled off the crown of their little hill. The horses neighed disquietly in their neighbouring stable — from which a shale tile presently tumbled to the dark earth.

He opened the gate and chained it to the pale wall for the moment. He waited a while longer, his wife coming out behind him to see for herself what mystery had delayed her man this time. A frown creased her furrowed brow and she folded her arms in the neat manner that had drawn her otherwise husband to her in long-ago years.

Then the dark stranger came to a steady halt some four paces from the gate. He leaned on a tall, black staff with one hand, but he was so weary that he bent also heavily on his knees, the breath making ghastly patterns before his hooded face. A cloak was wrapped about him, all leathery with the hide of an unknown behemoth. Darker than the leather, however, were the unmasked fingers of this well-wrapped traveller, marking him as one of those proud men that hailed from the faraway south.

"You have trekked here from the other-most end of the earth, brother! Come indoors and eat some dinner!" Said the watchman, adding slyly: "My wife will carry you in, if those well-worn knees are too well worn for walking,"

His beloved at the door sighed.

The stranger tried laughing. He seemed not to have enough breath for it, however, and so he gathered himself again. Finally he said: "Pardon me, friend. That was good. I take it she rules this hillock well?"

"Oh with an iron fist, brother," said the elder man with a jester's grimace and a shake of the head. "I warn you, you may dine with us, but then you'll have to enjoy it too!"

The southern stranger laughed again, and said, "This long journey has made me finally obedient, it seems. I will gladly join your table, and try to do so meekly. Fear not; my only weapon is this ebon stick, and my face is friendly by the light of homely hearth."

At this the stranger lowered his deep hood, revealing the black curls of a wayfarer's long beard and the wild hair of one that could do well with a bath. "I am Gaba, friends. Well met," said the southerner.

"Hail, brother. Come in and eat now. We are called Watcher by name, for our clan has been so long atop this hill," said the elder man, motioning his guest toward the front door. As they entered, Mrs. Watcher going to tend to the meal again, her husband continued: "This watch has been passed father to son to son's son for six generations!"

Mr. Watcher took staff, pack, and cloak from his guest, and laid them neatly on a bench near the door. "Here lie your things, should we turn to goblins in the night and the need for flight takes you." At which something tumbled from the stranger's leathery cloak, landing with a twanging sound upon the wrinkled floorboards. It was a wooden bowl of sorts with tines of metal bending over its mouth like glittering teeth.

"What is this?" muttered Mr. Watcher, more to himself than his guest as he picked the thing up in his hand.

"That is a device for playing melodies. It is a remembrance that was given me by one whom I love," said the southerner.

"Ah! Then I dare not tarnish it any longer with my unlearned hands! We are honoured to have you in our home, brother skald," said the elder man.

4

"Thank you," said Gaba the southerner. "Might it be that there is a seventh son to take over this hall from his father's care, where we speak of dear ones?"

"From mother's care, more like," Mrs. Watcher corrected with a stern glance, and they all laughed.

But then a sudden and solemn colour took the air — the fire pit's golden dimming somewhat yellow. "There was once such a son, who would have made much more of what we had than we could ever have. But our land is coarse, brother," said Mr. Watcher. "It will take from you what it wants, son, daughter, house, steed; and if you cannot stomach that …"

A long pause settled on the room.

"You will stomach this, I hope," said Mrs. Watcher finally, holding her hand toward the table that she had set for them.

"Most certainly!" said Gaba. "About your son, though, I am aggrieved to hear it. You are worthy parents in your care-taking, that much you have already proven."

"Yes, thank you, brother. Perhaps too good in the care-taking, and not enough in the carpentering. I think we could have weathered some of the softness from the boy, but such thoughts are futile," sighed Mr. Watcher, and looked sadly at his beloved. She returned a sad smile. "But he was a good lad until the end. He had a noble heart, and that is what the king remembers him for as well."

They sat down at the table. The Watchers sitting on a bench nearer the back wall, the southerner with his back toward the firepit. Before each was some bread and a wooden bowl of steaming stew.

"He was held in honour by the king? The noble descendant of Imnir that now sits in Glimwæth's hall?" Gaba said, astounded.

"Sooth," said Mr. Watcher with a proud smile.

"He stood against a long and dreadful shadow which in recent years has not grown shorter for all the brave blood that has spilled into it," whispered Mrs. Watcher, and let her grey head sink onto the shoulder of her man.

"What shadow might this be? Your lands have seemed friendly enough so far, I thought while adventuring hither that the king's thanes were mighty men indeed to keep such peace in lands that are rumoured to be so wild," said Gaba, leaning forward as he blew the steam from his spoonful. He shovelled down the bite hungrily, announcing his satisfaction as he punctuated his question with the words: "Oh, venison! Very good!"

He smiled merrily at Mrs. Watcher.

She smiled tiredly back.

"There is a terrible fiend about this part, brother. It is a creature as no other, though it has been here, then east, then here again; travelling as do the winds with the seasons. There into the east it often goes — into the steppes where the nomads roam."

"What kind of creature might this be?" pressed Gaba, he had lowered his spoon again, and his face was now intent on the watchman.

The elder man looked uncertainly at his beloved.

6

She shook her head slowly. Fear was in her eyes.

"Such things are better left for daylight, brother," said Mr. Watcher then.

"Haven't we borrowed some here?" Gaba pointed to the fire-pit with a chuckle meant to soothe them; but they were not moved. Their faces were still all with fear.

"By night, brother, this borrowed light is snuffed like a candle by the closer friends of dark," said Mr. Watcher.

The southerner nodded, raising his palms to his hosts in acknowledgement of their words. "Then I shall not press the matter further."

They continued to eat by the music of the fire and the singing of the winds.

"Your journey must have been quite some feat, brother. Tell us, what drives you so far into the dark world here north, where we all look as though we've sprouted from the snow?" the watchman asked when the silence might have become a strain.

Gaba laughed and shook his head. Then he nodded, as though noting something for himself. He looked kindly up at his hosts, and said, "Shadows as long as those you speak of."

Suddenly a thunderous gale struck the dwelling, causing its steady timbers to cringe and squeal with strain. The yellow fires flickered and the window-shutters came loose from their hooks, slamming a frightful drumbeat against the wall outside. The nets of garlic and the dried meat hanging from the rafters overhead whirled and rocked as though the building were at sea.

Then there was quiet.

The Watchers, who had flown into one another's embraces, came slowly apart and began to look with ashen faces all about the room. Then Mr. Watcher let his eyes land frightened on the traveller before them, and he uttered: "Was that your doing, master?"

"Go on calling me brother, master, for I am just as frightened as you seem!" said Gaba, climbing quickly from his bench.

"Whatever it was seems to have settled again," Mr. Watcher dared.

"Yet now outside is far, far quieter than it was just before," said Mrs. Watcher.

Gaba made his way to his staff, taking it into his hardened hands as though readying for battle. "I think your wariness does you credit, my lady," he said, still looking from one end of the house to the other. Presently some onions fell from the rafters to the floor, and Mrs. Watcher started, covering her face with her hands.

When nothing more happened she began to laugh at herself and her husband chuckled as well, patting her gently on the back.

"What power onion has over us simple folk! It makes us weep when it is cut, it makes us fright when it falls! All that's needed is a dim light and the proper noise, and we jump out of our socks," the old man laughed, shaking his head.

"As long as you don't jump out of your socks, Mr. Watcher! I don't want you catching a cold," said his wife recovering her sense for scolding after her scare.

But this time it was Gaba who would not be soothed, for the silence in the air outside was, as Mrs. Watcher had said, quite unlike the babble of the natural world at night.

"Oh, sit, brother, and finish your stew. It'll get cold if you don't!" said Mr. Watcher with another chuckle at this southerner's wariness.

Gaba was about to make his reply when a boulder hurtled through the doorway, striking clean the fire-pit and extinguishing the flames.

Darkness and noise.

There came the cries of the Watchers from the dark, and the sound of tripping and falling. There was desperate movement, and then frightened silence all around. The world here north was dark indeed, though tonight it was not for a long wintering as Mr. Watcher had meant it. The borrowed light of the firepit had been snuffed out. Outside the open door that led into the night, now faintly traced by light of stars beyond, a tall figure could be seen to lurk like a long shadow in the dark.

The southerner pressed his back against the wall near the doorway. He kept his breathing low and strained to hear with all his might.

A low growl issued from that tall devil in the dark beyond the door. Then there was the sound of metal on metal and chain linked with chain — a sound which Gaba had failed to hear with this creature's approach. The ground shook with every step the creature took as it strode toward the dwelling of the Watchers. It stepped again and again, and then the crushing sound of cracking stone broke on the air, for the beast had stepped onto the chalk-stone wall outside. It growled again, and Gaba dared to peek around the corner.

The creature stood some two men tall, he made out, with long and lithe limbs, and it appeared crowned by two curving horns as the mountain goats that take great care to move their heavy heads. It seemed to stand there an endless time, looking down as though the breaking of the wall had caused it pause. Then it stepped back with another growl and what sounded like a chuckle, and it strode back down the hillock, eastward, whence it must have come. Like so many strings dangling from forlorn gallows, the fraying cloth of its robes whipped about its lumbering form in the nightly breeze.

When Gaba could see it no longer, and the sounds of its footsteps could no more be discerned from the other sounds of night, the southerner dared to call out to his hosts.

"Watchers! Watchers, are you there? Are you still with us, or have you gone to join the six generations in the earth?"

A timid owl began to hoot somewhere in the trees below.

"We are still here," said Mr. Watcher weakly. "Though I feel as though I have crawled out of my own skin with fright!"

"You've crawled out of that hat I made for you, Mr. Watcher, and nothing else!" replied his beloved, and Gaba sagged with relief, sliding down the wall against which he was pressed until he was sitting on the floorboards.

"I would offer light, dear brother, but I fear that it may draw again the wrath of that long shadow," said Mr. Watcher apologetically.

"There is no need to worry, my friends," said Gaba. "I could sleep where I now sit, hearing that the night-birds have begun talking again. Perhaps we can call on your noble king when the daylight is less easily snuffed out and our bodies have rested from their fright."

"I like that thought, brother," said Mr. Watcher, "but our duty is to light the beacon when some danger has struck us, and we still have hands to do so. I have nothing left to lose — save my hospitality. But, for the sake of catching this shadow that has robbed us of so much, I will give up even that. Understand me without bitterness, my brother, but this is why we live on hither hill, and not within the safe walls of Glimwæth."

"I understand it, friend, and applaud it! That sounds like a captain's plan in battle," said Gaba. "I will even light the beacon myself. Now that I have measured the beast that dwells in these parts, I would even stand against it without shying. I was merely caught by surprise. Would you tell me where the beacon is to be found, then I will leave you to gather yourselves from the fright."

"The beacon is behind the stables," said Mr. Watcher, "just next to this house. Make sure it is fully ablaze, so that it is not mistaken by the wardens on the city wall. They will send out riders as soon as they see it; though I wonder whether they shall send enough. We in the meanwhile will go into the cave that is cleft into the western face of this hill. The hall of my fathers. I shall wait for you at the mouth of it when your brightling work is done. Unless the shadow can tear open hillsides, he will not catch us there."

For a moment Gaba stared at what he could make out to be the boulder the beast had hurled. Then he said "very well", flung his cloak about his shoulders, and went outdoors.

He crossed to the stables, where he found the doors to have been flung wide, and an uncanny silence to have settled. This caused him to stop with caution, but he shook himself and returned to the duty at hand, striding past the wooden building to where an ancient tower of moss-cloaked stone leaned like a warning finger into heaven above.

He near ran up the rungs until he could drag himself into the tower's nest. Here he touched his ebon staff to a vast well of stone in which a great piling of beams on kindling had been set. In the twinkling of an eye a great, white flame burst to life in the heart of the pile, and Gaba stepped back watching to make certain the fire spread evenly through the wood.

When he had finished his 'brightling work' (so 'brightling' that one may have mistaken the beacon for dawn's early return), he himself returned to the hill's rugged turf and was taken aback to find Mr. Watcher standing there with an open mouth and a make-shift torch in his hand.

"I thought that you might need something to kindle that blaze with, but I mistook you for someone who has made fires less often than I. That was handy work!" said Mr. Watcher.

"Some might have called it witchcraft," the southerner chuckled, amused by Mr. Watchers wide-eyed face.

"Some," Mr. Watcher agreed.

"I hear no horses in the stable," said Gaba then, remembering the eerie silence that had come from there.

"Oh, yes! The horses! They've gone," said Mr. Watcher lowering his now bitter face into his one free hand. "They must have bolted when the wind blew open their doors. A sad thing that, but we have more pressing matters to deal with, I think."

"I think so as well," said Gaba, and he followed his host down a hind path that led to the cavern of which he had been told earlier. It was comfortably arranged with beds and a firepit of its own. Perhaps it had been used for guests before. The buried fathers of Mr. Watcher must have lain deeper in. There the three of them waited to hear the sounding of the city watch's coming, speaking at whiles about what they had just endured.

"Is this the shadow which took from you your son?" Gaba asked at one time.

"Just so," said Mr. Watcher with a menace that the southerner had not thought possible in so kindly-seeming a man. "That shadow is a creature said to have sprung from the bogs in the east. It is a bandit called the Ibex, often said to be followed by a fell host of brigands. I am glad that it was alone tonight."

13

As night drew on, they began to doze, their heads nodding to their knees as they sat about the fire-pit. Eventually Mrs. Watcher climbed into one of the beds of the cave, and Mr. Watcher was not long to follow. But Gaba sat by the fire, leaning wearily against his staff. He had had many restless nights along the road; many were the burdens that were laded on his spirit's shoulders, pressing sleep away from his dark eyes.

Finally a grey light began to trickle through the cave's narrow mouth, and a horn could be heard to call out above. The Watchers sat up blearily in their bed, looking from side to side, slowly remembering the last night's dread, and then they recognised the horn that had been sounded as that of the city watch. The king's men had come.

Chapter Two
Sealed with a Kiss

As dawn broke over the glittering spears of the men newly arrived, the heavy sound of their approach and the sounding of their horn drove a raven into the waking heavens. From the top of the Watchers' house the raven lifted itself crowing upward on black wings. It climbed eastward, over the wooded hills that rolled away and down into the deep vales between the sheer country of the children of Imnir and the great steppes in the east.

There, finally, great swaths of a thousand different grasses began to stretch away before the black bird's careful gaze. From so faraway a height the sparse spinneys of aspen that clothed the edges of rivers were like seedlings in the dun of that vast land. There the corsac foxes hunted gerbil; ants that crawl amidst blades of grass to the raven's eye. Great elks roamed the broad moors, and in the craggy outcrops of jagged stone that pressed past the earth, where long-dry rivers once had done their work, brown bears roamed and groaned to make sure none dared bother their routine.

The further this raven pressed into those eastern steppes the more regular the sight of a tall henge became — a stone circle standing up like a dusty wheel of giant's teeth; waiting, waiting in the endless weathering of days; waiting, waiting for the final falling of the iron heavens above and the end of all things.

And then, like a broad wyrm that snakes across that distant land of lights and shadows, a thick river wound this way then that. From the north-west it rove into the south-east. From faraway seas of ice to the not-so-far Middle-mere, the sea along which all strands of the countries in the north meet.

There, along that river, the raven spied out what it had sought: a village with the smell of weirdness about it. There lay a village pitched of tents, smoking white clouds by campfires in the breaking of the morning light.

Yes, in this country rove great rivers through even greater steppes — a land of wonder and mystery, for here no king had yet claimed regency, and the roaming chieftains of the nomads looked more to their people than their land. Here a hillock raised its grassy head, there a bog raised its foul stench, as its filthy water bubbled in rhythm to the hidden tread of wild things. It was in this vast land, which would have easily been called empty by unwatchful eyes, that there dwelt a people that were of cursed blood.

To be certain all people, when they are burdened by the mistakes of their forefathers, regard themselves cursed; but these were burdened, not merely by the mistakes of their forefathers, but with their own nature. It was because of their nature that they had been driven out of the lands of their forebears, because they were the children of a bitter union: that of light and dust. They were called by most "the river-people", because they would settle for a time alongside a river, where the ground was good, and then they would move, when the time came, to another part of the river. Because of this, the river-people never built great houses, nor did they have many unnecessary ornaments. They were a nomadic people, ever on the move, and dwelt in tents of hide.

The raven circled down into the village of tents it had spotted from the cloud-speckled firmament above, coming to rest with a croak atop the boughs of a willow near the broad river. There it pecked at the bark of its new roost, now crying out, now warbling wordless murmurs.

Three women that were doing the washing of their families on the nearby rocks spared only a moment now and then to admire the boastful bird, before they returned to their tidy work.

"It reminds me of Authæn," said a little girl with red hair, helping her mother wring the water from a sheet.

"He also can speak much without saying anything," said another woman called Wingilin, A close friend of Authæn, and they all laughed, save the little girl.

"I meant because of its black coat!" said the little girl, not having understood the jest. The black-and-gold of her lion-like eyes flashed defiantly. All river-people had such eyes, set deeply in the smooth grey of their skin. Their hair was most often black, though sometimes they were found with red or yellow hair as well.

The young woman who was well-befriended with Authæn said with soothing words, "I was only jesting, kitten. He does have a handsome head of hair."

"Have you heard when he is to return from the henge, Wingilin?" the mother of the little girl asked.

"I thought that he would have returned for my father's birthday, but alas, he has probably been distracted by some aged stone or other along the road," Wingilin said, sighing and looking into the north whence the river rove. There somewhere lay the henge that was tethered to the father of their race. They were the river-people of the river Wirthaumuin, named after the immortal shepherd of their henge. Wirthaumuin, the shepherd under whom Authæn had taken up his lessons.

At that moment the sound of hooves hammered across the riverbank. The scouts had returned, their eagles descending to alight on their arms as they reigned in their stout steppe horses, bringing them to a halt not ten metres from where the women were doing their washing. One after the other they dismounted, weary for their hard journey.

"Hail scouts! What does the wold rumour?" Wingilin called out to them.

The captain of the scouts, a tall fellow with broad shoulders, looked up with a question on his brow. Who had called out to him? But when he saw that it was Wingilin, the daughter of his chieftain, his furrows drew straight, and he smiled, saying: "We saw nothing, and the eagles whisper little of importance, dear Wingilin."

"If you saw nothing, it is clear you were sleeping in your saddle, captain," said Wingilin slyly.

The captain's men laughed, but he was not embarrassed. The old wives in the village had whispered that he loved Wingilin, and she had done nothing to silence those whispers.

"Then it was grass we saw, dear Wingilin," said the captain, "grass that moved as though dancing in the wind. It's weaving as graceful as the great swans of the Mountain Queen. Grass moving as though dancing in the beating of eagles' wings. We saw grass, dear Wingilin, grass that caught the rain and washed its humble threads with care and gentleness."

Wingilin blushed, and turned away. The other two women smiled at one another knowingly. The men sported raised brows and nodded approvingly to one another as though they had all been fairly bested in some unseen contest.

"Grass withers and fades, captain," said Wingilin quietly.

"All things wither and fade," said the captain. His face was suddenly drained of the light that had only a moment before hung upon his eyes, and he looked past the lady that had long held his heart, into the river where she had been washing her threads. "It is the nature of that which moves that it should one day move away."

"Or towards," said Wingilin, taking a careless step out of the river, returning her eyes now glowing back to meet those of the callous scout.

At this the captain stepped suddenly back a stride, caught off his guard. Everyone was quiet. Then his features softened, and he strode towards Wingilin without further hesitation. She stood there, waiting hopefully, until he picked her up in his arms, swung her about and kissed her heartily on the mouth. Cheers broke forth from all that watched, and heartfelt laughter. This was a sight that many had not dared to imagine, in case the tensions between these two important people were to lead to feud; but here was joy and final, wonderful satisfaction. They had found happily into one another's arms.

"What is this treachery, Huthram?" boomed a voice that caused all merrymaking suddenly to cease. The chieftain of the village had come, Wingilin's father.

But Huthram, the captain of the scouts, held Wingilin in his arms, and did not let her go. She struggled against his embrace a moment, looking one way then the next in a sudden panic. But at the last she looked up into the eyes of the man that held her, and there she saw what stilled her hammering heart. He was trusting and trustworthy. He was there and not a motion in all his countenance betrayed the desire to depart.

"This is only treachery, my chieftain, if I now betray this one I love," said Huthram, and Wingilin laid her ear to his chest, closing her eyes, trying not to hear what would come next, listening only for the warmth of his wizened heart.

For a moment the stern features of the chieftain grew graver still. Then they gave and softened with the shadow of a smile.

"Then I shall perhaps still have a son, even in my old age. A son adopted by the solemn rite of marriage!" declared the chief, and again cheers broke out amongst his people. "Still," the chief continued, "I would have your report of the past few days' ride, Huthram."

"At once, my chieftain!" replied Huthram, turning his smiling eyes to meet those of his beloved's father, and Wingilin detached herself slowly from his arms.

Huthram joined his chieftain, and together the two great men made their way by the flapping tents to where the great table had been set near the middle of the village. This ornamented table was called the council-board, a place where all the most important matters of the village were discussed by the chief and his elders, and where the weekly moot was held. Above this heavy board of oak, a conical roof had been built, thatched in the manner of the western folk that often passed through this land with goods to trade. Those were the children of long-ago Imnir.

"What is the rumour of the wind, Huthram?" the chieftain asked gruffly. He was a man that looked in all regards to be a walrus, barely trying to hide himself in the form of a man, though he wore the stout wool that his wife knitted for him, and he was donned with the cloak of his fathers.

"It is quiet, uncle," said Huthram. "There is nothing more than the usual danger. No great bands of raiders were seen, no roaming wolf packs greater than the usual. All seems quiet this week."

"So quiet that you have decided it may be a good time to settle?" said the chieftain.

Huthram looked up at the other, a tense question tugging the strings of his mien. "It is a good thing that an eagle has an eyrie, and that a ship has an anchor," said the captain of the scouts.

"And that a tree has roots," said the chieftain, nodding unexpectedly, "for otherwise it can draw no food and no water from the ground. But let us regard the tree for a moment, my son, for that is what you are now, you are my son. Your decision has been made and now you must carry whatever burden it lays on you.

"The tree is manifold, yet it is one. It has branches to catch the sun and wind, roots to hold the earth below and draw up its nourishment, and it bears leaves at the right time, shedding them after. The tree, when it is healthy, bears much fruit; yet the tree does not eat its own fruits. Do you understand what I am saying, my son?"

"A tree should not be at war with itself," said Huthram.

"Perhaps, but more frightful: a tree at war with itself is a hideous thing, and yet possible; a blight on the land that feeds it. That is your charge now, my son. Do not be at war with your other parts. Carry out this marriage you desire as well as you have all your other duties, and you will bring blessing to us all."

"Thank you, uncle," said Huthram.

"Father now, Huthram. Father. We have a wedding feast to arrange, it seems," said the chieftain.

The news of the wedding spread throughout the village like fire through dry grass. It was always the first thing to be discussed when a group of villagers met, and the last thing mentioned before their gathering disbanded.

The village of Thænim on Wirthaumuin was not very large, being part of the smallest of the clans of the river-people. Wirthaumuin's river-people were eagle-bonded, where other clans were known for riding reindeer, taming wolves, or communing with the Queen of Swans herself when she descended from the mountains with her great birds. Therefore, when so large a feast as this stood afore, the whole village offered helping hands to make the most of the celebration.

Most of the families of Thænim began baking cakes and treats for the festival as soon as they caught wind of what was to come. Those skilled in carpentry, as well as their children and apprentices, began to shape wonderful totems that would be placed along the ritual ground according to the web of stars above, and according to the histories of the two lives that were about to intertwine. There was also the matter of a tent, for it was custom for the new beginnings of a family to be granted a new home by their village, showing that the village received them well.

For this task the great tent-maker had been summoned, Nimith the Arm. He was a man that dwelt in solitude, though never so far from the village that the scouts were unaware of his dwelling place. He himself had never dwelt in a tent, regarding it as unsuitable for one who dwells alone. "For those of us that are bound only to the earth we tread and nothing more, it is unfit that we should shroud ourselves from the witnesses of iron heaven above," he would often be known to say. Beside his strange living habits, however, Nimith was a rather friendly man, and he was glad to honour the newly betrothed couple with the tent in which they would dwell thereafter.

And so the preparations slowly came to a head, and a great excitement could be felt all about Thænim. The ritual ground of the village lay on the bank of the river, whence the tents circled like ripples, interrupted only by the village heart, where the great table of oak was housed, and where the four fire-pits were that were lit once a week for the village moot.

The ritual ground was the place of memory, despite the fact that it had, only a decade before, moved every summer and every winter along with all the rest of the village. Here newborns were washed in the tug-and-weave of Wirthaumuin to bind them to their father-shepherd; here boys were declared men, when they were sent up the river in boats they had crafted themselves, to test themselves against the world; here young men and women founded new families when they were joined in the rite of marriage; here the dead were committed to the river of their clan. They would be sent off when they had finally returned their last breath whence it had first been breathed — sent into the running currents on the boat which they had made to prove that they had come of age.

Finally the ritual ground was decorated with the totems that reflected how the stars stood in this season. In wonderful geometry the totems were divided into the reaches of childhood, coming of age, and what marked Huthram and Wingilin as contributing members of the village. This would also divide the members of Thænim, giving each member their place to stand during the ceremony: the family standing near the totems of childhood, the mentors and instructors standing near the totems of their coming of age, and the rest of the village standing as witnesses (along with the everlasting eyes of the starry night) amidst the totems that marked the couple as what they had marked themselves out to be by their own hands in adulthood.

Three days before the wedding, her mother discovered Wingilin sitting gloomily atop a stone along the riverbed. It was evening, and the sun was about to set.

"What in all the world has driven you here to brood like a thundercloud, Win?" her mother asked.

"I'm just nervous about the wedding, that's all," she said.

Having always known her a little better than Wingilin had permitted, her mother was not convinced.

"Now, we both know that you are more than ready to go through with the wedding, Win," said her mother. "You have never fretted yourself with the proceedings of our customs. You have moved through them all like a prow through water. Besides, you look less worried and more angry."

"Oh, once in a while I just get frustrated with the children that run about without looking where they go, mother."

"Now Win, I have only ever seen you so angry when it has involved men, not children."

Wingilin sighed, and her mother came to sit down next to her beside the sliding of the dark water. From the red west a dance of copper filled that rushing mirror before them. The mother laid an arm about the daughter's shoulders, and the daughter let her head rest on the shoulder of her mother.

"It is Authæn. You worry for him," said the mother at last.

Neither needed say any more. Both knew that it was true.

"I had hoped, though he missed Father's birthday, that he would be back by now. I don't want him to miss the wedding. It would not sit well with him, I think," Wingilin said quietly, toying with the dark braid that hung over her shoulder, the golden light of her lion-eyes dim with sadness.

By the dying of the light the two women seemed like two stone cairns for the greyness of their skin. Finally the mother said: "He cares deeply for you, Wingilin. I think so deeply that he would know such a thing as a wedding to be only another stepping stone along a far more treacherous and far more important journey. He would not be embittered for missing it, certainly."

"Yes, mother," Wingilin returned. "I know him well enough to see that he might think such a foolish thought, but he once said to me that such stepping stones are needed, because without them the making of needed steps cannot be done. They are important to him, our customs. Even though he sets his face like stone and makes himself their victim."

The mother whistled quietly. "That boy sometimes does have more than clouds in his head," she muttered, and Wingilin laughed.

"Only when someone pulls him back into the boots that he has left on the earth," she said. "It is difficult to see him have enough ground to him to become the next chieftain, yet that is what the henge is meant to train him for."

"Oh, when such men of light as he are captured by the dusty earth in a way that brings them courage, they are without equal," said Wingilin's mother.

They sat there a while longer. Behind them the torches about the village began to quicken to life. The sounds of dinner took the air, pots and pans being arranged for the night's meal. Children ran about laughing and shouting riddlesome rules to games newly conjured. Elders shouted with wagging fingers as they tried to keep their balance in the storm of play, only to melt to laughter at what the children unfolded before them, or at the comments that the children made in reply to their reprimands. It was far to jolly a time to be stern in Thænim on Wirthaumuin, and so the children played on, heedless.

Chapter Three
Something of Weirdness

The sun sank lower in the sky as Wingilin watched it with her mother; but it's red spilled into a world far larger than the little village on the broad water. It spilled into great grasslands that stretched on north and east, and fell (like Athiluz once had) into the southward sea. The wind whipped over the stout grasses of the plains, ruffling them like a vast head of hair. Dodging from boulder to rock, the foxes made their quiet way towards a small spinney not too far from an outcrop of dark stone. There anyone would have seen the light of a small fire, in the onset of dusk as it cast shadows of a man against the charcoal black of a stone circle.

The man sat crouched, stoking the flames of his brand with a still green twig. He hummed to himself a tune from childhood; a melody to which he had long ago forgotten the words. In a strange way a wooden lyre that lay half-hidden amongst his things seemed almost to hum a response to the melody. His heavy boots, iron-toed, bore the scratches of much use, covered a little by his woollen spats. The cloak that rested comfortably on his shoulders was lined with the feathers of ravens. Presently he stroked the long locks of his dark hair over the grey of his ears and out of his face.

Black-and-gold, his lion-eyes stared into a distance beyond the flames toward which they had strayed. Beneath these golden eyes a large beard, as that of a man long on the road, struck forth, mottled with the signs of long journeying. His callous hands, weathered like the claws of an aged lizard despite the man's youth, stroked along it in sombre memory.

As it so happened, someone did see the fire and the shadows that it cast there on that circle of black stone. A wayfarer in the wilderness who was crossing over the steppes into the east saw the warm glow, and thought to introduce himself to whomever had made camp there. He thought to himself, "We might as well spend the night camping together — for to be alone on the road is a treacherous business." And so the tired traveller stumbled the last few metres to his destination, leaning heavily on his ebon staff as the winds groped greedily for his leathery cloak.

Upon nearing the crackling glow, the wayfarer called out, saying: "Ho there! I come in peace! Would you speak with a weary wanderer?"

There was a moment's pause. The shadow that had been dancing on the stony surface sat up an instant. Then another voice, hoarse for lack of use, called back, "Come into the light! What would a weary wanderer want to speak about?"

"Perhaps about the breaking of bread, or the tide of the lands ahead!" the wayfarer replied, rounding the part of the rocky shelter that had hidden the fire-maker from view.

"Ah, he is a poet!" the man at the fire chuckled, rising to his feet from where he had been crouched to feed his hungry brand. He clapped the dust from his hands and drew them coarsely through his raven hair.

"Only by accident. Though I did come across a wandering minstrel not two days hence," the traveller said, lowering his furry hood to reveal his own aspect as a friendly, middle-aged one. He had streaks of silver amidst his otherwise black curls. This was one of those proud people that dwelt in the world deep to the south, beyond the great sea. Presently, he lowered his heavy pack and his black staff to the ground near the outcropping, and breathed a cloud of icy vapour into the air between them.

"You must have a long road behind and ahead of you, uncle," said the man whose camp this was, for he was not much older than middling twenty, or so.

"And you, by the wear and beard on you," replied the other. "And you have not even a horse to carry you!"

"Nor you," observed the river-person.

Momentarily, the man from the faraway south looked about himself absent-mindedly, as though perhaps he had forgotten whether or not there had been a horse with him at the beginning of his journey. "No, I prefer the use of my feet. The slower I go the more time I have to think," said he with an amicable smile, as though he thought himself rather foolish, but worthy none the less.

"Then you must be a greater thinker than the ancients by now. Come and sit down by the fire! Might I ask your name and your road?" said the river-person.

But the stranger from the south remained standing a while, staring at the flames as the river-

31

person had only a moment before. Finally he said: "I am Gaba. Today I come from Glimwæth."

"But you are no Glimwægian," said the river-person.

"No," said Gaba, and a smile creased his face. "No. I come from further south. I come from the world where the sun beats down on man so that it bruises him thus." The southerner indicated his dark skin. "A world of drought and desert, of flat mountains, of grassland and frightful beasts." There was a short pause. "What of you? You have a strange look about you. Who are you, and whither your path?"

"I am Authæn," said the river-person, "and I am on my way back to my village, Thænim on Wirthaumuin.

"Ah, a noble quest. To return home always lifts the hearts of those that have been waiting, and re-minds those that return of why they left to begin with," mused Gaba, lost, it seemed, in memory.

"I have already been away too long, but ..." The river-person seemed to wonder how much he could share with this stranger to his camp. "I do not know what to make of these stones, for they hold some ancient mystery, it seems to me."

At this the southerner noticed the markings on the dark outcrop. Indeed, as he turned to take in all the surface of the stone that surrounded them, he began to notice that the rocks themselves had an eerily precise lay to them.

"This is almost more the ruin of some long-lost story-house than it is a heap of boulders," said Gaba with a gasp.

32

At this Authæn looked up at him with a smile. "Those were my thoughts as well. Look here, uncle:" At this the river-person rose and pointed to one part in the markings that were riven in the stone. "Here is a giant depicted, it seems, surrounded by strange little men bearing strange tools."

"Indeed," muttered Gaba. "That giant has horns. And this above him, what are these? Ladies of heaven?"

"There are such stories in the songs of my people," said the river-person.

"Those sound like songs worth hearing," said Gaba.

"As much as they are songs worth singing," laughed Authæn, "but for those you must go to a reader of stars, or to a fully trained henge-man. I am only partway there, and I would make a mess of it, I'm afraid."

"I see," said the southerner. "Such star-readers and henge-men dwell in this village whither you go? How was it's name again?"

"Thænim."

"Thænim. *There* are those that could sing me the songs of the ladies of heaven?" Gaba pressed.

"Certainly," said the river-person.

"Then perhaps I ought to join you in your return," said Gaba.

"I would welcome it!" said Authæn, suddenly beaming. "There are few that I have ever met that would be willing to join me on such a whim! That makes of you a greater man in my eyes."

Gaba laughed. "Oh you are a delightful sort, Authæn. You find the slightest and strangest things overwhelmingly mirthful," he said.

"That is because I am the slightest and strangest of folk, uncle," replied the other.

Gaba laughed again, saying: "Oh, the joys of youth and adventure! How I had quite forgotten those long-ago days — days of wounds and wonder, where all the world still lays before one, shrouded in the mists of future and possibility. Oh, how alluring the world looks thus: where one only sees here a shimmer and there a hill in the vast distance. Writhing movements in the shadows. Pray they are not the writhings of a beast on the prowl after you!" A shadow fell over the southerner's dark features. "They say it is wisdom when a king uncovers that which has been veiled; but wisdom can be torment for the soul."

"And yet necessary, would you not say, uncle?" said the other uncertainly.

The southerner smiled at this. "Indeed, my friend," said he, and sat down near the fire to warm himself. Authæn joined him there, and soon they had unpacked dry bread and meat from their baggage, which they washed down by skins of water once they had chewed them swallowable.

When they were done eating, Authæn began plucking at the melancholic lyre that before had been concealed amongst his things. Now and then he hummed in harmony with it. Not long after, the southerner also produced from his many furs a plucking instrument with metal tines, and joined in the performance.

34

"Oh you have strange harmonies!" said the southerner, presently.

"These are the harmonies of my people," said Authæn in a sad way.

"I understand. Yours must truly be a sad people for such harmonies to claim them," the southerner continued. "But they are beautiful in their own light. I simply must tune my instrument anew. Give me a moment ... there!"

For a while longer the music went on, a mournful strumming and plucking, whilst the wind muttered peaceful poems in tow. A small family of foxes crept to the rim of the light that spilled from the fire to watch the performance with regal timidity; half-hidden by the rocks and longer grass beyond. Then Gaba began to sing, for he seemed to have discovered that some words he had learned on the road fit the rhythm they had now settled on. So it went:

Far and long the road that leads
To the end whither we strive.
Let the songs and melodies
Of those long past ancients rise:
Let them guide our weary tread
To lay down our dreary head
In our final resting bed.

Their melody came to an end, and Authæn said, "That is good, uncle: if we have harrowing harmonies, then you have sad songs!"

"Oh that depends on how well you understand them," said the southerner with a smile. "Sometimes there is no better end than to lastly lay your head, after toil and much dread, to rest … to rest in a way that quickens all the body to *new* life. The thought of it always brings back some of that scarce courage to me that I seem to have lost somewhere long ago."

Silence again.

Suddenly Gaba pushed himself up, and Authæn followed him with wondering eyes. "What now?" asked the river-man.

"What does this giant here bring to mind for you, young master? You are a native to these parts, so I would ask your rede on it," said the southerner.

"Does that carving stir you, uncle?"

"It stirs me."

Authæn stroked his beard again, a frown taking his features. "I must think on it some more, uncle. I cannot say for certain just now," he said at last.

Not long after that, the two did lay down their heads to rest, and the corsacs departed to hunt some rabbits in the veld. The iron heavens glistened with their countless faraway beads of wisdom; and their singular lunar eye, which opened and closed once a month, was altogether new with sleep.

The following morning, after rising and breaking their fast with meagre rations, Authæn and Gaba looked once more at the etchings in the stone only to find that the little men and the ladies of heaven that had surrounded the giant the night before were nowhere to be seen now.

"Was it a trick of the eyes?" Authæn muttered to himself.

"If you mean the men with their strange devices and the ladies that are no longer in the grain of the stone, I stand as witness for you. This truly is a place of the fey," said Gaba, stroking across the smooth rock with his dry hands. "I think that I will spend some time more here, young master. I will seek out the rumour of your village when my work here is done."

"I look forward to hearing of your uncovery, uncle," said the other. "As for me, I have been here too long already."

After this Authæn gathered his belongings, saying that he had seen no signs of danger on the roads he had taken, but warned the southerner against banditry none the less with the words: "There is one in these parts, uncle, though I am fortunate only to have heard the rumour of him, for he is said to hate the sound of running waters. I have spent my life about the waters of Wirthaumuin, our shepherd-father's river, and so this troll has never dared draw too near my people. I thought of this in response to your question of last night, you see, but I wanted not to say such things in the dark.

"The Ibex, they call him. He is a terrible fiend; a monster that is said to have sprung from the bogs long ago, who has gathered an army of men to himself as cruel and as merciless as vultures. These brigands hunt people, for their master does not need to sustain himself as do ordinary men, and so hunting people has become his sport."

37

"No need to concern yourself, my son," said Gaba. "Should any such brigands dare overstep their boundaries, they shall feel the crack of my staff." It was as though thunder rolled in the distance with the last of his words, and a fey light flared up in the southerner's dark eyes as he said this. "As for your journey home, may you have a blessed return."

"Thank you, uncle. Stay well," replied Authæn with a smile. He was glad to have met Gaba, though he doubted that their paths were ever to cross hereafter.

"We shall meet again, my friend," said Gaba suddenly. The southerner stood with his eyes closed, drinking deep the morning air. Then he snapped open his gaze, staring hard into Authæn's black-and-gold visage. "I see it in your eyes, friend — you have something of weirdness about you."

After overcoming his momentary surprise, Authæn said, "I do hope we see one another again, uncle; but all my kin are ill-fated. All our eyes look as do mine. As for the weirdness: I am a student under the henge of my people; weirdness is my business."

Gaba chuckled. "Weirdest of the weird," said he, and looked directly into Authæn's eyes. "Then our fates *are* bound up. But that is something you will understand only when it is too late. Go well!" And with that, the middle-aged man from the south turned back to the etchings on the wall, sitting down cross-legged before them, laying his staff across those crossed legs.

"Stay well, uncle!" replied Authæn.

Shaking his head after he had walked some strides from his new friend, Authæn looked once back, then set off more earnestly in the direction of his childhood home. Many hours passed beneath his weathered boots as he strode away the heaths and hills with purpose. At about midday he arrived on the ridge east of the shallow valley that descended to where the village lay.

There was the village Thænim on Wirthaumuin. Home had not changed much since Authæn's last return, so that he felt as though he were stepping into the fog of memory with each stride he took, leaving behind the hardship and loneliness that the road and his time under the henge had demanded of him.

Like a mother's embrace the tents of his home drew in around him, many a make-shift chimney abillow with white wisps of smoke. Here and there someone sat on a hand-hewn bench, billowing equally-much by a pipe of clay or wood. The white heads of elders, seated resolutely thus, were encircled by the many running, noising children of Thænim on Wirthaumuin — children that spoke with much cruel innocence, a speech that Authæn had long not heard. At the henge they spoke differently. And there, rising to the north, stood the tower that once his father had brought forth, seemingly by sorcery. It was the tallest thing for miles around, like a man that could weather all ages; built on an ancient black stone for its foundation.

But Authæn no one seemed to recognise as he entered amidst the large tents of his people. It was likely for his great beard and long hair, both of which were uncustomary for his folk. He had forgotten this custom. Many was a wary eye that came to rest upon him, bearing one of the few questions that his folk had posed often to strangers in his childhood: *Are you one of our kin or are you a no-good vagabond from a fallen tribe?*

Suddenly he heard his name called, and he looked up to see who it might be. At that instant many of the dark miens dissolved again, fading to relief and recognition. "Authæn!" she cried once more.

It was the little girl called Folgnuin for her red hair.

"Folgnuin!" Authæn laughed, catching her in his arms as she jumped up to welcome him.

"How are you? How is your good mother?" he asked.

"She is well. I am well too. I'm almost old enough to marry you now, Authæn!" she said with the innocence of a child.

"How is it that you think of marriage, Folgnuin? Are there not more important things for you to run after at your age?"

"What else should I be running after?"

"Perhaps… other boys of your own age," said Authæn thoughtfully. "Or hare. Have you ever caught a hare with your bare hands?"

"Why would I want to catch hair, Authæn? I have plenty enough on my head. You are a funny man," said Folgnuin as he let her down. Then she suddenly tugged at his hand, saying: "But follow me, Authæn! Follow me! I must show you a surprise! Your father's is my favourite, it is so delicate!"

As she led him by the dwellings of his clan he looked over the tops of the tents again, at the tower in the north, wondering what his father could possibly have carved that would win the affection of young Folgnuin so. "Delicate" she had said.

"Tell me about your day, Folgnuin," said Authæn as they walked.

"Oh, this morning I woke early, Authæn. I even awoke before ma! Then, because she was not looking, I slipped out onto the hill there to the east. That's where you came over just now, Authæn!"

"It is indeed," said the river-man, "but you know that it is dangerous for you to wander off alone like that, Folgnuin! Why did you do it?"

"I didn't want to tell you Authæn, seeing as we are going to get married one day," replied the girl, "but I've been meeting a man up there. His house appeared a week ago, and he has the most wonderful blueberries! They taste like all the colours in the rainbow, and they are far larger than any I have ever seen!"

"You have been meeting with a stranger?" asked Authæn sternly. "That is not wise, Folgnuin."

"Well he was hardly a stranger, I thought. He told me all about da, even some things that ma did not know," said the girl, "even things that ma had not told me. When I asked her about these things, she began to cry, and asked me how I knew. It made me sad. I have seen the man all week! But this morning, after I had gotten up so early, I

41

climbed the hill, and you won't believe what I found, Authæn!"

"He had stopped feeding you the blueberries in exchange for acorns?" the river-man sighed. He did not know whether the girl was to be believed.

"No, Authæn! The house was no longer there! And there wasn't any trace of it!"

"A dream, then," muttered the river-man, so that she could not hear it.

Passing the steaming cauldrons of lunchtime (and a group of men playing at horse-bone dice in lively wise), they moved through one ring of tents, then the next, past the council-board under its thatched roof, until they finally stood before the ritual ground on the banks of Wirthaumuin.

After the rush of Folgnuin's guidance, the flowing of the river was a peaceful sound, almost quiet in its soothing voice. It spoke with the familiarity of a grandfather, slapping a rock as an old man might his knee, or sniffing a moment as the same old man might have sniffed powder. "It is good to be home again," muttered Authæn.

Then he saw the totems rooted in the dark earth that lay bare before him, and all the many questions that had been hanging loosely before his spirit, began at once to fasten, much like glass after it has been blown and shaped.

"Folgnuin, how is it you think of marriage?" Authæn said once more.

"Because I am marrying, Authæn, you fool," said the familiar voice of a woman from behind.

Chapter Four
The Fox, the Eagle, and the Worm

The world grew dark, all light had bled from the horizon. Overhead a frightening spectacle unfolded itself like a thousand-thousand drops of silver, shimmering in the cast-iron vaults of heaven. The stars danced thus, and their patterns were like a history of the world, showing a towering city long-lost; one great hero after the next; perhaps a frightening beast; a great warship; a bear and its cub; the Queen of Swans. There were mirrored, like over the face of a lake, the many moments in the songs of the river-people, and on the dark earth beneath that cloud of stars stood totems, showing just the same constellations. Amongst those totems, were the many leather-wrapped feet of the villagers of Thænim, the children of Wirthaumuin, the clan of the eagle.

In the middle of the ritual ground stood a waist-high stone that had been hammered into a perfect cube. All those present were gathered about it. All those present had bled onto that stone as children, and had been washed in the waters of the now muttering river. This stone was a witness to all of their clan, having been hewn by their forebear, Wirthaumuin the Immortal, upon his landing on the southern shores. This was their remembrance of him, as he now resided in the henge of their clan, seen only by those that he took under his tutelage.

43

One such student under the henge also stood with leather-wrapped feet on the damp earth, drawing crumbing lines in its fertile surface with the toe of his wrappings. Authæn was glad to be home, though he had always been somewhat nervous about weddings. They reminded him that he was still without a wife, and he did not want to be alone in the work that lay before him. Now another two of his close friends were marrying, and he was still withdrawn into the wilderness and crafty quiet of the henge, learning according to the ancient ways of the shepherds as not even their current chieftain, the father of Wingilin, had.

Suddenly a drum thundered three quick beats, like those of a frightened heart, and a silence fell over that little, starlit world. The mother of Huthram, the groom, stepped toward the square stone, then, placing on its dark surface the cub of a fox. The cub had been caught only earlier that day by another friend of Authæn: Carbeth the Loyal, one of the best hunters in the village. Carbeth stood beside Authæn in the section marked by the totems of childhood. Besides Carbeth, leaning heavily on a wooden frame that he had made to support his weakening form, Authæn's father stood on his son's left with a weary smile.

For a moment the fox cowered on the top of the stone, glancing this way then that, testing the edges of the cube. Huthram's mother returned to where she had been standing. All watched in solemn silence. Then, just as the fox was about to jump from the stone, a vast eagle swept down and snatched the cub into the air with it, the cub yelp-

44

ing and struggling as it was carried into some low darkness across the river. When the two animals were out of sight, the drummer began to pound the drum again in a quick rhythm, until the chieftain brought forth his daughter. At their slow approach the beating of the drum steadied dramatically to the pace of their steps.

Wingilin was clothed in a clean linen dress, donned with a shoulder-cloak of fox fur. Over her head she bore a deep hood which covered most of her face. In the half-light of the torches nothing could be seen of her smile. Large, many-coloured flowers had been braided into her girdle, and hung in intricately patterned strings from her waist to the bottom of her dress.

When she stood before the stone, the drums halted again.

"Here I bring my sacrifice," said the chieftain grimly. "I lay it on the stone of our fathers, and I pray that it will become a tree, bearing much fruit as a blessing to the village. What say you, daughter?"

"Here I stand, a sacrifice," said Wingilin, but she said it as though she were the greatest of victors. "I stand by the stone of our fathers, and I pray that I shall become a tree, bearing much fruit as a blessing to my home. From the house of my father I am cast out, may a brave eagle catch me, that I might make for him a worthy nest, as I myself was raised in a worthy burrow."

Then the chieftain nodded stiffly, looked once more at his daughter with glittering black eyes, and returned to where his wife stood.

The drum began once more to beat, slowly, steadily, for now it was time that the groom should approach; but in that moment a cry echoed over the waters of Wirthaumuin — the screech of an eagle.

A murmur shuddered over the crowd there gathered as the eagle that had flown away with the fox returned with its prey. The cub was still alive it seemed, but a dark thing was snaked about the eagle's winged form. It lowered the fox onto the stone of fathers again, stepping to the other side of its smooth face. It was a viper that had wrapped itself about the eagle's body; some dark worm or other.

A collective gasp went forth from the gathering, for the snake then bit the eagle. Again the eagle screeched. Then, all at once, it clipped the head from the snake with one fell snap of its beak. But the venom of the worm made short work of the eagle. The bird lifted itself from the stone, climbing on the air in circles by its wings, then slid through the air as one drunk, crashing onto the ritual ground before the bride. The fox, seemingly unhurt, sprang from the stone and ran away through the legs of the crowd.

After another heavy silence, in which all looked at the stunned bride — for she had raised her hands to her mouth and frozen in observation of all that had happened — the drummer began anew with the beat of the groom's approach.

Huthram strode toward the eagle's limp form. He, donned in a cloak lined with the feathers of just such an eagle, bore a new garb of linen, dyed blue and pale grey. Atop his brow was set a circlet

46

of silver, adorned also with with the beak of an eagle. He placed the now dead eagle's form calmly on the stone of fathers, all eyes upon him. Then he raised his hand, and the drumbeat ceased.

There was a quiet in that place, so thick that it pressed the air from their lungs.

Finally Huthram said: "Let this be recognised as the sign of my love for Wingilin. Should any dread worm dare attack us, I shall clip the head from it to keep her from harm, though it should cost me my life. If our life shall be a slow dying together, however, then let me be just as ready to offer myself to you in life, my heart."

This was not part of the traditional ceremony, and yet it was woven into the unfolding of things so carefully and so honestly that it seemed as though it had to be.

Huthram turned now to the woman that had been left to him by her father, as once his own mother had been left to his father.

"Dear woman, I take you up as my own. Let us be as the tree: one being with many limbs. Some reach up to hold nests, others reach down to hold burrows. In this wise, we shall become a home to the homeless, and a bearer of fruit for those that are starved and in need," said Huthram finally, completing his part of the ceremony.

At this Authæn stepped forward. As a student under their immortal father of the henge, he was tasked with tying them together in the power of one who was greater than they both and to whom they both owed their loyalty.

He jumped nimbly onto the stone, placing either foot beneath either of the spread wings of the eagle's form which lay there. Then he said, according to the custom: "I am sent here by Wirthaumuin, and by his teaching I bind you, and bid you to share of the same spirit, the same breath, by uniting under a kiss."

Without hesitation, Wingilin jumped into her man's arms, and he had only just enough time to draw back her hood before she kissed him full on the mouth. He held her there for that long moment, and all those gathered burst into cheers. Authæn quickly dropped from the stone to rejoin his father and Carbeth the Loyal amongst his people.

When Wingilin finally released Huthram, he turned to the village and said: "Now all are welcome to join in feasting at the council-board! The fires have been lit; the food has been made ready!"

In a procession, Huthram's guild of scouts took up the torches that had been staked with hammers into the hard-pressed earth, and led the village towards the centre of their tents. There the four fires burned brightly, bearing on them each a spitted calf.

The council-board was set with many gifts for the newly-weds, foremost amongst which was the tent that Nimith the Arm had made for them. He stood there now, as the village fell into that place, all chattering excitedly over the dramatic ceremony they had just beheld.

When Nimith spoke, however, the village was quick to silence. He said: "It is custom amongst our people to dwell beneath the covering of a tent.

48

We grow up beneath its kindly shelter. We lay ourselves to thoughtlessness when weariness fells us asleep, trusting that it will keep danger from us. It is like a guardian and a shield. And, when the time for our oldest sorrow comes — that we are bound to wander these lands without settling — we are accustomed to take up our tents and move toward more welcome tracts.

"In many ways, a tent is much like our own body: it is a frame like skeleton, covered in the hide of an animal, and within is life that emerges into the day. Here I present to you your own tent, my dear friends. Let it be a parent to you, as we are all children of Withaumuin, so let this tent remind you of your own shepherd, from whom you went out into the world, and to whose river you shall return when your long day's journey is at an end."

"Thank you, kindly Uncle Nimith, for this wondrous gift; may it house us until our children have been granted tents of their own," said Huthram, walking to take the arm of the other in acknowledgement of his gift. Wingilin embraced the old man as well, thanking him.

Then the feasting began many smaller tables and chairs had been set in the broad turf between the fires, and some of the men and women of the village had been at work whilst the ceremony had proceeded to ensure the meal would be ready in time. All the while the bride and groom were unravelling gifts, and thanking those from whom they came. A woman who was particularly well-known for her bakery had filled a basket for them, containing their favourite treats. Someone had made for Wingilin a wooden comb, and for her man a bracelet marked with the eagle. Carbeth had gifted a new bow of bone to Huthram, and a full quiver to his wife, to which he commented loudly: "That is how a marriage should be!" to great amusement.

"And who draws the string?" chuckled Huthram.

"Let that be fate," replied Carbeth, shrugging, "and let the mark of the arrow deserve it well."

The village approved.

After many more gifts had been gratefully taken up, the table was empty, and the villagers looked towards the close friend of the bride and groom, Authæn; for he had not yet given them anything for this great occasion.

Taking the anticipation of the gathering as his call, he stood up before them all, and said: "You have all known me either the length of my life, or the length of yours," he looked a smile at Folgnuin, and the village laughed. "The gift that I offer to the bride and her groom I offer together with my old father.

"As many of you know, he has grown weary with age, and weak by some unnamed malady, but he is still the greatest among the carpenters here gathered. He raised the tower that now keeps watch from our northern boundary, and he raised both this roof here thatched, as well as the table we have all grown to revere beneath."

From somewhere in the crowd another carpenter, one who had long been in quiet feud with Authæn's father cried out, "He breaks our tradi-

50

tions! He makes that we want not move, but to wander is in our blood!"

"Let the man finish, this is not about your spats, Mauthaur," said a blacksmith called Auring, the brother of Mauthaur Handless.

"Thank you, Auring," said Authæn. "Your hands may be black of your work, but your heart is golden-red with honesty. And still our request may embitter uncle Mauthaur further.

"Near ten years we have wintered already in this bend of our forebear's great river. It holds us safe with water, with good earth, and with much game that makes the lives of our hunters easy. It is the way of most people that come through these parts along the trading road to wander — as is our way and our blood, it is true — but also then to return to a home. They return to a place that does not shift to another end of their country whilst they are away."

"But there are dangerous folk about, they would pillage us, should we grow fat here in idleness!" cried Mauthaur the carpenter desperately, only to be silenced again by his frustrated brother.

"Indeed, Uncle Mauthaur!" said Authæn. "It is for exactly this reason, that we offer Huthram and Wingilin the building of a hall, in which all of the hunters and scouts of our village may rest at night, and that may serve as a haven should brigands assail us."

"What are we, Authæn? Children of Imnir or of Wirthaumuin? Let the snow-foam have their halls! We dwell in hide-frames!" shouted one of the hunters from the crowd.

"This is our offer," said Authæn with finality, and he sat down again, beside his father.

The chieftain was frowning deeply, considering all of these things. Huthram had been looking to his father-in-law every so often to see how he weighed the matter, but still no resolute answer could be determined from the walrus-mien of that man.

"This choice is for you, Huthram," said Authæn's father horsely. "The chieftain is also in favour of our remaining here. He is in favour of growing like a tree along the water. He has said so often enough. Your house here may be what we need to begin settling this land as we should have a long time ago: as though it were our own."

"I ask until the moot-day to think on it, uncle. I thank you both for your gift, for it worthies the gift and the wisdom of proud Nimith," said Huthram then.

At this Nimith, who had been looking on in kindly indifference, suddenly seemed surprised, and said, "How so? I have made you a tent, and now you are offered a big log-house!"

The gathering laughed.

Huthram also chuckled and said, "It will make of your tent a sign that we all are born into our skins, and that we all sail into the river in a boat of wood, when our time of waking is done. So your tent will be the birthplace of our family, and the great hall of Authæn and his proud father will be the boat in which we meet an end. Not only our family shall meet an end there in the days of our old age, however; all of our ways shall meet an end in this great hall, to bring forth a fully new way of life in this land. We shall bring forth a way of life that is more permanently settled!"

The crowd burst into babble again, each considering with his neighbour what this all could mean.

"You shall have until the moot-day, Huthram, gladly," Authæn called over the noise.

"Let us have music!" the chieftain said shaking his head, and going to sit down near his two most trusted elders. It appeared as though he wanted to discuss this matter with them.

Authæn arose, went to the place where a small band of musicians had gathered, and took up his lyre to join with them. They had already begun playing in the harmonies that were most friendly to their people, and so he easily found his way into their play. After not too long a time, they were trying to find the limits of their quick- and cleverness, laughing both when their music suddenly failed them, and when they managed to draw something together that was of profound delight.

The night deepened. The people grew louder and braver, for the mead of the bee-smokers had begun to flow in golden rills from large barrels that now lay tapping on the tables. It was a good night for celebration, the weather clear and not too cold.

At perhaps the beginning of the fourth watch of the night, when many had lain drunken down into the grass, or had begun to grow tired enough to return to their tents (though this was usually not done until the sun began again to rise), the newly-weds departed, taking with them some of their close friends to help set up the new tent they had received from Nimith. Authæn and Carbeth were included in this group.

And with that, the wedding feast was considered finished.

Chapter Five
The Breaking of Bread

The sun arose over a sleeping village. From the fires of the night before, smoke was drifting ghastly over the conical roofs of the tents, like mist striding through the mountains. The winds that rode horse-like across the open landscape dove over the ridge that kept Thænim sheltered from the east, hammering down through the flapping leathers every now and again.

The horses, the cows, the camels, the goats, and the aviary began to noise in response to the bluing heavens. But the men and women were put to sleep by the heavy blanket of a late night, and they did not yet arise. At about the fourth hour after sunrise, a deer that had strayed from its herd, wandered in amongst the still tents. It began grazing, sniffing the air at whiles. It was about to turn and leave the settlement, when it suddenly squealed in shock, jumped up a little in horror, then fell to the ground, dead. An arrow stuck forth from its heart.

From the newest of the tents, where the entrance had been slightly peeled back, one could have seen two laughing faces peer out into the day. There, sitting in the nest of their bedding-furs, were Huthram with a smile and dear Wingilin, who laughing laid her head on his broad shoulder. He laid down the bow, and she put aside the quiver from which she had handed him an arrow.

After a moment, the scout captain sighed contentedly.

"Not a bad start," said his wife.

He laughed. "I hope it remains just as fortunate, even if it is unlikely to remain so easy. To provide you with what you need to keep a household will be my greatest joy, and my hardest task, I sense."

"Well, as I have said: It's not a bad start. Perhaps our parents can come to lunch for venison."

"Nothing would make me happier," said he, and they kissed.

Their mouths came apart, but they remained close together, and Wingilin said, "One day we shall live in a great wooden hall. It is difficult to think of. I have never been with my father to Glimwæth. I have not seen the houses of Imnir's folk."

"But you are not opposed to it, my heart?" asked Huthram, a little fear in his eyes.

She looked deep into those golden pools. "Such emotion lends a depth to you, my home," she said. "I could not be opposed to you. I take my father's teaching very seriously."

He looked outside again, a little embarrassed and smiling bashfully. "Of course. That is why I spoke so well of Authæn's offer last night, my heart. I think it would be good were we to strengthen our home somewhat. We dwell in a most dangerous land, held safe mostly by the river; but still brigands have assailed us in the past. We should not be careless to let them do it so easily again."

They sat there a moment longer.

"I must wash myself," said Wingilin then.

"I will begin work on our bounty. Then I shall also wash," said Huthram, and they rose from their furs stiffly, stretching and smiling. Then they went out into the middling day.

Huthram slung his prize over his shoulders, and began to wander in the direction of Carbeth's home. He had been walking a short while, when he found Authæn sitting on his father's bench near the entrance to the tent they shared. He looked dull, not only for lack of sleep, but heavy with some gloom. It was not uncommon for the student under the henge to look so, but when one knew how full of life and mirth the man could also be, it was rather disheartening. Especially for a friend so close.

"Do you eat venison, Gloom-bringer?" Huthram said, not unkindly. A sad smile drew into the captains sympathetic features.

Authæn looked up, startled from his dark considerations. Then a smile broke his solemn features.

"Call me Doom-bringer! I don't eat it raw, my friend. I trust you have now fallen over the precipice whence one should not return," said the hengeman.

"Into what precipice is that, I wonder, if I should not return from it?" said the other.

"Into manhood. The true shape of it. That's not a bad start," said Authæn, indicating the deer.

Huthram laughed. "Yes, I have been told that already."

"Oh," At this Authæn looked about uncomfortably, as though he felt a fool for repeating something that had already been said.

Huthram shook his head. "Do not be embarrassed, my friend, I like to be confirmed in my false strength!" laughed he.

Still looking away, Authæn chuckled as well. Then their eyes met again, both carrying laughter, and Authæn nodded, saying: "I do eat venison, but I think my father loves it more."

"Then bring him to lunch with us. Our new tent you must still regard in the daylight."

"It will be our breakfast, thank you Huthram. A truer friend..." began Authæn. Then he frowned.

"There is none?" Huthram finished.

"We'll have you say it, yes. Then you cannot quote me against my other true friends," said Authæn with a cunning smile.

Again, Huthram chuckled and shook his head. Then he bade his friend stay well, saying, "At least trim that beard, brigand!" and went on towards the tent of Carbeth.

The tent of Carbeth was at the furthermost end of the village, for his treatments of the furs and leathers he pulled from prey was a strong-smelling business.

Upon arriving, Huthram found his friend still sleeping. At this he was struck by inspiration. He carefully laid the beast on his shoulders into the furs beside Carbeth, its glazed eyes made to look directly into Carbeth's sleeping ones. Then he went back to the entrance, standing just outside. He had taken two pot lids with him from the sleeping man's tent.

Just as he was about to strike the pot lids together, he saw Authæn coming towards him, and motioned the other to remain silent. Authæn understood and did as he had been bidden, but a puzzling frown still sat on his brow.

Then Huthram slammed the two pot lids together in the entrance of the tent, and heard the sudden movement of one roused from sleep by fright. Huthram withdrew his hands from the mouth of the tent again, not wanting to be seen.

"Hello there, lovely," a bleary voice was heard to mutter from within the tent. "I can't remember it being my wedding last night, but I seem to have gotten the spoils of it."

Forgetting himself, Huthram suddenly burst out: "Take that back! Wingilin is no carcass!"

Laughter issued from the tent.

"I am just paying you back for your kindness, Huthram. A whole deer! By the rushing sounds of rivers. This is wonderful!" said Carbeth's voice, and his two friends entered the tent again.

"It's not for you alone, Carbeth! I used your bow to kill it this morning; the poor beast had erred into the village. I wanted to ask you to butcher it for us. We want to have venison for our midday meal, for which you'd be welcome to join us, naturally," Huthram explained.

"Oh my," said the bleary Carbeth, getting slowly to his feet. "How magnificent. And the furs?"

"I want to have a garment made for Wingilin from them," said Huthram. "If there is anything particularly good about the bones then I would also like some dice made of those. I have lost mine recently on the road."

"Dice of deer? Interesting," Carbeth muttered. "I will get to the meat first, and then I shall put the furs in the river overnight."

They all stood there a while longer, looking at the dead animal. Then Carbeth said: "Off with you now, I must wake up and work at this. Go frolic in the sun, that should straighten your playful mood, you children!"

The others laughed and took their leave, heading towards the river to wash the remembrance of long sleep from them; the remembrance that one day they would not waken from the dust.

How many days had passed? How long had this man been sitting amidst those dark stones, the curious, black staff stretched across his cross-legged posture? Had he eaten since the departure of the river-person? Had he drunk?

Yes, even now he took up his water-skin and poured some of the cool life that flowed from it into his open mouth. About the ring of blackened stone, the yellow grasses bobbed and dove as the wind slapped them about. Into the east the soil became sandier, and it looked by this day to be a desert. But so far north, and in a time that begins to tilt into Autumn, such desert places were still quite cool.

Suddenly the ebon man from the south arose. He did so slowly, stretching the long sitting from his limbs with a groan. The winds picked up, and heavy clouds that were rolling in from south and west brought a coolness over that land for a moment; foreshadowing the coming of a great storm. There, in that faraway west and south, a white bolt of fire fell from heaven for an instant, but Gaba did not see it.

The southerner was still considering the carving of the giant. The carvings of the little men and the ladies of heaven had not reappeared, and he had wondered if it had something to do with the shifting of the moon; but there were new carvings that now presented themselves when the sun set. Two crowds of people would appear at the heels of the giant every night: one, smaller, riding to embattle him with crude weapons on the left; the other, a mighty warband standing with him astride warhorses, on the right. He had also taken in more details as the days had passed, but was uncertain of what they might mean.

There had been some kind of boundary to the left — a river, perhaps? It had been surrounded by tents. On the right had been the great mountains along the eastern rim of the world. These were never named by the people he had visited in his long journeying for all the weirdness and mystery that haunted them. Then there had also been depictions of what he guessed to be the henges on some nights, rising like angry stone fingers into heaven. On other nights there had been strange mounds that looked like doorways into the earth. Atop the mounds had always been trees with seven branches.

"This is a land strange with lights and shadows of things that are and want to be," muttered Gaba, as though remembering these words, but he did not know where he might have heard them before. "But I think now that it is time to find this village and this river-people of that henge-man-to-be; is that not so, my spirit?"

He took up his belongings, slinging his pack over a shoulder, then, without looking back, he marched into the west, and south. He marched into the direction of the oncoming storm.

Venison was served over the long, low table of the newly standing tent of Huthram's home. At the head of the table sat Huthram himself, his wife to the right of him. Along the right side of the table sat his mother, then Authæn's father, then Authæn himself. On the left-hand side of the table sat the chieftain, his wife, and Carbeth, who had once been married, but had lost his wife. Another friend from childhood, Loangilin Green-grass sat at the foot of the table, bridging the space between Carbeth and Authæn. Her parents were recently become merchants that had left their tent to her since their departure into the east, where all trade went and whence it always returned the wealthier.

"Thank you for joining us, friends," said Huthram, taking up the silence that had fallen at Wingilin's motion. "We thank you also, not only for joining us at the table, but for joining Wingilin and myself closer and closer together like so many welders, bringing pieces of metal together that should otherwise never have fit to one another.

"This feast is not only to eat our morning bounty of deer," the gathering laughed, all having heard the story of how the deer had been killed, "it fell very graciously into our lap —"

"And very graciously into my bed," muttered Carbeth. Everyone laughed again.

"But also, Carbeth," Huthram continued with a smile, "to show that as much as ever, our home is yours. Let us still all be of one family, as we have ever been under the long-ago heritage of Wirthaumuin."

"Then let us eat!" said Wingilin, and everyone took food to their plates. Salads had also been brought by the guests, and some of the bread that the newly-weds had received the previous night was put out on the table.

As they began to chew down on the tender meal, the chieftain asked Huthram's mother how she was.

"I am well, thank you, my chieftain," said she with a tired smile. "I am all the better knowing that my son is well looked after by Wingilin. I wish by all the stars that watch us from behind the fires of day, that she does not suffer the same fate as I."

She looked at Wingilin, taking her daughter-in-law's hands up in her own. "Huthram's father was a man as good as your own father. True and brave, and always willing to meet the tasks that must be done. I hope that Huthram's father's blood is stronger in him than is my own, and I hope that your fortune is more gracious than was mine, that you may truly live until the end of long days in a hall of wood."

At this the attention was turned to Authæn and his father, those who would craft said hall. Carbeth sniffed in slight disapproval, but said nothing as he ate.

"You are still against the building of wooden halls, Carbeth?" said Authæn's father weakly. The wooden frame which the middle-aged man used to support himself as he walked through the village stood beside his seat, making him seem as though he was fading much faster than was true. Some sickness had been working at him as long as Authæn could remember, weakening him day by day, one small bite at a time.

"I am, uncle, but I love you all the same. Your crafts are marvellous, but why bring the ways of the Imnir-folk into our homes? Are our ways not proven? Are they not from of old? I understand that I am a hunter of the wilds, and that I have been betrayed by a daughter of Imnir, perhaps that is why I am against it. But I do not see it saving us from the likes of the Ibex or his horde."

"The Ibex cannot come near Wirthaumuin's waters," said the chieftain. "The sound deafens him, and the waters themselves are pure, not like those foul and rotting pools that spawned that beast."

"His men are not of the same weakness. Were we to grow fat, as uncle Mauthaur said last night, he would not hesitate to send his horsed warlords after us," said Carbeth, looking at Authæn's father, then at Loangilin as he spoke.

"Don't look to me," said she. "My parents are in the business of commerce. I go where the strength of our clan takes us. Besides which, Authæn is a student under our shepherd, he speaks with some authority in these matters."

"I do not," said Authæn suddenly. He had grown pale again, and looked unwell. "I had not seen the shepherd Wirthaumuin for three weeks before I departed. I still am his student, but he has never spoken to these plans of my father, though I have always shared them with our shepherd."

There was a confused exchange of glances around the table.

"Why did you not see him for three weeks?" asked the chief.

"He told us that he had to go to his elder brother, one of the firstborn of the Immortals, for council on a grave matter."

"There we have it, such a change to our ways is a grave matter!" said Carbeth with a proud grin.

"It was not regarding something so small as the quality of our shelters, Carbeth," said Authæn. The dead look in his eye caused the other's smile to fade entirely. "I wish that it were."

"What is it, Authæn? What has happened at the henge?" asked Wingilin.

"I will not say, I think," muttered the henge-man-to-be.

Huthram, who had been looking with something like concern at his beloved, now also turned to Authæn, asking: "Is that what kept you from us so long, Authæn?"

There was a silence of expectation, but it seemed to pass the student under the henge by. He sat there, looking listlessly at his food. Finally he said, "Call me 'Doom-bringer'; call me 'Weirdest of the Weird'."

The air in the tent seemed to draw taut with un-answered questions. Then Authæn began to tell his story.

"I had completed the tasks assigned to me un-der the henge, having just returned from the Mother-henge. Yes, you all gasp with right — there should be no reason for a student under a henge to travel to the Mother-henge. But something has happened to make dust of our teachings, at least as I had thought of our teachings. I thought of the Im-mortals in a way in which we should perhaps never have done, for they have never spoken of them-selves in this way.

"They are no more than creature. They have said over and again, as we have sung with their words from childhood, that they are no more than we, only longer lived. And so it was that I was tasked with bringing the shepherd's wife to her fi-nal resting place.

"I was given leave to see my village again thereafter, as were the other henge-students of the eagle-bonded, but I was told that a grave fate awaited me upon my return; one which only I would bear through to its end, or fail, for all hangs on however the path is set before me.

"I asked what fate this might be, but I waited for an answer three weeks, and none came; until the last day of those three weeks. On this day the elder of our henge came to me, telling me that our shepherd had gone out to the Mother-henge to meet his elder brother for council.

"I set out homeward then, as I had been bidden. I travelled through the hard grasslands, and the sandy basins of the steppe. And then I came upon something that seemed strange to me, though it shouldn't have in that land of rugged stone in wilderness: A circle of black rock; very unlike our own.

"They stood there, these black stones calling somehow to my heart. It was the lay of them that spoke in a way that seemed somehow contrary to the way in which the under-earth builds stone; contrary to the rains and winds, and how they shape the bones of the world.

"I spent near a week there, alone. But I did not realise how fast time had sped me by. There were markings on the stone, you see. There were markings that came and went, but always one remained. It was an etching of the terrible Ibex. A giant with the horns of such a goat. I have only heard the rumour of him, as I am sure you all have too, but the depiction was more terrible than what I had imagined, and since then it plagues my dreams.

"On the new moon's evening, a stranger came to the camp that I had made there, a southerner with ebon colours from his staff, to his cloak, to his own weathered skin. And though he had come from the other-most end of the world, his eyes were still bright with knowledge and wakefulness."

"One of the sons of Hamath?" Loangilin asked with wonder in her own eyes.

"Just so," said Authæn. He paused a while, drawing his features together to remember where he had left off. "Ah yes," he said, and then continued:

"The southerner desired to know more about the figures that then appeared, only those that were shown on that very evening. There were 'ladies of heaven' above the Ibex, as he called them, and little men below, bearing tools of strange design.

"I left him there the following morning, having broken bread with him. He was a friend, and I will ever call him Uncle Gaba. He wanted to come to our village to hear more about these 'ladies of heaven', for I think they may be the daughters of the moon that we sing of. When he plans to come here I cannot say, for he decided to stay behind and study the stones a while, but I look for his coming."

"You tell a dark tale, Authæn," said the chieftain.

"Indeed, if the ground beneath our feet was not already shifting sand, you make it sound so all the more," said Carbeth.

"Well, for today we have venison on the table for which we can be grateful," said Wingilin's mother distantly. She had never approved too much of topics that went as deep as this.

"This is true. There is much to be grateful for. I am glad that you have returned to us safely, Authæn," said the chief.

"Me too!" said Wingilin, smiling at her friend.

"Thank you," said he with a heart-felt smile in return. "I am glad to be here for the time being.

68

But my spirit also wanders back to the henge. Now that the wedding is past, and I see that all here is as well as it will be, I must consider returning. I do not know what burden awaits me, and it makes my spirit itch within me."

Chapter Six
The Moot-day

The moot-day was the first day of the week for the river-people. It was the day on which they gathered to discuss all matters involving the village. Matters of conflict and necessity, most often. All voices were heard; though sometimes, if a voice was generally unpopular, it was hushed. At the very least, the moot-day gathering about the council-board was good for making sure that word of what was to happen was spread throughout the village regularly.

Storm clouds had drawn over the land the night before, and the people of Thænim stood presently in a grey scenery. Their colourless clothes furling quietly in the wind. The four fires surrounding the thatched roof were aglow with breathing embers, whilst meat was being roasted over them on spears. All faces were turned to the chief and his twelve elders, as they stood before the council-board.

"We shall begin," said he, addressing the village gathered about him, "as is our custom. We shall begin with the retelling of our fortunes. We shall hear the history of our people. Today it will not be sung. Today I will tell it, for today we must be sober of mind. A turning of the tide is upon us; a wending of the world. We may not forget that, before our ways were established, our fathers wandered ways of their own. Before them, their fathers walked ways of their own. It is ours to honour our fathers, and walk wisely for ourselves.

70

"Let me begin, then, where it is most suitable, namely at the beginning. Our people were not always wanderers in the wilderness of these great steppe-lands. We did not even reside here in the great open grasses, amidst jagged moors, and broiling bogs. Our fathers, the great and immortal shepherds came from the south. They came from the city on the water. The city that now stands empty with curse. They came from the city on the water; the city in the shadow of the mountains in the middle of the world.

"There they were born to men who were not like us. Our immortal fathers were a curse upon the world, it was said, for they were the children of a bitter union: that of the lights of heaven, and the dusty earth of which all other men were made.

"Look into the eyes of your neighbour, and you shall see that what I say is true. Look at the grey of your own skins. Our fathers, the immortal shepherds were born to children of Othan, and so we are also children of Othan as are all men. But their mothers were the daughters of the moon.

"How did this come to be, you may ask? In the time of that ancient hithe's thriving, there were small, dark beings that came from out of the mountain above the city, who saw that the sons of Othan there adored the moon. Around this they made a covenant with those sons of Othan, for the dark beings from the fells above the hithe of our fathers also worshipped the moon.

"Together, they summoned daughters of the moon into our world. This brought the dark beings from the mountains nothing but knowledge, in which they revelled, for they could bear no children; but the men of the hithe saw the daughters of the moon, and forgot their own women. By these foreign beings they had children, and these children were our fathers.

"The children of light and dust were grey of skin — the colour that surrounds us on this cloudy day, reminding us that we are twixt-while creatures. Beings that wander between worlds. Beings that wander always.

"All of you still know the days in which we gathered our tents and roamed for a better place upon the banks of our river to settle. We did this to avoid dangers, and to find new abundance.

"Today we will hear only one matter, for it is a matter that shall determine our path forwards just as the nature of our fathers determined the path that lies behind us. We shall hear the matter of Huthram and Wingilin's wooden hall, which was offered to them by Thuineith the carpenter, through his son Authæn, student under our shepherd — one of those fathers that were cast out of the ancient hithe now mentioned.

"Our fathers once dwelt on the waters, but they were cast out because they were of a different breed. We now dwell on the water once more. We have dwelt here near ten winters, and still we thrive! Yes, we have endured loss, and we have been betrayed by our neighbours, and for this we wet our eyes with tears; but we will not tell the lie that elsewhere along Wirthaumuin it shall be better! We are our own people now. We walk on lands unclaimed. Let us make of these untamed lands a

72

home in which our children will rise like trees along the riverbeds — trees that give life to those that eat from them — and if our neighbours desire to take of that fruit, to take life from us, I say let them! Let them take from us, for it is a sign that we have what they need, and when they recognise this as well, they shall treat us well, to ensure what we have is not lost to them.

"These are my thoughts on this matter, my friends, my brothers, my sisters. I stand here with your elders, for I have spoken of this with them, and they have come to the agreement that, though it is against some of their views, they shall not go to war with the village, if this is what the village desires: no longer to be a village on the move, but a village with roots in the ground, as deep as those of an oak."

Many of the villagers were nodding their approval, many others were staring with open mouths. None of them had heard their chieftain unpack the matter thus before. They had all known his view on the matter, but now he had told it to them as though it was meant to be a part of their broader history, and this had kindled a sense of fate, it seemed. Even Mauthaur and those of like mind seemed to have been silenced by the power of their chieftain's words, and the authority that stood with him as the twelve elders remained silently observing their fellow-villagers at his side.

Huthram, who also stood near the elders as scout captain, now stepped forward to draw attention to himself. Said the scout captain: "Wingilin and I shall gladly accept the gracious gift offered us by Uncle Thuineith and our dear friend Authæn. We ask that the village support us in this, so that the longhouse may be a dwelling for any that need a roof above their heads, and that it not be a matter that divides us against one another. A tree at war with itself, as my father-in-law has taught me, bears no fruit, and is an ugly thing."

"You are all sipping at the same cup!" shouted Mauthaur suddenly. "Above your roar, oh lions, who will listen to reason above fear?"

It was a harsh word, and it seemed to strike the chieftain rather heavily, for his brow shot up, and his hand went to his breast as though he were struck with an arrow. It was clear that he had not intended the proceedings to appear as though he were forcing something on his people.

Before he could say anything, however, Huthram spoke, his face having become hard as flint. "Uncle Mauthaur, your views will be taken up as earnestly as any others. But what is to happen if you disagree with something that has occurred and has lasting consequences? Shall you cast out the children of our decision as our fathers were cast from their home?"

A collective gasp went up from the crowd. There was fear in some of their eyes now, for no one desired a feud. The feuds of their people had been few, but they had all incurred the wrath of the shepherds, and that had led to terrible loss.

"With your decision," said Mauthaur Handless sadly, "you have cast us out of our home, young Huthram. May that hang over your heads for as long as the rafters of your 'longhouse' hold up a roof. Do not forget this day, brothers; speak of it to your children, sisters, for it was the day upon which we of the true path offered up our homes for your childish ambitions. We will not feud on this. You are like the daughters of heaven that brought down a curse on us to begin with, becoming one with the settled dust, as though you belonged to it. But we do not belong to the dust. We belong to it as little as we belong to the full moon. What you say, my chieftain, is true! We are twixt-while beings, and my brother and I shall not pretend otherwise."

Mauthaur and his brother Auring turned then, and departed from the moot of Thænim, and a great many went with them — about a third of the village. The rest of Thænim remained, shocked by what had just happened.

"Your generosity will give us all grass to chew on in meditation, Mauthaur!" said the chieftain, little rills of sadness wetting his cheeks, and not for the sudden drizzle that had begun.

"Then it is decided," said someone from the other end of the gathering. All eyes turned to the place whence the voice had spoken.

"Carbeth!" exclaimed Huthram.

Beside him Authæn had also stepped forth in surprise. He had a place near the elders as forthcoming chieftain. "I thought that you would have departed with the rest!" said he.

"No," said Carbeth. "I met with Mauthaur and Auring, and this was the decision that we could not avoid. I said that I was loyal to you, not to the phrases that you sling around so well. If this is a mistake you make with your hall-building, I shall remain to make sure some of the burden is shared, for is that not also our way? Do we not also share in the mistakes of our brothers?

"They were glad to leave me here to take responsibility for this change, whilst they continue in the way of our fathers, having elected Mauthaur as their new chieftain. Today another small village of the eagle-bound have emerged, it would seem."

The gathering was stunned.

"Truly, there are few in all the history of our people, Carbeth the Loyal, who have been so true to the name that was given them to wander in. You wear it like a prized cloak," said the chieftain.

"Let it be a boon to us all in the times that lie ahead, my chieftain," said Carbeth.

There was no more that would be discussed, as the chieftain had announced, and the meat was being brought under the thatched roof to get it out of the rain. Still, there was reluctance to begin eating. There was too much food, and brothers that had once shared the table with the village had now departed.

"I have the sense that we should be fasting, not feasting," Loangilin said to Authæn as the crowd broke up to begin the meal. She seemed deeply troubled, and he took her under his cloak as they walked towards the council-board together, shielding her from the rain.

"You should speak with Carbeth on it. He has long lacked the listening heart of a woman," said Authæn.

"Hah!" laughed she. "Not all women have listening hearts, Authæn. But I'm sure old Wirthaumuin teaches you other important things under the henge."

As had been far too common for the student under the henge recently, his face was embittered for a black moment. "It was a woman that taught me this, Loangilin. I think no man, though he were of the meekest disposition, could have the same effect. There is a reason I shall never be called mother."

"I shall call you mother, if it cheers your black mood," said Carbeth from behind them, suddenly. They turned to him in surprise at his interruption.

Authæn laughed. "You always know how to make short work of my words," said he. "I would rather not be called mother, please. It was a figure of speech."

"You should choose words that are made of sterner stuff," said the hunter, sighing. "You carpenters will be my end."

"Or we will bring you new beginnings," said Authæn.

"The two generally go hand in hand, round and round, up and down. However you want to look at it. But still. There is only one truth. And in the end it will turn to dust what does not stand in its tent." There was defiance in the eyes of Carbeth as he said this.

Loangilin looked from one to the other, patted Authæn on his chest, and slid out from under his cloak. "Let me listen some wisdom into this man, then, Authæn. You eat. You will need the strength of this meal as the building begins."

Authæn smiled at them as she slid under the other man's cloak. For a moment more, they looked back at him expectantly. "He looks better with you than with that yellow-head, Loangilin," said Authæn, leaving them flustered as he turned to fetch something for himself to eat.

"Using friends to win me over is foul, Authæn!" he finally heard Carbeth manage. But Authæn had seen the way Loangilin had been looking at Carbeth during his visits over the years. He had seen how her eyes had settled sweetly on him handling the prey he had brought back after a hunt, how she had been more than willing to mend and wash his clothes when they became too worn, as they always seemed to be since that daughter of Imnir had left him in the night. It had been Loangilin that had taken his sorrow onto her — the deep sorrow that he would never have shared with Huthram or Authæn.

This had gone on for years, and nothing more had come of it, but perhaps that was all it needed to be, a profound friendship. But why not make one life of it, if that is what they both needed?

There was a quality to Carbeth, the quality of loyalty from which he had his nickname since his coming of age, which meant that he would not abandon the woman that had betrayed him until he had made of it something final. Perhaps she had known this, that daughter of Imnir. Perhaps she had known that she had captured his heart, and now ran about the broad world with the only key. Perhaps she was just cruel, and there was no meaning to it at all. But what Authæn had seen under the henge had taught him otherwise.

When he had taken a rib from the table, busily tearing the well-done flesh from it, Authæn went to stand next to his father, who was currently sitting on his walker frame.

"How are you father? I hope the tumult did not unsettle you too much," said he.

"I am well, my son," said the father. "I am not concerned over my fate so much. It was sealed before you were born, and I am still carrying it out. Ever towards the end. Make sure not to lose that friend of yours, Authæn. He is wise in the way that a bridge is. Many things can move by a bridge; the water, wanderers, wagons. But it lasts many generations. A bridge does not say anything. It simply stands, and yet it stands in a manner that speaks more mightily than any wordsmith ever could."

Authæn nodded. "And still, many need a wordsmith to point this out to them," he said.

"That makes the work of a wordsmith a low work, Authæn," said Thuineith the carpenter. "It is not proud work. It can only ever point at greater persons and greater works than those of the wordsmith himself. A wordsmith points at the truth, because he is most seldom true himself, and wishes others to look away from him."

"That is a growing sentiment in my mind since I have been at the henge, father," said Authæn. "I wish sometimes that I had been swallowed up by the earth after having been born. How much pain I caused you with all my strangeness."

"Stop moping, Authæn," said his father. "You do not know where you come from. You barely know your father." Thuineith chuckled, shaking his head. "Keep that hunter close, Authæn. He is true. And one day, you will know what that means."

"I sense that finally understanding truth would destroy me," said Authæn.

"What our young Huthram said of the eagle that died to save the fox at his wedding is also worth thinking on. Sometimes being destroyed is not the worst of fates, but it depends on the reason for your destruction."

"To be grass and water to the sheep," muttered Authæn.

"What is that?" his father asked.

"It is a saying of the shepherds, father. Nothing more. You speak in their language, it seems," said Authæn.

Thuineith's eyes lingered a while longer on his son, then they were brushed over to where Carbeth stood with Loangilin. The middle-aged man nodded, as though to himself. "Now our work begins, my son. The end of our beginning, as it were."

What those words were to mean, Authæn wondered to his last day.

Chapter Seven
Foundations of Stone

The very next day work on the longhouse began. Where and how it would be built, as well as the beams for it, Thuineith the carpenter had prepared weeks before already. He had anticipated how things were to run once the idea had been put to the village. Now it was to become a reality.

"This," he had said to his son on the day of the moot, as they had visited the site of where the building would begin, "will be my crowning work, Authæn. This will be that for which I am remembered among our people. And they will not look on it happily, I am afraid."

"Oh father, you are as gloomy as I. Think not so much about yourself. Think of the house. That is where your mind works best."

Thuineith had laughed. "Indeed, my son! You do say worthy things on occasion."

Now, in the rain, they were laying the stones of the foundation — stones they and a few other men of the village had quarried from near the river all morning. Carbeth had aided, to their surprise, saying, "I want to know the things I disregard, otherwise they may win me over by trickery."

They would have to go back to quarrying once they had laid the stones which they had now lugged from water to building site, but there was no helping it. Without the proper foundation the building atop it would come undone like a rotting carcass around ribs. Not too far from them the wooden beams lay covered in many furs and leathers, that they would not soak and bend in the wet.

Huthram and the chief were also there, heaving stones in quick succession, and then leaning back to give their weary backbones relief. Presently, Carbeth appeared next to Authæn.

"I am glad you are with us, Carbeth," said the student under the henge.

"That seems to be the only thing that people appreciate me for today," the other said through gritted teeth as he lowered another large stone into the mud. "Tell me, oh wise one, wherefore the stone?" Carbeth stretched his back, sighing.

"It is not common, I admit," said Authæn. "But my father has learned this from some mason that swears by it — a mason who worked on repairing some damage that was done to Imnir's hall when lightning struck it. Imnir's hall is built on stone. But that is an ancient burg, and it is far larger than what we build here."

"Ah yes," said Carbeth. "I had forgotten that you came with us to Glimwæth that time. I suppose I was too busy regarding ... something else."

"Some*one* else, you mean," Authæn sniffed as he prepared to lift another stone and place it.

"Yes," muttered the other. He had stopped moving entirely now. The rain had made of him a drenched statue. "Tell me, Authæn, have you ever fallen in love with a woman?"

Authæn placed the stone he had lifted, straightening himself again and scratching his stubble. He had sheered himself, finally, after the comments on his appearance had heaped to high for his favour.

He had shaven the sides of his head also, binding the rest into a bun atop his head. This was the common cut of his people, but it revealed the marks that wound about his temples. They were birthmarks, but they were strangely symmetrical, some said that it was a mark of the mothers of their race, for the shepherds all had such markings.

Once, whilst Authæn had still been a child, a weirding woman of the reindeer clan had said to his father on their travels, "The old blood flows strong in this one." To which his father had said, "That is why I bring him to you." After that they had left him alone in her tent to discuss something outside.

Presently, Authæn stood up on the wooden beams that had already been fastened to the wet earth to mark out the limits of the foundation, and to hold the stones of the floor more tightly together.

"I have," said he quietly.

Carbeth looked up at him through the wet and through narrow eyes.

"Tell me!" he said.

Authæn looked to where his father stood. The carpenter was issuing commands, then coughing bitterly as he held tightly onto his walker frame. "I loved Wingilin," said he.

Carbeth's eyes fell open, and his head tilted a little to the side. "Do they know?" he asked with concern that warmed Authæn's heart.

"Yes," said Authæn. "But you do not understand."

"Do I want to?"

83

"I think all you need know is that it would have been unwise, and that we are all glad for the way things have now turned out."

"I only wonder about you — I also marvel at you, if you want to know — that you have not settled with a woman yet. You have a heavy burden ahead of you. You have always had a great duty lying in wait for you, but you have decided to bear it alone."

"I do not know that it is so simple, Carbeth. Women do not simply fall into my arms as they do with you and Huthram."

"That is because you hold them at a distance, Authæn. Do you not do it purposely? They are scared that you shall turn them away!"

Authæn burst out laughing. "Is that what it seems like to you, Carbeth? Perhaps you are right, perhaps that is what I do. I think I am frightened."

"Of what? Another person sharing your confidence? There are many of us, I gather, and we are all glad to have you at our side. But you can only truly share your life's breath with one other. Look here at your carpentry a moment, and I shall explain," Carbeth suddenly said moving over to the corner of the foundation. "This beam coming in from the east, you see, is the man. The beam coming in from the north is the woman. Where they meet is their marriage, and from here a house can be built."

"And you decided that hunting was your business?" Authæn laughed.

"It is, I only try to speak in your simple ways so that you will understand, Authæn."

"Of course."

"Of what are you frightened then?"

Authæn looked over to where his father sat again.

"I am frightened of having to leave such a person behind," said the student under the henge.

Carbeth looked down with a frown.

Over the next weeks the building slowly grew wooden pillars, and a high, domed arch over the stone flooring. The outer shell of the hall was finally finished off with the same thatching that Thuineith had used for the roof over the council-board. In the middle of the stone floor, a pit had also been mortared in with flat stone plates. This would be the firepit. Along it, and around the edges of the hall, long benches were set, and furs were laid over the stone that the room might not be so cold. Even hooks were suspended from the rafters that held high the steeple-roof, so that the bounty of the hunters could be hung for smoking in the tall room. Finally some tables were also brought in — though none that rivalled the oaken council-board.

When it was finally completed, the village celebrated it into the final watch of the night. This time all hunters and scouts needed not return to their tents, but could inaugurate the bedding furs of the new hall.

Wearily, Authæn stumbled back from the celebration to the tent of his father. There he at once fell into his furs, as well as into a deep sleep.

White fire fell from heaven, as the clouds wound down towards the glistening grass in the spiral of a frightening storm. Again, a bolt of lightning, then another. Booms of thunder swept the steppes as out of the murk ahead a tall hill stuck from the landscape like a giant lizard raising its head in a plateau from the earth.

There, atop the hill stood the stones of the henge, reaching out toward the spiralling clouds as they slowly and determinedly descended. Thunder boomed again, as the landscape was painted black and white by the lights and shadows of falling heaven.

Suddenly Thuineith stood before Authæn, his back turned to his son. Authæn tried to run over to him, but his feet were caught in something, and he fell to his hands. As he looked down, he saw that it was between the stones of a vast foundation that his boot had been caught, and he tugged, trying to release it.

"Help me father!" he cried, for his father was now the man that Authæn had known him to be as a child, still strong, and not too worn by his sickness. But Thuineith remained where he was, staring at the spiralling clouds that descended on the henge.

Finally Authæn managed to free his boot, determined to reach the carpenter before him. "Father!" he cried, but now the mud was cleaving to him, trying to drag him into the under-earth, as he had once seen the bogs do to a camel.

"You do not know where you come from. You barely know your father," a cruel voice chuckled

86

over the seething air, as winds whipped about the icy rains.

But Authæn pressed on, finally breaking from the earth's hold. He drew closer and closer to his father, but now he saw that, with each move he made towards the carpenter, the man grew older. He was suddenly afraid to come too close to his father, and then the floor tilted up, causing him to slide over the wet earth, faster and faster, towards the now quickly dying Thuineith.

At the last, Authæn was hurled through the bony remains of the carpenter that had been standing before him. He wept, remaining where he was lying on the floor. Not desiring to move at all, though his boot was finally free.

"Where do I come from? Where do I come from?" he uttered between sobs.

Then he was suddenly thrown up. The floor fell away beneath him with a suddenness and a speed that left him reeling and he was above the clouds, standing uncertainly on their woollen vapour.

A light went up, and Authæn gasped as the full moon rounded out before him. Thence one of the daughters of heaven descended towards him in this over-earth where the raging of the storm was a distant rumour beneath. Here all was calm. Here all was quiet. The only sound after a time was the step of the daughter of the moon, which sounded like glass on glass as she strode across the air. Her eyes were endless, swarthy pits of everlasting observation. Her hair was silver lining.

"Are you ... my mother?" Authæn began.

At this the daughter of heaven stopped where she was. Her head tilted slowly to one side. A thin smile curled about the edges of her mouth.

You do not know where you come from. You barely know your father.

Suddenly Authæn plummeted through the clouds again, but after passing through hail, and shadow, and blinding lightning, he fell out into a vast, open darkness, a cavernous maw that seemed to have no end. He fell, and fell, and fell, and fell. It seemed forever, and he tried to catch on the air, if such a thing was at all possible. He tried to extend his cloak, and catch the wind, but there seemed to be no wind here, only stale air.

As he fell, the clouds above began to clear a little, and they began exposing a shape in the deep shadow beneath. He recognised far away grasslands, as though he were a raven flying at a great height, but then there seemed to be a mountain upon the plains; a glimmering hill. Only when the mountain arose, and took on the form of a horned man did Authæn recognise the etching he had seen on the black stone in the wilderness.

The Ibex looked darkly up at him, extending a black and metal talon towards the falling man. *Now our work begins, my son. The end of our beginning, as it were*, the very air itself seemed to say.

"Where do I come from?!" screamed Authæn as he fell to his doom. "Where do I come from?!"

Authæn awoke with a start, feeling as though he had just hit the ground from a great height. The words "Where do I come from?" still hanging on his lips. Had he actually uttered them aloud? He looked about, suddenly. He was drenched from head to toe, and the odd breeze that drifted through the rocking tent was like an icy spider crawling all across his body. At the same time he was too warm, and he flung the furs from him, looking for his father.

Thuineith was not there. Outside lightning struck, and the thunder rolled by his tent with a grim shudder some heartbeats after. He quieted his heavy breathing and dressed himself, belting his tunic, pulling his iron-toed boots over his breaches, fastening his spats over those. He tightened the bracers on his arms, and drew his raven-cloak over his shoulders. Then he pulled the hood over his face and cast off into the dark without.

Almost at once he was run into by a tall, furry shape, and nearly lost his balance. The shape into which he had walked, also stumbled back, regaining its balance.

Authæn looked up at this figure. It was a man dressed in furs. A stranger. The stranger had a spear in hand. The stranger was lifting the spear.

In a desperate movement that thrust itself through his entire body from somewhere deep in his belly, Authæn jumped at the bandit, kicked out one of the enemy's knees whilst grasping his spear with both hands. The right leg, with which he had kicked, landed on the muddy earth, and he used his new footing to fling the bandit wholly from his weapon, onto the ground.

Without hesitation, Authæn spun the spearhead to face his assailant, and drove it through the fur-clothed bandit's open mouth until it was so deep in the earth beneath that the spear held up the dead man's horrid face on its own. Authæn stepped back in a panic. Only with the utmost effort was he able to tear his eyes from the dread work his hands had wrought.

At this, he noticed that another figure was trying to sneak towards him without capturing his attention.

Authæn did not even look properly. In the back of his mind he recognised the movements of the man there, and his body cast itself with a knowledge that he had not expected into an attack. He spun to his left, grasping that man's spear near the head, pulling his enemy in closer.

This bandit had a short knife in his other hand, and a growing smile the nearer he came to Authæn.

At once Authæn leapt to the side, avoiding this brigand's swipe of the knife.

In one fell motion, Authæn flung his cloak from his shoulders, over his opponent, kicking the spear from the other's hand, then pushing him to the ground. Still covered in the cloak, the bandit fell back struggling against the net that had been cast over him.

As soon as the bandit managed to free himself, he sprang up, but into his death; he had leapt stomach first into the spear that Authæn had held at the ready.

The wind was knocked from the bandit's lungs, and he fell to his knees, crunching closed his pain stricken face, until he was limp and dead on the ground.

Authæn had taken up his cloak, cast it about his shoulders again, and began to run towards the tower which his father had built. There a horn hung from the roof of the nest that was meant to be sounded in times of danger.

The great hall they had built stood not too far from the tower, and, as Authæn passed it by, he saw there also dark, furry shapes encircling the longhouse. But it looked as though they had not yet found their way in. The doors were likely barred from within.

Quickly the river-man clambered up the stairwell that wound its way about the tower's sturdy frame, and when he climbed the last short ladder to the top, he immediately grasped for the horn where it hung.

Only just quickly enough.

An arrow shot by him, passing him by but a hair's breadth, severing the bands that held up the horn, causing it nearly to fall over the edge into the dark wetness below. But Authæn managed to hold onto it, dragging the cold metal into the nest. At once he caught some breath and pressed his lips against the mouthpiece.

He failed to sound it for his panic. He tried again, gathering himself a moment before.

A low drone went out over the village. Long, slow, pronouncing threat. Then came another sounding of the horn, and another, and another. Roars of defiance could now be heard below, and the clashing of steel. There was the thudding of arrows, screams in unfamiliar voices and tongues tangled over the air. All the while, the horn sounded in the dark.

When he could sound it no more, Authæn's whole body slackened and he slid onto the floor, lying there as though paralysed, breathing hard.

He heard creaking suddenly coming up from the ladder, and he tensed. The face of another bearded bandit peered attentively over the edge into the nest of the tower. The bandit's eyes widened, and then Authæn's boot smacked into it, casting the man down to the earth so suddenly that he had not even the time to scream. The heavy sounding of his hitting another part of the stairwell on the way down came uncomfortably to the riverman's ears, and he shuddered, drawing himself back again, against the rail of the nest.

The battle below raged on. Then, suddenly, there was a golden explosion, as though fire had burst forth from the earth.

The longhouse was in flames. Fast in their sleep, the hunters and scouts had not heard the scraping of tar onto the thatch of their new hall. Now, having been awakened by the sounding of the dread horn, they had flooded out into brutal combat. They did not even seem far from overcoming their enemy, when one of the bandits had lit an arrow and sent it like the sun goes to dawn, into the smeared thatch.

Despite the rain, the fire caught in the gap where most of the tar had been smeared, between the roof and the ground. From there it seemed to dance with a will and a malicious life of its own from one part of the roof to another. A terrible blaze burst forth golden, and then great pillars of smoke climbed towards the heights, embattled against the darts of the weeping clouds.

Within, Huthram was staving off five of the assailants with a broken bench that he swung about with his lithe limbs.

"Begone with you!" he cried in shock at this sudden attack on so wonderful a night.

Behind him Wingilin held her distance, looking from one part of the hall to another for some way to help. The room grew steadily brighter and warmer, and above the thatch was seething with smoke. Soon, parts of the thatched roof began to collapse into the hall, letting in the rain.

The fires above distracted some of the bandits. One fled for the safety of outside, another called angrily after him in the language of the warlords to the east. Over this one's head, Huthram broke another part of the bench he held, and the bandit collapsed to the floor.

As Huthram picked up the fallen bandit's axe, he was grazed badly along his side by a spear he had tried to deflect. He swung the axe that he had picked up with a mighty heft, cleaving the arm of his assailant open, and Huthram brought down a finishing blow on the bandits head.

Another of the three remaining leapt forward, seeing an opening, but Huthram took the spear of the newly fallen brigand, driving it through the throat of that one.

Two remained now, wearily estimating their opponent, circling him in opposite directions in order that one might flank, and strike his open back. But he did not let them circle far enough. Seeing their plans, Huthram at once leapt towards the one, catching the shaft of the spear with both hands. He rammed its holder away, but it was only successful in that it momentarily stunned the brigand. Now they stood, close together, both tugging for control over the spear.

Wingilin screamed Huthram's name, and he at once flipped the brigand with whom he struggled, to stand as a body shield between him and where he knew his other enemy to stand.

It had been a fortunate manoeuvre, for the other had drawn his shortbow, and set loose a dart in Huthrams direction.

The arrow bored through the heart of the man he held as a shield, piercing Huthrams own shoulder on the other side. At once the man-shield went limp with death, dragging the scout captain to the floor with him.

Huthram roared, falling to his knees for a desperate moment, struggling in his spirit to rise again from the bodies that carpeted the floor around him. He looked up at the archer before him.

Suddenly the captain of the scouts clasped the spear he had now wrested, rolled forwards, and used all of the motion he had built up in this swing to jump into his last aggressor with a deathly thrust of the javelin.

The last bandit was flung up a little by the power of the blow, then fell like a drunkard to the floor, and was dead.

Once more, Huthram fell to his knees. His wounds stung horribly, draining him of much of the last strength left to him. He panted in his sweat, sensing the drawing nigh of his beloved Wingilin.

She would not let him lie down here to sleep forever. She screamed words at him that he did not know, but loved. He drew on them the strength to lean on her as she helped him deftly to his feet. Together they stumbled into the bright world of flames without as, behind them, the crowning work of Thuineith crumbled to its foundations of stone.

Chapter Eight
The Worm's Kiss

In the red of the great hall's glimmering carcass, Carbeth had begun screaming at whatever villagers were near enough to hear him. Their enemy seemed to have fled, if they did not all lie dead at the feet of those that were meant to have been their victims. As the hunter flailed his arms and his words alike in fury, all he said was punctuated by the pillars of the hall that leered into mourning heaven like whale-ribs behind him. The grey of dawn had begun to light the clouds above as well, bleakening the scene with grim revelation.

Authæn had just come down from the tower to hear the tail-end of something his friend had shouted into the frightened face of Folgnuin, who stood all alone before him with wide eyes.

"—those carpenters and their great plans of prosperity! Look at what has become of us! We are lesser than we have ever been! We have fallen drunk into the arms of our enemies; drunk, not on mead, but on complacency! What was I thinking! What was I thinking!? Why can I only ever choose what is cruel? Where is some health in this burnt world? All is a charred and bitter breakfast — a waking to the knowledge that we were drowning in Wirthaumuin from the first, never to stride out of its jealous bed!"

Carbeth fell to his knees, roaring. In him Authæn saw all of the sorrow the man had borne in the past years well up and flood out in this single dreadful display. The hunter's hands relaxed at his sides as he began to sob pitifully, and Authæn saw blood-bitten axes slide limply from both of them.

Seeing the henge-man, Folgnuin ran into him, clinging fast to his legs. He laid his callous mitt onto her rubine head, unaware that he was looking for her mother; unaware that he noted for himself not to see her amidst the gathering before him. Unaware, and yet thinking that her fate might be to become the child of another river-family according to the law of Wirthaumuin.

His eyes locked with those of Carbeth then.

"What have you done? What is this, monger? What works do your hands set up as witnesses against you?" whispered the kneeling hunter.

Authæn only stared at him coldly.

Then Wingilin burst into the gathering, a heavy Huthram on her shoulder. She tripped and stumbled forward, bringing both herself and her man to their knees near Carbeth. The hunter saw them, gasped, forgetting all of his complaints, and crawled over to where they were. Wingilin sat down now, weeping, Huthram rolled onto his back, breathing heavily. Carbeth tended to his wounded friend in an addled way.

All the while Authæn only stood there, looking coldly on the scene that played out before him against the background of that cindery skeleton.

"Where are you, father?" he muttered. Perhaps Folgnuin heard this, but he could not have said. His mind was adrift between dreams and waking. He thought then to hear again the haunting words:

*Now our work begins, my son. The end of our be-
ginning, as it were.*

At that moment the chief arrived, panting,
painted in the blood of those he had laid low. He
looked down to where his daughter and Carbeth
were tending to his son-in-law in the mournsome
mud. He looked to Authæn with a curt nod. Then
he looked at the burning longhouse, shaking his
head and gritting his teeth. Closing his eyes for a
moment, the chief seemed very quickly to come to
terms with what he was faced by.

Then he said, addressing all of the villagers
that had gathered there: "My brothers! My sisters!
A terrible thing has befallen us this night! But we
do not yet know the extent of our danger. We cannot delay with putting our hands to the necessary
tasks. First of these tasks is to bring the wounded
to the council-board, so that our *mith-aumuinan*
can look at them. Then it is to find those of us that
have fallen in the night. We must commit them to
the river with the setting of the sun today.

Slowly the village began to rattle itself from
the sleep of sorrow, making their way through
every body strewn over the sodden ground. One or
two of the bandits that had fallen on them in the
night seemed still to be alive. These were bound
tightly, and brought to the ritual ground with the
dead. Those of the bandits that were dead were
stripped of their belongings and cast hatefully into
the dwindling flames of the burning hall. The sick
odour of death was everywhere one went.

Authæn went at once back to his tent to seek
out his father. He told Folgnuin to be brave and see

if she could help or learn from the *mith-aumuinan* as they tended to the injured. His father was not in the tent just as when Authæn had awoken to the assault, and he tried to remember whether the old carpenter had even been there upon his stumbling into sleep here after the celebration.

Thuineith had certainly been in the hall with the opening of the celebration; he had still spoken of how the great hall marked the end of one way of life, and the restoration of a true way of life for which the river-people were destined. Had he left early?

He stepped out again, looking for any sign of the old man. He returned to the hall, where he asked a young man, who had once been apprentice to the blacksmith Auring, whether he had seen anything.

The young man, who had been staring mournfully at the wreckage of the hall, looked through glassy eyes at Authæn. He blinked a few times as the question that had been posed to him sunk through his broad brow, then he shook himself, wiping the tears from his eyes.

"Your father, the honoured carpenter. Yes, I thought I saw him go out that way, into the southeast, soon after he had said his part last night." The blacksmith pointed to the south-eastern corner of the ruin, near which a door led out of the village.

Authæn hesitated, then thanked the blacksmith. He strode carefully over to the place that the apprentice had shown him. There he found the tracks he knew well to belong to the walker-frame of his father. They were covered by the many tracks of men and women that had crossed here in search of their loved ones, or in flight from the brigands, but he knew the marks of the walker-frame so well that they caught his eye at once. The rain had done little to wash them away.

After following them some hundred metres from the village he found the walker-frame broken and cast aside. Desperation gripped his heart, and he looked up to where the ridge arose to make a near horizon against the brightening sky. He began to mount the ridge, hearing a call from behind and ignoring it.

He followed the tracks of his father's straining boots into a place where boulders made a narrow pathway to the top of the ridge, and upon reaching the top he finally stopped. It was as though ice had come into his blood.

"Authæn! Authæn!" came the voice of Loangilin from behind. Then she stood beside him, frozen just as still as he. She laid a hand onto his chest, not turning from the sight on which both their eyes were locked.

From the boulders whence he and Loangilin had just emerged, a round green of turf spread over this part of the ridge, in the middle of which had been placed a square-hewn stone, akin in likeness to their own father-stone. Atop it, laid as though into a burial boat, lay Thuineith the carpenter. From his chest protruded a long, cruel dagger of black metal like the sting of an oversized hornet.

Without words, Loangilin closed her embrace around her friend, laying her head onto his breast, and sobbing quietly. Small rills of wetness also flowed from Authæn's eyes, and not for the drizzle to which the rain had now subsided.

Now our work begins, my son. The end of our beginning, as it were.

Wingilin watched fretfully over the sleeping Huthram, who was now wrapped in bandages where he had been hurt. Next to her stood Huthram's mother, weeping for her son (and silently praying that her daughter-in-law would not fall to the same fate as she had suffered these long years). Huthram had been laid under the long oak of the council-board. Atop it were those patients still being treated by the healing *mith-aumuinan*.

Carbeth sat against one of the pillars still grumbling. Presently, he muttered: "Look at what these carpenters have done to you, sweet Wingilin."

But Wingilin would have none of it. She strode over to where the hunter sat, who stared blearily up at her, and struck him across the face as hard as she could. He tumbled to one side, getting quickly to his feet. Many of the *mith-aumuinan* had stopped in their healing work to look on in wide-eyed caution. Huthram's mother gasped in shock.

The hunter stared at her with a raised brow, injured in pride more than in face, though a rare red mark began to glow upon his cheek. "What has come into you?" he whispered.

"Who built this roof to keep us dry!?" she screamed at the top of her voice, and it broke. She gathered herself, and continued: "Who built this table on which the *mith-aumuinan* now heal our wounded brothers and sisters? It was the carpenter you curse. Now be silent. This horror was brought on us by devil-raiders that were trying their luck. They have paid sorely for their folly. Do not follow their dice-play; it was a gamble they lost. You have spoken yourself about the importance of those carpenters. Do not speak against what you have said, otherwise the ground will turn to sand beneath your feet, and the river will wash you away."

She turned as though to return to the table, then she looked back at Carbeth, tears streaming down her muddied grey countenance. "I do not want that you be washed away, Carbeth," she said, and then she did return to her husband, leaving the hunter shaken and alone in the rain.

When the sun was kissing the horizon, the village gathered along the ritual ground. Tonight there were no totems to decorate the dark earth. There were no animals that were brought to display the ways of the flesh, for here, rocking in boats that had long been kept in the boat-wagon of Thænim on Wirthaumuin, was the uttermost end of the way of flesh.

Here, rocking in the rushing of the father-river's swollen current, lay the dead of Thænim on Wirthaumuin. Among them lay the great carpenter, Thuineith, and the mother of Folgnuin, who was silently weeping whilst clinging to Wingilin. There were others. Faces and names which had been known in the village as well as any. Now they would be sent down into the ever-moving waters of the river, themselves never to move again.

103

Before the gathering the chieftain now stood, draped in the dun colours of the ferryman.

"We are come to the edge of the river," said he. "Who of us shall turn back?"

The gathering responded to this with the well-known words: "We are come to the edge of the river. The living shall return."

"But here on the edge of the river the ferryman waits on his barge," said the chieftain.

"The living shall return."

"But here on the edge of the river, his barge is filled with our kin."

"The living shall return."

"Return to the ways of the water, my brothers and sisters long-tired. Return to the ways of the water, to the one who sent you into this life. Return to the ways of the water, and when the days come to their end," said the chieftain.

"The living shall return," responded the village gathered there.

Then, one after another, the boats that these departed villagers had built with their coming of age were unbound from the riverside, and drifted swiftly away with the current.

For countless hours beneath the waxing of the moon, which peered from time to time through the curtains of the clouds, the village looked on after the loved ones they had lost.

"The living shall return," said little Folgnuin, and an elder woman in the gathering began to weep heavily.

Then a scout that had been sent out to look for any threat on the horizon returned, riding almost onto the ritual ground with his steppe horse in his haste.

"What is this foolishness!" pronounced the chieftain of Thænim angrily.

The youth on the horse was too frightened to show the expected decorum. "There is grave danger on the horizon, my chieftain!" said he.

"Get down from that horse, boy!" demanded the chieftain, and the boy did just that, in a manner that showed the weakness of fear was on him. "Take the horse away to the stables. Come with me, boy. Wife? Bring us warm tea. This young man is in need of it. Put lots of honey in."

"Th-there is no t-time!" screamed the boy, looking at everyone's feet, not daring to look into the eyes of his fellow villagers. His pale grey skin shimmered with the jewellery of fear; the black-and-gold of his lion-eyes darted this way then that, his dark bun atop his head bobbing now here now there as he looked about in panic. His spirit was crawling into itself. His woollen garb was drenched through with sweat, but not from the riding.

"What is it, boy?" said the chieftain, his patience thinner than any had ever seen it; perhaps he too was afraid.

One of the twelve elders finally managed to wrest the thong of the horse's reins from the boys clammy hand. The boys eyes shot up with an urge to fight the elder of a sudden.

"JARAUR!" the chieftain's voice finally managed to break through to the scout by means of the boy's name, and Jaraur's eyes snapped to look into those of the chief, which were now stern though not unkind. Meanwhile, Authæn asked the rest of the village to head in the direction of the council-board, where the news would be shared when the scout had found his voice. At the back of the crowd, Authæn saw Carbeth. Their eyes met, but Carbeth quickly looked away, and departed with the crowd. Authæn returned his attention to the boy. Only he and the chieftain still stood before Ja-raur, the elder with the horse having returned the mount to the stables.

"It was like a thousand red eyes, settled on the hillock, my chieftain," Jaraur was saying. "The torches of what looked an army in size. They were gathered, ring after ring, horses everywhere — horses armoured! And then …"

Jaraur's eyes grew in fear, and he looked past both Authæn and the chieftain into the night bey-ond. The two men spun about, thinking that there was perhaps something behind them, but Jaraur had only been reliving what he had seen whilst scouting. The chieftain patted his shoulder, taking his arm gruffly to regain his attention.

"What did you see, Jaraur?" bade the chief again.

The boy clenched fast his jaw a few times, nodding as if encouraging himself to say the words that would conjure the horror now wormed into his mind; as though trying to suppress the need to be sick then and there at the memory of it.

"It was a giant," said the boy, looking up dir-ectly into Authæn's eyes then. "It had the horns of an ibex curling from its tall helm, long limp rags covered it, but I saw beneath them a black armour, battered as if with much heavy use. It ..." Jaraur struggled with himself again. Then he regathered himself. "It slew those that had returned to it. The fur-clothed bandits, they had been slaves, sent to scout out our home. It slew those that returned to it. It said ..." Again the boy must overcome himself. "It said that it had wanted the carpenter alive. It wanted to know who had killed him."

"Who killed him?" Authæn demanded suddenly, taking a threatening step towards Jaraur. The henge-man was momentarily very aware of the blood only recently washed from his hands, and he battled to keep them at his sides. A bloodlust had suddenly burned a zealous ardour in his veins. "Who killed my father?" said he more calmly and more frighteningly.

"I don't know," the boy whispered frightenedly, shaking his head and looking from Authæn to the chieftain and back. "The monster killed the bandits before any of them had chance to speak. I ran then. I rode as fast as I could. I wanted nothing more of that nightmare, but I can't escape it," Then Jaraur began suddenly to weep, falling to his knees.

At that moment the chieftain's wife returned from her tent, bringing a pot of tea and some cups. Authæn left before she could offer him any. The chieftain looked after him warily, his wife looking a question at him.

"Leave him. It was a heavy blow he received today, my heart," said the chief.

Authæn wandered as if caught between a dream and the waking world. Visions of what he had been and done under the henge seemed to return to him from a great distance.

To be grass and water to the sheep.

Sometimes being destroyed is not the worst of fates, but it depends on the reason for your destruction.

"What was the reason, father? Why were you taken from me?" muttered the henge-man to himself. He drew forth the black dagger which had been lodged in his fathers breast on the stone square atop the ridge to the east. It still bore his father's blood on it, but he could not feel the loss as he thought he should. There were only questions and a pressing weight on his spirit as something crying out desperately to him, but he could not understand its language. He had looked down into the burial-boat of his father, but had found himself thinking of old Wirthaumuin and the duty that awaited him at the henge.

How had the Ibex known of his father? Had the great wooden hall drawn this dark attention from outside? No. There was something greater at work here that he could not understand. Perhaps he really had not known his father, and having heard these very words from his father's own mouth caused a bitterness and a sense of betrayal now that his father seemed to be bound into a much bigger web than merely the finery of Thænim's circle.

"Why did you never speak to me of these things, father?"

Authæn found himself climbing the tower. It had been the first of his father's great works, and the one of which Thuineith had been most proud even when the building of the hall had commenced. When he reached the top, he lifted the horn from where he had left it on the grooves of floorboard. He tied it to the roof of the nest again. Then he turned east, where he now knew the Ibex camped on some hillock, knowing exactly where their village was to be found. He stood there for a long while, then he slid to the floorboards along a post that held the roof aloft, wrapping his cloak tightly about himself.

As he waited there for some daughter of the moon to perhaps descend from on high, to take him to another world, Authæn saw Wirthaumuin before him in memory. The shepherd himself was some two men tall with a long beard of the same hue as his skin woven down to his knees. His grey hair had been tied in a bun atop his head, much like the one Authæn wore now. Along the sides of the shepherd's head there had been markings, but they were different to those of Authæn.

"They shall change with you, my son," the shepherd had said. "They shall reflect who you are, always. Do not hide these markings, for they are your testament to the world. You are no ordinary son of dust. You are a river-person, and that is a far lower thing, and therefore all the more important. What house can stand without a foundation? Is the foundation not the lowest part?"

Chapter Nine
The Rede of Eagles

Authæn woke with a start, the sun casting its rays like darts into his burning eyes. Someone was clambering up the stairs of the tower, and he raised his boot in preparation of kicking without meaning to. Suddenly the face of Loangilin appeared from over the edge where the ladder climbed into the tower's nest, and he relaxed. Collapsing to sprawl over the hard floorboards again.

"Authæn!" she cried, exasperated.

He started into a sitting position at the urgency in her voice.

"The village has decided to take up the pilgrimage again," she said, clambering up into the nest, and sitting down beside him. Her face was drawn with sadness that made her look much older, and in a frightening way much more beautiful to Authæn. Perhaps it was because he felt sad as well; he felt it somewhere in a place of his spirit that would now be empty evermore.

"Pilgrimage to the henge?" he asked horsely, and cleared his throat.

She nodded.

"That used to happen only every hundred years," said he.

She stroked her hand over the floorboards as though clearing dust from them.

Authæn put his hand on her shoulder and she looked up at him with a raised brow. He nodded at her. She smiled and nodded back, then she went back to swiping the floorboards with her hand.

When he drew back his own hand, a bitterness suddenly shook his whole body, and he said, "Ugh."

She looked up at him again, her face waxing with concern.

"I must go and put together our tent now," he explained. "I have the sense that I must not mention him, but he is gone, and I don't want it to be so!"

She squeezed his shoulder sympathetically. "I will help you with your tent, if you help me with mine, henge-man."

"That sounds good," said he.

Upon reaching the bottom of the tower, he suddenly said, "Now that I think on it again, Loangilin, I want to do this alone. I shall join you when I have done with it."

She nodded an understanding smile at him, and they headed off on their separate ways.

When he reached the tent a sense that all the world was slowly tilting to one side made Authæn feel somewhat unsteady. The light of the sun seemed to dim and yellow from its prior golden-red, and he felt a chill as fire crawl over his skin, leaving him feeling unwashed. He noticed then that he was unwashed.

"Your sleep clings to me father. May it be more peaceful than my waking," said Authæn to his spirit. Then he ducked into the mouth of the tent.

He went through his father's things slowly, remembering as best he could how the clothes had

111

hung on the carpenter's form during a time in which he had been sounder of body; thinking back to the way he had once smoked his pipe, and how he had played the lyre which was now in Authæn's possession. He looked at the polished wood of the instrument, but all desire to play it had fled him.

The henge-man sighed. Then he began to, methodically and orderly as he could, pack everything into the wooden chests that he remembered his father making after their fifth migration between camps. Their old chests had all fallen into the bog in which they had lost their camel. Now they … Now Authæn owned only his father's steppe horse. He had never had a horse of his own, for it was not the way of the shepherds to ride. They were called to wander the lands by foot.

For a moment Gaba the wanderer returned to Authæn in memory. Then Authæn looked down at his own hands as though the blood of the slaves to the Ibex he had slain still clung to them. There was much about him that marked him as anything but a shepherd. A shepherd was meant never to take a weapon to hand in combat. He had leapt into the fray like a wolf, suddenly revealing himself to be a brutal killer, no peaceful scholar of his people's songs.

The dead face of the bandit with a spear through his mouth resurfaced in the quiet horror of his mind, and all at once, Authæn felt like he had died a long time ago, and a stranger now wandered the waking world in his body.

"Authæn?" he was suddenly startled back into the present. The walrus-head of the chieftain peered through the flap of the tent. The face waxed from hesitant concern, to a kindly smile.

"Come in, uncle. I am just gathering our ... *my* things," said the henge-man.

"Take what time you have, Authæn. The enemy is sure to come for us here. We must find safe haven," said the chief, entering and patting the chief-to-be on the back. "I am truly sorry for what you have lost, Authæn."

Authæn's lips smiled but he did not look up. "The river flows on."

"The river flows on," repeated the chieftain, nodding. "I will leave you to it, then." And he departed again.

And so Thænim, which had had the desire to be permanently settled along the banks of ever-flowing Wirthaumuin, began to roll up its tents that had so long stood on the soil of that place. Chest after chest was filled and loaded onto wagons, some of which had now grown green with uselessness.

The camels were once more loaded with the treasures of their masters, the horses readied for a long and weary road. The herdsman began rounding up their goats and cattle with familiar cries, sending their dogs out to keep the order amongst the livestock.

Autumn was drawing into the land as well, with chill westerly winds drumming over the wold every so often, and so the children had to be dressed warmly, to ward off the cold.

What crops had been quietly cultivated about the tents of folk more green-fingered were now harvested, whether ripe for the scythe or not. Dried meats, and meats hung in temporary smoke houses were prepared for the journey ahead, and whatever could still be baked amidst the upheaval was baked.

And so, at about the fifth hour after noon, the village had been packed onto wheels, as it had often been in the days of old. If one were to have paid close attention, one might have seen the chief sit a while, despondent atop a boulder not far from his village, speaking to his spirit with the words: "What have we done, dear Mauthaur? Were we so blinded by the lights that our brother brought with him from the south? Were you right to leave our gathering? Now we are pressed into the mill of our fathers to be weathered by wandering for the rest of our days, despite our brave resistance."

The village began to roll out of the valley in which they had so long been settled. There was no way upriver along the bank, and the sun was moving into the south, leaving the world to winter in the north. Thus they would have to wend out into the east, and then make their way across the open plains northward, toward the safety of the henge.

They rolled from out of the valley, wagoning, into a broad land, undulating with emptiness to unconcerned eyes. Not much more than the copses of aspen and the outcrops of rock amidst the odd and jagged plateau crossed their way today.

In the middle of the procession on long, open wagons, the injured from the prior night's battle were borne, ever attended by the diligent *mith-*

aumuinan. Wingilin sat there, Folgnuin sitting quietly beside her. Wingilin's mother, and the mother of Huthram were also there chattering nervously as the day gave and the sun fell westward into rubine sleep. Huthram was still asleep. He had not woken since the day of his injuries.

And then an eagle swooped down, casting up the dust with its mighty wings, landing on the gloved hand of its bearer. It was the eagle of the scout second in command, who had sent it to gather tide of the lands ahead.

In its screeching language he conversed with the bird a moment. Then he rode to the fore, where the chieftain was riding his own steppe horse.

"My chieftain!" said the scout, calling forth the walrus-man from his moody reverie.

The chieftain saw the stern glance of his scout, and the anxious eagle on this proud man's arm, and said: "Tell me."

"The enemy moves on us. They have four-hundred horsed archers at least. Each of them seems to be outfitted in some black metal, so that our attacks will glance from their armour easily."

The chieftain paled.

"How did they know that we move?" he asked.

"They had sent ravens to watch us, chieftain."

"What are we to do?" the chieftain muttered, more to his spirit than to the scout that rode beside him.

"Become the river," said the rider, despite the fact that he had not been asked.

The scout's chieftain looked up into his eyes. Both aspects were hard as flint then, both knew from personal scars what this would mean.

"Gather the willing," said the chieftain with so much command in his voice that it made the scout attending sit up straighter in his saddle when he nodded his assent.

"As you wish, my chieftain," said he, and rode in amongst those that looked fight-worthy.

Within the half-hour a fine company of men and women with the will and wherewithal to be dangerous to their enemy departed from the village, headed by their chieftain. The rest of the village was sent with its twelve elders towards Glimwæth, for which they would have to turn back, and ford Wirthaumuin to the south, before crossing into the country that grew steadily more forested, and more sheer to the west. The pilgrimage to the Henge would not be possible with the enemy towards the north.

As the warband of Thænim's chieftain thundered northward with the ardour of vengeance, Authæn found himself riding shoulder-to-shoulder with Carbeth.

The hunter looked across at his henge-man friend awkwardly, as though trying to apologise with his eyes.

"You have a hairball, methinks," said Authæn without expression.

At once Carbeth's mien broke into a painful grin.

"I am sorry, Authæn," said he, and now his smile faded at once. Tears came to his eyes, though

Authæn could see that Carbeth hated himself for it. "I cursed you and your father in the shadow of his greatest work, before it was even cold. I was set upon by my demons. And now I shall never be able to tell him how I *did* revere him, despite our differences. Forgive me, brother."

"Let us say, brother," said Authæn, "for us the waters of Wirthaumuin are thicker than blood. You still live. Don't you leave me as my father did. Not just yet."

At this Carbeth laughed aloud (or cried, it was not certain) with relief. "Today we become the river, and the river flows on through all ages!"

"We become the river!" Authæn repeated.

"We become the river!" chanted their whole host of a sudden. "We become the river! We become the river! We become the river!"

And then they rounded the bend of a slightly taller hill, and found themselves charging a teaming army of black upon black — metal on horseback, bearing bows.

Their enemy was visible, yet distant, and the suddenness of their appearance caused the entire warband of Thænim to come to a clumsy halt under a rumoured wind of fear. Some of the horses neighed rearing, and some of the riders shouted. But then their chieftain cried a command, and they came steadily to stand at his attention once more.

There, in the dying of the light, the chief looked each of those there gathered before him in the eye. They were some twenty-three men, and seven women astride all manner of steppe horse, bearing bows for hunting, and knives for skinning.

Some bore other metal instruments, and a few even bore weapons they had salvaged from their assailants in the night of the raid.

Then the chieftain nodded proudly. Even he now had a tear in his eye.

"My brothers! My sisters!" he began. He was quiet then for a long time, taking a while simply to look at them again. He seemed not even to be looking for words. Once he nodded to himself, as though he were confirmed in some quiet deliberation. Then a new-found certainty flowed from him over his people.

"Today," said he at last, "we BECOME THE RIVER!" and he raised the spear of his fathers high.

"We become the river!" his warband repeated, though his certainty was still somewhat weak within them. Behind their leader they were being charged by folk the like of which they had never dreamed up in their worst nightmares. Jaraur could be seen to bead again, as did many others, with the pendants of fear, remembering the dark night in which he had first seen these frightful foes.

"We are each a droplet," said the chieftain of a sudden, and he had their attention, for he had said it without the slightest fear in his voice. Now they all looked to his smiling eyes as he rode from one end of their company, then turned his mount to ride back to the other end again. All the while he smiled like a man at peace.

"Alone," he continued, "a droplet falls into the sand, and where the sun does not lap it up at once, the dust shreds it and divides it amongst itself.

118

There is far more dust here than there are droplets, brothers, sisters. And the grasses also want their share. Shall we scatter, like a brief pretence of drizzle?"

Some amidst the warband were shaking their heads, some whispered the word "no". Some smiled back at their chieftain with growing resolve.

"Bring one droplet together with another," said he. "Then add another. And another. And another. And ..." he turned his horse to face the enemy, "another!"

"And another!" the warband began to chant. "And another!"

"Today water is thicker than blood indeed, brother," Carbeth chuckled beside Authæn as the chant continued and waxed in its intensity. Soon they were all shouting it, as though their war cry were more effective a shield than any of the darts that their foes could send out toward them could pierce.

"And another! Become the river! And another! Become the river!" the shout suddenly changed, and the chieftain spurred on his horse, leading his warband to glory, whatever their forgettable end might be. The thunder of their little band in the face of that deep, dun cloud that gathered at the backs of their enemies would have been laughable, were it not for the shout that even almost the wind seemed to join then.

AND ANOTHER! BECOME THE RIVER! AND ANOTHER! BECOME THE RIVER! AND ANOTHER! BECOME THE RIVER!

The two unlikely forces were two hundred metres apart, when a wind like a storm cloud suddenly spiralled in from the heavens above.

The warband of Thænim came steadily to a halt again at the command of their chieftain. "Here is the answer of our shepherds, my friends!" he cried.

"This is not the work of the shepherds," Authæn whispered to Carbeth, and the other looked from him, back to the falling pillar of black cloud with a concerned grimace.

Within the whirling of the stormy limb that had suddenly gathered from a prior clear heaven, white fire now fell into the ranks of the warlord army ahead, scattering them like a wild ocean of beasts. A great tumult and uproar came from their enemy, all the while more fire fell from heaven, making ash of their assailants. A fire caught brand in the grasses of that place. Some odd trees that had grown on boulders, and in the sheltered bends of the plain, were cleft down as well. The lightning took on more and more the quality of a blood-lusty axe, which clove away anything that dared draw too near.

The cloud bent, as though blown by the wind, over the seething remains of the army then. And fire continued to fall there, chaos continued to drive the dark-clad forces to destroy one another in sheer horror and panic.

Finally a terrible roar, some command, went out from amidst the writhing black see of horse and man. There was a partial response amongst those mounted archers.

Another roar, and now the enemy regathered itself, despite the death that loomed above, returning to some formation as best they could.

Not slowly, the storm suddenly began to clear. The heavy winds that had been swept up now swept away the wonder that had brought them forth, and even stars appeared above.

All there saw a man, then, where the cloudy pillar had touched the grassy plain. He was cloaked in dark leather — his hood cast back by the gale — and he bore an ebon staff in his right hand. Beyond the man who seemed so small before that quickly rearranging army, another figure suddenly grasped the dreadful attention of the onlookers.

Tall as two men he arose from the midst of his black-armoured warlords, there he had been drawn in a carriage. Now he climbed onto a vast chariot, driven by two large warhorses. His servants parted as he descended through their ranks and came to a halt before the ebon man with the ebon staff.

There stood the great and terrible Ibex upon his dread chariot.

Chapter Ten
Black Iron on the Anvil

The voice was like stone grinding iron and like a mountain falling in on itself all at once. "*Gaomun-gâlak butum iztunaoz-nagi ukunagidlazg,*" uttered the voice of the giant as the very shattering of the air. It disembarked the chariot, setting itself directly before the man that had commanded the storm. The words it had spoken were directed alone at the southerner in a language foreign to all others there gathered.

In the bleak twilight it all seemed more a nightmare than it was. Behind the Ibex, the many torches and the burning of the world cast out a hellish landscape, and at its head stood this monster: it stood tall as a tree, its high, angular helm bearing the horns of its namesake, yet there seemed to be no holes in the helm for eyes; only along the side of it, narrow vents let out the creatures vaporous breath. It's narrow limbs were bent all with well-fitted plates of an armour the like of which none of the river-people had ever seen — onyx, well-worn, and drawn over with curling lines of meaning that was too dark and too far beyond them. But over that dread shell there hung the limp grey of a forgotten garb, long weathered beyond its original cut and hue, now serving only to frighten and to remind of the decay of all things.

"*Ûmûdlazg iztunaoz-û, agûbiliz izkaotizkuluz,*" returned the southerner in a voice that could only just be discerned amidst the roaring of the fires.

In an eerily precise movement of the head, the Ibex tilted his visage slowly to the side, regarding the man who travelled storms with helm-hidden hatred.

Then, in the twinkling of an eye, the beast made to swat away the southerner with its trunk-like arm, only for the southerner to catch the limb with his staff.

Lightning leapt from the earth, pounding like a hammer against the midriff of the beast, and its many dangling cloths began to blaze. It roared with agony and stumbled back a few steps.

"Kill the fool!" cried the Ibex then, his iron-barbed tongue making of those the most fearful words on earth.

At once all the anxious horses in their dark regalia, and all of the riders, having drawn curved swords for the near work of butchering, surged towards the southerner. They fell in atop him, so that he was quickly hidden from view, and then the horses began to fall over one another, their riders crushing under the weight — a most horrid spectacle of the fear of men, and how it drives them to folly. Only a fraction of the four hundred that had at first charged the river-people remained.

Beyond the terrible undoing of his horde, the Ibex was seen to leap onto his chariot and flee into the north-east, where the wold stretched and then eventually dipped into a land of boggy mire. On the western end of the chaos, many of the black-clad horsemen made for an escape.

"We are safe!" cried the chief. "We are delivered!"

There was wonder in the eyes of the river-people, and fear; but at the words of the chief they cheered. "For Thænim! For Wirthaumuin!"

Then from somewhere amidst their little warband, a voice began again to chant: "And another! Become the river! And another! Become the river!"

The entire party joined in with the shout once more, and their chieftain roared with laughter. The ritual shout that they had sent out demanded that they see this work finished, and as the hordes of the Ibex had clearly been defeated, the river-people now charged the fleeing giant's warlike wagon.

At the same time lightning seemed to strike out of the starlit sky, to a place not far from where the chariot charged on, casting another red glimmer over the lands, as new fires grazed on the hard turf at the Ibex's wheels.

"I see the storm-rider there!" cried one of the scouts.

"Then he has survived! That is good news! I would speak with him!" called the chief over the drumming of their hooves.

"I think I know that man, my chieftain!" said Authæn.

"All the better!" returned the chief.

For another half-hour they thundered after the chariot, and then it seemed to slow. The Ibex halted in a great open plain. The hills amongst which they had first met for combat now standing to the backs of the river-people. A gust from the east heralded the rot of the bogs, but in this light they could not yet be seen.

"You are brave, little water rats!" boomed the voice of the Ibex. "You did not think that I was fleeing, did you?"

At this, the shadowy figure of the giant moved in the light of the half-moon, and Carbeth cried out, "He fires!"

But it was too late.

The chieftain slid limply from his horse, dragging it to one side with his dead weight. Yet the river-people charged on, their chant raised once more.

Become the river! Become the river!

The Ibex now roared with laughter, releasing three arrows all at once from its cruel bow. All of them hit their mark, and one of the horses fell, the others having been pulled away by their dead riders, causing another to stumble over it. A few more of their number were lost.

Still the river-people surged on.

"Such fury," uttered the Ibex's tremendous voice in the dark. "Such revengeant lust." And then the giant laughed like the shattering of stone.

They were nearly upon their enemy, when lightning struck the earth before it, and the horses veered off to either side, splitting like water parting for an island. The river-people circled about again, as of one mind, but they brought their mounts to a halt, for where the lightning had struck, the southerner that had saved them now stood.

126

"Halt!" said he, though they stood still already. "He would crush you! Have you not already need-lessly thrown away too much?"

"If not them, then I shall crush *you*, my false shadow!" chuckled the Ibex, making to strike the southerner again.

"Down, worm!" cried Gaba, and white fire leapt up again from the earth, striking away the gi-ant as though he were a fly. Then Gaba took the staff in his hands like a club, and swung it thus as well, sending a great hammer of streaming fire into the bones of his contender. Then he slammed the staff onto the earth, and a great breath was held on all the air, before a bolt fell from heaven, breaking over the now flattened Ibex as iron flattens on an anvil. New flames roared up about the gathering, throwing dark red light over all that moved here. The horses neighed and reared; the riders strug-gling to handle themselves, never mind their mounts.

Authæn quickly slid from his saddle, and left his horse to run, if it would. It cantered off to the side nervously, but it was too well trained to fly far from its master. Authæn himself tried to move closer to the battle between the great powers before them.

"Back now, dear Authæn!" cried Gaba, sud-denly looking over his shoulder and throwing the river-person flat to the ground with a movement of his free hand. The power of it was like the tail's whip of a water-dragon, gruffly carrying him across a long space, so that he remained where he lay for a while, dazed.

127

Before Gaba the Ibex arose again, now like an orange-glowing skeleton, freshly forged in the smelters of the under-earth. The air about that once-so-dark yet now-so-bright form of the giant shuddered with the heat of his smouldering armour. Not a forlorn cloth was left on him, only chain and plate, and these were fusing yellow, even as the gathering watched.

With renewed vigour the Ibex lunged at his enemy, but Gaba thrust forth his ebon staff with both hands, as if shielding himself. The Ibex was caught against some unseen force of air, and he could not move forward, though he ducked into its assailing powers dug his heels into the crumbling turf beneath. Ripples of white-yellow to blue coursed across the now cooling shell of the beast as it contended against a wind brought forth by the staff.

"*Úzkudlinaz-zîk?*" shouted the southerner through gnashing teeth, ire and despair mingling in an unknown question.

"*Bûgnaz îzgushikiliz-laoz!*" returned the voice of the Ibex, though it seemed now to hold more the quality of a loose bow of horsehair on untuned strings.

For another moment the two figures as those from a strange and power-hungry dream stood thus, an unpronounceable force pressing between them. Then, finally, Gaba slapped away the other with the staff, bringing the Ibex to his knees. There the tall creature panted, now ashen-grey and steaming in tendrils of white after the damage wrought by the elements on its metal hide.

The southerner stepped tiredly towards the beast, breathing heavily. "*Ûzabaz îbaoz?*" said the southerner wearily, leaning on his staff, and putting his other hand as a fist against his hip.

The Ibex only raised his head slowly to stare without eyes.

Suddenly wroth, Gaba lashed at the faceless mask with his staff, and it cracked in twain, shedding the Ibex of his horns. Beneath was a face of charcoal grey. It's eyes pale with blindness. Its mouth a ghastly seam of lipless teeth from one ear to the other. Without any emotion it stared unseeing into the face of its conqueror.

"*Ûzabaz îbaoz?!*" the southerner demanded once more, now with less patience.

The Ibex's eyes dropped then to where they would have regarded Authæn if they were to have had any light left in them; but they were blind. "If you want to know whom I serve, my shadow, only follow the trail you have already picked up," muttered he. Then that great terror crumpled forward and into itself, collapsing into a cloud of ashen dust. A sigh went up from the place where it fell into itself, rising upward to be caught on the fell breezes of the bog like a reluctant whisper.

The southerner breathed in, then sighed the depth of a world bygone. "So passes the last of an order," said he, looking a moment warily at his staff, then turning finally to meet the eyes of the river-people he had saved.

They were all silently staring now, frightened by what this strange traveller on storm's wings might have in store for them.

Authæn had now arisen once again and stood beside Carbeth, who had brought back to them the lifeless body of the chieftain on the back of his horse. Their other fallen comrades were presently also being returned to their company by others. A tall, dark arrow stuck from out of the chieftain's chest, yet his features were peaceful, his eyes closed as though he had only laid down his head to rest. At this, Authæn began to speak the words of the song that he had learned from the southerner at their meeting, laying a hand on the breast of his past chieftain.

Far and long the road that leads
To the end whither we strive.
Let the songs and melodies
Of those long past ancients rise:
Let them guide our weary tread
To lay down our dreary head
In our final resting bed.

"So be it," said Gaba with a sad smile. "It was a fool's errand, hunting ancients such as this, but so we are brought to meet once more, my friend."

"I thought that you might one day come to see our village," said Authæn, smiling back sadly, "but the days of Thænim on Wirthaumuin seem to have come to an end with their chieftain. My people move for Glimwæth, where they hope to find shelter beneath the Shoulders of Imnir."

"Indeed?" said the southerner. Then he turned to address the rest of the river-people company. "I thank you all, my friends, that I needed not go through this battle alone! You have paid a heavy price by offering up what few lives you had to spare. Their bravery will not go unrewarded."

"What now, Authæn?" said Carbeth suddenly, glancing a moment at the southerner with wide eyes. "We must commit these dead to the river."

For a moment Authæn stood without moving, looking down at the place where the Ibex had fallen. He was chieftain now.

"My duties call me away, Carbeth," said he finally. "I must return to the henge, where some untold duty awaits me. I will guide this man there, our deliverer, for he desires also to know more regarding the birth of our race, and of the mothers of the shepherds.

"To you, my brothers and sisters, as the man that should now be your chieftain, for our past chieftain has fallen, I say this: I am not yet trained, and I have been called back to my training under the henge. When I return thence, alone then shall I be worthy of guiding you through this wilderness. For now go to the rest of the village. Where you ford Wirthaumuin, commit these heroes we have lost today to the river. Then take up your dwelling amongst the people of Imnir's land. Be a boon to them, that they bless you.

"Carbeth shall be your chieftain until Huthram is well. When he has healed from his wounds, Huthram shall be chieftain, and the elders shall be his guides; but Carbeth shall be his right hand. So Carbeth and Huthram together will command what our beloved chieftain once did."

Carbeth was stunned.

"Let it be so! The chieftain has spoken, and we have heard!" proclaimed the scout second in command, causing Carbeth to start.

"Let it be so!" the rest of the company said.

"Then," said Authæn, "under the countless witnesses of star-beaded heaven above, and under the … fifty eyes here gathered," Authæn looked uncertainly back at Gaba, for his two were among that number. "I am witnessed. Let me be true for your sakes."

Authæn embraced Carbeth, then sent off his people, bidding them to hurry and not leave the travelling village defenceless. His eyes lingered sadly on the chieftain's body. "Take my horse as well, Carbeth. If I now return to the shepherds, I should do it in their manner, without a mount to carry me," said the henge-man. His friend nodded.

"Take even this with you, good Carbeth," said Gaba of a sudden, raising the two horned halves of the helm he had smitten from the Ibex out of the dust, and offering them to the river-man. "In Glimwæth you shall win the personal favour of the king, if you show him this helm. It is known and hated well in that country."

Carbeth nodded his thanks warily, taking the fragments in his strong grip and tying them to his saddle. Then they made off.

As those brave river-people rode again into the darkness whence they had pursued their dread enemy, not understanding the danger and the deliverance that had lain in wait for them, Gaba laid a heavy hand on the shoulder of the henge-man, saying: "Thank you, Authæn. Thank you for what you have given today."

"I have not given as much as those that even now wait for their true chieftain to return to them, uncle," said Authæn, turning to smile gratefully at the southerner. "But it is good to see you again. The sight of a man so noble and so powerful strengthens me against that which still lies ahead of me."

"And what may that be, my son?" asked the southerner.

"I must confess to my teachers that I have broken their law," said Authæn. "I have slain men. I have ridden to war. I have not lived by their teachings, and so I am unworthy of them, but they also wanted that I return to them, because they desired to belay me with a task on my return. Let us see if they are still of the same mind when I have told them all of my crimes."

"Whatever they decide, Authæn, I shall stand by you," said Gaba.

And so the henge-man and the ebon man began their quiet journey northward, where the world was growing daily darker.

Part II:

of   Respite

a   n   d

Remembrance

Chapter Eleven
Ghosts of the Past

It arose from the bubbling mire like a dragon's yawning maw; its jaws were like the everlasting bones that hold up the high places of the world. About it clung heavy carpets of moss like a hide of coarse furs: a monstrous cavern in the western mark of the bog. The song of the many thousand insects of that mist and mysterious world drove on from place to place with the high jumps of green hoppers; gurgling and sliding underlined the melody as great serpents descended into bubbling pools of emerald-cloaked water, and the croaking frogs punctuated the rhythms of that heather-held world from bridges of stout grass. The lair of the Ibex beckoned. The work of the black staff was not yet done.

Before the western edge of the bog, atop a jagged cliff that looked down onto the landscape of many waters that dwindled into the grey, Gaba and the young henge-man, Authæn, were gathering their things to continue on their journey. They had made camp there for the night, and having now arisen to the foul stench of decay, they were unable to tarry longer.

"Uncle, you said that you must go after the lair of that terrible horror which you slew. Wherefore?" bade the henge-man.

"For that I must explain to you the history of the Ibex, and the tale of why I have come into this northern world of yours," said Gaba.

They finished packing together their things, strapping them to their persons to the best of their ken. Then they made their way down from the cliff by narrow, slipping water-ways, until they stood with their feet lapped by murky pools.

"Here," said Gaba, "follow the heather, but let me go at the fore; it may have grown in a thin cloak over the water, and you would be sent into the bubbling depths, were you to step on it. I will test the walkways with my staff."

They began wading into that veiled world of fogs and sounds unseen, slowly treading through the dripping grass until they themselves were dripping from the clouds which hung about.

"The story of the Ibex," began Gaba then, having considered a long while how he should begin, "is bound to the forging of this ebon stick I use to fare me far across this barren world. It is a story that tells the beginning of my order, for my order began with the beast you knew as the Ibex, and his brothers, but their way led to corruption, and ours to cleansing."

Authæn listened carefully to every word, wondering what world this southerner must have come from, so full of orders, and he was frightened of a sudden at the thought that the man he had trusted into the mire was bound somehow to the giant that had only a day before threatened him and his people with destruction.

138

"There were five of them, though I know not what happened to the others. They still linger in the far corners of the world, I gather. Each of them was bound to one of five such staves as I here tap in the blind world ahead of us."

At this, Gaba suddenly stopped, raised the stick above his head, and slammed down with it on the heath before him with terrible aggression, and again, and again. Authæn, stumbled back a way, nearly slipping, wondering what fell vapour had slipped into his companion and possessed him to do this. Finally the southerner quietened again.

"A viper," said the other, holding aloft the worm he had beaten dead. Then he drew out a thin knife from his belt, cut off its head, and hooked the limp length of snake to another part of his girdle.

"Where was I now?" muttered he, staring on ahead.

"You were saying that there were five of the Ibex's race," said Authæn.

"Yes! There it was! The Ibex and his four brothers. The Five. The Giant's Hand, they were called. Though that was in a time in which they were still men. Why this Ibex grew into such a ghoulish monster, or how he left behind the body of the man he once was, I cannot say. I know only that he was stripped, as were his brothers, of their weapons, and they were banished from our lands, for they had begun to grow greedsome in their use of these powerful artefacts.

"When word reached us of this Ibex, we knew that he must be one of the Hand, for he spoke with the tongue of our people in his mouth, and there

139

were other signs. You see, dear Authæn, the Ibex had been sent up to this corner in search of a mighty weapon. The quest for this weapon was his exile, the rumour of which said that it could fell even the old beasts that wrothe in the water at the beginning of the earth."

"Tell me, uncle, was that the speech that went between you and it at your meeting?" asked Authæn.

"'Twas, my good man, so it was."

"What was it the beast said? It sounded so fierce, and yet you answered seeming much angrier than it."

Gaba remained silent a while, as the road they were taking became somewhat trickier. Then he said, "When it saw me, it recognised not only that I was of the order that had betrayed his own in his sight, but that I was bearing this staff, which once belonged to him. These weapons are mighty, Authæn, and they are bound to the very spirit of those that wield them. If such a weapon is turned against its prime wielder, it is as though the wielder's very own spirit has turned against him."

"Is it by this ebon stick that you can fare even on the wings of storms?" Authæn asked.

"'Tis," said Gaba, "but to return to the words with which I was greeted, the Ibex said, towering in all his menace before me: 'And now they send my shadow that I might be devoured by it.' To which I replied: 'If you are devoured by your own shadow then you have lived far too long a time already.'

"Still he fought, though he knew that there was no defeating himself; for this was a battle against his own betrayal in the past, not against me. He fought against his betrayal of our people, and he fought against the task to which he had been appointed, namely to serve our people with the power of this staff. In truth, what remained of him is in this staff, and the troll that we have sent back into these swirling mists, not quite dead yet, was his shadow, but he saw it as being the other way round."

"How do you say 'not quite dead yet', uncle? I saw him fall like so much ash from the pot of his broken armour," said Authæn.

The southerner chuckled and looked over his shoulder for a moment, then returned to forging forth the path ahead. "I must ask your pardon, Authæn. I have been on the road long, and I have forgotten my prior sense of answerability to those around me. A sad thing, because without the people that have carried me along the road, I would not have gotten much further than those faraway borders of my home.

"The truth is that this staff cannot remain whole if the spirit of its prime wielder yet lingers in the world. I am almost certain that the Ibex's last breath has fled to his lair here in the bogs. I can hear his spirit's lonely song calling to the staff. I am bound to follow it, and to finally make an end of this menace. That is why my order sent me here, so that it is not by the hand of our people that yours must suffer."

A strange warbling and rasping as that of the chattering of goblins came to their ears from not too far off.

"Then we are blessed by your coming, uncle. But uncle, will not the staff fade away when the spirit of the Ibex is defeated?" Authæn asked.

"Indeed," said the southerner simply.

They walked on a while in silence. Then, from out of the fading mists arose the cavernous maw of the lair. The sun of the day was now cleaving vengefully at the earth-clinging clouds with its discerning gaze, revealing more of the flat shape of the bogs. Here and there a dead tree or a drooping willow stood like a grim shadow in the bleak dance of the vapours, rising like a bastion for all that sought not to drown in a world that was slowly being pressed into a wet suffocation. And now the two travellers saw upon all of the trees near the lair sat rows upon rows of glistening black ravens, chattering and complaining in the dew.

"What do your people call this land, Authæn?" the southerner asked suddenly, frowning at the river-person through glittering eyebrows.

"We call them the *Noal-withaur*," said Authæn. "The Waters Breathless. But the traders and kaupmen that travel these parts on their wayfaring into the east call it the Murkwing Mire, for it seems strange with its own breed of these black treacheries." He indicated the ravens.

"Interesting," said Gaba. "Thence comes the call to the staff; from within the grotto there."

"Then we need not delay, uncle," said Authæn. "If you are ready for the task at hand. I for myself

142

desire to return to the henge with all haste. My crimes weigh on me heavier than these mists weigh on my cloak."

And so they came to the mouth of the raving maw, the black birds still speaking, one over the other, with their mad chatter. The raving subsided somewhat as they stepped into the cool dark of the mouth, striding carefully deeper over carpets of slimy yellow and green. Little things scattered before them, but the two travellers were concerned with darker, less visible forces at present, and paid little heed to the beasts that scurried by. Finally Gaba let a little light flow forth from the staff; its pure blue like a cleansing balm on this ragged place.

It was not a very deep cavern, and they did not have to look with great care, before they came upon a thing of interest to them both. There, in the back of the cavern, lay a large, round stone. It was black, and its surface was the size of a house altogether.

"It was on just such a stone that my father built the first and only tower of our village!" cried Authæn suddenly, leaping forward to study the melalith more closely with his fingers.

Only just did the rills in the skin of the tips of his fingers brush the stone, and a sudden light pierced its face, causing the river-man to step back and the ebon man to step forth.

Pale lines, as with the light of the moon began to draw themselves like tears in glass across its obsidian surface. At first it was all as senseless as a hasty spider's web, but then it took on a character

143

of meaning, and in not all too long a time figures as those etched along the wall of the stone circle in which Gaba had first come upon Authæn presented themselves.

"Terrible!" gasped the southerner, for there, upon the now line beleaguered stone were the images of the tale he had just told Authæn regarding the history of the Ibex. "Could it be that these dark stones in your country listen to those that speak near them, and take up what has been said?"

"I cannot say, uncle. The stones that bear witness amongst my people are less talkative," said the river-person with a quiver.

"It is usually a foolish thing to do, touching one artefact of power to another, but in this case I am too curious to see what will happen if ..." Gaba reached out toward the circle with his staff. At its touch a great wind swept into the cavern, and the earth began to rumble and shudder as with the waking of a mountain's ire. The staff turned to powder in the hands of Gaba, and he cried out in dismay. Then the lights of the stone began to fade, and slowly the world grew quiet — quieter than it had even been before. The warbling of the mad birds was stilled.

The companions stumbled from the dark, returning to the mouth of the cavern, and stepping back onto the now sun-touched heather that stuck like the hair of armpits from the walkways of the bog. With noon-tide the land looked much more peaceful, though the hiddenness that remained at the edges of sight did not undo the unease that this place laid in the belly. Nowhere all around did they now see a single raven.

"They must have been frightened away by the shaking of the earth," noted Gaba.

"Perhaps," said Authæn. "Unless they were bound here by the powers that have now been un-done. The staff is no more, which must in turn mean that the spirit of the Ibex is no more."

"Indeed," said Gaba sadly.

"Why are you sad about this, uncle? Is it not a good thing?" asked Authæn bemusedly.

"It is, my son," said the southerner, "but I am left as though naked now. I have no further weapon to carry me through the wilds. I knew that this day would come; but I had hoped in my heart that the leave-taking would be more gradual. Whatever the case, we ought to leave these sinking lands and make our way toward that henge of yours.

"The thought of learning more about this land heartens me, for ... I still do not know what powers the Ibex served here. Clearly he was under the power of some shadowy threat, and I think that image of the little men, and the ladies of heaven are the key to the riddle."

"Of your 'ladies of heaven' I can tell you some things as we journey on, uncle," said Authæn. "They were the mothers of our race, and so our people are bound up very closely with them."

"The mothers of your race?" muttered the southerner. "Perhaps that is what the Ibex meant. I have struck upon some path that will lead me to answers. I hope that they do not lead into another miring cavern."

"For now at least they should not, uncle," said Authæn. "The henge of my people is north, in the lands that lie higher up, nearer the mountain root that stretches inland from the west. It lies near the source of the river of my people, the river Wirthaumuin."

"Ah, a river," said Gaba. "An important river to the henge-folk. This all aligns with the circle of black stone at which we met. I saw many things in the days of my studying it. But never again those etchings of the mothers of your people."

This time in thoughtful silence, they returned to the edge of the bog and mounted the lands that quickly climbed there to open steppes again. Above, the sun shone according to the second hour after noon already.

They began the march northward through those broad, dun lands again. Now it was Gaba who asked and listened, as Authæn explained the history of his people to him.

"Our history begins with the history of all men," Authæn said, "but it becomes our own, the history that has left us bruised as your own people but with a grey of skin and eyes as those of the lynx, with the arrival of the daughters of the moon."

"I see, then that is their name," said Gaba.

"That is how we know them from our songs. But we have never met them ourselves, and some of our people have forsaken our ways, thinking that all such stories are but idle myths.

"But the daughters of the moon are no phantasms, or else we would not look as we do, singular amongst the children of Othan, and we would not have been driven away from our homes."

"Where was the home of your people, before you were driven out?" asked Gaba.

"In the south. On the eastern shores of Murmur-mere, they say our city stood — the city of our fathers. But our fathers, seeing that we were cursed, maltreated us, and finally cast us out, driving us into the north to find a home apart. For their own failure they have punished us. It is all the more why I cannot deny that I have failed my own fathers, the generous shepherds, and must return to them. I cannot make the very mistake that led to our exile; that led to us ever wandering and never settling. Where our way is breached, the price must be paid."

"I see," said Gaba. "And these daughters of the moon, whence did they come to the fathers of your fathers? What became of them?"

"They were creatures of twilight, and creatures of the dark veils of night. They were called forth by the ancient magics of some unknown folk that dwelt in the mountains above the city of our fathers. All of that people worshipped the moon. I have heard some of the shepherds refer to them as the Ghouls of the Middlemost Fells."

"The Middlemost Fells?" asked the southerner.

"Those mountains that lie in the middle of the world," said Authæn.

"Ah," said Gaba. "I have sailed across Murmur-mere, for I had to cross its glassy deserts to reach the high halls of Imnir's folk, but I did not stay along its eastern shores. There was the shadow

147

of a tall berg in the distance there though, now that
I think on it."

"Then you have seen the home of our forebears, uncle! That is wonderful!" exclaimed Authæn.

"No, Authæn. I saw only the shadow of mountains. We did not sail near enough to see what lay
amidst their roots, or what crawled along their
shoulders. Murmur-mere is vast, you understand. It
takes many days to cross it's muttering mirror-
scape. But it must be those mountains of which
you speak. Then they have a name for me as well
now. The Middlemost Fells."

"Indeed, uncle, the Middlemost Fells," Authæn
said thoughtfully. "Perhaps I shall still see them in
my short years, those mountains and that forsaken
city."

"The city stands empty?" asked Gaba.

"Oh yes, uncle. It was forsaken not long after
my fathers were driven from it. Some curse lingers
over it," Authæn explained.

They climbed presently up a ridge in silence,
keeping their breath for the tall steps that they had
to take to rise. Upon reaching its crest, a vast country was set out before them like a dinner table, and
at their feet a small forest of pine and birch made a
stubbly embrace of the curves of their hill. From
this height, in the distance ahead, they were shown
the slow beginnings of folding stairs, as if fashioned by giants, though they were in truth the work
of a shifting world. They looked like great
wrinkles in the landscape, climbing from one to the
other, riven sometimes by narrow, winding streams

and waterfalls that looked from this distance to be no more than silver chains. They were called the Giant's Stair. Beyond those rising fells, there could be seen peaks, but these were not the heart-mountains of the great towers of stone in the west. These were all only foothills.

To their left and west, the great body of Wirthaumuin ran in a winding meander from those foothills, also descending into the south-east by a great waterfall that cast a foam into the air.

"The daughters of the moon, uncle," said Authæn, "departed as soon as their children were born to the men by whom they had been begotten, and those men, who had forgotten their own mothers, wives, sisters, and daughters, began to die as though their life's breath had been taken along with those heavenly ladies that had shared in it. The men of the city under the Middlemost Fells were left with children that they did not love, and the Ghouls of the Middlemost Fells had lost the ladies that had brought with them the secret knowledge of the heavens. And so the ghouls returned to their mountain-homes, and the men of the city began to bicker and war, driving out the children that reminded them that they had failed their own people."

"It is a sad story, Authæn," said Gaba, "the story of your people."

"Let us hope that in us, its children, it finds happier satisfaction," returned Authæn, smiling at his companion.

Chapter Twelve
The Secret in the Steppe

It took them four full days of wandering in that flat land, a thunderous wind hammering across the plain all the while, before they reached the feet of the rise they had seen from the ridge. Amidst the roll and jagged breaking of the lands that stood between them and the climb, they sometimes lost sight of their mark; but they knew ever to head northward and slightly west. The nearer they came to the Giant's Stair the more forested were the moors that now began to tumble upward.

Amidst those moors, the two travellers came again upon the weeping wade of Wirthaumuin's waters. Near its familiar babble, having followed it to the shower of its fall from some cliffs above, they decided to make camp for the night. As Gaba built up the fire Authæn went to see if he could pike up any fish with a spear that he had fashioned from a straight sapling. All around them the trees grew tall, and amongst their roots the first falling colours of autumn had begun to conceal moss and fern. Using Gaba's knife, Authæn had whittled away one of the ends of the pike into a sharp stake.

Visions of the raid on Thænim had burst across his spirit as he had shaped the pike, and he had seen again the face of the man whom he had stuck with a spear through his mouth. His appetite faded, but still he went to work, seeing as his punishment that he did not desire the food that his body needed.

"I will climb a ways up the waterfall, uncle, to find rocky pools along the water's path," said Authæn to Gaba. "I shall not be away long, and I will not be too far, if I can help it."

Gaba nodded, having looked up from his work, and so the river-man departed, leaving his cloak and boots with his companion. He climbed easily up the jutting stones that heralded the beginnings of the Giant's Stair. When he was above the level of the trees, beneath which they had made their camp, Authæn found a place where the water had hollowed out many pools in the stone. Here Wirthaumuin leapt from over a crag that reached a ways over the pool beneath, allowing for a large hollow to form, curtained off behind the silvery fall.

Curious of what treasures might be found within, Authæn stepped lightly from stone to stone on his way to the waterfall, pressed himself against the grey of the rising shelf alongside it, and slid past the shower along its edge. Behind the waterfall was a large island, from what he could make out in the dark. It was made up of stone and dirt, and the floor of it crunched beneath his bare feet, but he saw nothing here, other than the low ceiling of the stone above, rising in an alcove towards where the water sprang from it. He looked over the dirt and stone beneath his feet, and spotted what looked like the remains of a fire in the middle of the island.

"How old are you, I wonder?" muttered Authæn to his spirit, and he knelt down beside the charcoal and half-burned branches heaped together

152

there. "This is surely not a wise place to make a campfire, visible to all that approach from without, whilst none approaching from beyond the curtain are visible to those sitting within? Or what if there is flooding on a stormier night?"

Idly, he brushed away the cindery remains, wondering if there was anything in them that would give a clue as to who might have stayed here the night. Suddenly his fingers came across the cold of metal, and his hand quickly withdrew of its own accord, uncertain of what the icy touch had belonged to. With a closer look, he realised that something was buried there.

"Can't be all too deep," he muttered, and began to excavate it by means of his pike. Soon a small, shallow chest sat before him next to a hole in the ground and a mound of river sand. It was square, an ell in length and breadth, and about half that in depth.

"But another secret in the steppe," said Authæn, scratching the short beard that already clothed his chin.

"Not one meant for you though, weird-eye," said the deep voice of a stranger.

Authæn span about, but there was no one behind. He looked around desperately, wondering who had spoken, but he could not make out much in the dark. Frantically he began to crawl back to the place whence he had entered that curtained hollow. Nothing came in his way, and he quickly escaped, clambering back down to where the southerner had gotten a brand to burn.

153

"Uncle! Uncle!" exclaimed the river-person breathlessly.

The southerner looked up with a raised brow.

"What has happened, my son?" he looked at Authæn's spear. "I see that it has kept you from fish, whatever it may have been. A bear?"

The other shook his head, breathing deeply so that he would not simply shout words that had no string of meaning to them.

"There was a voice," he finally managed, "but I did not see its owner!"

"What did it say?" asked Gaba, rising to his feet and patting the dust of work from his hands.

"It responded to something I had said to myself in my thoughtlessness."

"What had you said?" pressed the southerner.

"I found a campfire's remains above, in a cavern beyond the river's fall. There I dug and unburied a chest. I thought to myself that this was another amongst the many curious riddles in these steppe-lands. There have been so many strange things to surface here in the last days. Then the voice responded, saying that this was perhaps another secret, but that it was not for me!"

For a moment the southerner thought about this, then he said, "We must know whence the voice came. If it is a bandit or so he may come over us in the night and do us harm. I would not want that."

"But we have no protection against threats!" said Authæn.

"We have this spear of yours," said the other. "I have been trained in warcraft, my son. Give it to

154

me, and stay near, and nothing should go too far awry."

And so they returned to the hidden place beyond the waterfall where the chest lay, this time each carried a burning torch made of some cloth wrapped about a branch. Gaba sidled in first, taking care not to douse his torch, and calling out, "Ho there! We come meaning no harm!" Authæn stood close behind, his eyes darting from one corner of the now illuminated cavern to the next.

"You say this secret is not for us," said Gaba, drawing nearer the chest that still stood in the middle of the island. "Why do you not show yourself?"

There was only silence as a response.

After having looked around a few times more, Gaba knelt down before the chest as well, holding his torch over it, and guiding his fingers across its design. It was a simple box, yet bound by stone instead of iron, and along the stone that held the dark wood of it in place were designs so delicate and detailed as Authæn had never seen in all his life.

He also drew nearer to catch a sight of the depictions, and his brow rose in astonishment. There, along the stone edges of the chest, were depicted many histories and terrible battles of a stout folk, armed with strange devices, and another folk, smaller, stranger, as without proper faces.

"I recognise these," said Gaba.

"The little folk from the stone circle," said Authæn.

"Indeed, those wielding these devices. But there is a smaller folk than they against whom they

155

battle! How strange. But even here, my son, observe these mounds. They are like barrows, mounds of burial that the sons of Imnir raise for their dead, yet they all of them bear trees atop them — trees of seven branches."

"Then this may be a chest built by one of these stout folk that seemed opposed to the daughters of the moon!" said the student under the henge, also crouching down before the box now.

"But what have they to do with the Ibex, I wonder?" said Gaba.

They continued to study the finery that was chiselled as though by needles into the stone. Then Gaba rose again, looking about.

"Are you certain that you heard a voice, young Authæn?" he asked.

"I ... was deep in thought," said the river-man. "It also did not speak again after I heard it at first, and so it is possible that my mind had mistaken the sounds within for sounds without."

"I see," said the southerner. "Then this is your final chance, oh voice in the stone, or in the water! As this chest has been unburied, we shall unbury the secret within this locker."

"Are you certain, uncle?" asked Authæn, but Gaba only knelt down again, and attempted to lift the lid. It did not come open, and he sought out a keyhole, but found none.

"There must be a mechanism somewhere to open this box," said he.

Then, suddenly, a profound voice as deep and rumbling as that of a giant thundered into that place from behind them, saying: "WHAT ARE YOU DOING?"

They span about, Gaba holding the pike at the ready, Authæn raising his hands in fists in case he had to defend himself.

Before them, not much shorter than an ell itself, stood a shadowy figure, garbed in grey. They saw it for but an instant, before a frightful wind blew into the cavern through the waterfall, drenching Gaba and Authæn, and extinguishing their lights.

"I posed you a question, gentlemen!" thundered the little creature again.

"Remarkable!" said Gaba.

"What are you?" cried Authæn.

"No! I ask you my question first *and* you answer, and only once this ritual is complete shall I consider deigning you with a response, weird-eye. I asked you: WHAT. ARE. YOU. DOING?!"

The very stone of that place seemed to shake with the force of its voice.

"We are in search of answers, and this chest seems to contain them!" said Gaba quickly, casting aside the wooden steak, and raising his hands to indicate his mild intentions. Seeing this, Authæn also opened his fists to be less threatening.

"That chest, as I have said, gentlemen, is of no worth to you. It is a secret better left buried; and now I have to find a new place to bury it too! DO YOU EVEN THINK?!" boomed the voice, and there was what sounded to be a dangerous crack in the stone above them. "OR DO YOU ONLY ACT WITHOUT HEED!"

Another loud crack.

At this, Authæn felt Gaba pull on his arm, and they both ran and dove through the wet curtain, into the pools beyond, hoping that the water there was deep enough, and not to strike any stones.

As soon as they had felt the cold of submersion, and had battled into the current that swept towards the waterfall, there was a tremendous crash behind, and a swell of the water caught them up, casting them dangerously close to the edge of the hurtling drop.

They both came to the surface of the foaming waters, clinging to stones that protruded above the fall like teeth in a massive underbite.

"Authæn!" cried the southerner. "Authæn, climb up, or you shall fall!"

"I am holding on, uncle!" said Authæn. But then he realised that the strange sense of movement he was feeling was not only due to the rushing waters, but also because of the coming loose of stone to which he clung. It dropped remarkably again, causing him almost to lose his hold on it, as some stray root or other seemed to catch on it again. He took a deep breath. Shouted a wordless cry.

Gaba saw with horror as his guide to the henge fell from the edge of the waterfall, the stone to which he had so desperately clung tumbling alongside him into the roar beneath.

"Authæn!" he cried out of sheer horror. "Authæn!"

He must get down, he thought. Then he looked up, seeing that the stone beneath which the chest had been hidden had collapsed, and that this was likely the reason for the surge in the current that had thrown his companion over the edge.

"Blasted, shrunken, treasure-hoarder!" the southerner screamed, struggling back to a better foothold, and then regathering his breath before he made for the way down.

When he dropped the last short distance to the forest floor, Gaba stumbled to get a better view on the place where he had seen the river-man fall into the water. It was too dark. He would need to light another torch.

He turned quickly and made his way to the fire, only to find the dripping figure of the river-man standing there, shivering, his arms pressed under his armpits.

"Authæn?" cried the southerner.

The other only stared into the flames.

Gaba ran up to his companion, grasping his shoulder coarsely.

"Authæn!" he repeated.

The other was startled from his state of shock, and recognised the face of the southerner.

"What happened, Authæn? I was worried!"

"There was … some great hand in the water, uncle. It caught me, and hit aside the rock. It … It had a face!" exclaimed the river-man. "It reminded me of …" But the river man could not bring himself to finish.

"What did it remind you of, Authæn? Authæn!" pressed the southerner.

"It reminded me of my shepherd. But I have never seen our father do such a thing. If it was he, then the henge will know of our coming ere we arrive. Has he watched me all this time?" again the river-man drifted into the thoughts that were locked away behind his eyes.

"Rest now, dear Authæn, rest. You have had a terrible fright ... a terrible fright," said the southerner, and fell down into a sitting position by the fire himself, forgetting that he was no warmer than his companion.

The following day neither Gaba, nor Authæn awoke, for neither had slept. They had lain down to relieve some of the strain on their backs. When they had begun to truly feel the bite of the cold, they had stripped most of their clothes, to let them better dry near the fire, wrapping themselves in their cloaks. Then they had tossed about in the frightening furling and ravelling of their thoughts.

Now the sun brought a red glimmer into the heavens, showing that its singular eye was just as stung as those of the sleepless two. In silence they gathered their things, and then, just as they were about to return to their journey, they looked at each other, both knowing that they had to return to the place where the cavern had been collapsed by that strange goblin garbed grey.

They clambered up the side of the cliff again. In the sunlight, they now saw that the ruin of last night had caused the water to spill even further than before, so that it now splashed beyond the original river's path, wetting the earth outside the banks. There it had already formed new rills and ways by which to flow.

They did not approach the place, for fear of further strangeness. "Whatever is bound to that chest seems cast in strange magics to me," said Gaba.

"Strange magics for a strange folk," muttered Authæn.

"Indeed."

Their journey continued into the highlands that rise towards the west, out of the vast basin-country that formed much of the eastern nomad lands. As the day progressed, both Gaba and Authæn began to recognise the signs that they had caught a cold.

So they halted for lunch, and Gaba made a tea. They still followed the waters of Wirthaumuin, and it was from the father-river's waters that the tea was brewed. After this they made a trap for fish in the water, building a small cove of rocks with a narrow entrance where some boulders had made it easy, after which they lay down to rest and let the tea do its work.

Authæn woke first, but with a start. Looking about, he saw that it was near four in the afternoon. He could not remember what dreams had driven him to waken, but he was suddenly reminded of the fish trap by his rumbling belly, and so he went to see if it had caught anything yet. There were some trout swimming about in the cove. The fish opened and closed their mouths, uttering silent questions, swimming round and round the little pocket in the river without much success in finding their freedom.

After watching them a while, Authæn waded into the river a ways, closed the entrance to the cove with a few larger stones, and then proceeded to corner and catch the fish with his hands. As a river-person this came to him with ease; though he thought that perhaps the water moved to guide the fish to him as well.

"My mind is yet dream-addled," he muttered to his spirit.

He slapped the fish that he caught against a stone to end their suffering, and then cast them onto the ground not far from where they had made their camp.

When he had done with this, he rekindled their fire, and began to gut and clean the fish, then to spike them over the flames with sticks they had gathered along the way. Soon some eight fish were roasting over the fire as Authæn sat by and let his mind drift towards the dreams that had caused him to panic so. Perhaps they had been brought on by the cold, but the tea seemed to have done its work well, and he did not at all feel fevered.

And then his mind suddenly drifted to the far corners of aged memory, the memory of his early childhood, memory that he would have thought lost were it not to have returned then.

He remembered travelling with his father — the smiling face of his father returned to him like the benevolent aspect of grace itself. They had gone from village to village, his father had always asked regarding the markings along his temples. They had gone to all manner of weird-folk, but

162

none, not even the weirdest, had known what these symbols had meant.

"Call me 'weirdest of the weird'," he muttered to his spirit then.

Most of the weirding men and women that they had visited had asked who the boy's mother was, after having looked at him closely, their frowns always deepening, such words as 'impossible' falling less and less carefully from their lips.

"She was a vagabond. She was tribeless," his father had always said. "She died bequeathing him to me."

"Why is it impossible, da?" he had once asked his father.

"It isn't, my son. The weirding folk learn much from the shepherds, but they do not learn everything. I am certain, however that you will."

"How can you be certain, da?" Authæn had asked.

"Because none of the weirding folk of our people could tell me that you were not destined for the tutelage of the henge," his father had replied.

"But one of those bearded men told me that all who go to the henge become weirds, da!"

"Not you, my son. That bearded man also ate more mushrooms than any other weird I have met. He might have gone slightly beyond wisdom in his exploration of *the* beyond."

And so Authæn had been brought to the henge of his people. He presently wondered whether he had crossed this exact spot on that first journey. Perhaps he had washed in exactly this bend of the river; though he doubted that the bend was still exactly the same as it had been those dozen odd years before.

He had been brought to the henge when he was only seven years old. Still some years too young for the trial by boat that all children of the river-people must endure, but upon their arrival at the henge, and as soon as great Wirthaumuin had opened the low door that descended into his sunken home, the shepherd's eyes had settled on the markings on the sides of Authæn's head, and he had at once asked them in without any questions.

Before the shepherd had said anything else, he had bidden them to sit, asking his wife to bring some tea for their guests, and then he had swooped down from his towering height to crouch playfully before the young Authæn, saying: "You are blood of my blood, and bone of my bone. More than any other of my children, you carry the doom that was put on us, and so, in you may lie the satisfaction."

"Satisfaction ..." muttered Authæn. Later he had learned that the shepherds hoped for a new generation to arise from out of their river-people children, that would guide their children back into the city from which they had been cast, bearing the power to lift the curse that had made it impossible to dwell there.

"Satisfaction ..." Authæn turned the word once more on his tongue. If there was great tension in the muscle, all that was needed to release it was a needle in one precise point, and all that pent up tension would slacken and find peace.

"Satisfaction ..." said his tongue as if by an own will. He had crimes that bore down heavily on his shoulders. Wirthaumuin had been stern from the first, but always true in his judgements, never unfair, and his mercy had always overwhelmed Authæn where it had come. It was as though the shepherd had herded him, the sheep, to recognise why truth must stand, and how to stand so that one does not come in its relentless way.

He had failed that teaching.

Chapter Thirteen
From Briars Arose

There had been long darkness. A pall as that of cold, stale air pressing down on the lungs had lain over her for what now felt like years, though at the time it had felt a passing sleep. Now there was a stiffness to her, a weight that caused her every limb to hang on the cool earth beneath. As her mind began more and more to waken, she grew more and more determined, yet her body lay motionless.

Finally she managed to move her jawbone from one side to the other, and from there it was as though her still body began to recognise the command of her spirit. At last it was as though all of her members heard the one call:

AWAKEN!

And life flooded her lungs like a gale tearing through a cobwebbed attic; her eyes snapped open and were drowned in the yellow-white of a misty midday. Her arms lifted, shivering; her back arched, stretching the long lying from it; her knees were brought up, aiding her into a sitting position. She reached out as far as she could, feeling those once so powerful shoulders shudder with the returning memory of their many labours.

Then the earth shook and, above, dark, winged shapes flapped their feathery forms in uncountable multitudes over her slowly adjusting vision — ravens rejoicing for freedom.

"I sing with you, ravens!" she called after them as a child might have. "I sing. My breath is a song

166

near forgotten to me," she sighed, tempted to lie down again. Then the thought came to her that she may never awaken if she lay down to sleep now, and she sprang from the stone coffin that had been her bed — her long-grown hair falling in golden waves over her shoulders — and landed barefoot in the soggy grasses just beyond.

She continued to stretch her waking form, clothed more like a boy for travel than a woman. She wore a tunic and breaches of wool, and a cloak of blue with the emblem of the eagle upon the brooch that held it about her shoulders. These had all been a gift from her father, she remembered, before she had come to this land. She let her hand slide along her woven belt of leather thongs, seeking out the scabbard and the sword, but they were not there. Then she remembered the long jabbing at her side from her years of sleep, and looked into the stone casing that had held her. The stone was all surrounded by briar and bramble, but above it: a single rose as red as blood. Beneath it lay the weapon she sought; the sword that her uncle had wrought for her.

"No smith is your like, uncle," she laughed, and bound the scabbard to her belt in the manner of her people.

In the coffin lay also her boots, and she pulled them over her feet, sitting atop the stone edge.

In the distance she thought she heard voices, and, pushing aside the many questions that gnawed at the frayed edges of her mind, she quickly, sometimes slipping, sometimes tripping, made her way towards them. There were two voices to her ear, somewhere near the large hillock that jutted like a great mouth from the slowly drowning pools of the Murkwing Mire. But when she thought that she should stumble upon the speakers, she came to the mouth of the cavern, and found that there was no one there.

"Strange," she muttered to her spirit. "But then, I may still be half caught up in dreams."

Not wanting to think on it any more than that, she decided to make her way through the bog until she came across something of interest, whatever it may be. She felt particularly unbound at this moment in time, and she would make the most of it.

For many hours she wandered, slipping and swearing, through the splashing and the bubbling world of Murkwing Mire, sometimes ending a choral croak by stepping on it, sometimes beheading some serpent that dared threaten her. Once the sword was drawn and bloodied she kept it out, her hand had almost forgotten the pleasant weight of it, and she would idly toss it from one hand to the next, as easily as one might have a leather ball.

"Now why am I in a bog, I wonder?" she said to the wind, not wanting her spirit to respond. But her spirit was slow to understand today, it seemed, and memories like images cast on the still pools of her joyous mind began to flow past her inner eye. There were images of a great, horned horror, roaring at her in a foreign tongue; there had been long journeys on the road; many tricks on bandits in the steppe — and the consequences. She shuddered, feeling ill.

The image of a man flickered on her sight: he bore a bow of bone, crouched low in the tall grass beside her. She was only watching him, love she thought she had felt then, but now she felt sick, and she screamed, not caring what attention such a noise might draw, trying to clear her mind of these things.

"Very well," she sighed, breathing heavily. "A bog then. I do not care how I have come to end here. I have found a new beginning, and that is what matters. Did I not waken from a tomb ...?"

Again visions of the horned monster came into her mind. She, paralysed with fear, being lowered into the stone enclosure. A lid sliding over its top.

She shook her head again, this time not screaming, and at last some melancholia had found a perch along her eyes.

"Well, I have a new beginning now, I should not doubt," said she. "Let us try how resilient this bog is to defy me!"

Again she leapt forwards, now charging. Her eyes keenly focussed on the heathery places, avoiding the pools of emerald slime, and she ran deeper and deeper into the mire, the moisture of the air clinging to her hair, her face, and her clothes until they altogether began to drip, and she to slip more and more often. Then she stepped onto a place where the moss and heather had grown in thin imitation of a bridge over the waters, and she fell into the murky stench.

At once, she surged up, kicking with her feet, whipping her arms about, slapping down on the broiling surface with her hands, gasping like one caught in a nightmare. She caught a hold of some dead tree's roots, and slowly began to draw herself out of the water. Moaning at her misfortune.

"Oh! Why must it be a bog?! Of all the places in this middle-earth, why?!"

And then she heard a low drone drift over that foul land, as the call of some lonely beast in the murk.

"Is that a monster that I might slay?" she wondered with her mouth.

Forgetting her slick state, she sprang up again, and travelled — more sensibly now — in the direction from which she had heard the groan come. She told herself that she could not run now, otherwise she might chase away the dragon, or whatever it may have been that had growled so menacingly. And so she steadily came to a more swampy reach, moody trees looming up about her, looking long-faced down at her.

Here there was barely any heather for a walk-way, and none dared venture so far into this fright-ful wilderness to tame it, so that she now had to wade through waters knee-high to traverse it.

Again the rumbling drone issued over the wa-ters, causing them to ripple by her. She felt some-thing sinewy slither through the water near her foot, but she was not concerned about that.

Before her, the trees of the swamp were begin-ning to shudder and break, as something vast came marching towards her from beyond. Again it growled, now deeper in its throat. Then the thing emerged: a young water-dragon, tall as her shoulders, though it wrothe close to the ground on

170

its four horned legs. Its large, leathery wings unfurled before her in a frightful and final warning.

But she did not heed; or perhaps it was the
beast that ought to have heeded this daughter of
Imnir's dauntless raising of her iron. It saw the action, as she clasped the leather grip in the woollen
embrace of her weathered fingers, raising the sting
of the blade to point at it.

"Strike me, I dare thee, lizard! This is iron
from the mountain's heart, hammered by the Bear
of Glimwæth into a sting of woe! Cringe before
mine sting, worm, or thou shalt cringe upon it,
barbed!" proclaimed the yellow-haired lady. But
she did not wait for the beast, and charged much
rather, causing it a resentful pause, as it curled its
snake-like body and drew back its lengthy neck.

Then, just as she drew into its reach, the head
of the dragon snapped forth, and she dropped, sliding down under the surface of the water, the head
of the dragon snapping shut just above her. Her
sting thrust forth from out of the water, into the
lower jaw and through the tongue of the beast. She
pulled back the blade, and black blood flowed like
a stream from the wound, yet the beast's skull had
not been punctured.

She, having felt this from below, arose from
the swishing green mirror, and hewed at the long
neck of the drake. It stumbled to the side, slamming down its wing onto the water in an attempt to
stun its little foe.

The torrents that the wing cast up swept her
from her feet, knocking her heavily against a tree,
so that her head and back smarted a moment. She

171

blinked the water from her eyes, shook the hair from her besmirched face, and raised the blade once more with a terrible war scream.

Then she charged again.

The dragon, wary now, and a little frightened by the horrid blows that bled from it, recoiled, but it was caught in some trees and vines in a way that it had not anticipated, stumbling and rising up on its hind legs with desperation's wrath. It roared again, this time so mightily that she had to stop in her stride with the cold that gripped her belly. Then she spurred herself on again, hacking at the leg as though it were the only tree suited to kindling.

The foreleg of the beast, which it had raised in rearing up, now slapped across her shoulder, and she was flung away again. The dragon seemed to be fleeing back into the trees whence it had come. There the water grew quickly deeper, and it dove under, leaving a dark cloud of blood to discolour the wake it left behind.

Staggering once more to her feet, she screamed weakly after the beast, then she stumbled toward a tree, falling into unconsciousness just at the right moment, so that the low branches of it caught her up.

There she hung, like some gathering of vine and yellow moss, her sword leaving growing circles on the water where it had fallen. Above, the sun strode across the heavens and began to descend. It was late afternoon before she awoke again.

"Still deathless, am I?" she asked her spirit, which was angry within her. Perhaps she had angered it with her carelessness. In the face of that inner fire she laughed, then she frighted, seeing that she had let her sword fall. When she bent down to search for it, she suddenly and momentarily lost all sense of orientation and fell face first into the cold water. Spluttering she resurfaced, and held up the blade that she had let fall, triumphant. "Not yet sting-less either!"

Like this, she stumbled towards the place where the dragon had submerged. Now she went from tree to tree, seeking by which way she might walk, sometimes finding no way forward for half-hours at a time. And then she came upon the large form of a dead lizard, washed into shallower waters. One of her blows must have done terrible bleeding damage.

"Come now, beast. Perhaps this water was given me that I might drag you back to land with!" said she. But the dragon would not be moved, no matter how she tugged at it.

She sighed. Then she began to carve scales from it, one at a time. She tied her cloak into a satchel, and placed what scales she could into it. She also took some of its teeth with her tireless hacking. Finally she sought out what bones of it might be good for making dice of, or perhaps some other furniture. One of its many horns she certainly took for a drinking cup.

At the very last, she drew a bottle of crystal out from beneath her tunic that hung about her neck on a chain, drank some of the drake's blood, and filled the vial with some more.

And so she departed the Murkwing Mire, laded with two large leg bones over her shoulder, her sword now sheathed. In her cloak was a hoard of scales and teeth. It was near middle night when she left behind the foul vapours and gurgling ponds of that realm of decay. Now she sought a travelling pedlar that was headed to the east, so that she might sell some of her new treasure, or at the very least find company for the road.

Along the trading road that stretched from the easternmost havens on the water, all the way to Glimwæth, a small camp had been set up amidst a small cluster of poplar. Camels yawned and grunted, in the firelight, and their keepers played at dice around a low table near the fire.

The men around the table were three; one seated at each edge. One of them wore a heavy fur coat and a fur-brimmed, conical hat. He was a large man, wide of girth, but mighty jolly of disposition, for he never allowed himself a moment outside of pursuing the life he considered most adventurous: that of a merchant and kaupman. His dark eyes glistened as he presently laughed. He was winning, and was rubbing his brown hands together gleefully.

Another at the table was a guard; one of the two that had been brought along from Glimwæth. His round helm sat in his lap as though it were the spearman guard's own child, looking out from almond eye-holes at the game.

The third was another merchant; thin, with angular features and a patchy, black stubble. He wore a weathered greatcoat — an article that only his people wore, and even amongst the easterners, these were only common amongst the wealthy merchants.

From not too far away, a fourth, taller man with wild, golden curls of hair leaned against a tall standing stone bewritten with runes, smoking a long warden pipe. His magnificent beard cast him in the image of a lion, and for this the people of his city called him the Lion Pen-tooth. But it was not only his hair that gave him the visage of such a fearsome predator, behind the dark lenses that had been ground into circles to hide away the shape of his eyes, the Lion Pen-tooth had eyes unnaturally akin to those of a lynx.

"Oh, what is that smell!" exclaimed the easterner merchant with the greatcoat.

"We are not too far from a great mire, Qeremun," the jolly merchant with the fur-brimmed hat chuckled. "Oh, and you will not so easily distract me from the gamble! It is interesting, however; the mire is fed by the waters from the melting snows in the heights, and, though it begins pure, it descends into the bog, that pure water becoming a foul cesspool filled with all manner of dark lurker."

"Nor shall *I* be distracted. This is nothing in comparison to the stench that sometimes flies into the nose when walking the streets of Glimwæth," said the spearman with his helm in his lap, stroking his beard. He had just cast his dice, and was wondering if he should withdraw from the game, hoping at the same time that this was not visible on his face.

There was a sudden scream from the edge of their camp, and the spearman that had been playing at dice jumped to his feet. His spear was ready in his hand, its head aglint with the lightning of quick reflection. The merchants scrambled towards their goods, in order to shield them with their lives, if it had to come to that. Then they, too, drew their blades; both wielding curved daggers.

The Lion Pen-tooth pushed himself from the stone onto his feet, and strode a few steps nearer the firelight. He took the pipe from his mouth, which slowly formed the 'o' of a surprised frown, and stopped. A smoke ring puffed through his lips, and he tilted his head to one side.

From the shadows another guard, garbed as the one that had been at the game, ran into their midst, then his breaches fell down about his ankles, and he tripped, landing on his outstretched hands.

"*Draug! Draug!*" he squawked.

Behind him a ragged figure lumbered into the crackling warmth. The wool of her tunic and breaches was torn, her boots were scratched and battered, but not so much as her face. And she smelled as though she had just crawled from the gutters of the wooden city itself.

Presently a large pouch of *clack*-ing things landed heavily next to her feet. It was a cloak, the Lion Pen-tooth saw then, but filled with some hard treasure. More gruelling than anything else about her, however, were the two fresh bones of surely some giant's limbs that she then also let fall like chains after long imprisonment to the whispering heath.

"Treasure bearing camels!" hissed Qeremun with a scowl. "Is that blood along her chin?"

"Leave her be!" commanded the Lion Pen-tooth then.

"This is no time to sit down with a fen-spirit to tea, Pen-tooth!" chuckled the larger merchant, his hand holding his metal to the ready.

More of the guards arrived then, and looked from the newcomer to the Lion and back. They were under his employ, for he had offered the merchants protection, if in exchange he was allowed to travel through the steppes with them, back to his home in Glimwæth.

"I think she shall sit down all on her own in a moment," said the Lion through the weave of his magnificent beard, "and not to tea."

He was right, for just as he had said it, the lady that had encroached on their dice-play flopped to the ground as if dead.

"What is this? Not a spirit?" muttered Qeremun the easterner.

"No, but she does bring treasure with her, it seems," said the other merchant, replacing his dagger.

"Payment for the privilege of the journey perhaps?" asked Qeremun swooping down over her, not in a threatening manner.

"I think that payment enough shall come to you for returning her home," said the Lion Pen-tooth.

"You know this woman?" asked the spearman, turning to pick his helm up from where it had fallen to the earth. The nose-guard of the helm had caught up some of the dark soil and grass where it had landed, and the spearman cleaned it gloomily.

"This is the daughter of the king," said the Lion. The guard looked up suddenly with wide eyes. "Niece of the Forge-bear. We had thought her long dead, slain by those river-people that she fled her father's ire with."

"The king's-daughter of Glimwæth? Out here? Bearing the bones of a giant into our camp in the middle of the night? She looks more a wild boy out to traipse through the country meadows!" exclaimed Qeremun in disbelief, folding his arms.

"Look more closely at her sword, friend," said the Lion Pen-tooth. "It bears the mark of the Forge-bear, and the runes that grant his favour for its use."

The easterner needed no further encouragement, and dropped down to draw forth the blade for study. His eyes widened as the runes revealed themselves to him, hammered into a manifold weaving pattern in the metal. "These are even runes that determine what her quest may have been in these parts: to slay a river-dragon!"

"It seems she has done just that," said the guard who had fallen down around his pants. He was on his feet again, presently tying up his belt in a way that showed he hoped no one would remember his embarrassing display in a couple of days time.

"How many are the years that have passed since she has been seen in the wooden city?" asked the merchant with the conical hat.

The Lion strode up to her fallen form, and the merchant that had been studying her blade pushed it back into its scabbard, withdrawing respectfully. Pen-tooth knelt before her, stroking the hair from her face as the lines on his own deepened.

"Seven."

Chapter Fourteen
The Brothers in Darkholt

The stars turned over the roof of the world as though they were moving by a great tooth-wheel, and then the fires of heaven's forge went to their bluing work, emerging blazing with the brilliance of dawn. Beneath, the camels had been roused to begin again the long journey to the wooden city of Glimwæth, their saddles rattling with the many wares from the east.

The Lion Pen-tooth was charged with ensuring the safety of the king's-daughter, who was in a fevered sleep, and shifted between silent dreaming, and disquiet thrashing. There were two tall camel-drawn carriages and from one a space had been cleared, covered then in furs, to make for her a bed. Onto the same one her treasures from the bog were loaded, so that she would see them upon waking, and not ask any unnecessary questions.

They rattled along the dusty road, passing by great boulders in great plains, over the dry gullies in which rivers had failed, they ascended hills, and forded rivers that yet flowed.

When they had just emerged from a path where the road drove in-between the two sheer faces of a great hillock that looked like it had been cleft in twain by a giant's axe, the spearman, who was head of the guardsmen the Lion had hired, said, "This journey seems not too much in need of our handiwork, Master Pen-tooth! I can hear my axe rusting at my side."

They descended into a little wood, the breeze rustling through the leaves, and then a great brown bear stepped out into the bespeckled light of the forest floor. The sun grew brighter, and the shadows starker, and then another bear strode out, sniffing the air. With them were three little cubs.

"Halt! Halt, I say!" exclaimed the larger merchant, now no longer so jolly.

"Well it is not every day that a man sees Jithron of Tall Hithes so afright!" mused Qeremun, though he himself had clearly only put on a wary pretence of boldness.

The caravan did draw to a stop, but the mother bear had already seen them with a threatening growl and a shaking of her fur. The camels began to draw away in fear, and the riders seemed momentarily disquietened.

"You spoke of a rusty axe too soon, it seems, Garhelm," said the Lion, looking a smile at the spearman.

Garhelm laughed heartily, dismounting from the saddle, and taking up both spear and shield. "Let me show you that the blood of Imnir flows in my veins! Perhaps I shall tame one of these bears as he did, and ride it back through the gates of my burg!" he said.

"Ho ho!" laughed one of the guards from behind. "I think the king would leave you his throne if you went so far, Garhelm."

The spearman steadily approached the she-bear, not unaggressively. She looked angrily at him, growled again, roared, then charged without further fuss.

181

She was fast, but he was quicker; raising and casting his spear like a javelin to strike where the neck of the beast met its shoulder. It stuck, and the bear stumbled, still roaring. It had not been enough. Exasperated Garhelm sighed. A familiar gloom took over his countenance, and he aggressively tore his bearded axe from his belt. He shook it next to his ear a moment, and asked it, "Are you still sharp, my beard?"

The bear's mate was now also almost upon him with a roar and a rearing thrust of its claws, but he stepped smoothly out of its way, almost striking its head, when it lunged into him unexpectedly, and all seemed like it would soon be over for poor Garhelm.

"Stop!" came the voice of a woman. It was *the* woman. The king's-daughter had awoken, and she at once had drawn her sword, now holding it up so that it caught the light of the sun on its many folds. As the light danced there in heady glitter, a ringing as that of hammer on shrill bell came into the ears of the onlookers, who had all frozen in stunned disbelief.

From the frenzied, dirty woman, thrashing about in fevered dreams, she now seemed to wax with majesty and power. Her face seemed wholesome, her arm strong. The bears cowered, and began to slink away, leaving the mother bear to suffer an inescapable terror with the spear that seemed to have crippled her.

"Make an end of your pretence, iron-skull!" she commanded.

At once Garhelm clambered back onto his feet, taking up his axe. The glitter of sweat on him could be seen beneath his helm as he quickly darted an uncertain glance at his king's-daughter. Then he let the axe fell a harsh *crack* on the skull, and the animal slackened into the darkling puddle beneath it.

Jithron, the larger trader from the Tall Hithes, laughed merrily, clambering from his camel with customary difficulty, and guided the spearman's mount towards him. Garhelm pulled his spear shamefacedly from the bear's corpse.

"Now you will perhaps heed what I had said near the beginning of our journey, dear Garhelm," said Jithron to the son of Imnir, "about the manner in which one speaks of a lady, whether she is listening or not. Think of how she might speak of you now, were she a lower woman."

He nodded silently, taking the reins of his mount.

"Wait, spearman!" said the king's-daughter then, having heard the words of Jithron and having seen the shame of his current bearing. "You are clearly a worthy fighter. I would have a trophy of your prowess."

"Anything, king's-daughter," said Garhelm sadly.

"A cloak from that bear's skin."

"Oh, now that would fetch a fine price," mused Qeremun, stroking his face dreamily.

The king's-daughter looked at him a moment with bemusement. "Who are you?" she asked.

"Qeremun, my lady!" the easterner bowed in his saddle. "A humble trader on the trading way."

"Thank you, and all the rest of you, for taking me up in my need. But I must ask: whitherto?"

"We are headed to Glimwæth, king's-daughter, to the hall of your fathers," said the Lion Pen-tooth, watching her carefully.

She swore loudly with the tongue of her fathers, and collapsed back into the furs, silently weeping. The sound of skinning came from where Garhelm had gone to work.

"Then it is true, king's-daughter? You ran from your father's wrath, into the arms of the river-people?" inquired the Lion.

"Do you want to write a history of my life, Pen-tooth?" she said as though it were an insult.

"I want to write a history of all that passes in the line of Imnir. There are so many strange secrets tangled in his blood," said the other calmly. The Lion even smiled as if with pity.

"You disgust me, Pen-tooth. For all that scribbling, you have no real teeth!" she spat out, sitting up again, but weakly.

He laughed, again with pity in his voice.

"Do not look at me as though I were a helpless child! I could slay you where you sat!" she raised the sword in his direction, her eyes ablaze, her teeth gritted.

"You have slain drakes in the tracts unwalked, king's-daughter," said the Lion. "You could lop my head from my shoulders and be praised for it. I will do my work only where I am left to do it."

She sagged into herself again. "You will get nothing from me!" she hissed, and then flopped back into her furs.

The Lion shook his head. Qeremun and Jithron looked at one another, and Jithron shrugged with a resigned smile.

They waited for Garhelm to finish his work on the bear, and when he had harvested it they spurred the caravan back into motion.

They came into rain as the day wore on; it drifted in from the west, where they could already begin to see the steady climbing of the faraway moors.

"When does one see these forests you spoke of, Jithron. I see only grasses, stones, and the odd shrub!" said Qeremun of a sudden.

"What, did you not see the trees for the bears before this hateful spit began to pepper us? There was a bit of wood!" the other replied.

"That was not how you described it, my friend, you said that the hoary green of it lay over the world like a blanket that covers all the west! We've gone past that blanket housing bears, and we are still in the west!" returned the easterner.

"Oh, Qeremun, Qeremun, you must understand, the west is far smaller than the east!" Jithron called back. "We went through the blanket, and have come out in the east again! I'm quite afraid we've forgotten to stop in Glimwæth."

"If only that were true," said the king's-daughter, sitting up again beneath the temporary roof that had been pulled up over her carriage with the beginnings of the rain. Faraway lightning struck some poor tree, splitting it down the middle. The

185

thunder of that one-sided conversation rolled over them like the breath of their newest companion's fury.

"Perhaps you would describe it to me, my lady?" Qeremun bade.

She sighed, letting her head roll from one shoulder to the other once, twice, thrice. "Very well. I will tell you of Darkholt. Sharpen your ears and your pen-teeth, Lion. This will kill your prey for its flavour."

At once the company drew in closer to her carriage, all now piqued with curiosity.

"It begins with a king sitting on his high chair in his high hall," said she. "He had two sons and a young daughter. Upon a day, his sons came to their father, asking him: 'Father! Father! Where is it best to go on the hunt? We wish to test ourselves against the wilderness in order to prove that we are men worthy of our high station!'

"To this their father, who was considered wise in his council, said to them: 'my dear sons, this is a worthy thing for which you strive! Go forth and tame the dark holt that lies at our door. Hunt in the vale just over the ridge to the north, that is a bountiful place; but be ware, my sons! For if you choose this path, neither I nor any of my men shall come to your aid for all your most desperate summons. By doing so you honour me, and the blood of aged Imnir that rustles in your veins.'

"And so his sons descended from the high hall of their father, and they went by all the burg's folk, which cheered them on as they walked. And they came into the vale, having climbed the verge by great efforts.

"But a black magic lies like a pall over that land of deep forest, and at once, having come to the edge of the vale, the elder of the brothers, Mathydras, turned on his younger brother, who hight Svæn, and a madness glowed in his eyes, and he said: 'The greatest hunt in these woods, brother, is the hunt after *thee*!'

"The younger, not bewitched as yet, stumbled over the edge of the cliff on which they had stood themselves, tripping by the struggle with the elder, and fell to his death. At that moment the spell lifted from Mathydras, and he was aggrieved for what he had done. So terrible was his shame that he fled into the heart of that vale, and there, it is said, he was devoured by the ogre that haunts those parts.

"the young daughter of the king, realising that her brothers were gone far too long, and wondering whether they had founded a new proud burg in the woodland, thought to set out after them one day. She cloaked herself in the guise of a boy, stole a sword from the workshop of her uncle, the great smith who is known as the Bear of Glimwæth, and charged into the forests north of her home. But the woods were a place so thickly knit together above that she could not see after a while, and she began to weep, and to sing lonely songs in her despair.

"At this the birds came to her, for what I have not yet told you, proud gentlemen, is that the king's-daughter was bathed in the blood of a dragon at her birth, and so she could hear and understand the tongue of the birds.

187

"It was the birds that told her of the dark fate of her brothers, and so she returned to her father, bearing news that would change the bright hall of the Nornburg over Glimwæth into a mournsome place ever after."

White light flickered again as fire fell from heaven in the distance, and the only sound to accompany it was the creaking and thudding of the caravan's steady tread over mud. None dared speak, for a great emotion sat like taut lines on the face of the king's-daughter. It was some mixture of purest wrath in the face of most gravely lacking reason.

The others all looked down or otherwise away; only the Lion looked hard into that grief-stricken countenance. What thoughts lay behind his black-and-gold eyes only he saw reflected in the dark eyeglasses that sat atop the bridge of his nose.

"That is not the story as I have heard it, or perhaps I have sharpened my ears too much," said he.

She looked up at him through a scowl. "What you have heard bears no weight," said she.

"What I have heard comes from the king," said he.

A whisper of surprised and disturbed movement went through the rest of the company.

"Tell us then, great scrivener, how shall it have happened otherwise?" asked she contemptuously.

"At first I should point out that there are no water-dragons in the country of Imnir, and that they, like their blood, are a rare thing. You would not have been bathed in it as a child, unless I am unaware of yet another secret in the dark web of

188

Imnir. Then I should like to point out that the daughter of the king never went into that part of the woods, for there would have been great commotion if she had. Finally I would like to say that I knew your brothers well, king's-daughter. I will not have you lie about who they were and why they were sent into the dark forest."

She bared her teeth, turning her face away, it having taken on the constitution of stone.

"What was the reason, Pen-tooth?" asked Jithron with a frown. "I believe I met the young men as well in my time, but that seems rather a harsh banishment!"

"It was!" the king's-daughter snarled, looking daggers again at the scrivener's dark eyeglasses. "What kind of father would send his sons into the wood without their permission? What kind of father, regarded wise in council, would forget his wisdom in the face of the mistakes of his children?"

"Any good father!" roared the Lion Pen-tooth suddenly, sitting up tall in his saddle. It was as though his hair stood on end then for a moment, but he sighed, shrinking back down into a more slouched position. He looked ahead, moving his bearded jaw as though he were chewing on a bitter thought. "Any good father that makes mistakes," he added. "How was he to have foreseen what came of this decision? His sons had committed a grave offence. His rule would have quickly diminished were he not to have been as fair with them as he had been with all other cases that were brought before him during the Thing. Do not lie to justify your father, king's-daughter. Forgive the truth of his actions. Forgive the truth of your brothers' actions."

"I will take advise from you when my blade is blunt, Pen-tooth," said she.

"With a fury like yours that will be soon, king's-daughter," returned he.

She was silent again. The storm still felt as though it was bound to her temperament.

Jithron and Qeremun looked at one another uneasily.

In a similar way, over the course of the following days, their journey continued in bouts of silence, banter, laughter, grim exchanges, and silence again. Another week this continued, as they climbed over the hills and finally wound their way through the tall eaves of Darkholt.

At first Qeremun had been cast into a wonderment by the appearance of the large, dark ocean of sighing green that sailed into sight when they had crossed the moorlands. The further they pressed into its oppressive shadow, however, the less wondrous were his eyes, and the more he seemed to shrink into his saddle.

The groaning and the sighing of the trees surrounding was like enduring the disinterest of ever-watching spirits, each creak a dissatisfied complaint about how the caravan was progressing on its journey. Beneath the tread of camel and wheel, dark earth was ground up, mushrooms were crushed into powder, and the greedy fingers of the ferns were whipped aside. At twilit hours there seemed even to be the looming shadows of lurking monsters, moving languidly in circles around them as though watching and waiting for one of the company to become isolated.

Eventually the forests became scarcer, waning away as though retreating into the north. All the while the hills and fells of this country caused the rising and falling of their winding pathways. They had come to a place, where a large, grey fell jutted slanting from the earth, a river bending itself liquidly about its mossy feet, when a strange chatter came to them from ahead. Here the trees were somewhat thicker again, but had a milder atmosphere, and the waters of the stream ran clear and soundly over lichenous stone.

The noises ahead sounded at first like the chatter and laughter of a large travelling troop. There were the voices of children, of men and women. Then there came a scream, and a strange gurgle of voices joined the fray. In a short moment the sound of warfare drifted over the merchant caravan.

The king's-daughter arose from her place in the furs, drawing her sword and jumping to the hard-trodden earth of the road beneath. She wore the bear-skin about her shoulders, which Garhelm had treated and shaped under the guiding hand of the Lion, who knew of such things. The merchants had also offered advice, as well as a little of their wares for treatment of the pelt — Qeremun always with a misty look in his eye. She had also been granted new linens and leathers by Jithron, more becoming for a traveller of the wilds.

"Gentlemen, It sounds like battle!" said she, striding out past the camels as they moved slowly on. "And my hand twitches for the blade after all your tiresome prattle!"

The merchants and their guardsmen drew their caravan aside, tethering the camels to trees. Then they joined the king's-daughter in her march towards the sounds of battle.

The fighting took place only just around the bend of the jagged fell, but the sight that there met their eyes was far stranger than they had at first anticipated: There was a large host of grey-skinned river-people — an entire village of one of their clans, it seemed. Their caravan, carriages, camels, horses and livestock had been brought to a standstill alongside the babbling stream (perhaps for mealtime) but strange little creatures had begun to pour from a crack in the tall fell.

The creatures were a dirty white, their hide was battered and callous. Their heads were bald, or sometimes tied with tails and weaves. Their little eyes were like black beads, their teeth like oddly placed stones in the wide seam that presently garbled out foreign curses.

"Imps!" cried Garhelm, and charged to aid the river-folk with his spear held high. His guardsmen followed.

But the king's-daughter had stopped in her steady march. She looked out across the fighting and, at the other end of it, a man that had just run dry of arrows looked up to meet her eyes.

"Carbeth," she breathed in horror.

The eyes of the hunter at the other end of the battle widened. His back straightened, and he seemed to forget the storm surrounding him. On his lips was shaped a name in return. The name was called Ystrith.

Chapter Fifteen
Aface of Music

White fire fell from heaven, as the clouds wound down towards the glistening grass in the spiral of a frightening storm. Again, a bolt of lightning, then another. Booms of thunder swept the steppes as out of the murk ahead a tall hill stuck from the landscape like a giant lizard raising its head in a plateau from the earth.

There atop the slanted hill stood the stones of the henge, reaching out toward the spiralling clouds as they slowly and determinedly descended. Thunder boomed again, as the landscape was painted black and white by the lights and shadows of falling heaven.

Into the highlands rising toward that henge, Authæn and Gaba were struggling through the heavy rains. They were travelling along the road of a high pass, and there were no trees large enough to shelter them nearby. Finally they came to a place where a great rock slab leaned against a monstrous boulder, forming a steep roof beneath which they could refuge themselves. Atop the boulder a stout pine whipped about its branches in the wind.

Once they were beneath the rock, Gaba took the dry kindling and wood out from where he had tied it to his back beneath his leathery cloak. It was still dry enough to their relief, and the southerner got to work in that dark shelter, as the weather continued to war around them.

Soon they were warming their shivering limbs about the brand, chewing on dried meats. Without wanting to, the student under the henge looked out towards the place where the henge stood, a stark shadow against the backdrop of whirling clouds. The stones of Wirthaumuin's home stood like a heavy judgement, biding its time to crush him at precisely the right moment.

We wait for your coming, it seemed they were saying, *we have waited long, and can wait longer still; but when you come, whether soon or late, you shall atone for the crimes against our law.*

He shuddered, and drew nearer the fire, wrapping his raven-cloak tighter about himself as thunder sounded again, and the fog of heaven's war was lit white a moment.

"Are you well, Authæn?" asked the southerner.

The river-man looked up at his companion, and said after a hesitation, "I still feel my doom hanging over me as though it were a mountain set to fall." Without thinking, he let his hand slide to where the dagger that had slain his father was concealed beneath his tunic.

"A wound?" Gaba asked, following the movement with his eyes curiously.

Authæn's hand quickly fell away again, and he looked into the fire. "I did not want to speak of this with you, uncle. Not out of a lack of trust, understand. You have shown well enough that you would care for me as for any close member of family, but the grief that I carry here beneath my garb is a grief that I desired to share first with the shepherd; the father of my fathers."

"I shall not come in the way of your customs, Authæn," said the southerner.

"For that I feel, perhaps, as though I should share this with you, uncle. I need to think this out loud before the final judgement stands afore," said Authæn.

"Show me then, my son," said Gaba.

The river-man drew forth the dark steel, curved and cruel. Again it reminded the river-person of the sting of a hornet. He laid it into the extended palms of the southerner, and the other looked closely at it.

"Is this the weapon which you used to kill?" asked the southerner, not looking up as he did so.

There was no response.

When he looked a question at Authæn, the southerner then saw that he had been wrong. There was a harsh bitterness on the mien of the river-man as he shook his head; the golden eyes ever lingering on the now dull black of the weapon.

"It was used to slay my father," said he then.

Lightning framed them blinding white again, and a dreadful *crack* as that of a whip tumbled over the world.

At once the southerner laid the blade down before Authæn, wiping his hands on his breaches as though they had been dirtied by the metal.

"For what reason?" asked the southerner.

"The Ibex seemed to be after him, and yet a scout from our village said that it was not intended that he die. My father was a remarkable man. He travelled much of the lands surrounding Middlemere. He even once touched prow to Murmurmere, having sailed the Jagged Strait, but his in-

196

terest in his wandering was to find a way to make easier the hard life of the river-people. We have been wanderers from the first, but in Glimwæth, I think, he saw that it needs not be so. There are wooden halls of comfort that remain standing from one generation to the next."

"And you think it is for his knowledge and his ken that your father was sought by the Ibex?" Gaba asked.

"I do not know. He was a carpenter, and it could also simply be that he sought him to build war machines for him. The Ibex's horde had been growing rapidly before his demise. I had the sense in those days that he was preparing for some great clash of powers, but which powers I cannot say. The nomadic plains are not united enough to pose a threat, and the children of Imnir and his brothers keep mostly to their country, seeking adventure more within their marks than without. The old kingdoms along the southern strands of Middle-mere are waning in their reach."

"There are powers further to the south; my ancient city is one such force. But my people are only interested in the north when it strikes us as glaring danger in our direction," said Gaba.

"Or if there are mighty weapons to retrieve here," returned Authæn unexpectedly.

The southerner raised his brow in surprise. "Yes," said he, "I suppose that is what it must look like. But the weapon of which rumour reached us was not one made by the forge-craft of men; it was not even hammered on the Bear's anvil in Glim-

197

wæth. Rumours spoke of it as being hidden in the wilderness, a forgotten relic of yore days."

"Then perhaps my father had knowledge of it. That was the quest of the Ibex, after all," said Authæn. "He did not speak much, my father; though he would always answer my questions. When he did speak of his own accord, he would say such riddlesome things that I never knew what to respond."

"Was it his wish that you go to the henge?" asked Gaba.

"Not at first," said Authæn. "My father was wary of weirds. He would call them half-baked bread in an oven made for forging steel. Still, he took me to all weirds of whom the rumour was whispered among our tribes.

"Every weird said the same things, or similar, and this both confirmed my father in his views, as well as winning him over for the training they had gotten under the henge — weirds are trained under the henge, you see uncle."

"What did they say of you, my son?" asked the southerner.

"The weirds? They claimed the old blood was strong in me, that I was more akin to the race of the deathless shepherds than ordinary river-folk," said Authæn.

"And you say that it was under the hand of the Ibex that your dear father was slain? You are certain of this?" asked the other.

"Yes, that is what our scout reported at the least, and I have good reason to believe him honest."

"Even the honest can err," said Gaba.

"To the detriment of all others," muttered Authæn.

"Wise words!" chuckled Gaba.

"They are the words of the shepherds."

For a time there came a thoughtful quiet over them, full of uncomfortable shifting. Questions that had no words in them lay hanging in the air like the wisps of smoke now issuing from the fire.

"You are a hurt man, Authæn. Badly injured in spirit," said Gaba sadly.

"There is healing for all things."

"There is; but it does not always look as we expect it to," said the southerner, stoking the flames, and laying another branch onto the brand. "So I think, anyway. I am grateful to have met you, and to be sharing this journey with you. I call you again Weirdest of the Weird, Authæn, for you are not alone a weird, but something more."

The storm quietened after some time, and they put out the fires to continue on their journey. It was only a half-hour's struggle upward now, and then they were sure to have reached the henge. As they drew nearer, the standing stones that made a circle there seemed more and more threatening.

Presently one could also see that there were other buildings surrounding those tall fingers, and, though they were broad, they sank low into the ground, with roofs of turf to keep in the warmth. There roofed chimneys of stone sent up spirals of smoke to join the rain's vapours. Somewhere animals could even be heard to grunt and bleat. Then they saw figures sitting in the middle of the henge, they had sat as still as stone, and had at first been mistaken for just the same by Gaba, but now a song could be heard to rise against the rain, and the moon suddenly drew back the drizzling veil above to shed further light on the sight.

There were the students of the henge, sitting in a circle about their shepherd, who was at once recognised for his tremendous size, and his purple robes. He sat, presently, with his back to those newly arrived, as he led his students in this song:

Now middle night has swept its cloak
Over the hills the weaving fields.
Let those upon a midnight road
Journey safe till dawn reveals
All that in shadow evil hides;
Away the dark,
Bring forth the light!

A journeyman – his hands are honed –
He works at that which in employ
Received from masters that him owed
The labours with which none should toy.
Let masterfully masters work
Their midnight craft;
Which is oft shirked.

This craft is that of singing song
— A song that long forgot has lain —
Let those that now remember long
What laid away is evil's bane.
Let masterfully masters work
Their midnight craft;

Which is oft shirked.

Now look about, have not all gone
Away into the land of sleep?
I call my brothers, sisters on,
But they cannot their hour keep.
Let masterfully masters work
Their midnight craft;
Which is oft shirked.

It is with this that proof is giv'n:
The sleeper sleeps, and he is all;
Save one whose eyes with tears are riv'n:
The watcher on the wall so tall.
He is alone at middle night
He sings for them
In heart held tight.

Now middle night has swept its cloak
Over the hills the weaving fields.
Let those upon a midnight road
Journey safe till dawn reveals
All that in shadow evil hides;
Away the dark,
Bring forth the light!

By the end of the hymn, Gaba and Authæn stood at the threshold of the great standing stones, waiting for someone to notice their presence. Neither of them dared disturb this ritual song. There, in the circle of the standing stones, the grass was dry, and well-groomed, and lines went out from its centre that were in alignment with the stars of the wintered north.

When the song had come to an end the students arose first, then stood waiting for their master. The aged shepherd raised up a great crook-staff, bearing many marks that were akin to those that Gaba had seen along the shaven temples of his road-companion. Then the shepherd turned himself to face the newcomers. He took a few steps toward them, and only then did he notice that his way to the sunken houses was barred; and it was only then that Gaba saw beneath the tall, purple hood that the shepherd was blind.

"You return to us, my son," muttered the soothing voice of the great shepherd like a river flowing in the hills. "But you do not come alone, and you yourself do not return unchanged."

Beside the southerner the river-man could be seen to cringe with a veiled despair.

"Do not be dismayed, dear Authæn. For beings as transient as we, change can be good, for it may bring us nearer the eternal," the shepherd said.

"I am afraid, great shepherd," said Authæn with great effort, "that this is a change for the worse in me; though the stranger I bring is a friend to your children. Many of our kin has he saved from the dread horror of the Ibex, for it is this southerner that has made an end of the bog-dweller."

"All things shall be weighed against truth. What there stands a chance without truth's mercy?" said the shepherd, and a thin, benevolent smile curled on his lips and crunched about his eyes. Suddenly his voice boomed, as he reached out with his hands, saying: "Welcome, Gabazi *kadonazd-Manutuz*! the birds have whispered much of your road here. It has been perilous; but let your stay here at the henge be one of respite, and wholesome remembrance. Come with me! I shall show you a place to lay down your heads for the night."

The travellers let the shepherd pass them by, falling in behind him. Behind them, the silent students now departed the ring of the henge, dispersing in frightful order to their own rooms in low houses at the far end of the settlement.

"How is it, great shepherd, that you know my true name, and the tale of my road, if I may ask?" bade Gaba then.

"I have listened to the song of the birds, Master *kadonazd-Manutuz*. They have revealed much of your strange flight. You are said to stride heavy clouds, and to call them as though you yourself were a shepherd, but of the heavens. No man has lived that has not dreamed the same," the shepherd said, then he stopped, turned as though to look at the southerner without seeing him. "Does that frighten you, man of the secret south?"

There *was* fear in the eyes of the southerner. Indeed, his eyes were petrified in wide horror — the only movement a bead of fear running down from his ebon temple, along his cheek and neck, and staining his hood barely darker in a small spot. "It does, oh deathless one!" said he, falling to his knees.

Never had Authæn thought such a response to be drawn forth from a man so mighty as Gaba, and he stepped back in shock.

The shepherd laughed, and said, "You recognise me, master dragon hunter. That is good. Then there is hope for your order after what you unleashed upon us in the terrible wrath of the Ibex. My own children are fortunate never to have to fear me as you must. But are not all children so fortunate?"

"Not all, oh deathless one!" said Gaba from where he knelt in utmost reverence.

Pain coursed through the ashen features of blind Wirthaumuin, changing it like a river might change a landscape. "Oh, dear Gaba," said the shepherd then. "You truly are like one of my own. Arise, and know yourself more welcome here than you ever would have been in your own father's house, were you allowed to return to it alive."

Now it was for pain to torture the face of the southerner. He looked up, into the blind, smokey features of Wirthaumuin, tears streaming from his shrinking black eyes. "Why?!" he coughed as though stifling a sob. "Why can you know this?!" he pressed the words through his teeth as though they were desperate to be freed from behind those bony bars.

"Waters run far, my child, and on them many whispers. Come now. Fall into the embrace of the home that you never knew to have. Fall into the flock and graze on the songs of the yore days, in which all of our troubles began, and since which we have all only built on them." The shepherd turned again, and descended the steep stair into his home. He had to duck beneath the door after he had opened it, but the two newcomers walked through it upright, for the shepherd was at least some two men tall. Embers glimmered in a hollow stone pillar in the middle of the round dwelling, above which a chimney, held up on four pillars, led the smoke to the heavens beyond.

There were three great beds in the room, one on the other-most end of the house from where one entered it, one along the left wall, and one along the right. The floor was of stone, and Authæn seemed to have stopped, staring at it. There were, otherwise, wooden arches that went out from four beams near the centre of the room, holding up the roof, and between these four beams, benches formed a square around the fire, so that one might sit comfortably to warm oneself.

Two of the benches were taller — likely for the shepherd. Two were shorter — for visiting students. The pillar of stone within which the shepherd now rekindled the flames, was as tall as the knees of an ordinary man, and where the pillar met the floor, iron bars seemed to allow for openings through which further heat flowed into the room. There embers fell through a grate on which the fire had been made, and air could flow to heat the fire from below.

"Sit, my children," droned the shepherd's soothing voice. "I shall make some tea as a remedy for your sorrows. I know the stories that you come to bring. Both of your stories. Still, I would have you offer them to me in words, for the sake of your own spirits. There is no need to keep caged within that which may do the world without a great good. Share your sorrows with me, and they shall become a fountain of hope for many others.

Authæn and Gaba settled on opposite ends of the fire, each sitting on a shorter bench. Meanwhile the shepherd hooked the kettle, which already seemed filled with water, over the fire to boil.

There they sat a while, the shepherd still as stone; the other two wrestling with themselves not to burst forth in horrid recollection all at once. How were they to begin telling their stories?

Chapter Sixteen
Remembrance

They each sat huddled about the crackling of the fire, holding a wooden mug of hot tea between their heavy hands. Authæn spoke long into the night of his breaking of the laws of the shepherds, having taken up a weapon in battle to slay his foe, having ridden after their foe to put an end to him. He brought forth the blade with which his father had been slain, laying it on the lip of the fire-pillar, and spoke about the horror of finding his father's body on the stone altar that had been placed on the ridge just east of their river.

When he was done, the shepherd said, "Your honesty is a joy to behold, Authæn. In it you are greater than all students that came before you. Let it set in your heart like stone. As for your judgement, that we shall leave for the moot-day. But I tell you now, Authæn, my son, yours has always been a fate far lower and more important than that of any of your forebears. Who is to say what shall come of it?"

The river-man sighed relief, shaking. Now, finally, after having told the tale of his failure in the hollow drone of inescapable recognition, the floodgates burst open in his eyes, and they welled with relief. His river-father had not denied him. He yet had a place in this world, not outcast, not vagabond, but one of the children of Wirthaumuin.

The shepherd then turned to Gaba, and the southerner, who had listened silently to his companion's account, straightened where he sat, closing his eyes and breathing a deep sigh to gather himself for his own retelling. When he opened his eyes again, he looked hard into the milky, blind gaze of the shepherd, and knew that he could hide nothing from those eyes, and for the first time since his exile he did not want to.

"I am Gabazi *kadonazd-Manutuz*, of the city of Manutuz. I am the last of the sons of his house, the last male heir of the house of the long-ago king of the Bulwark in the South. But, since his death, and the queen's assumption of the throne, our throne has only ever been one for the daughters of Manutuz; his sons are her wardens.

"I was chosen to join the Order of the Dragon Hunters, an order that has stood since the time in which the great wyrms were driven from our country, and the city of my fathers was freed from their draconic tyranny. The first of my order were five. They were *the* Five. The Giant's Hand, named for the giant of whose finger-bones the five staves were made.

"One of these five founders of the order was the creature that we all know as the Ibex. In that time he was a man, a son of the city, and chosen by the Child of Olam, the order's head, to serve and to protect by the power that was bestowed on him.

"He failed this charge, using this power of his to cut out for himself a swath of our country in which he reigned as a warlord. But the order had grown since then, and though the five were still at the head of the order, the Child of Olam had begun to notice a heavy corruption on his brothers — he even recognised this illness in himself, drawn from the rot on the finger-bones of the giant which they wielded. Too much of their spirits had flown into these artefacts for all their use.

"It was by command of the Child of Olam that all of the Five be banished from the Order of the Dragon Hunters, as well as from the South. With their altogether effort, the newer members of the order did just this, stripping the Five of their weapons, and sending them each on an impossible quest into faraway lands. What has become of the others, I do not know. Indeed, I thought that the Ibex was long dead, for the day of the Ibex was indeed a yore day.

"Today my order stands to ensure that no ruler of the city rules as once did the dragons, for this we have very sacred, very rigid rules ..."

Gaba looked into the fire now, his jaw working his teeth carefully against one another in bitter memory. The southerner shook his head then, and drank a few draughts of his tea. Then he continued.

"Many ages hence, I failed my order, and I was cast out. I, too, was stripped of my own weapon, which I can even now feel calling to me from faraway places — it is a wound never healing on my heart! In place of my own, I was laded with the staff of the ancient Ibex, and banished to my own impossible quest.

"Word had reached us, you see, of the rise of the Ibex; scouts that had gone to seek out roads by which we might ourselves join the trading road of the northern world. There they had seen the 'bog-dweller' from afar, speaking in our ancient speech.

It is my task not only to end him, in which I have succeeded, but also to ensure that such a monster never again arises outside of our borders. Until that task is done, I may never return to my home, and even if I were to, I doubt greatly that I would be received back a friend of the city, never mind brother to our queen."

"Thank you," said the shepherd, "for sharing with us this difficult tale, Gabazi son of Manutuz, but why then have you been brought to this henge by its son?"

The southerner drank again, then looked into the milky eyes, saying: "A long time I hunted the rumours of the Ibex, oh deathless one. Then I met him one dark night, atop a signal hill near the wooden city. I departed that place as soon as I could, to hunt after this fiend. Along the way I met upon this, your son, in a circle of black stone, in which came and went the images of this land's memory.

"Along the black stones was shown the Ibex. Below him were a strange, stout folk, bearing instruments the like of which I have never seen. Above were depicted what I now understand to be the daughters of the moon; the mothers of your race in particular, oh deathless one."

"You needn't call me deathless any longer, Gaba, my son." At this the shepherd turned to face Authæn. "Will you tell him, Authæn?"

The student under the henge looked up at his river-father, then at the ebon man across from him. Between them the heat of the fires bent the air.

Said Authæn: "Where we met along the road, uncle, I was on my way back to my home after having undertaken a long journey into the tundra land. There lies the Mother-henge; the heart of our people, since their coming into this land. To that place I brought one that was more a mother to me than whatever woman bore me."

The river-man looked up at his shepherd grimly.

"It was my wife," said the shepherd with a distant smile.

Authæn continued: "I went along, guiding the carriage bearing her body by two stout horses. Into the broad grasses even tougher than those of my home, I fore. There, where the great mountains of ice melt away, cleaving at the lands and forming them anew, there I came upon a sight so wonderful and terrible that my heart nearly froze: the Mother henge!

"Where the other henges of our people are more or less great circles of stone — many are the secrets of them that not even their student knows — this is a house of stone, builded in a great plain. It has great arches, held aloft by vast pillars, and none of the shudderings of the earth have toppled them. Then, in its middle, there is a rounded dome with many tall doorways that lead into the heart of the henge.

"There only shepherds may enter; but seeing what I brought to them in the carriage behind me, the brothers of great Wirthaumuin permitted my entrance. There she was laid to rest, the shepherd's wife, and I saw that she was not the first of those that we had called Immortals to be slung down in mortality."

"Then even the ancients are beginning to dwindle?" asked Gaba with horror and disbelief on his voice, looking up at Wirthaumuin again.

"The time for my brothers and I to pass on seems near. New shepherds have been called forth," said the tall river-father, indicating Authæn. "He is of our race, though I had not thought it possible for a long many years. And yet there was a hope in my heart as that of a child. I only wonder if there are more like young Authæn to take up this mantle, and guide our people back into the forsaken city."

"But tell me more of the daughters of the moon, great shepherd!" Gaba bade. "Is it still as Authæn has described it to me, that your people worship the moon at your henges? Did we not only some hours hence see you call her forth in her bewitching beauty?"

"Why do you wish to know, my son?" asked the shepherd. "Is it because you think that the Ibex was in some way bound up with the moon and her daughters?"

"Would that be possible?" asked the southerner.

The shepherd leaned forward, his long beard flowing from his lap to dangle to the floor. "It may be; but I have not seen a daughter of the moon since our first arrival in this country, many ages hence. They were all about the henges in that time as though to guide us; but, just as after we had been born to them and handed over to our fathers, they departed from us, and we were left with the light of the new moon."

"How would one call forth such a being, great shepherd!" begged Gaba. "If I could only ask of one such daughter whether she knew of the Ibex, then I should be able to find out more about what power made of him such a menace in these parts."

Again the shepherd hesitated. "Be careful, dear Gaba," he said after a thoughtful pause, "that your quest does not cause you to tread down what goodness is laid in your path along the way. By doing so you may well tread away those that only you had the power to aid."

The southerner shrank away a little from the fire, nodding to himself. "Forgive me, shepherd; I was hasty. I have been long on the road, and I have forgotten what it means to walk alongside others."

"You are right to ask your questions, my son," said the shepherd, "but it is the manner of your asking that may end you wretchedly. None the less, to find the daughters of the moon you would have to find those that first called them forth from the mirroring sheen of Murmur-mere: You would need to find the ghouls. They too dwell in this country, hidden away in their corrupted barrow-forges, which now slumber few and far between."

"Barrow-forges?" said Authæn suddenly. "Are those perhaps the mounds straddled by trees that you glimpsed in the stone ring, uncle?"

"They are mounds bearing the beacon trees that shine a light in the mists to guide the lost toward them. Often these beacon trees are shown to have seven branches," said the shepherd.

214

"Those are they!" said the southerner. "Yes, then we have learned much more already about the world whence the Ibex was brought forth. The stone circle must have shown these ghouls to stand below the Ibex and the daughters of the moon to hover above."

"Perhaps it is also along this line that one may understand why the Ibex was marshalling such a troop at his ankles," said Authæn.

"You mean at the behest of these two powers?" asked Gaba.

"Or at the behest of one of these powers against the other," said the shepherd, and he sat up tall again, a dark shadow crossing his mien. "There are those among us shepherds of the henges that believe our mothers departed not to spite the sons of Othan that had reached out to them, but to flee the avarice of the ghouls. It may be that they, as daughters born of light and water, remade this Ibex by the foul pools of the *Noal-withaur* to fight dust against dust, the Ibex against the ghouls."

"Then I have disarmed the mothers of your people against the dark creatures that seek to harness them for unknown purposes. Was it a mistake?" said Gaba, and he let his hand glide over his face in a moment of deep conflict. "The Ibex … what a terrible life to have led, and yet he may have only been redeeming himself after all," he muttered to his spirit.

"Regarding all of these things we shall have to find more certain proofs. Let us retire for the moment. You are both in need of long sleep. When

you waken we shall look for answers," said the
shepherd.

With that the weary travellers removed much
of their gear, laying it aside, and they each took a
bed for themselves. The shepherd, meanwhile,
took their cups to wash them out with the water
from the kettle in a bucket. As he did this he
hummed a while, and then began again to sing the
song which he had been singing at their arrival. So
it was that they fell into a sleep unlike any they had
slept before, carried by the words of Wirthaumuin.

Now middle night has swept its cloak
Over the hills the weaving fields.
Let those upon a midnight road
Journey safe till dawn reveals
All that in shadow evil hides;
Away the dark,
Bring forth the light!

***

The moot day came four days after their arrival. As
the days drew like curtains by, the clouds above
also departed, leaving the ever-diminishing sun of
autumn to sprinkle happy yellows over the high
meads. The foothills further to the north-west,
could now be seen, cloaked as their first snows had
buried them in a piercing white. The cold would
roll down thence, causing the students under the
henge to walk about in heavier robes, hunched and
huddled most often about the fires in their low
housing. At certain hours of every day, however,

they would still gather in a circle around their shepherd in the middle of their henge, and sing the songs that told of their histories and of their many laws.

Authæn, though he greatly desired to join his siblings under the henge, had been bidden to hold himself from their rites for the time being, as his doom still hung on the pronouncement of the moot. And so he had shown Gaba about these lands, taking him even to the house that had been built around the source of Wirthaumuin's river. From its flat roof Authæn pointed down into the great, pine-speckled tundra beneath, to where the river flowed into a much greater stream that came in from the north.

"If this is the source of the river Wirthaumuin, what river is that?" asked Gaba regarding the greater stream.

"That is the other source of our river, for much of its water flows into it from the great bergs of ice further north. Those which one sees from the Mother-henge," said Authæn.

The dawn of the moot-day was red, and as the sun arose all were found gathered for the moot already. Amongst the students songs had already begun to settle their minds into a mode of reverence and honesty, so that whatever matters were brought forth would be decided upon well.

They began with simple matters, such as the distribution of stable duties and accounting for things that had been lost or broken in the past week. Matters of firewood and whether more

217

needed harvesting and drying, and who would go out on the hunt this week.

Finally they came to the matter of Authæn, and he was called forth to stand before his brothers in the middle of the henge.

"Authæn, the son of Thuineith, brother of the henge, you stand before us this day as accused. You have said that you need no accuser, but would rather stand and accuse yourself. What are your crimes?" asked the shepherd, standing at the far end of the circle gathered. Beside him stood the elder of the henge, and those students with the highest responsibilities.

"I stand before you brothers," said Authæn, "guilty of the crimes of slaying a man willingly, in order to defend myself before his weapon, and in so doing I have robbed him of the chance to turn from his wickedness. I slew three men. Two by their own weapons, one by kicking him from the top of a tower. To this day these actions haunt me."

"Were these bondsmen, or free?" asked one of the older students. A great murmur was beginning to rise amongst the gathering.

"Was he not chosen of the shepherds? Look at how he has failed us!" another of the students cried out.

At this Wirthaumuin strode into the circle, raising his hands, and a slow silence finally fell again. Then said the shepherd: "We have treated this, your brother, as we would any other student under the henge. He has been here since the age of seven years! He knows all of our customs and all of our

songs as well as any could hope to; in many cases
he is even better versed than one may hope.

"But make no mistake." The shepherd turned
to face the accused. "He is not like any of your
brothers. He is in blood far nobler. He bears the
mark of the shepherds, as do I and all my brothers.
You must judge him fairly; but if you fail to recognise him for that which he is, you shall pay a bitter
price, my children. Do not forget that all of us fall
short of the love of our fathers, and that this is why
we have been cast into the wold, to roam in circles
about our henges."

Then, Wirthaumuin returned to where he had
been standing, and many of the faces of the students were downcast as though reprimanded.

"Continue, son," said the henge elder.

"I ..." said Authæn, but he faltered then, the
words catching in his throat as he struggled to contain himself. His face was void of emotion but pale
and he shook his head once, then caught his breath,
then shook it again. Finally he continued: "I have
ridden into battle against the foe of my village, the
Ibex, with the intent to destroy him."

"Then you had vengeance on your heart? Or
did you seek to protect the village in the name of
your chieftain?" pressed the henge elder.

"I had vengeance on my heart." The gathering
burst again into disturbed chatter. "I sought to
avenge my father, who had been slain!" Authæn
cried over the tumult, and would have succumbed
to his dread and despair, had he not looked into the
still face of his shepherd. There he gained fortitude
again, and he stood tall, clenching to his jaw.

When the noise subsided the henge elder was the first to speak. "You have acted boldly, Brother Authæn. You have fought for the sake of your village, and you have succeeded, with aid, as our shepherd has shared with us, to undo this great threat that roamed our lands. For this you should be heralded a hero."

These words seemed not to quieten the accused, however. He seemed, rather, to wax in his dread. "But ours is not the way of the hero," he whispered, and yet the hiss of it carried all across that ancient circle.

The onlookers seemed mostly amazed at this. Now it began to dawn on many that this river-man, their brother under the henge, truly understood their way, if they had not trusted it to be true before. Indeed, many of them, in this moment, were brought to understand their own ways in a manner they had not yet before.

Authæn fell to his knees, finally overcome with a fatigue of the spirit. The glittering exertion along his brow and nose, and his laboured breathing showed the toll that the truth of his failure demanded from him. His eyes darted from one of the vast, blank standing stones to the next as though they were speaking dark dooms over him.

"It is as your brother under the henge says," declared the henge elder, and all saw that there was a hold that even this old man was struggling to keep over himself. "Ours is not the way of the hero. For that you may go into the world, and learn to play its bloody games under its warmongers. Therefore, Brother Authæn of the race of the shepherds as none have been before you since the shepherds themselves. We acknowledge that our plans for you are not the plans of Truth, and that you are being shaped by broader tools than alone what we have to offer here.

"You know our ways, Brother Authæn, and we would bid you steer by them, but by breaking from our codes you have broken from our brotherhood, and we must declare you a brother in Wirthaumuin's river, though not a brother under the henge. Be not bitter too long against us, and find the fate that has fallen from the stars for you."

Again the gathering burst into a dismayed uproar, and into all manner of debates. How could one who had so perfectly understood their way err, and how could he be punished despite his recognition of his mistakes. Meanwhile, the river-man, no longer under the henge or its laws, arose in silence and strode away from the gathering. He did not go into the house of the shepherd, he simply walked in the direction of the river's source, and the house that was built around it.

Chapter Seventeen
Respite

There, above a world so calm and busy with its little plays, Authæn was glad not to be noticed. He felt as though the world had shunned him, as though it had declared him lesser. A low creature.

Suddenly, the words Wirthaumuin had spoken to him as a child returned to him: *Do not hide these markings, for they are your testament to the world. You are no ordinary son of dust. You are a river-person, and that is a far lower thing, and therefore all the more important. What house can stand without a foundation? Is the foundation not the lowest part?*

"The lowest parts carry all others on their shoulders. Is that not even your name, river-father?" Authæn mused to his spirit. "You are the river that carries all others in our clan; even me. Yet I am the capstone, I sense. I am laid at the very pinnacle, worthless, no more than weight for the greater river-folk to carry. Marked out to be strange am I, all for the sake of strangeness and nothing more. I cannot keep to our laws, I am a worm in the grasses, sneaking and striking the weakest enemies, fleeing before the strong, unless kindled to a lack of restraint!"

Authæn kicked a bucket as hard as his iron toes allowed it, and the wood gave at once, so that the bucket stoved in and clung to his foot. This surprised the river-person, and he lost his balance, falling to the roof of the river-source's house on which he had been standing all day. The bucket still hung on his toe with a large, splintering hole in it.

It was evening now. The sun was setting behind him, casting a light over the shimmering white patches of the world of all his failed history. He roared into the heavens, shaking his fists as their iron eyes began to glitter and wink at him with some unbearable shrewdness. He kicked the bucket from his toe with the other foot, then rose and kicked the wooden thing doubly hard in a way, that it flew like a cannonball into the distance below, breaking in pieces as it tumbled through the chill air.

He tensed all his strength into a silent scream, not desiring to be heard by those at the henge. The sounds on the mountain carried across these open lands. He had learned that long ago. And so he paced in one large circle about the flat roof of the house, looking at whiles into the darkling heavens.

Finally, when all his ire was out, Authæn lifted his hands, breathed a long sigh of resignation, and said: "Now I am yours." Words of an ancient ritual that his fathers had sung upon departing the city of their birth. And he collapsed again to his knees as he had at the beginning of the day. He was now never to be a henge-man. All of his father's efforts to bring him here had been undone.

He closed his eyes.

His chin rested on his breast.

He was defeated.

Suddenly, despite the dark of his shut lids, a light seemed to brighten that darkness. Authæn opened his eyes again, and looked up, for thence came the light. In his spirit the image of the daughter of the moon had caused his heart to falter for a second, he could not bear the coming of such a creature at this hour.

But it was no daughter of the moon. Above, where heaven was now starlit, the golden dawn of northern lights was playing out its wondrous sight, to soothe a stricken soul in need of comfort. It wrothe there in all manner of hues from the reddest of reds to the bluest of blues, dancing and weaving in similar fashion to the boughs of a great tree; or was it in the manner of a river's lithe tide?

The lights began to tangle themselves into shapes and patterns that the eye desired to meet, as though they were filled with meaning, filled with guidance. But then, when the eye had thought to catch the shape there brought to bear, it was nothing and meaningless. Or was it? The eye would search again, always following, and never understanding.

"Who are you?" said Authæn as a child might have.

I am the End.

The voice rolled across the mountaintop and into the grasses below, a thunderous revelation at the least expected moment. It was all so clear, and still he did not understand it. Had that voice truly spoken from the night-time dawn above?

Below the hills were rustling in the wind; the many groping fingers of the tundra reaching with all their length toward the bejewelled heavens. There, above, was an ocean of jewellery; and, presently, where the stars had always stood still, so that one might navigate by them, they began to dance with one another. They bobbed and weaved above the northern lights, and in a dizzying display, all the heavens were aglow with light that seemed devoid of sun and moon — a frightening, chaotic, senseless light; whilst below, the earth still remained dark, and the grass strained for what life it might eke from the careless heavens.

Then the blades were set against one another in bitterness and spite. The grasses went to war, each blade with its neighbour! They began to consume one another as though they were serpents with nothing more than their own kin to feed upon. Finally, the hills were a reflection of the stars, all awhir with war.

The great, rolling downs began to tumble about against and amongst one another, so that soon, all was an ocean — for indeed! the deeps burst open, and great waters poured forth, covering the lands with a tumultuous shadow. Soon there was only a fiery heaven above, and a railing sea below.

And Authæn was clinging to a single staff that stood up straight out of the water to stay above the heaving tides with all a helpless child's desperation.

He clawed upon it like a cat — and, indeed, in that moment he realised that his hands were claws. He *was* a cat.

His narrow claws dug deep into the wood of the staff, so that it began to bleed sap. Hooking one claw after the prior, he slowly made his horrified way to the top of the staff, only to find that it was a tree with seven branches.

He swung himself heavily onto a branch (he thought, in the back of his mind, that his weight was far too great for the size of his body). From here he looked panting out over the storm of brilliance and its terrible reflection. Great winds rent the waters, and laughed as though they were dragons. The tree swayed from this side to that.

Look around, Authæn. See that which you fear; this is fear itself!

The voice had spoken again, and now he felt that this was the only voice that mattered. "Make that it ends!" he screamed.

I am the End.

"Authæn!"

Was that still the voice from the dream? He felt cold, and uncomfortable. He could not feel his legs, and he felt as though he would fall over if he moved his head.

"Authæn! Awaken, you foolish child in the body of a man!" demanded the voice of Gaba, and he came to, swinging his head up drearily, and then falling over backwards onto his shoulders. Above him the sky was starlit, but the northern lights were no longer there. Then he felt the pain in his legs, for he had fallen back onto his feet. He had fallen asleep whilst kneeling.

He groaned in discomfort, and the southerner helped him up at once, seeing his awkward position on the planks of the roof. "You will catch your death by cold up here, you fool!" the southerner shouted as Authæn found his feet again, slowly swinging the feeling back into them.

"I am sorry, uncle," the other blurted out in an uncontrolled manner. "I am only very sad."

Looking into the dark face of the southerner, Authæn saw his sadness reflected there, and he felt as though not all things in the world had shunned him. Here he was well understood. Perhaps here was even truer sorrow than in his own eyes. This man had not only been banished from a henge, he had been banished from his country, and durst never to return, save his quest be complete.

He looked away, but he was now less ashamed than ever. The vision of his dream still burst like a whirlwind on his soul, and he felt that any life would be better than that cosmic nightmare.

"You have found him then, my friend?" came the voice of the shepherd.

"Just as you said I would, great shepherd," said Gaba.

"Leave us a moment, Gaba," said the shepherd then. "Go already towards the house, and make some tea, if you would do us the honour. I see stars in young master Authæn's eyes that were not there before."

"As you will it, shepherd," said Gaba, and after nodding and smiling a concerned smile to his road-companion, he returned to the stair which he had only just ascended. Below the water drowned out the sounds of his departure.

"Did you see the gold of northern lights to-night, shepherd?" asked Authæn as they watched their southern friend go on his way. He wondered now where the dream had begun.

"That is a strange question to ask of a blind man, Authæn," the shepherd chuckled, and took a seat at one edge of the roof where a bench stood. "But I heard none mention it."

"I sometimes think that you can see, if I may say it, river-father," said Authæn.

"You have keen wariness," said the shepherd, "perhaps as keen as that of an eagle."

"I had a dream now, shepherd. It was a terrible nightmare," said Authæn.

"Regarding what?" asked the shepherd.

"The ending of the world, I think. The falling of the heavens, the rising of the seas, and the war of all that lay inbetwixt. It was as though therein somewhere lay a terrible call to me. A voice spoke from out of the northern lights."

"That truly is the token of a dream, my son. There are no northern lights so far into the autumn. Are they not the sun's farewell?"

"It said, this voice I heard: 'I am the end'," Authæn continued, and now the shepherd seemed more thoughtful, perhaps only because the dream seemed to bother his child so.

"Do you fear being without purpose, young master Authæn?" asked the shepherd in rhyme with the river.

"I do," whispered the other.

"What say you of your fellow traveller's purpose?"

"I do not know what to say of it, shepherd. What would you say of it?"

There was another long silence, and the shepherd drew out a pipe that he had stowed somewhere in his belt until then. As he packed and lit it, smoking out the weave and dance of endless mysteries in blue smoke, he seemed to weigh out careful words. Still nothing came forth.

"I simply do not yet understand his purpose well, shepherd," Authæn said. "That is why I ask."

The shepherd nodded his head slowly, sympathetically. After puffing out another cloud of richly scented smoke, he said in a faraway voice: "Every quest, if followed through to the end, will cleave from you what will stand in the way of its completion; if it tries to take from you what you will not let go, then it will tear it away, and do even greater damage than was first necessary. But the quest that has been put on our Gabazi, the quest that has replaced his identity with the title of 'dragon hunter' and then stripped him of it, has replaced a vague life with one of absolute purpose; and absolute purpose claims the *whole* life. He cannot stop, save at whiles to rest, until he has reached the intended end."

"That is a hard saying, shepherd," muttered Authæn.

The shepherd hummed a part of the melody to the song he had sung when they had arrived. "You only find it a hard saying, because you want to follow him to *his* intended end, young Authæn," thrummed the shepherd then, in a low, quiet, smiling way. "But it may be that you have your own ends to meet, apart from those of the legendary Gabazi *kadonazd Manutuz*. Yes, his is a cosmic story, but that is *his* to give. Yours may be far more humble, and far more meaningful than ever the very wise could tell. For those of us who know much, are often also blind to much more."

He drew again on his pipe. Then he continued.

"You want to be a great hero, Authæn; I sense it in your actions. It is why you tried to wrest your life from the hands of those slaves to darkness. I do not judge you for it. Is our whole way not but another shape of clinging desperately to life. You consider your own life worth more than that of those that seek to claim it. It is no foolish thought; though perhaps it is so deeply buried in your heart that you have not even considered it.

"You are destined still to be the chieftain of Thænim, a village that is all but in the wind. It has fallen away from the rest of our clans, sent into exile amongst the children of Imnir to wait for its chosen leader to return. But why should he return, Authæn? Why should Thænim be spared? Has it not fallen from the road that we walk as much as you have? It has drunk deeply of the promises of your father, Thuineith. In you they see these promises should be fulfilled."

The shepherd drew again on his pipe. Authæn had placed his head between his hands as his thoughts reeled. These words of the shepherd cut into him as iron bites bark. He did not want them to sit so well in his rind, but there was such a truth to them that he could do naught but sit in still horror and hear carefully every drop that fell from the tongue of his river-father.

Eventually the river-man managed: "I followed the trail of Uncle Gaba, because I was certain that I would die until he came to our defence. In him I saw again a way to live. But now I see that even his road ends with ... death. I think, now that I have seen also his mortality and not only his power, that I should have remained with the village, and learned amongst the elders there how to govern my people. You had summoned me back, but I knew that I was no longer a brother under the henge. I thought that I might learn to be a greater leader than they could teach, if I followed a greater man than they could ever be; but now I doubt my judgement. I thought to be a hero, but I am, as you have often said, low."

"Do not mistake me, Authæn," said the shepherd with a sigh. "That makes you greater than many another man I know! Greater even than I and my brothers, for in our time we were those that preserved our people. You shall be the one to deliver them!"

"But it is as you say, shepherd!" retorted Authæn, suddenly and bitterly impassioned. "I desired to be the hero where something 'lower' and yet 'greater' was needed! I should not have followed Gaba; I should not have sought to gain from the powers which he wields!"

The shepherd laughed. "Why not? You have seen the good, shall you not also know the evil? For if you are to be a leader then you are to fight for what is good for your people. If you know not only the great good that can dwell in men, but also the great weakness, you will have a compass that is

231

as great as you hoped. It will take on a character the size of the world that you have come into conversation with," said the shepherd between streaming tendrils of tobacco blue.

"I only fear ... to discover that the good that man can offer is little, when compared to the never-ending evil there; to discover that, even what little good there is, may be corrupted by duplicitous desire. What if any aim to which a man sets his mind is wrong?" said Authæn.

"That," muttered the shepherd, "is most often the case."

A long silence settled in, and then it appeared.

In the heavens above, like the great boughs of a living tree, wrothe the many limbs of the northern lights. Their dance was one so ethereal and divine that in that moment, all else was forgotten. This was the great reminder to the river-people, that they were not only made of dust, but that in them was also light beyond the dust; veiled and burdensome.

"Perhaps," chuckled the shepherd, who seemed, despite his eyes, to know the lights to dance above, "this is the answer to your question, my son! That which is good in us, is poured into us from without, and drawn out of us from without — like light is poured into the eye, and knowledge is teased out of the heart. The question is not whether you can make goodness within yourself, but whether or not you can trust that which is good to be good, with and without you, and to be grateful, when it rears its friendly head, that you may be its witness. For in bearing it's witness from time to time, even you may bear its good from time to time. Yes … gratitude for what is good. It is a simple peace."

When the pipe of the shepherd was done, he cleaned it and arose, and Authæn followed him down the stair back to his house. As they went, the shepherd began again to sing this hymn that even Gaba now knew. "Sorry," muttered Wirthaumuin. "It is my favourite."

Now middle night has swept its cloak
Over the hills the weaving fields.
Let those upon a midnight road
Journey safe till dawn reveals
All that in shadow evil hides;
Away the dark,
Bring forth the light!

And above, the light had been brought forth, pointing out the many lines between the constellations that only forgotten minds had ever observed.

Chapter Eighteen
The House of Noth

The following morning Gaba, and Authæn were awoken by the busy movements of the shepherd before dawn. The kettle was singing over the fire, and the smell of breakfast hung in the air. For a moment an icy wind swept through the house, as the shepherd cleared the entrance of snow. There had not been overmuch in the previous night.

"It is time to rise, my good friends!" declared the shepherd, knowing by some secret sense that they were awake. "The House of Noth has been seen!" A joy was in his voice that Authæn had not heard for a long time.

They arose, and dressed themselves in their newly washed garments. They had planned to leave today, after teasing more answers from Wirthaumuin over breakfast, for the doom that had been spoken over Authæn caused the henge to feel like a prison for him. He did not want to think of those that were once brothers under the henge with him, he could barely think of facing them day after day were he to remain here any longer. He was far too ashamed.

"Let us go together to the House of Noth, my friends," said the shepherd. "From there you may depart again. The questions that you have shall be answered there better than I could ever answer them here."

"Who is this Noth?" asked the southerner.

"He is a wanderer," said the shepherd. "much like our people; but he is far older than any of us shepherds. It was under his guidance that we were led to the Mother-henge, and by many of his teachings we taught our own children."

They ate on in silence, washing down the meal with hot tea. Then they climbed the stone stair out of the low house, into the twilight of just before dawn. Even in this bleak light, however, the three could see that they were not the only ones awake at this hour. Along the road that led down from the plateau of the henge stood a long, silent line of the henge-dwellers.

Under their watchful eyes the three began to depart. Authæn did not dare meet any of their gazes. Then he heard the voice of the henge elder: "You are witnessed, Authæn! You are witnessed, blood of our blood!"

At this the banished river-man looked up. He saw that the students that now stood alongside his road were smiling at him, nodding their encouragement, and he felt overcome. Somewhere nearer the top of the gathering, where their departure had begun, a voice began to chant: "Become the river! Become the river!"

And at once the rest of those once brothers under the henge joined in the cry: "Become the river! Become the river! Become the river!" And they beat their chests as they shouted, and all the while the shout thundered over the low plains that had only a moment before been silent with the language of graveyards.

And so was Authæn son of Thuineith dismissed from the henge of his people, and from the tutelage of his fathers to become the clay of broader potters; a needle that navigates a wider compass.

Their journey now took them south along the river's course. They crossed the sprinting waters at a place where they crashed over some sturdy stones, and then their company went into the west. There the lands were also more mountainous, and there were many needly trees of green and cone that ruffled themselves in the shuddering breeze.

Beneath the trees, tucked into the sheltered nook of two meeting fells, they found the fabled House of Noth. It was not what either had expected, seeming nothing more than a steepled roof of lichenous shale that reached all the way from the earth to a presently smoking chimney. Beneath the roof was a mossy, wooden front, with a window set in the centre of its gable. It was a window of coloured glass set in leaden framing. Beneath this was a crude, wooden door with no handle.

"That is a long triangle," said Gaba. "But shall we all fit inside?"

The shepherd laughed, and said, "This is where I shall leave you to find an answer to that question yourselves, my friends. I must return to my duties under the henge."

"Then we thank you, great shepherd for housing us so generously!" said Gaba, reaching out and gripping the shepherd's arm in greeting. The other responded in kind, stooping, and laying his free hand on the southerner's shoulder.

"Go well, Gabazi of Manutu's city," said he. "May your paths end in peace."

"Tell me one thing before you leave us, great shepherd," bade Gaba then, as their arms came apart. "I would still know whether or not you worship the moon as did your fathers, and as do the ghouls to this day."

A hearty smile drew itself into the shepherd's beard then, and laughter danced on his eyes. "You worry that we fall into the same folly as those that came before us, Gaba — a question that is heavy on the road that you yourself must walk. We shall all fail in one way or another." The shepherd turned his visage towards Authæn. "But we do not worship the moon. We recognise it for what it is."

"What is it, then?" asked Gaba.

"It is the shadow of the sun," said Authæn.

"Indeed," said the shepherd. "It casts light that was given to it, bringing to the children of the world light, even in dark night. Nor do we worship the sun, though that may be thought of as less foolish than the worship of the moon, but we recognise that it brings to light was has long tried to hide away. Nothing can hide from the sun forever, for it shall outlive us all."

"What then do you worship at this henge? Is it memory?" pressed the southerner.

The shepherd seemed surprised. "That is an interesting thought, my friend," said he. "But no. Here we worship the Truth by witnessing it."

"I see," said the southerner. He seemed troubled. "I thank you again, shepherd, and bid you also farewell."

"And I, my river-father. Do not forget me," said Authæn.

"You will become a stone of remembrance to all our children, Authæn. Do not doubt this, but do not think that it will be by your own hand that your greatness shall be achieved," said the shepherd with an enigmatic smile. Then the great, grey figure turned its purple robe, and began its return to the henge of Wirthaumuin.

They stared after the shepherd's lumbering movements in the snow a while, then they turned to face the glowing gable before them. "Let us see if there is someone to tend to that fire within," said Gaba, turning to smile at his companion, and patting him on the back.

They strode towards the house, and as they did so, clouds must have swept over the sun. All seemed to grow a little duller, a little darker. The green of the soft grasses beneath the pines became a withered grey, and the rustling in the trees was like the sound of an ocean's rising tide. The timbers of the house aface of them began to crack with loud groans in the shifting of the weather, and the light of the singular round window above the door seemed to grow brighter, staring out at them like a singular eye.

Gaba knocked at the door three times, and they stepped back from the threshold in expectation of a response. Behind the lighted window a shadow seemed to flicker, and then the shape of a man's head appeared there, looking out at them. It fell away again, and then the door clicked, and swung open. There was no one in the doorway to invite

238

them, but the glow that flowed into the outer grey where the two travellers stood was invitation enough, and they stepped into the house.

When they stood inside, the gentle click behind them signalled that the door was now closed again. They barely took note of this, however. Before them, the house that they had seen as small and weathered from the outside, was revealed to be no more than a stair-house, and as they descended the stairs into the candle-lit earth, they came down into the world beneath; into a great, circular room like a tiered stage. In the middle of the circular room was a large, round table, and in the middle of the table was a small tree aglow as if with its own radiance. It grew from the middle of the table like a fresh shoot might begin to grow from the stump of a vast tree.

At four opposing ends of the room, four brilliant firepits burned, lowered by circular coves into the tiered descent. Above each firepit was a stony tunnel into the ceiling that must have guided the smoke to the little chimney over the stair-house. Along the tiers were littered all manner of tome and handiwork yet incomplete, or complete and abandoned in the middle of some even greater project.

"This reminds me of the council-board. This reminds me of the moot of Thænim!" Authæn marvelled.

"Yes, son of the river. It was I that showed your father how to build your moot," said a man that now revealed himself, descending from the opposite end of the tiered descent, and the travellers no-

239

ticed then that there were doors cloven into the earthen walls over the uppermost tier. Roots stuck forth from the dark earth there, repurposed to hold candles, whilst here and there stones had been arranged to support the stability of the earthen surroundings, but there were no pillars going up from the centre of the room to hold high the earthen ceiling.

When the man stood at the far end of the table, he looked up to them, smiling, and said, "Join me, my friends! Wirthaumuin has told me all about your quest." And he motioned them to sit with him at the round table.

Warily, they descended, for this seemed almost an ordinary man. His hair was dull, as though it were meant to be black as onyx, and yet it was grey. His skin seemed to intend the colour of olives that grew along the southern shores of Middlemere; and yet it was also grey. His eyes could have been the colour of hazel nuts — but they were the grey of the sea — and his heavy robe was also tinted with the hint of bright colours, yet they had all forgotten exactly why they had once been so.

"Are you Master Noth?" asked Gaba, pulling back a high-backed chair, and carefully sitting down on it. He laid his things onto the ground beside him. Authæn sat down on the southerner's other side.

"I am," said the other, smiling at them again. "Might I offer you a drink? Are you perchance hungry?"

"We do not intend to stay much longer than it would take for you to answer some questions that we have, Master Noth, if that is not an offence to you," said Gaba.

"You want to know why the roof has not yet fallen in over our heads?" the colourless man tried.

"That was one of my questions," chuckled the southerner.

"Perhaps you want to know how Wirthaumuin and I have spoken if he has not left his house ex-cept to guide you here since my house was sighted?" the colourless man continued.

"That was something I had wondered," said Authæn, now frowning.

Noth leaned forwards over the table, though with the distance that the great piece of furniture put between them it made no real difference. "Birds!" he said. Then he leaned back in his chair with a grim face.

"You said that you taught my father, Master Noth. Did you mean Wirthaumuin with those words?" asked Authæn.

"No, I meant Thuineith. The carpenter was a good friend. It is sad that he has been slain, and for such a dark purpose, too!" the grey man shook his head.

"The birds must have been heavy with tides this morning," whispered Authæn.

"Oh, this I knew long before you returned to the henge, dear Authæn." The grey man looked at him, his face entirely drained of feeling, as well as colour.

"How is that possible? Did the birds spy out the attack on Thænim for you?" demanded Authæn, forgetting himself, and standing up with his hands flat on the table.

"No, dear Authæn," said Noth, smiling sadly. "I was there."

The river-man sank back into his chair with wide eyes.

"And you had no power to stop the death of Authæn's father?" asked the southerner, now with a frown of his own.

"Of course I did," said the grey man.

The southerner folded his arms, his eyes narrowed, and a look of great scepticism took his features. "I do not know if you are the greatest fool, Master Noth, or if you are to be feared more than any other."

"No," said Noth, and another sad smile twitched at his mouth, never reaching his eyes. "You do not, Gabazi."

"Please, Master Noth!" said Authæn then, desperately. "Please tell me why my father was slain! What was the meaning of it all? Why the stone of fathers upon which he was slain? It all makes very little sense to me. I feel as though I never truly knew my father."

Said this grey Noth to his guests: "I will tell you what I will. The stone upon which you found your father was a stone hewn by the ancient servants of the ghouls. They are called 'gnomes', or also 'grons', and they are also those that raised much of the ancient and forgotten architecture of this land. The grons built the barrow-forges, and they built the passages that lead into the under-earth. But they no longer serve the ghouls."

"Is that what we saw depicted along the rim of the chest that was buried beneath the waterfall; there where that strange creature rent the stone with its voice?" Authæn asked Gaba.

The southerner thought for a moment, and then nodded. "I can think of no better explanation."

"Then those stout creatures were the ghouls, and they were at war with the gnomes in that depiction," said Authæn.

"Ah," said Noth. "You have found one of the relics of their war."

"Found and lost," said Gaba.

"It is better that way," said Noth, "for the time being."

"But why was this done to my father? Had he angered the grons? Was it these gnomes that brought forth the Ibex as a means to war with their masters?" asked Authæn.

"No, not the grons. They have all scattered over this northern world into pockets and clusters of their own. Some walk alone — as alone as a gnome can. They have no great designs over the world."

"Then why?" Authæn begged.

Pity came into the eyes of Noth, and he said, "Your father was pierced by the hand of a ghoul. Hold forth his killer, Authæn. Yes, there is their black metalwork. Does it not remind you of something, good dragon hunter?"

"It did, from the moment in which I saw it. It reminded me of the Ibex and the armour in which he was clothed."

"But it reminds you of something other, as well. This dagger is familiar to you, in a way that pierces your soul," pressed Noth.

The southerner looked at him with the same fear-stricken eyes that had looked up at the blind shepherd upon their arrival at the henge. "This is a strange country, where no one's secrets are safe, and the things said aloud are remembered by its stones forever after!" whispered he.

"What does it remind you of, Gabazi," demanded Noth.

"It reminds me of the staff that I wielded. It reminds me of the weapons that were stripped from the Five."

"Yes. It reminds you of the reason you came to this country, a land strange with lights and shadows of things that are and want to be," said Noth with a friendly grin.

"What are you?" hissed the southerner. "Where did you steal those words?" And now it was Gaba's turn to forget himself, snatching the cruel dagger from where Authæn had placed it on the table, and jumping to his feet.

"Arise, Authæn! We must leave this place. He is a strange kind of wizard! He can see things that none should know; not even the birds!" cried the once dragon hunter.

"Gaba, I desire to know of my father's fate!" cried Authæn. "I have met weirder than this man! Am I not the weirdest according to your own judgement? Let us hear what he has to say, he has not yet drawn a weapon on us, and he has taken us into his home, offered us to eat and to drink!"

"No doubt poisoned!" barked the southerner.

Noth looked down, as though to contemplate all of these things. Then he looked up again, smiling as though he understood, and said, "Would you perhaps like to try something to eat or drink now, and make of a theory a fact?"

This stunned the southerner, and the river-man looked from the grey man to the ebon man trying to say something, but spitting out only many silences.

"Come now, it is a simple question. Someone's poison is another's remedy, and these are fruits of goodness!" pronounced Noth, and before the seats of both Gaba and Authæn, a little vine began to sprout, then blossom, then bear abundant bunches of grapes. "They will only wither, if you do not eat of them."

Slowly Gaba sat down again, though he did not eat, nor did Authæn.

"Hmm…" said Noth, seeing their reluctance. "The only condition that I have is that you enjoy it."

Gaba cried out again, though Authæn did not understand why.

Noth laughed.

"Come then, let me tell you the tragedy of Thuineith, that you may be at peace, dear Authæn," said he then, and again, all at once, his face was drained of emotion. "The ghouls slew your father, because he had met with a daughter of the moon in the ancient home of your people. Indeed, he had seen the city of your fathers. I was there with him, in fact.

"The ghouls fear your people, Authæn. They know that one day the children that came of their great disobedience shall overturn their designs. They do have designs, you see, unlike those that once stood in their service."

"Would it be possible for us to speak with such a daughter of the moon?" asked Gaba.

"You ask, because you desire to meet with the ghouls, Gabazi," there was a long moment in which the southerner and their host stared tensely at one another.

"What of it?" asked the southerner.

"It is strange how some desires make us bravely foolish in the face of that which we know to be greater than ourselves," said Noth. "That is 'what of it' I think. Still, it may be good for you to meet her. There is one daughter of the moon, who comes with every full moon to a place which I shall ensure you are shown; but for me to show it to you, you will have to eat of those grapes."

Gaba had not let his eyes drift from the grey man.

Authæn looked again from one to the other, then he took a single grape from the vine that had sprouted before him, wondering by what power it had been conjured, and laid it reluctantly into his mouth.

It burst like a thousand colours over his tongue. With each drop that rolled down his throat of the grape's juicy contents, it was like his dearest memories and smells returned to him, and wove together in his mind the laughter of a woman he felt he should have known. There was comfort in that

246

laughter, and then he thought he heard the voice of his father. There was a movement in his heart, as something sinking into profound depths. In this moment he knew something important, but he shied from putting it into words. He did not want this nostalgic joy to fly from him. In his spirit's heart, he begged that this moment would never fade away. But it did.

And then he looked sadly down at the fruit before him. "It is the memory of joy — of true peace and contentment — as if made real in this very moment," the river-man muttered without wanting to.

Gaba looked a frightened way at his companion, shook his head, murmuring something that sounded like "This is not a good idea", and followed in the example that Authæn had set for him, bringing just one grape to his mouth.

A bitter expression coursed across his features, and he cringed into the back of his chair; he coughed a little, but tried to stifle it. Then there came something like confusion into his features, and then his mean cleared, his brow lifted, eyes still closed. And then a tear rolled down his cheek, and he nodded slowly. A moment later a frown creased his brow. He opened his eyes.

"Good, good!" said Noth. "Then you will stomach the wine that I have prepared for you. It will speed you along on the road to the caverns of Lyn Ithæm."

"What are the caverns of Lyn Ithæm?" asked Authæn.

"They are caverns," said Noth, and grinned, "of Lyn Ithæm."

Chapter Nineteen
Second Impressions

The scree beneath the rising snows was ground down by horseshoes. The gnashing of the mountain's many fallen teeth resounded from the tall shelves of stone that surrounded them. Gaba and Authæn had climbed their mounts into the rising chalk of the foothills that lay in the direction of Glimwæth. In this direction also lay the caverns of Lyn Ithæm, a daughter of the moon. The horses they had received from Noth, who had led them into an underground stable through one of the doorways above the circular descent of his main hall. He had also laid great saddles with saddlebags onto the beasts, sturdy mountain horses that were not all too tall.

"They shall guide you through the forests as well, once you cross the mark into the vales of Darkholt," the grey man had said. Then he had given them some new travel gear, along with new rucksacks. These were also filled with dried foods and skins of the wine from the grapes they had eaten.

They had thanked him, and he had said that they were far beyond that, laughing.

"A strange man," muttered Gaba presently, adjusting himself carefully in the saddle. It was snowing again.

"You are not accustomed to riding?" asked Authæn.

"I have simply not ridden for a long time, but as a dragon hunter I would spend more time with my horse than with my family!" laughed the southerner, allowing the joy of the memory to flood him for the moment. Authæn smiled.

"What do you think he was?" asked the riverman then, scratching his head. "Or what is the matter with his house? The shepherd said that he was a wanderer, which I believed well enough when I saw the house from the outside; but within it seemed an endless warren of mysteries."

"Beginning with that table of his," said Gaba.

"Indeed. But then his house also simply vanished after we closed the front door!" said Authæn.

"Yes, how strange it was. I can't even explain it by saying that he hid the entrance. The house was there when we stepped out, then we closed the door …" began the southerner.

"We turned around and began to lead our horses away, and then there was that noise!" Authæn continued.

"I thought the building had fallen in on itself!" said Gaba.

"But we turned around, and there was nothing there." Authæn finished.

"Even this speaking with birds has me a little wary. Do they truly speak with the birds of the air, or is that some turn of phrase here in the north?" asked Gaba.

"Not a turn of phrase. It is an ancient custom among our people," explained Authæn. "Our scouts are the only ones that now observe it, for it requires a great deal of discipline or single-mindedness. The speech of the birds can only be bestowed upon those that drink of the blood of a water-dragon, uncle."

"And your people hunt these fiends on a regular basis?" the former dragon hunter seemed terribly bewildered by this news.

"No, uncle!" said Authæn. "The shepherds alone know how to make and end of them, and of all the river-people it is alone Wirthaumuin's children that participate in the blood of the water-dragon. The captains of our scouts, when they are chosen, must venture to the henge, and ensure a supply of the dragon blood for their underlings. This way they are also acknowledged by our river-father."

"I see."

They rode on again in silence, on either side of them the tall, brittle shelves of a gorge stretched up. To their left was a sheer drop, and much of the scree and snow they now trotted over tumbled into the faraway below. They kept themselves as near the right side as possible, wary of the danger that the loose stones might slip out from beneath the hooves of their horses and bring them sailing to a fateless end.

Eventually they reached the other side of the kloof, turning now right to where a crude pass continued into a heathery height, on which their horses might find better footing. This was another broad country, which stretched on for miles around, only at a distance could any other bigger mountains be seen.

"What did Master Noth say again, regarding the place where this Lyn Ithæm might be found? He told us to follow the river below, was it not so?" asked Gaba.

"Indeed," said Authæn, "we must keep it to our left side, until we come to a narrow shelf. This in turn will lead us to a door that only opens on the full moon."

They brought their mounts down into the highlands here between the tall fells, and let the horses graze a while. Then they continued again, keeping the river ever on their left. Still, it seemed that they would not reach the cavern this day, for they were still some distance from the next rise that promised what they sought. And so they made camp for the night amidst a jagged outcrop.

There they ate and spoke, and Authæn missed his lyre as Gaba brought out his strange instrument, but enjoyed the songs that the southerner then played from his homeland. He played memories that sounded so joyous, and yet they would sometimes dip into desperation, or into pride. Yet always the joy of victory would ring forth again; victory over the wyrms of long ago. Finally they drifted into sleep.

Authæn was roused from dozing near their little fire by the sound of his baggage clattering and rustling, and … was it speaking?

"No, not that one!" hissed a little voice from the general vicinity of his travelling gear. "Not that one either!"

"Well what shall we take, then?" another retorted. "We might as well have stayed away, if you're going to be so picky. The lion-eye will waken at this rate!"

"He shall certainly waken, if you shout so!" said the first.

"You're the one who's shouting!"

After a particularly violent rustle, a small, fat creature was thrown into the light of the fire from the open mouth of the rucksack. Another leapt out after him with an angry scowl clothing his face — an ugly face.

"I'm not shouting!" — it was shouting — "You are" — it struck the other with a fat little fist — "SHOUTING!"

"NOOOOO!" screamed the other. "YOU AAAAARE!"

It was a full on fist fight, without restraint. The blows landed every time (these two were clearly creatures of experience in the art of fisticuffs). Every strike seemed to reverberate on the air with its intensity, yet neither seemed really to take any injury from the other's blows.

Their little contest continued for a few minutes, during which Authæn sat up and watched with an interested and puzzled frown. "You must be brothers," said he, when he thought that the mystical scene might lose its charm.

They stopped in a deadlock, their little black eyes twitching over to where he sat, and their heads following suit on their stout little necks. They weren't fat after all! They were as taut as stone. Were they of stone? After a tense moment, they untangled themselves from one another and stood abreast very proper-like. They were clothed in dun cloth that was very intricate in some places, and very rough in others, but both were donned with long liripiped hoods. They must each have been about an ell in length.

"You say so," said the one.

"Unfortunately," said the other, baring unnatural large teeth for so little a beast. The teeth were all worn flat at the edges and white as pearls. The pause stretched on for an uncomfortable few seconds, after which the one pointed at the other, saying: "He's dumber!"

The other turned slowly and malignly toward his brother, and said, "If *I'm* the dumb one, then how is it that we are here, after doing what *you* suggested!"

They were about to fly into another fight, when Authæn interrupted, saying: "Your voices are familiar, is one of you the wight from the waterfall, if I may ask before you settle your differences?" He, in fact, could not discern any difference between them, and wondered whether they were perhaps twins.

The two little wights looked up at him for a moment, ponderous. Then the one gripped the other by his rugged attire, and punched him so hard in the face that a third of the heavy little creatures popped out of him like a reflection pops into water.

"Oi!" said the third angrily. "I was SLEEP-ING!" and charged the other two, landing a tackle heavily on the one, whilst kicking the other thoroughly in the face with a free, wagging foot.

"So, by no mere chance, was I!" thundered Gaba of a sudden, rising to his feet.

In a strange sensation, Authæn realised that this was not another of his dreams. In his shock, he suddenly cried out to the newcomers to their company: "What are you, and what do you want from among our things?"

"Treasure-hoarders!" Gaba proclaimed them, having now also recognised the little creatures as being of the same race as the wight from the waterfall.

The meanwhile triplets stopped fighting, and arranged themselves once more, though this time in not so orderly a fashion.

"What, have they stopped singing the songs about our kind along the river's rind? You seem so at a loss about what we are!" said one of the three.

"Yes, unless they no longer aptly describe your kind," said Authæn.

"Oh, that's a crying shame," said another – he was actually shedding a tear from his now scrunched-up eyes and baring his overlarge teeth in lament.

"You two ALWAYS avoid the topic presented. PULL YOURSELVES TOGETHER!" roared the one that had furiously not been speaking until then.

"Well, if we must," the other two chimed, and in the strangest spectacle that Authæn had ever observed, they walked into one another until only one of them remained before Gaba and him.

"To the topic at hand, then, just for you, weird-eye – oh how they shimmer, those eyes! You wouldn't happen to be looking to get rid of them by chance?" A horrifying grin.

"I still need my eyes for the road that lies ahead of me, but I will take your words as a compliment," said the river-person stiffly.

"Very well. Then to the question: I am a gnome, that is the name of our people, but we are oft called grons, according to our class. Others call us ... by other names."

"And have *you* a name, master grin?" asked Gaba, stepping closer.

"Gron. It's GRON! As to the name: Yes. In fact, I have many names."

"But certainly there must be one that catches your ear more than any other," said the southerner impatiently.

"Oh my, you are a daring, bunch of apples. That name is a secret, not the only secret you will not lay hands on. Suffice it for now, that you might both call me "Grin", as you seem to find it fitting."

Authæn flinched as the gron grinned with even greater voracity than before, its teeth glistening in the firelight like polished ivory.

"Tell us, Grin, what did you seek in our bags? Is your hidden treasure box of ancient relics not enough?" asked Gaba.

"Ah yes, the 'treasure box'. That seems to have caught your attention, son of Hamath," said the gron. "I was simply looking to see what secrets you might be keeping with you. But you seem simple and trusty enough."

"Then you may know what secrets we keep, but you must remain a mystery?" scowled the southerner.

"Just so, gentlemen, just so," said Grin.

"And is there something that we can do for you, treasure-hoarder? You nearly caused our death at our last meeting," the southerner continued, crossing his arms angrily.

"I think," said the gron with a cunning smile, "that I might be able to help you."

Neither of the other two about the fire seemed convinced of this.

"You seek the cavern of Lyn Ithæm," said the gron, his face falling for not having teased a response from them.

"And you know this because you speak the language of the birds?" Gaba laughed in disbelief. "I hope that even I begin to know as much about strangers when I first meet them, if I remain in this country any longer!"

"Oh, but this is our second meeting, son of Hamath," returned the gron.

"Very well. You will guide us then? Have we a choice? Would you even leave us be if we threw you into the river?" said the southerner.

The gron only chuckled.

The following day they broke camp early, intending not to spend another night before reaching the cavern. The landscape did not change much as the height of the fell drew near within which the gron had confirmed Lyn Ithæm's hollow to abide, its tall grey like the broken spires of an ancient burg.

"Did Master Noth send you, Grin?" asked the river-person after the silence of an early start had gone on long enough.

"My, my, weird-eye; you have a dwarf's mind! Wit as keen as a leaf," the gron replied, not turning to look at Authæn as he said it. "I came to him with news that the chest you two stick-fingers had been 'studying' … with your hands!" Grin made an exasperated motion with his own broad little hands. "I went to him with the news that the chest is destroyed. Its contents safer under the fallen stone than it may have been in the chest. So you have done me a kind of favour, though I give you gentlemen no credit! Hiding it had been my task, and now it is rather well hid."

"And you will still not tell us what lay therein, treasure-hoarder?" asked Gaba bitterly.

The gron shot a dark glance at the southerner, and said simply, "Stones have been moved before, Hamathian."

Without stopping for lunch, except to take some of that wondrous wine that Noth had bestowed upon them, Gaba and Authæn were led to the place where the ravine beneath grew more sheer again. The tall hill of Lyn Ithæm stood before them now, a narrow shelf skirting along its side above the ravine to their left. Above, a scarce cloud hung about the brittle heights of the fell. It was snowing again, and the breaths of the company were as veils of vapour before them.

"The moon was waxing," said Gaba. "I had thought either tonight or tomorrow shall be the full moon. If I am wrong, then we will have to wait here a month longer."

"Perhaps that is why Master Noth so graciously laded us, uncle," said Authæn.

The southerner chuckled and nodded wordlessly. He was staring up at the imposing loom afore. Night was settling grey and quickly darkening about them.

"Tonight should be full moon; yet I wonder whether she shall show herself for all of these clouds," said the gron. "It is the month of the blue moon, if you didn't know! One moon on the first and one upon the last! Let that be a token, if you want to find any, gentlemen!"

"We count our months by the new moon," said Authæn.

"But then you can never have two full moons in the same month! How terrible!" cried the gron, laughing immediately after in his stark bass. "But let us find this door now, my good apples. I was told it is likely of gron-craft, and so I may be able to get us all through with or without full moon."

"What? You can undo the door's lock?" said Gaba in surprise. "For once I am glad that you walk alongside us, Grin!"

The gnome smiled great teeth up at the southerner, like one who knows that he is wanted.

They followed the little creature up the skirting shelf, having tied their horses to a stout juniper tree. Pressing their backs to the wall, the two men sidled along, whilst the gron strutted forth as though there were a rail.

"You are a fearless one, master gron," said Authæn.

"Oh, I fear what ought to be feared, weird-eye," said the other. "And you are right to fear the fall."

At last there came a recession into the hillside. There was a crude alcove that bent down from a great height towards the doors that now stood profoundly before them. Their surface was of a clean, white marble, from which had been hewn the shapes of so many little figures, all gathering about a single tree at the middle of the depiction. From its branches hung both sun and moon, and at the edges of the door, the newcomers now saw that the branches and the roots of the tree met, and made the closure in which all other things depicted played their plays.

"Remarkable!" whispered the southerner. "Such a thing I have not once yet seen in the north. Here most things are cleft of rugged planks by the hands of men more interested in their own fame than in the beauty of their work."

"This, oh gentlemen, is the handicraft of the grons," said their little companion, sighing with admiration. Grin stepped towards it then, suddenly parting, so that there were two of him, then three, then four. Two climbed onto the backs of the other two (who complained about it bitterly), tapping and listening to the stone, then shifting their position. Another gron popped rolling out of a Grin that was being used as a stepladder, and climbed to the top of the second, so that they stood three atop one another.

Eventually there were nine of Grin in all, and they were looking at the stone whilst rubbing their chin, whilst tapping it with their rock hard fingers, whilst licking it for the taste of the work, whilst moodily trying to go back to sleep, whilst pressing gently against the detailed figures with the pads of the fingers.

Suddenly, with a loud *crack* as that of a whip, a seam split the middle of the door, and ever so slowly the stone came apart to reveal a passageway into gloomy beyond.

The southerner and the river-man looked at one another, having recovered after the start they had suffered with the sounding of the *crack*.

"That is the strangest switch I have never considered in my life," said one of the Grins, apparently shocked. His hand still hovered where the switch had probably been. The others sighed, or shook their head, or groaned and rolled their eyes.

"Go on then, back together," said another one. "TOGETHER, I said!" repeated he, and the nine quickly became six, became three, became two. The one who had found the switch was still standing, frowning at his finger. He looked up with a raised brow as his twin approached him, and patted him gently on the shoulder. "It was a strange switch, but we should come together, if you don't want to be left here on guard duty."

At once there was only one gron standing before them again, and the company, in hesitant pursuit of the gron, began to descend into the passageway.

It was soon too dark to see, and the two men pressed against the walls about them, swinging free hands forward in the dark, hoping that there were no traps in this place, or worse than traps.

Chapter Twenty
The Righteous Moon

All was shadow, all was tenebrous doubt. Feet shuffled in the dark, the patting of hands echoed from the cold stone of the walls surrounding them. Sudden blue light flared up in silent brilliance before them, and the two men had to cover their eyes.

"You should have brought some torches for yourselves, seeing as you can't see in the dark, you cabbages!" laughed the voice of the gron as their sight adjusted to this sudden illumination.

As Authæn began to lower his hands and look towards where the gron had conjured sudden dawn from, he saw that they were in no natural cave. The walls were hewn as though by many chisels, but to represent the waves of the sea. Every here and there great sea-beasts could be seen to rise from the glittering, stony waves on either side, captured in perfect stillness. Below, the floor had been cobbled neatly to guide the way; above, the ribbed arches that held stable the ceiling were swallowed in lofty darkness. But, beyond them, the faint hint of a bejewel imitation of heaven betrayed its presence by winking back at Grin's lamp.

"What is that?" asked Gaba, kneeling down before the gron who held out the glowing stone now clutched in his hand.

"This is a moonstone, son of Hamath," said he. "Take it if you will; my eyes are still young and fit for seeing in the dark."

The southerner took up the stone carefully, treating it as though it threatened sudden explosion at any moment. Behind him the gron stuck out his tongue at Authæn gleefully.

"How is this possible? Is it a star fallen from heaven?" asked the southerner.

"What? The ... the moonstone?" asked Grin. His playful face had set like stone again with confusion. "No, Hamathian, that is a stone I picked up from the floor here."

"But it glows!" said Authæn, also picking up a loose stone nearby. He was disappointed, however, when it did not also burst into sudden brilliance.

The gron chuckled, his features softening again. "I see," said he. "Give it to us, river-man!"

Authæn did as commanded, and placed the stone he had picked up into the little palm of the gnome.

"Perhaps not so dwarfish a mind after all, eh?" chuckled Grin as he carved something into the rock with his thumbnail.

"What are you doing?" asked Authæn.

"This," said the gron, still busily carving and momentarily blowing the dust from the stone, "is the dwarfish word for 'moon'." He held the stone against the light of Gaba's moonstone, so that his companions might see the one under construction:

"I do not recognise the writing," muttered Authæn.

"Nor I," said Gaba.

"You needn't. I just thought I'd show you apples how magnificent I am," chuckled the gron. "It is pronounced *lûn*."

"And what makes it glow?" asked the southerner.

"Just a moment there, old man. It will begin in a minute. I wouldn't have let you stumble about in the dark any longer than I had to, you see. I do like to laugh at folk, but that would have been cruel. The stone merely — dense as myself — takes a time to comprehend so lofty words as those of our masters."

"I thought the ghouls were your masters," said Authæn with a frown, at which the stone in Grin's hand suddenly flared into pale, blue life.

"My, what a marvel!" cried Gaba.

Grin handed Authæn the stone, and began to continue down the passage. They followed.

"Those that you call ghouls, master stone-plucker," said Grin, "were once dwarfs. They were once the great masters of the language that can string together webs of truth, and make them hard as glass in the hand. That is what you have just experienced with those shinies of yours."

"But what were the dwarfs, if they are so no longer?" asked the river-person.

"There still are dwarfs," said Grin, "in fact the ghouls are far fewer in number than their wiser kindred in the Veiled Hills. How it came to pass that they fell from reason and began to worship the moon is a mystery even to those of us that served directly beneath them, building all of their mighty dwellings and workshops for them in the earth.

265

Like most of the agents of evil, they likely decided that it was time to enforce their own desires, rather than accept truth as it stands about us; but if you do not, in truth, have the power to decide how things are, all you do is break yourself against the sharp blade of ... well, against the sharp blade of how things truly are."

"And who does decide truth? The dwarfs with their runes?" asked Gaba.

"No, truth is not decided. It is witnessed, and testified to. That is the work of the rune-workers. They tell the truth," said the gron.

"But this is no moon," said the southerner, waving about his lamp with a frown.

"And yet it glows with the moon's light," chuckled the gron. "I am no dwarf, master Hama-thian. You must ask them regarding their myster-ies."

"I am certain young Authæn can appreciate your view on the matter, treasure-hoarder," said Gaba.

"It strikes me how similar your words are to those of our shepherds," said the river-man.

"Does it really?" the gron challenged. "The ghouls were one of the reasons your fathers came into being. Is it so strange to think that some of the dwarfish ways might rub off on them too? Besides, it was the King of Grons that raised your shep-herds. What wisdom they have came from him, I am certain."

At last the tunnel along which they had been descending came to an end, and they stepped out into a great and open space. Here the very air seemed to vibrate on the ears, like a sound just beyond hearing. It was a great, circular chamber, lit from above by a vast hole in the ceiling. Through it one could see the jagged, moonlit tines of the hill within which they were. No clouds were blocking the window into heaven as one might have thought them to from without, and presently the full moon tilted over the edge to spill its glorious light into the cavern of Lyn Ithæm. At the centre of the chamber was a broad yet shallow pool, also round, raised on a steep dais in the centre.

The adventurers strode up the stair to stand at the dark edge of the shining pond; the rim and the base of the pool seemed to be made of black glass, so that the moon was caught in a perfect reflection on the crystal water.

"A shadow of a shadow of day," muttered Authæn, staring into the water and then up at the moon itself. "Lyn Ithæm. Is that name dwarfish, Grin?" he asked of a sudden.

"Ha! You must have two brains in that head of yours, weird-eye: one dwarfish, the other ... simply fish," said the gron, stepping to look over the edge of the pool next to the river-person. "It is a dwarfish name, it means the full moon: *lûn ithâm*."

Suddenly the waters in the shallow basin began to glow, as had the moonstones (now redundant in the hands of their hands). The light of the full moon was working its charm on the water — but now something more happened: through the milkiness new runes were seen to glow.

Almost at once more of the writing appeared, but now on the surface of the water, then at different depths within the liquid. The letters began to move as though reading themselves — as though in conversation! More and more was written, until one saw pictures playing there like memories, though somehow stranger and more distorted — perhaps it was a pool of dreams.

Then A figure began to knit together amidst the imagery, like a scarf. It was a gown, and then it was filled with the figure of a woman. Slowly, with all elegance, she arose out of the stony depression, adorned in robes of simplest grey. Her eyes were black and endless as all the starless heavens. Her skin was as snow, an unrelenting celestial that glowed with the moon's essence. Her hair was silver lining. Nothing of her was not otherworldly.

Gaba fell to his knees, cowering with his hands held up to shield him, he seemed to feel the eminence of the daughter of the moon's presence more sharply than Authæn. In this moment the hum on the air bent into a thousand harmonies.

The river-man, on the other hand, stepped forward, and she looked at him with a familiar smile bent on her lips. He shuddered with some aftertaste of memory on his tongue. She seemed so familiar; as if this were all a dream...

"You are Authæn, son of Thuineith the carpenter, according to the law of Wirthaumuin," said she. At this it was as though something that had held all tension in him snapped. He was calm at that moment, though he should not have been. He saw into her eyes and was unafraid.

"You have been watching the henge," said the river-man.

"You have seen me?" asked she, clearly curious.

"Only in my dreams, I think," said he.

"I am tasked to look after you, son of Thuineith. It was the task he bound me to with this dark chamber."

"You do not seem overly desperate over the matter," said the river-man.

Her head tilted slowly to one side.

"You have been interesting to observe," she returned.

"Then my father sought you out so that one of the daughters of the moon would watch over me?" asked Authæn. "He desired that I would have guidance in my studies — guidance in becoming what he thought I must? He thought that you would guide me to become a true shepherd, like your *other* sons? A shepherd he wanted me to be; I, your son!

"And where were you, woman?! I had no guidance from you! I dwelt amongst our true shepherds, and even they never knew what a mother's embrace was, save by great speculation and staring at the moon! And here we are, all staring at the moon. But I do not fear you. Why should I call *you* mother?"

"Oh, you have grown so suddenly!" she beamed with a light that drove Authæn to narrow his golden eyes, but he would not let her cow him. "And you truly do have no affection for me. I am… enthralled."

"You are a shadow, and not that of mother-hood," said the river-man. "You are a grain of sand in an hourglass, measuring every passing moment; waiting with baited breath for the last of moments to arrive. You seek control from afar — to control the tides by your magnetism, never actually dipping your fingers into the brine. You are a pale imitation of life. How life was ever brought forth through you is a true wonder!"

"Your tongue has venom in it; like that of the viper," she chuckled. "And yet you speak truly. It is a shame that I have no hold over you. I desired so to bend you to my will. I desired so to make of you my dream in waking flesh! But instead I was fastened here in glass upon glass, bewritten by the world-wrights. No control was left to me. But what control did I ever have that did not lead to destruction. You, the fruit of my womb, may yet be a leader to freedom for those long seeking it. For that I have something no other sister of mine has."

"And what is that, moon's-daughter?" asked Authæn.

"A name in this world; for behold: I am Lyn Ithæm, mother of the deliverer of the river-people! All I did for this great honour was marry into captivity."

"Great lady!" Gaba managed hoarsely.

"It speaks!" she gasped.

At this the southerner arose with difficulty. "I must ask what you know of the Ibex and his ravaging of this land. It is of great importance."

"The Ibex, that metallic hollow!" she snarled, then her face was lit with malicious joy again. "A plaything of the ghouls. Oh how they sucked every service out of him before the end. As they shall with you, dragon hunter. In your calling they have you as a friend. Did you know that the Ibex had found a path towards redemption through their crafts? Do you still feel like a hero for slaying your brother of old now?"

"How? How was he to be redeemed?" cried the southerner desperately.

"Oh, you have a weakness! This I must remember. It will be a floodgate into your soul. He was sent to find the bane of wyrms, was he not? He was sent to find an Unth—"

"DO NOT SAY THE WORD!" thundered the voice of the gron, suddenly, and the radiance of the daughter of the moon dimmed somewhat in surprise.

"Ah, and here is it's failed protector," she smiled again, now wider than before. "I am met today by the trine failure!"

Gaba's eyes snapped onto the gron. "The chest," he whispered.

"It is lost, south-man!" growled the gron. "Do not go lost along with it."

"It is my charge! With that I can return to the city of my queen!" roared Gaba in a frightening loss of control. "What would you do, gnome, if you could return to the crafting of such halls as these, but for your intended masters, the dwarfs? Would you not do anything?"

"The dwarfs are perhaps my masters, and I would still serve their every whim ..." the gron

271

trailed off, his face, a moment before the picture of anger, now grew regretful as he looked at Authæn.

The river-person looked back. He had not expected this from the gron. Why pity? Why now? What other great revelation lay in wait?

But the gnome shook himself, and said again, "The dwarfs are our masters, but the grons have a king of their own, and they serve him before all others. I know my place, southerner; you have yet to find yours here in the wilderness!"

"Stop!" cried Authæn. "She turns us one against the other, like children squabbling over the last cake on the table!"

"Oh, you came to blows all on your own," said Lyn Ithæm. "But I do not want you to stop now, it was such a marvellous unravelling of matters that were trying so hard to remain hidden! Let me prod some more! Tell him how you slew his father, gron!"

Authæns eyes widened, and shot a glare at Grin.

"I did not kill him, weird-eye!" said the gron with such stern earnestness that the river-person felt foolish for having fallen into the hands of the moon's-daughter.

"What was this look of pity you gave me?" asked the river-man.

"The ghoul that slew the carpenter slew him for having me aid my kin to build this prison. Yes, I helped build this place, but only a small part of it," said Grin sadly. "He disguised himself, that wretched ghoul, as one of the red dwarfs — one of the dwarfs that are not ghouls. He came to me, and

272

I hewed for him a block of stone as one that Wirthaumuin had made for your village long ago. I have never questioned a red dwarf, my dear, dear fish-brain, it is not our way. Upon that altar he slew your father.

"But it was the King of Ghouls," said Grin, turning in ire to oppose the daughter of the moon, "not I, who slew the carpenter."

Again her light faltered a little; she seemed even to be somewhat afraid of the gron as she remained silently smiling. The southerner also regarded the gron with a newfound reverence.

"Forgive me, Grin," said he. "Until this moment I did not recognise you as that which you are."

"Oh? What am I? A potato that stayed too long in the earth and grew too many roots?" the gron asked, turning testily to face the ebon man.

The other burst out laughing. "Yes!" said he, shaking his head. "Yes, a wonderful potato, Grin."

The gron smiled in his honest way, and then he turned his attention to Lyn Ithæm again. "Tell us of the covenant that bound the Ibex to the ghouls!" he demanded, his face like flint.

She scowled, but relented with reluctance, saying: "The Ibex was offered the armour that he wore; an armour that made of him a draug — deathless, as long as his soul-stone remained in tact. For the armour would forge itself anew atop the soul-stone that was laid into his lair, were he ever to perish despite wearing it.

"He did perish; but then something happened that not even the crafty ghouls had seen to-fore: a

273

hunter had been sent for the Ibex. A hunter once of dragons, now of brothers!"

Gaba closed his eyes in a painful grimace, lowering his head into his hands.

Lyn Ithæm smiled cruelly again, and continued: "This brother-hunter brought the artefact, which held more soul than the soul-stone, in touch with the other, and both were undone. The spirit of the Ibex was freed as the breaths of all mortals shall be in their last moment.

"As for the weapon that both this and the past southern stalker of these lands sought, it was promised to the Ibex as soon as it could be found, but now it lies buried amidst the tumbling hills of a waterfall. The ghouls are unlikely to find it. You are cursed to wander these lands until you also breathe your last, noble dragon-hunter-no-more!"

Whilst she still spoke these last words, the gron had turned and begun already his departure of the cavern. When she was done, Authæn followed, and lastly the southerner also walked away, head bent low.

She did not call after them, she simply resumed her smiling posture, waiting for the night to end, as she had and would on every night in which the full moon touched that shallow pool.

Part III:

of the Return

to the Beginning

Chapter Twenty
The Spendthrifty Offspring

Tall and dark, the forlorn banners of a house fallen
to despair limply licked at the smokes that curled
upward from the long firepits at the middle of the
hall. Though people stood in tight gatherings about
that dimly lit chamber, their voices were a quiet
murmur, all of them speaking about the man that
had bidden them here; he that sat now in the high
chair at the raised end of that place. His wan face
was empty of the joys in life, his eyes drooping in
the manner of men that have seen too much and
endured barbs of hell. Here the king of Glimwæth,
proud son of Imnir, tamer of the bear, bearer of the
hammer of his folk. Here brother to the Forge-bear
of Glimwæth, who shaped the metal of stars into
works fit for their ancestors. Here a man with no
children left.

That is what they were muttering about him
there in their groups. To his weary eyes they
looked like bunches of grapes. He was a failed
king for his lack of offspring. Why did he still sit
in this chair? He moved his greying head to look
down at the similarly greying bear slumbering by
the foot of his dais. He chuckled to himself, leaning forward to stroke the beast, and all murmuring
stopped as his guests turned to observe their generous host. From above, the light that fell like pale
silver into the room flickered, and the moats of
dust that had been exposed there could hide again a
moment.

The king's eyes snapped upward to see two little, glowing orbs staring back. If he were alone, he may have simply waited to see what the bearer of those little lamps would have done next. It was some goblin that had come in for a visit. Its red eyes reminded of those long-ago raids into the under-earth that the king of Glimwæth had endured beneath his father's rule. The blood of Imnir was strong in his family; but in his children only that ancient bear-tamer's madness had come to bear.

Without saying anything, he arose, took his hammer, which leaned heavily against the dark timbers of his armrest, and swung it over his shoulder. The bear was roused by this, the people in the hall alerted. He walked by his guests, a weary smile on his face. He did still love them, but he was tired of their manners. They bowed as he went, for he was a greatly renowned man. He nodded in return. Then they followed him out.

Like two well-greased gravestones, he swung forth those high doors of oak with a boom, leading his court out into the light of faraway yellow in the south. There the sun was looking on a warmer world. Here was autumn, and the leaves had begun to fall. Here was the high entryway into the Nornburg, the king's seat in Glimwæth, and down there, where the stairway led, were the smoking houses of his people and his kin. They, too, had their firepits aglow, though with warmer company than the king's hall, thought that hero of old gloomily.

And then he was reminded of why he had stridden out into the day; why he had left his dark reverie: the goblin in the rafters — a forest imp. Below he now recognised teams of them swarming through his streets, all under the guidance of one great, lumbering figure, the sight of which brought a kind of sense to his heart that had long been lost to him. It was the memory of dread.

The goblin hosts were being led on by a great beast of ruddy fur, it waded like a man toward the climbing stair, but it did not ascend, and where it stopped its little horde also ceased its march. The king's people had fled the streets at the sight of this monster. They now all peeked frightenedly from their windows. Then the ogre of Darkholt turned its head upward, and its sickly yellow eyes met those of the king.

"High king in your dark hall!" shouted the beast in a voice as harsh as granite. "How goes thine slumber? Hast thou not yet been o'ertaken by the spry of bone?"

"How should I have been!" the king called down into his fore-burg. "You keep slinging down the worthy and leave my household empty."

The ogre laughed an ugly music into the air, and what few birds had remained in that place now fled. "'Twas greed that slung them down that day, my dearest greybeard king; not that this was to thee a matter, or to thy loyal Thing!" Bitterness flared suddenly on its flat nostrils, darkening the mien that it bore further. "But banter aside! I bring a challenge for you, to test if even you are worthy still to slouch upon that throne!"

"It sounds as though you'd want the seat, and make of this your home!" returned the greybeard king. There was a disquiet in the gathering behind him. He had spoken in rhyme.

The monster smiled unprettily, and a glimmer of sweat appeared on the brow of the king. "I think I now know why, after so long an age of dredged idling, my dread has once again announced itself like a visitor to my heart. I know you, monster. I have seen your face before. That red of hair is like the licking tongues of sunlight not long ago I ruffled with mine own... hands!"

"Oh!" swore the ogre. "And here I held the hope so tightly that irony was all that sped those words of heirlooms from thine maw; a maw that has slung down mealtime after mealtime, brought forth by hands that thou thyself hast long neglected to provide with food, with mead, with goodly fireside! That throne beneath thine weathered hide, dear father old and dried, is mine by right, since long a tide. I am thine only heir remained, after mine old fratricide."

"SILENCE!" boomed the voice of the king, and the bear at his side roared a dreadful calamity onto the wind. "Your dark web of words will not find roots here — the dark wood lies beyond my gates, and until you sit over my tombstone in this hall, your seithing words will be pressed into its many murky eaves!"

"Thou ask'st not even, father mine, how goes it with this son of thine?" grinned the ogre through ivory tusks.

"Svæn!" the king screamed then, the eyes that had many years looked as though they had been made of glass began now to shed that glassy exterior, and to bleed with briny waters. "You break me! What is your challenge?"

"War," said the ogre in a grumble, and it beckoned for something that lay hid above the kingly gathered court. There the goblin that had heralded this grave, oncoming storm from the rafters of the mead-hall now plummeted to the floor, and to the fright of all there gathered. They, in turn, swung back their furry mantles to undo their bearded axes, swinging them like toys of steel from their unweathered belts.

But the king stepped lithely backward once, and the spear which the goblin had held, bedded in the floor, the goblin smacking on the stone, and flopping down the stairs, dead. From the spear unfurled a banner then, the banner that bore the sigil of an aged custom, not yet known by the bairns of this old city, for the fathers of this city had built on its foundations of war a tightly pressed peace for nearly four generations. So old was this bear-taming greybeard that was tired of his rule.

"The deeps return to claim the middle-earth again, as once when darkness fell, father mine. The under-earth is teaming now with youths as spry as wolves."

"So I see," whispered the king, still weeping. "Where is my Pen-tooth, when I am met with such a foe!?" He righted himself again, dashing the tears from his bearded cheeks, and clearing his throat with a roar once more. "You there, son of mine! I claim you as my heir, but then you must survive this! You must survive me!"

The court gathered about was all awhir with bewilderment, for they had not foreseen this.

"If you," the king continued, "can best me, then, as a son of Imnir — though foul you have grown — you are entitled to this throne!"

"Why did he say it in rhyme!?" cried the earl of Urmingwey, a haven to the south. "You have spun a web of seithing words, my king! Why!?"

The king bared his teeth, grasped the earl of Urmingwey by the furs, launched him up against a pillar of the hall, held him tightly there. He gave a grim twitch of his mighty limbs to make sure that this young noble listened well.

"I will not betray our customs, Urmingwey," said the king with a snarl and a glare that glinted too much like steel on his grey eyes.

Then, unexpectedly, Urmingwey kicked the knee from out of the king's stance, and the man that held him high was fallen low in groaning.

At once the bear of the king came growling to do vengeance for its master, but the old man held it back, shouting: "No! No, stupid bear! You are too loyal, it will make short work of you, though you have never been so tall for all the lying about you do. No, Yrsa! Hold!"

Urmingwey stood ready with his twin axes, both had tasted the blood of bears, but they had never been stuck in the belt for the taming of one.

With eyes as dead as driftwood, the old king then said: "Stand with me, and one of you shall be proven more rightful than this—" the king turned his head to shout back down into his town, "SON OF MINE!" And the king began to weep again.

The ogre chuckled like mountains moving, and began himself to wade away again. As he went he sang this song, his minions chiming in at whiles, singing "With-in! Turn in!" and "No-where! Despair!" at the appropriate intervals — though the song was itself altogether inappropriate.

Within, within, we look within;
The world without is noise without win.
Turn in, turn in, we turn within;
We seek the answers none may find:
An endless road that leads nowhere
And yet all roads lead to despair.
Within, within, we're caught within;
Left with the lies that we consider win.

Outside the city walls the song was renewed, and this time a thrumming thing raised a droning melody into the air, and the heavy press of wheels was heard to tread away into the shadowy eaves of Darkholt. The challenge had been made. War was coming on Glimwæth. It would arise from the pits of the under-earth, a long-biding enemy of Imnir had finally brought into line its dark devices.

Chapter One-and-Twenty
To See and to Say

The creatures were a dirty white, though their skin was battered and callous. Their heads were bald, or sometimes tied with tails and weaves. Their little eyes were like black beads, their teeth like oddly placed stones in the wide seam that presently garbled out foreign curses.

"Imps!" cried Garhelm, and charged to aid the river-folk with his spear held high. His guardsmen followed.

But the king's-daughter had stopped in her steady march. She looked out across the fighting and, at the other end of it, a man that had just run dry of arrows looked up to meet her eyes.

"Carbeth," she breathed in horror.

The eyes of the hunter at the other end of the battle widened. His back straightened, and he seemed to forget the storm surrounding him. On his lips was shaped a name in return.

"Ystrith," said he in barely more than a whisper. "Ystrith! My Ystrith!"

But the king's-daughter had turned away again, and bolted for the forest. She was fleeing, just as she had those years ago.

"Ystrith! Ystrith!" cried Carbeth, and dashed after her in reckless abandon, treading over the nearby toes and heads of the short imps, kicking them wildly aside where they dared to come in his way. Soon he was a whirlwind tearing through their throng, and they sprang from his path as he raged by them, weaponless, save for his dart-less bow, and his hunter's knife.

Ystrith, daughter of the king of Glimwæth, burst through the ferns, pounced atop a boulder, and sprang forth into the gloom of the wooded beyond. She was climbing ever up, upward towards the height of the hill that had risen to the right of the battle; upward towards the top of the fell from which the goblins now streamed. What barred her way was slashed by side with her quickly strength-ening sword arm.

Up and up she ran, clad in her furs and linens, her golden hair a banner for fear in the winds of the rise. The trees here grew scarcer, and she emerged from the eaves, into a rocky shoulder. Here she clambered up and sprang from rock to rock like the goats of mountain climes. A little wooden rail could be seen above, where the rocks had formed a comfortable watch, and there she could now hear more imps, though not engaged in battle.

Finding her way to the stair of the imp-watch, she rushed upward, and suddenly came upon them. There were some five imps here, huddled about a bubbling cauldron. It sputtered out a ghastly gruel into the makeshift fires beneath, causing the flames to cough out their ashes.

With one hew, she cleared three of their heads, before they could even properly recognise what terror had descended upon them. The other two sprang to their feet, one to fumble for his club, the other to run away. But this daughter of Imnir cast her blade to pin the flighty one to the floor, whilst she tore the club from the other's grip. The last of the imps, seeing her raise the club to slay it, lost no time in simply slinging itself over the rail — its nearest escape. It landed six metres below, much like a cat, then scrambled into the brush, shrieking as it fled.

With a quick eye, Ystrith scanned the nest for anything that might have value to her. She found that there was a trapdoor that likely led into the hill, where the imps most probably had their lair. Other than this there was nothing for her, and she took up her blade, and flew again, the furs of the bear billowing like the leaping figure of a wild animal at her back.

The climb eased now, and she came to the heathery head of the hill, whence she could see the battle raging below. The work of her rescuers had made a notable difference: she now saw the merchants kicking and cleaving at the little beasts with their curved daggers, laughing in the revelry of battle. The Lion Pen-tooth had drawn an ancient sword from the saddle of his camel, when they had tied down their caravan, and he was presently swinging the weapon deadly about, so that the imps lost bits that strayed too near the flashing steel — tongues, heads, fingers, feet, arms, shoulders, and darkest of dark blood.

Then she heard a commotion behind her — more of the forest goblins must have arisen from their shelter in the stone, and there they had found some resistance. The sound of battle came from the imp-watch she had cleared. Not long after, the noise died away again. Then he strode forth from the weathered rise that she herself had climbed only a moment before. Much like herself, he was out of breath, filmed in a sheen of sweat.

"Carbeth," said she, and the image of the hunter flowed over her memory again as she had watched him stalk and kill his prey in the grasslands to the east, and the memory of love fell over her like a thief in the night, piercing her heart again and again, as though the beating of that drum in her chest was barbed on a dagger with every beat.

He said nothing, staring at her as one transfixed. His eyes were wide with disbelief, his arms hung limply at his side. Finally the words fell from his lips: "You ran away."

Perhaps they were only words to him, but to her they were the strike of the doom-hammer. Like the thud of a king's judgement, she felt struck in the throat. No words could trickle by that stranglehold to help her.

He took a step towards her. Then another. Then another, and another, and another, and then he was striding boldly, his face full of relief. He was certain now that this was no dream set on by the brewery of the forest goblins. He reached out to her, her eyes growing wider and wider in horror, for she dreaded his approach.

In a sudden flick of her wrist, the blade of the Forge-bear sung the melody of metal between them, and Carbeth halted, held back by the shivering point of its manifold tongue. He took a step back, wariness growing in his features, then determination.

"Why did you run after?" she hissed. "If I run, can there not be good reason?"

"At least tell me how I have failed you!" cried the hunter in dismay.

"The world is bigger than you, Carbeth. It is bigger than your river-people," said she.

"And you would try to sling it all down in one bite?" he demanded.

"You do not know my quest," said she.

"Then tell me!" he bellowed, pressing his breast against the tip of her sword.

For a long moment her eyes lingered in his. Then they greyed like the steely aspect of her father, and she bolted again, charging down along the opposite side of the hillock.

"Ystrith!" roared her husband. He looked after her as she went, looked down towards the battle of his folk below. He roared into the heavens. Authæn had made him chieftain's right hand. He could not leave now.

Carbeth looked one last time to where his heart fell away into the descending landscape, out of sight beyond that near horizon. Then he made his way towards the trapdoor that had been in the camp of the imps. He would ruin their dark lair, and if that would take his life from him, he would be glad. For the moment, there was little that he did not hate.

With his arrival at the imp-watch, the trapdoor flew open again, and a greater goblin than those that had been there before arose from it, the words still trailing from its tongue: "What on earth are you doing up here, you hill-lice! Get back to your armpits!"

Then the eyes of the greater goblin and those of the river-man met. Those of the hunter remained cool with wrath; those of the goblin widened in disgust and recognition. It looked about at the carnage that had been wrought here, and then it leapt forth with a gurgling roar, brandishing a stone mallet in its right hand.

It swung at the river-man, who stepped to the side, treading at the imp's head, taking it to the floor with the force of his boot, and crushing the skull against the rocks. Then he took up the goblin's hammer, lit a torch by the flames of the fire, and made his own descent into the darkness below.

In the shadow of the hill, the fighting was renewed as another wave of imps surged from the cracked mouth of their hollow. The arrows of the hunters had been all used up now, and those that had a strong arm were amidst the fray. The newcomers were at the fore, the guardsmen of Glimwæth hewing frightful flurries into the seething horde that pressed against them.

Still, the goblins were trickling through the ranks of the river-people, finding a gap here or there to near the wagons on which the ill and the *mith-aumuinan*, many of the women, and the children watched on in frightened tautness.

Then a band of five imps did burst through the battle, and made for the carriage atop which Loangilin now arose, letting go of Folgnuin. She strode forth, staring down at the oncoming imps. In her right hand she held a pot of clay, stopped with cork.

"Stop!" she cried. "By the waters of Wirthaumuin, I command you!"

For a moment the imps ground to a halt on the sands of the river, looking up at the pot she held above her head now with a threatening stance. At first wary, they now looked dark frowns at one another, and then began to chuckle, then laugh heartily, beginning their approach once more.

She cast down the pot, and it struck the nearest of the imps, who had looked down to laugh. The pot broke over the creature with its weight in such a way that the beast lost its balance and fell onto its side, unconscious. There water now gushed over the sands and darkened where it sank away into the ground of the bank.

The goblins had jumped back again, now wary. They had thought the threat a ruse, but now they were uncertain. When nothing happened, they began to charge the wagon on which Loangilin stood again, renewed in their spite.

A shrill scream went up into the air, issuing forth from the bottom of her lungs, but the goblins were almost upon her in their now careless ire.

The nearest of the remaining four was reaching for the wagon, when a jet of water suddenly shot through the sand beneath its feet, striking it in the face and forcing it back. The stream broadened, until a small pool was swilling at the feet of the panicked imps, and then the sand began quickly to pull them under, as though by many watery hands.

Now it was the forest goblins that screamed, and a commotion went all through the fight, for many an ear had been caught by Loangilin's scream. The goblins in the fray now saw their companions captured by the strange craft of this river-woman, and their eyes widened with fear.

At precisely this moment, Carbeth broke from the crack of the cave, holding the head of the impish leader in his left, and the hammer of stone in his right. The morale of the imps was broken, and they began to flee into the forests beside the hillock that had been their home.

The river-people cheered, but did not chase their enemy. The guards that the Lion Pen-tooth had brought with him did rush after them, however, wanting to rid the borders of their land of as many of these fiends as they could.

The villagers of Thænim had already begun to gather their dead, and to bring them to a wagon that lay empty of used rations. Another group was amassing in a circle about the place where Loangilin had cast the waters of Wirthaumuin onto the goblins. There now broiled a shallow pool.

When the dead had all been gathered the caravan of the merchants was brought about from where it had been tethered down, and all assembled round the wagon on which Loangilin presently wept on her knees. Beside her the little girl Folgnuin sat, embracing the river-woman, trying to comfort her.

Carbeth stood at the head of the elders, who had formed a half-circle before the spluttering pool. Huthram, who was still amidst dark dreams still knew nothing of his new charge as acting chieftain.

"Surely there is no need for this!" cried a woman from out of the gathering.

"She has spilt the waters of Wirthaumuin willingly. The laws must stand," said one of the elders. Carbeth looked grimly at his friend as she wept.

"She did this in order to save the young one," said Carbeth bitterly.

"Still," said another of the elders. "We have bent our laws enough under the rule of our prior chieftain, Carbeth. If we were to utterly break them now we would deny our inheritance — the same inheritance that allowed these two lives a long home until this day."

"So be it," said Carbeth. "Then I revoke my inheritance and join them in exile."

A great gasp went out over the gathering.

"You would reject the ruling of your true chieftain?" exclaimed yet another of the elders in disbelief. "He that you called friend; he that bade you to be a steady hand for Huthram, who even now depends on you to do what he cannot. You would so easily disregard Authæn?"

"I act now as Authæn himself has," returned Carbeth angrily. "Did he not lay aside the rule of the shepherds to warn us of our danger with his father's bugle, thinking of us before the shepherd's rule? Did he not kill to warn us? Did he not ride with us to battle, thinking of our ire before the shepherd's rule?"

The gathering was silenced.

"He acted boldly as our chieftain, though it was not according to the way of the henge," muttered the elder that had last spoken.

"Then I will act boldly, so that you may know these daughters of our village are well-guarded in exile," said Carbeth, and he stepped around the sinkhole that the waters of the clay pot had formed, helping Loangilin down from where she wept. Folgnuin sprang nimbly after.

Together the three exiles departed. Wingilin leapt down from where she had been weeping beside Huthram, embracing them each, and bidding them be brave. Then they went on their way, wandering in the direction in which the goblins had fled.

"Thank you," Loangilin whispered into Carbeth's shoulder as he held her near in her weeping. To his right, Folgnuin silently held his hand.

"Do not thank me," growled Carbeth in return. "I do it out of wrath, not generosity."

In shocked silence the village caravan now stood where they had watched the exile transpire. The elders gathered together quietly, and began to discuss what this would mean for the leadership of their village. They were, by the right of the eagle-clan, not meant to rule. They were only there to offer council to their chieftain.

"It seems we came at a bad time," muttered Jithron to Qeremun. Near them the Lion Pen-tooth sighed.

"Are these your folk, scrivener? They have your lion-eyes," asked the easterner then.

"They are my mother's folk. My father was a son of Imnir," returned the scrivener. He bent down, then, to pick up a piece of an imps garb, using it to wipe clean the blade of his aged sword.

"Where did you pick up that crafty tongue of death?" asked Jithron of Tall Hithes.

"In a tomb," muttered the Lion.

"For a writer of histories, you can be very wordless," said Jithron, laughing to himself. "I like you, Pen-tooth. Much silent strength flows from you, even without a weapon in your hand, and now you bear forth a sword that might have jumped from legend."

The Lion looked up at Jithron and smiled tiredly. "It is a sword from legend, Jithron. It is the blade of Athilan."

The merchants looked at one another with raised brows, then back at their companion with the blade.

"You weren't looking to sell it, perchance?" said Qeremun.

The Lion shook his head, still smiling.

"But it fell with him, did it not?" asked Jithron.

"Indeed it did," said the scrivener, righting himself again, sheathing the sword, and hiding it beneath the saddlebags.

"I am suddenly far more inclined to read the histories you have written," laughed Jithron. "The way you sell them with your silence is simply unbearable!"

"For that we shall first have to reach the wooden city," said the Lion.

"You are also seeking to travel to Glimwæth, masters?" asked a voice suddenly. It was a river-woman who had approached them without their notice.

"Indeed, young lady! I am Jithron of Tall Hithes, and this is my partner, Qeremun of the East. As for our bespectacled companion ..." said the merchant.

"Your bespectacled companion can speak for himself," said the Lion, striding forth to take her hand and kiss it gently. She turned a slight shade of grey darker at this.

"You are too kind, masters. I am Wingilin," said she. "I am the wife of the acting chieftain."

"Is that not the man that only just departed? Did he not just exile himself? Why would he have left you behind?" asked Qeremun bemusedly.

"Not so, masters!" said she, sadly looking in the direction in which her friends had wandered off. "No, but he was a good friend of my husband and I. My husband was stung by a poisoned spear, and is currently still battling the kiss of the worm in his sleep."

"Ah, we may have a remedy for that," said Jithron, touching her lightly on the shoulder. "I shall look about our medicines, and bring possible cures to him. Do you have skilled healers that may work with such remedies?"

"We have our own guild of healers called *mith-aumuinan*," said she. "If there is something amongst your wares that will speed his recovery, I am certain our elders will be more than happy to repay you!"

"Then let me have a look for something that may tread down on the head of the worm, and bring back the breath to your man," said Jithron, disappearing amidst the camels of their caravan.

"Where is the king's-daughter?" asked Qeremun then.

"She ran from the man that stole her from her father," said the Lion Pen-tooth. "The man that has put himself into exile."

"Ystrith was here?" asked Wingilin suddenly.

"Just so," returned the Lion. "But she has spent her whole life running from the truth of her family's history. It seems she is not yet out of breath today."

"You did not run after her, Pen-tooth? I was hoping for a king's reward upon our return to the city!" cried Jithron's voice from where he could now be heard to rifle through a bag of glass vials.

"There is no stopping her. Her will is too strong for that. Even her husband seems to have stood aside at their meeting. I saw it there above. Though an odious spirit hovers over his mood now."

"There is no surprise in that," said Wingilin horsely. "He has never forgotten her in all the four years of her absence."

Chapter Two-and-Twenty
The Wooden City

With the falling of day away into night, the bodies of those that had been lost to Thænim were committed to the river alongside which they now found themselves. From here the prayer went out that their bodies would find their way again to the waters of their river-father.

The night was spent where the battle against the imps had been won. When Garhelm and his men returned, the caverns of the hill were thoroughly searched and cleared of whatever remained of the forest goblins. They named that place Imp-watch, and the scrivener made a note of it for the king's cartographers.

"Here, one Carbeth of the river-people laid low a warlord of the imps," muttered the Lion Pentooth as he stared into the river running by, "and was subsequently banished by his own will, so that two daughters of his village would not go defenceless into the eaves." He removed his dark spectacles for a moment, rubbing his eyes.

"A brave act," said the voice of a man weakly from behind.

The Lion donned his dark eyeglasses again and turned to see who might have said this. He did not recognise the man, but it was a river-man, dressed simply in fresh woollen blue.

"My name is Huthram," said he. "I am the captain of the scouts of this village. I hear I have also been charged with the duty of chieftain whilst our true chieftain seeks to fulfil his training else-where."

"And what might I offer you, Huthram of this village?" asked the Lion Pen-tooth.

"It is I that would like to make an offer," said the other humbly. The river man walked carefully to sit down near where the Lion was. The scrivener saw then that the man was barefoot, and he re-membered that this must be the husband of Wingilin, who had been ill.

"It is good to see you on your feet again, Hu-thram chief. Your wife is a charming woman," said the Lion.

"Yes she is," laughed Huthram with true joy as one only sees after great malady has been over-come. "Oh, how I would be truly forsaken without her. And now I stand in the shoes of her father. That is no easy chore."

"Her father was chieftain as well?" asked the Lion.

"Yes," said Huthram, smiling at the scrivener. Then he looked down into the running of the water, and lowered his bare feet into it.

"What is it that you would offer me, friend?" asked the Lion.

"My thanks," laughed the river-man. "I am afraid that is all I have. But know that it is a true thanks, as that of age-long friends."

"Perhaps you will take back your thanks when you see my face unveiled," said the Lion Pen-tooth, removing his glasses again, to bare the black-and-gold of his lion-eyes. "I am one that has forsaken your codes."

"By the rushing sounds of waters falling!" muttered the acting chieftain. "I thought you were some noble son of Imnir!"

"In a sense I am," said the scrivener. "The king trusts me to record the histories of his people, and allows me, from time to time, to seek out histories beyond his borders. In so far as I am in the king's favour, I am noble. In as far as my father was a son of Imnir I am also that."

"From what clan came your mother to Imnir's land?"

"From the clan of the lynx," said the Lion.

"Ah," said Huthram. "Another clan of farsight. But the members of your clan have long not been seen by any of our folk. Where do they settle nowadays, for the river of your shepherd is not always so far off from ours, is it?"

"My clan is no more," said the Lion. "Our shepherd and his wife perished many years hence. They found only his wife, however, grossly slain. Whatever happened to the shepherd, the beast that slew them must have dragged his body away. We had thought it impossible. For our folly, our lot was to be scattered into the winds like so much chaff. My mother's folk were, that is."

"I see that you were close with your mother. Perhaps in you the children of your scattered clan will be healed of the deep wounds that motherlessness left our shepherds with," mused Huthram.

The Lion chuckled. "I was close to my mother. You are not surprised to hear that a shepherd's wife has died?"

299

"Our shepherd's wife has also passed into the lap of the Mother-henge, though our shepherd himself yet remains to guide his children."

"And what has brought him to guide his children unto Glimwæth?" asked the Lion with a frown.

"We have been sent away for our own safety," said Huthram. "We are without our true chieftain for the time being, and we were driven from a place — where we were trying to settle more permanently — by the terror of the Ibex."

"And so you have been bidden to seek refuge in the shadow of the Shoulders of Imnir while you wait for your leader's proud return?" asked the Lion.

"It is as you say."

"That Ibex is a troublesome spectre," muttered the scrivener.

"He is slain," said Huthram simply. "I have heard this only now from the elders as they spoke to me regarding our journey and my new duties."

"What? How so?" said the Lion.

"There was a stranger, a man from the south, I believe. He came to our aid in the battle against the Ibex, and slew him. Our chieftain has taken this southerner to our henge."

"If there were some proof ..." began the Lion.

"Our village carries the fragments of his helm in a strongbox. We intend to win the favour of your king with it."

"That favour shall be easily won," said the Lion. "If you truly do hold the helm in your possession, that is. Between the Ibex and the ogre of

300

Darkholt many of those that my king had considered fit replacements for his rule have been slain."

"There is an ogre in the Shadow-wood?" asked Huthram.

"We should be glad to depart these trees. I am glad that they already grow scarcer. The forest is his domain. They say that he rides through it faster than horse can carry man. They say he rides upon a siege engine of sorts. It is a great wooden lyre on wheels, droning out a dirge wherever he goes. When you hear it, you must flee, or he finds you and takes you back to his dark spire in the northern reaches."

"Terrible," said the other with a shudder. "Let us hope never to cross his path!"

For a while they stared out into the darkness, listening to the water run by. Above, the stars glowed brightly; sometimes so brightly that they burned out and fell from the heavens.

"Tell me, Huthram," said the Lion then, "were you well-befriended with this Carbeth?"

"Yes. Very," said Huthram. "Do you ask because of the king's-daughter that you lost today?"

"Your wife also has sharp ears, I gather," chuckled the Lion.

Huthram only smiled.

"I wonder if he has the mettle to find her and bring her back to face her past," muttered the scrivener.

"No. He has no hold on her," said Huthram after a short pause. "Sadly. He loves her too very,

301

but she has always been a woman entangled in some unseen tapestry."

"She seems to have been in league with her uncle. He sent her out here to slay a river-dragon."

"What?!" now it was Huthram's turn to be surprised. "Such a thing can only be achieved by the shepherds!"

"Then she is a shepherd," said the Lion, turning his gaze now humourlessly on the other.

Another silence benighted their company.

"Who was her uncle?" asked the river-man finally.

"He is a smith under my king," said the scrivener. "One who forges the metal of the star that fell into the Shoulders of Imnir long ago."

"What would he seek the death of a river-dragon for, and why send the daughter of the king? Why not send one of his heroes?"

"I do not yet understand it myself," said the Lion Pen-tooth. "I hope not that it is a plot against my king. The Forge-bear is a good man. Perhaps he simply had a weakness for the girl and sought to send her off with a gift to her wedding in the steppe. It was the rune-work on her blade that gave him away, but I do not entirely understand what to make of it. She brought with her many of the beast's scales and two of its bones — leg bones, I think. What she wanted with those I do not know."

"Do such trinkets sell well on the trading road?" asked Huthram.

"There you will have to ask my friends the merchants, Huthram. They know of such matters."

"Very well. I think I shall, and bid you a fair night until sleep takes you," said the other, drawing his feet from the river, and rising carefully to make himself on his way.

"Good night, Huthram chief. Until the dawn."

With dawn the village was alive with movement and business. Everyone was willing to return to the road, for they knew that beyond this point they would be moving steadily out of dangerous country, into the lands under the thanes of the king.

By midday they had rolled out into the open country where the woods had long ago been cleared away by Imnir's children, only to be replaced with course heath. Here they often passed by small steads, and they came onto roads that were much broader and well-travelled. The world seemed less empty, and the sense that they were nearing the end of a long journey began to draw laughter and careless chatter from the river-people. The merchant caravan rode near the wagon on which Huthram and his wife drove. The acting chieftain was not yet well enough to ride, but they spoke much with one another, the merchants regaling with the many adventures they had endured whilst about on business. All the while, the guards in the employ of the Lion Pen-tooth rode half to the fore and half to the hind of the village, ensuring their safety further.

Like this they went on some days. From time to time they would stop and visit a town, buying from their markets, or spending some of their coin

in the public houses and inns that dotted the landscape.

Finally they marched through a lightly wooded
hill country, passing a hillock to their right, then
crossing a river, and emerging into a vast vale, at
the other-most end of which arose the mighty
Shoulders of Imnir, the foothills to the great mountains beyond. And on the nearest of the great foothills stood the wooden city itself: Glimwæth.

"There above, is the Nornburg, the house of the
king. That was built in Imnir's day," said Jithron to
Wingilin, who had never laid eyes on the city herself. She only marvelled, and said to her spirit: "Is
this what drove you, Thuineith?"

They crossed the plain, camping near a river
for a night. The river was called the Nither, and
flowed down from the Height of Imnir, a place far
up in the mountains where a star had smashed a
small sea into the stone.

"Thence comes the metal with which the
Forge-bear works," said the Lion.

"From the mere atop the mountain?" asked
Wingilin.

"Indeed," said the Lion. "That is why they call
that little sea 'Steornufol', for there the star fell
from which all of the weapons are forged that the
kings of Imnir's house wield. Even now the king in
his high hall bears the mighty hammer with which
Imnir himself would ride into battle astride his
great war-bear."

The following day brought them lastly through
heavy frost to their end. There the broad causeway
leading to the southern gate of the fore-burg met

their feet with a welcome clatter. The foundations of this city, along with its walls, were made of that ancient stone that was so very uncommon for the children of Imnir, likely reaching out of the days in which the forgotten forest folk still dwelt here. Beyond the walls the steep shale roofs of the houses could be seen, puffing up white clouds in the settling cold.

Their caravan came to a halt before the great oaken gates, which were closed. Above they saw the glittering spears of watchmen. After a few moments the overest of the watch appeared, and called out to them: "Who wills to fare into our fore-burg? What is your business in the stead under Imnir's house?"

"You seem to have waxed warier in the time after my last departure, Gildolf!" said the scrivener, spurring his horse forth, so that he stood before the gathering. "We bring the head of the Ibex for the king to hang on his gable."

The watch-overest seemed greatly taken aback. Then, when he finally managed to recover himself, he said: "These are tidings well received, Pentooth! Our watchmen are indeed worn with their watching. Day and night we look out from here above, straining our eyes for sights of the ogre. He hath challenged the king with war, Pen-tooth! Oh, thou shouldest have been here, scrivener! It would have been thee a behoof! But come in you all! Open the gate!"

A great creaking and groaning sounded out then, and the great oak before them, held together by curling iron framework, was slowly swung outward to greet them like the arms of a father, thrown out for the embrace.

"Welcome back to Glimwæth, Pen-tooth!" said Gildolf, and then turned to a runner for the king's hall, sending him off with the news of this unlikely company's arrival.

The caravan now entered onto a large, low square of cobblestone. This square alone was the first tier of the city, out of the middle of which climbed the highway to the king's house, and along the walls of which were stables. The highway climbed at once into the second tier, sporting a public house on both sides of its ascent. The stables were directly below the inns, so that the company could now find a place to tether their animals, and park off their wagons.

Some of the river-folk wasted no further moment, and made for the inns to indulge in some festivities after a long time on the road. Many others waited to be directed by Huthram, as he was slowly helped down from his wagon by Wingilin and the Lion Pen-tooth himself. The growing gathering of Imnir's folk that watched the company arrive saw this with surprise, wondering aloud whether these were somehow relatives of the man whose mother had belonged to the river-folk.

Whilst they were still organising themselves, the river-people suddenly heard a great commotion. It was sounding from the streets above, up in the higher tiers. As the sound grew, however, it seemed to be drawing nearer them down the highway, and then some dozen horses suddenly emerged from behind the public houses, and came into the entry square.

They were mighty horses, spurred with regal shocks of fur, their manes all woven to look all the more menacing for battle. Astride the horses were men well clothed, and fierce to look upon; their hair all cut in manners to make them look more sullen, their beards to match. The lines drawn over their weathered white faces were the lines of seriousness, and their sky-lit eyes looked a bright blue into the world around them. Only one had grey eyes. All of them looked thus, some of them with black hair, some of them with white, and others with anything in-between.

In the middle of their dour company rode a greybeard bearing a circlet on his brow. Presently he slid from his horse, holding a great hammer in his hand, swinging it onto his right shoulder.

"You meet us as though for war, my king," said the Lion Pen-tooth.

"I was told you bring dark elves into our home, my Pen-tooth. I was concerned that *you* might meet us as though for war. I perhaps even dared hope you meet us thus," said the greybeard.

"You have been challenged," said the Lion. "Gildolf spoke of it."

"Just so," said the king. "And whose honour do I rob by meeting them this day?"

"This is Huthram, chieftain of this village of Thænim, my king. And, though you may rob him of honour with your presence, he has come to honour you, and give your name a trophy of greater worth than any other thane before."

The king's brow rose.

"It is as your servant says, my king," said Hu-thram, bowing wearily. "Forgive me, I have been on a hard journey, much of my time spent battling dreadful illness. I am still on the mend."

"I await with breath in bite to hear how it is you honour me, chief of dark elves," said the king.

"Such a thing is better shown than said," de-clared Huthram, and motioned that an elder bring forth their village strongbox. One did, bearing it forth at once, and holding it out, that his acting chieftain might open it.

"It is either your great fortune or your great misfortune, then, that such a throng is gathered here to witness you, my friend," said the king frowning at the box. "Trinkets and treasures are more the stuff of the scrivener here than of my ilk."

"Great fortune for you, my king; and greater still for me, I hope, who has far less to spare," said Huthram, and he lifted the lid, having unlocked its clever mechanism.

A great uproar and fright seized the crowd gathered, and they all began to speak at once, filling the square with mad cacophony.

The king only stared with eyes as broad as mir-rors, his brow rising into the heavens above with disbelief. His lip trembled, and he withdrew some steps. Shaking his head, he managed to stutter: "By what conjury did you slay the beast, dark elf?"

"I did not," said the river-man. "This was gran-ted as a gift to my people by a southerner who did the task. He said that it would win us your favour.

If it is fighting men you need for your war, the imps along the road have given us a hearty warming for it. My men are yours along with this wall-hanging."

"Ah," sighed the king in realisation, a frown bringing his brow back into the world of men. "Then this is the gift of Master Gaba, who not long ago came through our lands. He has held true to his word, and shames me for my diligent mockery of him. Still we gave him house and hearth for the time that he needed, and revelled greatly in the company he offered at the fireside. If only he would return, then perhaps we would hold the burg against the beast that beckons. Pen-tooth, the ogre is Svæn, my son!"

The Lion Pen-tooth paled. "It cannot be," he whispered.

"It has torn the very lungs through my back," scowled the king. "I am glad you feel with me, my friend."

"No, my king, you mistake me. This is not the only one of your children that we thought dead, yet remains alive!" said the Lion, grasping the arm of his king desperately.

"What mean you?" demanded the greybeard.

"Your daughter, my king. She lives. Ystrith king's-daughter lives."

309

Chapter Three-and-Twenty
In Dark Reflection

Ystrith king's-daughter lived. She breathed. She ran through the great moorlands that dominated the wolds of Imnir's folk. The animals would flee before her, for she ran through the country like a storm, only to fling herself into the tall grass with sleep; only to waken with a mind bent on running. She did not know where it is she ran to, as long as it was away. She dreaded more than anything the face of that hunter again, a man of so little understanding, despite his great passion.

She shook the thought from her head as though it had gotten caught in her hair like a bat, and ran harder. For food she harvested the wild berries that she loved so well, and she caught rabbits in traps; though she sometimes found herself running alongside some unfortunate prey on occasion. In those moments her star-forged blade would lick the life from it like a tongue of dancing, blue fire.

Only in cases where she had caught meat would she halt to set blazing a fire, and to roast her catch. Then she would sometimes sleep the digestion from her for a half-hour, and begin to run again.

Finally, when the mountains began to present themselves in the faraway west, and the mark of the forest began to draw nigher in from the north again, did she come to a steady stop. Before her stood a standing stone of old, a tall square-hewn pillar, upon which were writ the runes of some ancient wanderer. There she read aloud the words, for they were in a strange dialect that she did not fully ken: *Til we ov nider thiz lothzom læzt ovkomnir, lauknir we ov faur tilbaka.*

Then she saw this mark carved into the stone directly beneath the runes:

"Until we escape from of this hairy burden," she thought to understand it then, "look we back from afar off."

She frowned.

Then she mounted the pillar, dangling her legs from atop it, and breathed, taking a moment to rest. However many days she had been at her running, she had lost count. To her it was all a blur, but now she could run no more, and the thoughts of her ever wrathful spirit seemed never to have been much slower than the might of her spry legs, catching her up in every dream.

"Come then spirit mine! Speak with me! What have I done that so angers you within me? Would you rather I stay with the hunter? Should I forsake my quest and run after idle things? No, I must set

312

right the house of my fathers. My brothers are fallen, and I must revenge them against the ogre! How better to do this than the way our uncle has shown us? What better way to find the ogre without his war-drone, than to listen to the whispering of the birds? I can hear them even now, and the dragon's blood which I have drunk makes sense of these shrill chirps for me."

For a moment the icy winds from the wintering mountains dashed over the lands like a herd of horses, but the king's-daughter's blood was still far too hot for such a thing to bite at her.

Then a voice suddenly spoke to her — a voice that responded like a woman to her questions.

"Is it wrong to be angry?" said the voice.

Ystrith froze, not wanting to turn about like a fool frightened of what she was faced with. She waited, wondering if the voice had been real, or if it had only been the play of the wind.

But the voice spoke again, saying: "Who has told you that I am angry with you? Perhaps I am angry at this hunter. Perhaps I am wroth with the house of our fathers. Perhaps I desire destruction, rather than the setting right of things. Let that which has fallen burn. Let rise newness from out of the ashes!"

Ystrith stood up on the pillar, making sure to sweep the area all about her with her eyes. This voice seemed to speak for her spirit, but she did not hear it from within.

"Then you would say my quest until now has been idle?" said she.

"No, it has been but a forerunner, the road that leads to a definite end … and new beginning," returned the voice.

"And what beginning would that be?" asked Ystrith, continuing to look about her. At last, she thought she saw a shadow amidst the dark trees of Darkholt to the north — a shadow beckoning.

She hesitated, then she sprang from the tall stone, and began a slow march in the direction where she had seen it. When she reached the place, however, there was no one there. Nothing.

Ystrith began to whistle the notes that a cuckoo was piping from somewhere in the wood. "It is just the weariness," she muttered to her spirit, then she joined in with the cuckoo again, walking along the mark of the wood.

Suddenly the birdsong was silenced, and a whisper came to her on the wind. She turned to look in amongst those dark oaks again, and then she did see it, the figure of a woman with bright red hair and skin the colour of milk, beckoning, then fading away among the trees. Drawing her sword she strode into the shadows there, wondering what on earth this all meant.

"Forget," said the voice of the woman on the wind. "Forget! All you desire is to forget! But that is the cry of a weak and witless child. You are a woman grown. You are slayer of the dragon, drinker of its blood. Bird-whisperer are you! Traveller are you! You have dwelt among dark elves and seduced their greatest warrior. You begin to realise your potential. You speak of the house of your fathers, but see how your mother has suffered at the hands of those bumbling fools!"

At these words the ire of Ystrith brimmed, and she clenched fast her teeth to hold back a sudden frenzy. The memories returned to her, just as the muttering of a brook drifted towards her.

"Yes," said the voice of the red lady, "you hate him, that grizzly greybeard. See how your blood boils red within you — the colour of true life. But he would rob you of it! He would press you into your bower above the burg. He would tame your blood to trickle blue and thin, like this water beside you."

She met the brook and followed its silver waters into a climbing forest. On and on went this way, and she had to scramble irritably over rocks and through the rotting mulch of many bygone autumns. And then she came to a place where the waters pooled beneath another such stone as she had sat on near the borders of the forest. The same runes were etched into it, and the same strange symbol as the mournsome face of a monster. The waters that had formed the brook were flowing from what appeared to be the mouth of the symbol-face into the pool beneath.

"A weeping stone?" muttered Ystrith. "This sight disturbs you, my spirit, surely?"

"Disturbs? It causes me to look down!" said the voice on the wind.

Ystrith looked from side to side, but could not see the red lady anywhere. Then she did look down into the pooling shallows. There she frighted a quick moment, swinging her sword out before her.

From the dark water, staring back out at her, Ystrith now saw the red lady as though it were her own reflection.

"But the only reason that you have to hold so tightly to the house of your fathers is your brothers, whom you seek to avenge," said the lady in the pond.

"I am sent by the Forge-bear himself!" screamed Ystrith. "This blade was his final charge to me! And with it I will make short work of the beast that slew my monsters!"

A cruel smile bent the white face of the red lady. "Your *monsters*, dear Ystrith?"

"My brothers!" she cried out, trying to correct herself. "My brothers!" she repeated faintly, but faltered, falling to her knees. The blade of her sword dug into the soft forest ground. "My brothers! My brothers!" she said again.

"You see it, dear Ystrith. You have for a long time. Those fools were full of the 'blood of your fathers'; of the blood that flows like a rich fountain from your one common father!"

"Imnir!" gasped the king's-daughter, looking again at the stone. "Those are Imnir's words!"

"Now you see clearly," said the lady in the water.

"No!" screamed Ystrith. "No, I see as though through a heavy mist. I feel pressed down, as though I am caught in a ... tomb! Wrapped! I feel closely wrapped, as though by death-linens!"

"SILENCE!" hissed the red woman, but Ystrith did not heed her, she had begun to weep loudly. "Silence, Ystrith. Lay by side the title of king's-daughter. The title of king's-wife did nothing for your mother. She was only turned into that raging beast for her loyalty to the house of your fathers."

"She could not have escaped that fate! That is the curse of our bear's blood!" sobbed Ystrith, striking at the water's surface with a fist.

Dark ripples went out over the pond.

"Is that what you would say of your brothers as well? They were violent fools only because of their bear's blood? An easy release from the prison they deserve! Far too easy! The one they now have is far better for them. But you could make of them the end that would be fit for them. Or have you forgotten? Have you forgotten how they sold you out to the kings of the west so that they might grow mightier in this blood that haunts you?"

"SILENCE!" screamed Ystrith now.

The red lady laughed at the irony. "And why should I listen, where you did not?" she chortled. "What did your father do to save you from marriage to the half-giants in the fjords? There blood flows over the cliff faces, blue as the ice that those misbegotten beasts revere so."

"SILENCE!" repeated Ystrith, rising to her feet again, taking up her sword.

"Very well. If you will not listen to my wisdom, then I shall find another to fulfil the fate of your household for you!" screamed the voice of the red lady of a sudden, and from behind the rune bewritten stone, a great crow flew away into the deeper wood.

"No!" cried Ystrith. "Leave them be! Leave them be!"

She ran a ways in the direction the crow had taken, but her legs soon took on the weight and flexibility of lead, and she stopped. "My brothers …" she muttered looking bleakly into the darkness ahead. "Why should I not forsake the memory of them? It will haunt me. It does haunt me. I must put an end to them, perhaps. I must slay the ogre, and free Mathydras from the tower's heart. Will I there find a new beginning? Ah, but who am I speaking with? My spirit has flown away in the form of a crow!"

She stood there, still as the stone that bled dark waters not far behind her. For an hour, perhaps, she stood thus. Then she began the slow pilgrimage. She would march on the ogre's spire. She would find his haunted vale and make an end of the blood of the bear.

Ahead of Ystrith, the crow continued in its flight, piercing the canopy above, so that all of Darkholt suddenly sprawled before it. Then it glid over quick winds to where it heard rumour of another traveller. He bore upon him the heavy scent of the bear's blood and its doom. He was not alone. The crow dove down to where he wandered beneath the dark canopy, holding a woman under his cloak, and a girl by the hand.

Carbeth was humming a tune to which he had often fallen asleep. In the chill and dark gloom of the bare forest, the melody was like a small light, spilling through lantern glass, shining on their way forward. He had walked with Loangilin and Folgnuin, at first sheerly wroth. As they had pressed through the first few days, mostly in despondent silence, they had fallen into a homely rhythm. Loangilin knew mushrooms, and so she had gathered those whenever they had made camp. Folgnuin would fetch water from the stream that they presently followed. Carbeth would make fire, and had begun to prepare some traps and craft some arrows for his bow. He still lacked fletching and string. Neither had he any iron heads. It was the law that the banished should go with nothing more than they had on their person.

Loangilin suddenly raised her head from where it had lain on Carbeth's shoulder. "What lies before you Carbeth, now that you are exiled?" there was a tremor in her voice, and it caused his humming to come to an end.

They walked a long moment in the sound of crunching leaves beneath their boots and the melodic murmur of the water at their side.

"I had not thought clearly on it, Loangilin. I realise now that I have been trudging in the direction in which I saw my wife run," said the hunter finally.

She laid her head onto his shoulder again, and said no more.

When another long time had passed, he asked her, "Where will you go, now that you are unbound, Loangilin?"

"I do not know, but wherever I do go, I shall take Folgnuin with me," said she, smiling down at the girl. Folgnuin looked up at Loangilin, but she could not smile. Her wide eyes were dull with sorrow.

"Thank you, Loangilin," said Folgnuin, despite her bleak look. "I am adrift like the leaves."

Carbeth drew her in closer, pressing the girl's shoulder to his side. A tear slid from beneath his blinking lids. At length he began again to hum the melody from before.

"Do you know the words to that melody, Carbeth?" Loangilin asked after moment more.

He continued humming a while, using the time to consider whether he did or not. At last he said, "No, Loangilin. I have forgotten them. To me the one who sang the song was more important than the song itself. It is the way of a child's mind that brings it back to me. I think of my mother who sang it when she worked the loom at night."

He continued to hum again, their walk moving slowly onward. Then they came to a place where some trees and larger stones made a more sheltered nook in the forest. Here they decided to make camp for the night, and at once each went to do their duty. Loangilin went after mushrooms or any other thing that might yet be found to grow on the forest floor; Folgnuin went to fetch water in the pot that they had found on the second day of their journeying, half-buried in the ground; Carbeth sought out kindling and some dried twigs to set a brand ablaze.

Above a crow croaked out its mournsome drawl.

The brand was acrackle, when Loangilin returned with the mushrooms. She set them down near where Carbeth was stoking the flames. He smiled up at her.

320

"Where is Folgnuin?" asked she, her own smile fading suddenly.

He looked about himself in turn.

"Surely, she should have returned by now!" said the river-woman, somewhat more frantically.

He leapt to his feet, taking up the stone mallet which he had taken from the goblin at Imp-watch.

"There is a strange rustle that was not amidst the underwood before!" he hissed.

A scream echoed back to them, that of a little girl.

"Folgnuin!" cried Carbeth, leaping from the place he had held at the fireside with a burning torch in his hand, Loangilin close behind.

They ran through the dark, scattering shadows of long limbs in all directions as they swung about the red eye of their torch. They ran in the direction from which the scream had come, and then they stumbled into a broader opening, at the other end of which a greater oak than those surrounding stood grimly.

To the aged trunk was pinned the lifeless form of the red haired girl. Before her stood an angry Ystrith, screaming threats into the air.

At once Carbeth ran to her. Loangilin called after him to be wary, but it did not sink into his mind.

"Ystrith!" he screamed desperately, frightened for what she had allowed herself to do. "Ystrith! What have you done?! What madness has taken you?"

The king's-daughter grew suddenly quiet. She turned to the man that had spoken to her, her eyes

321

wide with horror as they had been at Imp-watch. Her eyes followed the path of the man whom she so desperately desired to hate. Her eyes saw as he fell to his knees before the girl, weeping, testing her to make sure she was truly dead. Then his head fell onto his breast, and he shook bitterly with tears. It was then that some smoke seemed to clear from Ystrith's vision, and she recognised the little girl, not as the red lady, but as the girl Folgnuin, whom she had often shared apples with when she had still dwelt in Carbeth's tent.

Then the silent rain of remorse racked her as well, and she collapsed into a pile next to her husband. She had killed a girl out to do her duty. The pot yet lay next to the sweet, lifeless thing, upset, having wet the forest earth.

Blood was mingled therewith.

From behind, Loangilin strode forth, removing the etched steel from the body of the child. She laid it at the knees of the king's-daughter, taking the child's body into her arms, and holding it there.

Together they knelt in the shadow of that sodden oak, weeping, waiting, as though for the passing of an everlasting storm.

"And, Ystrith Bear-blood, are you now ready to burn down a rotting world?" issued the cruel voice of the red lady from the side of the clearing at which the hunter and Loangilin had emerged.

Desperately, the king's-daughter looked up at the other two — her eyes darting from one to the other — as she said, "We knew each other once, dear husband! We were such good friends once, dearest Loangilin! Please, forgive me! Forgive me! Forgive me!"

The other two had looked in the direction whence the voice of the red lady had come. "Who are you, woman?" cried the hunter.

"Forgive me! Please, do not let her take me! Do not let her take me into her cruel embrace! Or I shall be what has undone the child this day! I shall be fast in the cruelty of her plots and ploys!" cried Ystrith, raving.

Carbeth took a long moment to look at his wife, then to look hard at the red lady, who stood still in the dark, her hair like dancing fire, her white skin like milk, falling through the shadows, her eyes like the green of emeralds, flashing with malignancy. Then he looked sadly into the face of Folgnuin. He stroked the girls hair, seeing then that it was so very similar to that of the red lady. He began to understand the madness of his wife.

"But you have taken a life so sweet, so young, so shapeless and yet still so full!" whispered he. "How can we forgive? Will our pardon undo this death? Is our pardon enough?"

"Surely, the screaming of my spirit within me is a burden enough!" cried Ystrith desperately. "Do not let me become like those monsters I must fell!"

Carbeth did not fully understand her words, and it showed in the furrows of his brow. "I am lost," he muttered, and she screamed into the heavens, sending distant birds into the air. Then she fell flat on her face, and continued to sob.

"Now you have no further bulwark, little but-tercup. Come into my arms," said the red lady, marching slowly into the clearing.

"Halt your step woman!" groaned a voice amidst the trees that of a sudden swirled in a wind new-conjured. It spoke as though from beneath the earth, and caused the world a slight tremor. The red lady shied back a ways, returning to the darker shadow of the trees.

Said the voice from beneath the earth: "You have done enough to those that were without a moment's regard for their crimes. But this girl has re-cognised the blood that screams up from her hands. You cannot take her against my command. Return to haunt her brothers, if you must. Your time of fire-play is almost at an end!"

At once the red lady spun about and was caught up in a strange movement. She was a crow in the next moment, and then she flew and was away.

Then another figure stepped out from behind the oaken tree. It was a man, a man that seemed somehow colourless in the dark, and very coarsely clad. He stooped and raised the girl's dead form from out of the hands of Loangilin. Then he looked down at the river-woman that had held her, then at Carbeth, then finally at Ystrith. "Find the ogre's spire, and there I shall call her back to waken from this slumber."

He turned and made to leave, when Ystrith grasped at his cloak, holding him back. He looked down at her once more, a question in his mien.

"Who are you, master?" she bade.

He smiled, and said: "I am Noth. I shall take her into my house, and I shall meet you at the tower when you have found it. Only follow this stream that goes by the roots of this besmirched oak, and you shall be led there speedily. A great storm is about to break over the house of the Bear. And whatever gold was ever in it shall burn forth, red with refinement."

"A doom day then," muttered the king's-daughter.

"Let the doom-hammer strike hard, Ystrith. Let it strike true, for your sake," said Noth, then he vanished again into the trees behind the oak, and there was the sound as of the falling of a mountain.

Then silence.

Chapter Four-and-Twenty
Dinner for One

The pines were hoary and aged, their sinuous bark
as the skin of leathery beasts, and ever did they
bend and growl from beyond black beards. Their
limbs drove into the earth and made of the trees a
fast and steady watch; their loyalty shown in the
density of their loam. There were stones and rocks
and hither a boulder, all styled with the growth of
glistening moss, and all about were the many eye-
less fingers of the inquisitive ferns that whispered
about the forest floor to one another — one always
knowing better than the other. All of them were
dressed with snow.

All the while, in the days of their journey,
dense fog seemed to have been roused and rose silently from amongst the dark wood to heights of
void; there it consulted the sly breezes of deepening cold. Hither an elm, an ash, or (more often
still) a bare birch stood skeletal and contemptuous
of those that might tread near; its face that of a
man with a whip and a bad temperament.

The river-woman and -man, and the estranged
wife, the daughter of the king of Glimwæth, now
walked into the deeper part. They wondered as op-
posites, a line of trees always between them, as
though grown strong by the years of their aperture.
The one walked with an uneven, unrelenting
trudge, filled with all that was not grace, nor was it
regard, but all that was opposed to such thoughtful-
ness and care. The other two walked with a keen

observance of that which surrounded them, for they were afraid.

Thus the humming of the river-man's forgotten melodies had been replaced by silence, and the silence with the lonely crack of twig and bark and fern; all the while, the ancient and wild trees scratched one another's backs with rude laughter at the bumblers in the below.

Many suns and moons had risen and fallen away, and the wood had shed its coat of leaves, standing stark in a rising blanket of bone-white and emerald green. After a moment's lingering at what had felt the end of the world to all three of them, they had turned their faces to the place whither the grey of the westering light always trickled. It trickled like the paint of a fallen pot over a masterwork canvas.

The world was waning in murky veils, but the distant sun seemed always to lay its indicative finger on a mound that stood like a unicorn's pate at an ambitious distance. So began the walk into night-country as stridden by Loangilin, Carbeth, and the battered Ystrith; their forms against the pallor of winter like that of three bent crows, tumbling through one gale and then the next. As they forged on, it grew a weary hour for the trees as they only watched on with the drooping of branches and the last sighs of the autumn's terrorising. Asleep, the ancient holt was a memory to the three wanderers; a memory of the little girl that had been killed in their care, no matter in what direction they let elope their eyes.

327

Along the road to that sombre hillock's mason crown, all manner of newness was brought to the senses of their party from an infinite intimacy; there were thin grey lines that groped at the twilit world like the many tensile strings of a spider's harp, playing a silver tune over some toadstools, or some coral growth in the frosting edges of forgotten pools; there was the everlasting sigh of the many waters that slid through the clefts of too many spilled tears in the night; there were the hard faces of many old men that were the rocks in their austere closeness; there was a path that laid itself in with many unequal stones, guiding now in the direction that this trine failure wanted to walk.

And then they stood on a tall rise looking down onto it, onto the place where had long ago been built a spire of black stone; stone like vulcan glass. There in the vale was built a heaven-held tower that could harness the sun, and bear its children.

From here Mathydras had once sought out a lady of heaven until he found one, and then he had tried again to speak with her, for he had desired to share himself; to no longer be nothing and alone — his brother Svæn, whom he had thought slain, had had no ears, nor a heart to receive his sorrows, and there was an ancient and lost nobility with the daughter of the moon that had shown herself to him in his dreams in days long lost. But the woman that his tower had brought down on him had been another.

The ancient knowledge that Mathydras had desired was borne somewhere in the heart of the woman that had sought after the murder of his brother.

It lay in the knowledge of something firm, which he desired to observe also — something truer than the life he had spent running after the power in his blood. And so, with every rising of the sun, the tower had also risen higher, glassy stone by well-shaped stone, the tower also reached for the zenith, until tower and sun had met in the pivot of the day.

There Mathydras had grasped the orb that had given day its name and encased it in an iron en-closure, so that night had fallen at once; casting the world into a long, cold dark. And the red lady had appeared to him, climbing from that orb. So, at least, sang the birds which accompanied the three companions along their sombre road, and every twitter of it Ystrith guarded silently in her broken heart.

When they finally stood on that rise above the tower, having been so long on such a desperate road, walking together, yet in spirit always having been alone, the three were shaken from a kind of torpor that had laid itself over them. They found themselves cold and hungry, only a single torch that Carbeth held for light between the three of them. Presently he handed it to Loangilin. They had forgotten themselves in the face of their great task.

"Think you really that dear Folgnuin can be awoken from her death as a child is woken from sleep?" asked Loangilin quietly as they stared to-wards the stony obelisk in the vale before them. The question was one that sought only an honest and reliable answer from her other two compan-ions. "If you say yes, then I go with you both into

329

the very heart of that tall hell, and do whatever I can with my meagre hands!"

"Your hands have lifted up and kept alive more than just that sweet child, Loangilin. They are not meagre mitts," said Carbeth. "And I say yes to your question! If not, then this exile of ours has been a curse, but we trust that the laws of our people are good, that the rulings of our shepherds are a healthy guide in the wilderness! We are nomads, and whatever trials may come, we shall wander them away."

"And I," said Ystrith, gritting her teeth in a powerful grimace. "I say aye also! I must undo the evil in which I have bathed my hands, and if that Noth master had the power to drive back the red lady that has plagued my family so in my generation, then I shall trust whatever clue he hands me to escape this shadow that threatens to settle on my soul."

"Then we make for the tower!" said Loangilin boldly.

But it was a little over-bold. In that moment a faraway droning alit on the crisp air. A low tune was heard all throughout that region as the low droning of mountain men in song, but the words that were sung were old and, though well repeated, they had been forgotten and had lost the weight which they had clothed.

Ystrith felt herself drawn to it in the dread of a before unknown addiction — as water through a straw! She had been so very alone here in the wilderness of trees; in the wildernesses before the trees. This voice was one of an age before she had risen in the mire; before she had even known the man that stood now so unknown beside her. It felt bound to her, this song, as iron bands might have been used to bind a chest of greatly valued belongings.

Within, within, they look within;
The world without is lost and thin.
Turn in, turn in, they turn within;
They seek the answers that are mine:
An endless road that leads somewhere
For all true roads lead to despair.
Within, within, they're caught within;
Left with the lies that have taught them to sin.

A violent shudder went through all of their bodies at once. Never before had they ever heard such horrible thoughts put so frighteningly to words, and with the eerie sound of the deep lyre to accompany it, it seemed all the night about them was enchanted with a strange and dreadful magic.

Suddenly a monotone thunder on a heavy set of twin hairs was struck up from not too far away. A sombre song in an ancient tongue was raised once more into the shades above; yet now there was a tremor in the very earth as two voices sang in harmony, and the world's breath shuddered with a primal violence.

It was distant, but drawing steadily nearer; rising, then falling, then rising, then falling: a dreadful rhythm, like the tread of a wheel. Then one heard squealing, like that of iron oiled against iron. Beyond the trees in the dark of the wood a faint, white light — as that which glimmers through lantern glass — could be seen to sway about.

The droning had suddenly taken on even more profound harmonies, and now Ystrith recognised it as the melody of some kind of winding lyre. It must have been a big instrument, for the droning was deep as no lyre she had ever heard in all of Glimwaeth. The poets of her home had performed in the city's middle square on occasion, under Glimwaeth's oldest oak, and she had quite liked the sound of their skaldic strings.

The nearer it drew, the more the voice that sang sounded old, as though there were cobwebs fluttering in it with every breath it took.

The light beyond the trees disappeared.

Suddenly, the droning came to a halt.

The sound of a great movement rumbled in the dark. Then there was the heavy *thud, thud, thud* of vast feet running. Now they ran this way, now that way.

Unseen, the vast creature drew nearer ...

and nearer ...

There was a moment's quiet ...

A *ROAR* thundered across the scene from all around them.

Thud, thud, thud ...

Silence.

The three came together, circling and circling, staring out beyond the trees that surrounded them, all back to back, so that they were a triangle of eyes pressing out into the gloom. Loangilin held

Carbeth's mallet in her free hand, the torch still in her left. Carbeth held his bow and make-shift arrows at the ready. Ystrith raised her sword, to aim it at the wilds, her face white and sleek as marble as she looked into the dark.

Thud, thud, thud …

Silence.

The light of the torch, that before had flickered red, now dimmed to a sickly yellow; so pale that the world felt colder, simply for being less with colour than before.

Suddenly the horrid voice that had sung deep as the hollow earth spoke, so that the very trees trembled: "Pleasant? No; terrible was this light: weak and sick-like. I thought such a light is that of a crooked fellow, for truth! Was it a light you saw, brother, then? Was it truly a light there in the deeper part?"

Then something happened that made all the hairs on their together bodies stand on end. The Creature that lurked beyond sight stepped nearer the circle of light their torch cast out, so that its shadowy figure could be recognised as similar to that of a man in form, reaching all the way into the high branches of the aged trees surrounding. It's eyes flashed with the same sick, yellow light that the flickering tongues above their upturned heads had now adopted.

Then the beast said: "Fetch me my dinner, man, or I shall eat you alive!" But then, without waiting for a response — as though it had only said empty words, and not issued a command — the towering creature trudged into the light, its curling, red fur bouncing with each step. It's lurid, yellow eyes shimmering with the delight of the power it held over these little creatures.

"Please!" cried out the hunter. "Take all the dinner we have left! Only leave us be!"

The hulking creature crouched down, looking the man in the eyes as near as it could. Slowly a grim smile spread over its horrid features. It looked very like a man that had lived a hundred years in the wild and had never stopped growing both in height and in hairiness; only, it had a bald pate atop its head.

Then it said through its ivory tusks: "Are we not all dust, brother mine. Come then, brother! Come then! Let us find this scoundrel and twist their legs into pretzel-bread! Haha!"

"Which scoundrel ... brother?" stuttered Carbeth in return, Ystrith's hand found his shoulder like the talon of an eagle, tightening so that he could feel it despite even the harsh cold.

The beast chuckled lowly. "Hmmm ..." it said, as though its voice were rising out of the ground like a vapour. "I have no more hunger. Then I will take these, I think. I will take them to your tower, brother! Yes, brother, company would be nice, would it not, then? I think so."

At this, Ystrith stepped out between the river-people and the ogre. At once the light in its eyes faltered as it saw the king's-daughter, it reeled backward, falling over, crawling backwards on hands and feet. It mouthed many moaning nothings. It pointed, shaking its head. Its before so malign face became the mask of pain.

"No! NOOOO!" bellowed it. "NOOOOOOO!"

Ystrith cast down her blade, she beat her breast, she cried out: "Oh Svæn! What has happened to you? What dark power has laid hold of you and made such monstrous talons of your before so simple and so gentle paws? Were you not always one who whittled wood, chirping happy melodies to the song of the starlings? What has happened to you? What have you become?"

She wept, and the lower she sank into the collapsing snows with grief, the more upset the ogre seemed to become — the more frantic its looking about for escape, and the more desperate its need to aid the lady that was distraught before it. So torn, the river-people had never seen any before, and never would see any after. It was here that the monster's innermost being was broken, more broken than any of the hearts that had been broken with the news of Svæn king's-son's death.

Then, as if by the enchantment of the skeletal forest surrounding, the king's-daughter sobbed herself into a sleep of despair. The encounter had been too much for her.

The ogre quietened, the only thing in its face fear. "Is she ... but no, brother! No, she cannot be dead. Nonono! Is it not as you said, brother, then? Hear you that brother? No, brother, listen! Listen! Can you not hear? There is a lady in the wood! It must be an old and long lost huldra, having wandered away and down from the mountains. She must be here and in need of some friends! Brother, come! She may not be left to despair — alone and forgotten by a loud and idle world."

All at once, not giving the other two a chance to react, it picked up the three wan companions as though they were snared rabbits, and it took them back to the thing that had brought forth the iron squeal and the frightening harmonies of a deep lyre. Carbeth's arrow went astray, and his bow fell away to lie somewhere near the star-forged blade of his wife.

The mechanical steed of the beast was a large tricycle, built up of frost-blackened, mossy wood, and glistening wrought-iron. It had a large, wooden shield hammered along the front of it — as though it were meant for besieging a castle — and onto the back was mounted a strange, mechanical device, which had long strings extending from it, and cogs and wheels that danced in rhythm with the turning of the pedals. Built into the bottom of it, near these pedals, was a large cage, which the ogre of Dark-holt now unfastened to drop his prey into. Then it climbed astride and began the journey to the tower that had made the hill in the distance so resemble a nightmarish unicorn.

At once the droning akin to the play of mountain men rolled out through the otherwise silent wood. Nothing dared venture near the ogre's passage. Caught there in the cage, in a situation unlike any most mindful folk would ever even dream up in the worst of their nightmares, Loangilin and Carbeth were quite beside themselves with terror, and it was all they could do, with slipping grip, not to lose their minds. Each of the jarring bumps in the road were like the shaking earth that shook apart foundations once thought to have been of sturdy stone.

Most bothersome of all that long, dark journey, however, were the words that the ogre now took up in song again and again, until they had lulled the unfortunate river-folk into a horrid, hypnotic kind of dozing. So often they heard them repeated, that they at one time found themselves waking up, singing along with the ogre!

Then came the veiled grey of forest dawn, then its red, like a great, angry eye rising on the southerly horizon, scattering all its malice through the clammy morning air. The winds whispered amongst the ferns and needles up above, and the bare trees squawked and creaked beneath their wrinkled bark as they were shaken momentarily from winter's sleep.

And then it stood so near before them that they were altogether awake again: a great, black spire wrought of vulcan glass and metal arose from the pate of a hillock in a clearing. Riding into its shadow was as coming out of one oppressive landscape into another. At the top of the tower hung many gibbets, and there was also a great metallic device there, all with glass lenses and shutters, centred with a great, dark orb that seemed to have been singed terribly by a fire once.

The stream which they had been following issued forth from out of the hillock on which the tower was built, running down the steep stone stairs to one side. There the forest descended into the north-east.

The tricycle was drawn up right near the entrance to the tower, and the ogre was quick again to haul out his cringing prey. Then he brought them inside. Here all was tall and shadowy, and the now gilding light of morning was pale to trickle through the narrow glass of the high windows. A kind of incense seemed to be going up from a table on which many strange and cruel instruments lay strewn.

They were carried through the rest of the middle-dark building, into a cellar below, where the high windows were dripping with water and bearded with moss. It was cold here, though torches burned along the walls to bring more light into the place, and between every two torches was the door to a small, barred cell.

Opening the cage with which the ogre had brought them in, he now carefully drew out Ystrith, and crudely shook the other two into such a small cell built into the wall of the chamber. Then the beast lumbered out, still holding Ystrith in one hand and the tricycle's cage in the other, muttering to itself: "No, brother, listen! Listen! Can you not hear? There is a lady in the wood! It must be an old and long lost huldra, having wandered away and down from the mountains …"

Carbeth and Loangilin listened to its departure up the spiralled stair along which it had descended into this low place.

Then it was gone.

Release was a collapse into one another's embraces. There Loangilin wept for all the gruelling horror she had witnessed in the last few days. So fresh from the safe boundaries of the river-people, and already they were captured in the clutches of a monster beyond compare. "Who will save us from this bower of death?" cried she.

All the while Carbeth stared at the room beyond the barred door of their cell. In the centre of the room he saw a great, black stone circle. It was raised like a table. all he could think of as he stared at it, was the foundation to the tower which Thuineith the carpenter had built when first the village, Thænim on Wirthaumuin, had thought itself worthy of settling permanently along its river's rind.

Chapter Five-and-Twenty
The Fall and Climb

There, white upon white, where the brown of the trees was painted black in the frost, the iron-toed boot of the river-man trod down on something hard and loose in the snow. He crouched down to extract it. His companions stopped and looked back at him, the ebon man bringing the horses that he led on by their reins to a halt. From the squelching powder the henge-man-no-more drew forth a glittering blade, the blue steel of which seemed to hum in the dark northern winter, and to tug on the desperate vestiges of light in this vague daytime of forest shade.

As Authæn arose, the light in the blade seemed like the distant and high ring of a bell, and all about it darkened for the metal's own brightness.

"Do you read the runes of Imnir?" asked the river-man. The gron looked up at the southerner.

"I do," said the ebon man, holding out his hand. Authæn laid the steel into that dark mitt, and the other carefully studied the weave laid into its surface. Then he looked at the runes carven near the hilt. "Here is the sign of the Forge-bear of Glimwæth. Then there is an address to any that might find this blade. It was forged in the nostrils of Imnir's city for the king's-daughter, Ystrith. She is sent with this blade to slay a river-dragon, to bathe it in the blood of the beast for a final temper. The blade itself is called Birdsong."

"Ystrith," muttered Authæn, shaking his head. "Is this where she came all those years ago? But no, the snows covering the blade were only a few days old. What could this mean?"

"What of this?" said the gron a few paces away, drawing forth a shortbow.

"That is one of the bows of my people!" said Authæn. "Now that I draw closer … give me this, if you please, Grin. Thank you. If my eyes do not deceive me, this is the bow of a hunter of my village, Thænim. No! It cannot be!"

"What now?" asked Gaba, moving over to stand near where Authæn was, to look down at the bow. The coarse fingers of the river-man were picking the dirt from an engraving upon the grip of it.

"This belonged to Carbeth the Loyal. My good friend. He would never have let it fall — where wakefulness still had him. Is he no more?" Authæn asked his spirit as though it might conjure an answer from the trees surrounding. "Why would they have come here? Did they catch the rumour of one another after so long a time, and come to blows?"

"Or perhaps they laid down their weapons to kiss in the shrubs," suggested Grin.

The other two looked puzzlement at the gnome.

"I have seen it before," said the gron, shrugging with his characteristic grin. "I see the wisdom in your approach, however, my apples. If only we could whisper to birds. They would surely tell us whitherto."

"Both a fight to the bloody end, or what our gnome suggests would have been possible for these children of the wilds," muttered Authæn.

"If the birds cannot tell us, then perhaps the Forge-bear can. We are almost to Glimwæth. The king will also rejoice to hear that his daughter ..." Gaba trailed off.

"Do you think that they yet live, uncle?" asked Authæn, his grey features crunching into a grimace amidst his snow-flecked mane.

"We can only hope, my son," said the southerner, patting the other on the shoulder.

They bound these two items to their horses, and then they sought out some stones. The light of the sun was waning, and when it no longer shone they could carve moonstones to light their way; save a bright full moon were to shine, in which case the stones would be less convinced of their lunacy.

But the moon was quickly waning.

"What is that?" asked Authæn suddenly, having looked into the vale that fell away from where they stood. He pointed to where a tall, dark obelisk rose from a clearing in the whispering trees. He looked to Gaba, then they both looked at Grin, for they thought the tower looked much like the architecture of Lyn Ithæm's bath.

"That was not built by gron hands. It is far too crude. It was made by a man, by the look of it. He had the help of the dwarfs. Or perhaps ... It may have been a light-touched fellow. Like you, weird-eye. There seems to be something to catch sun rays at the top of it. Very crude, if you ask me. The sun

343

looks better where he goes to his smith-craft against the branches of Day."

"Should we venture that way?" asked Authæn.

"No, I think it would be wiser to inquire after the tower and these weapons under the roof of King Vinnytlas. There is a dangerous horror said to roam these woods, and I would not like to encounter it."

Their journey took them across a muttering brook, edged in ice, but they did not follow it into the west, they followed the lights that died along the southern horizon. There they would have to cross the foothills, beyond which the wooden city lay.

"What does it mean, uncle?" asked the riverman, when the gron had lit their stones by the words of truth's witnesses.

"What does what mean, Authæn?"

"What does Glimwæth mean?"

"Oh, now I shall have to think a bit. It is a name that reaches from out of Imnir's day: a yore day in which words were different for all men. But I think it comes from the word for glimmer, and the word for meadow. And so I should think that the city's name is called Glimmer-mead. I should think they named it for the friendly glimmer of its many hearths, which one can see from the meads below its stone walls. I have seen that glow from the fields myself, and have been happy for it. A beacon in the dark."

They presently continued into their cold dark of night, finally relenting to build a fire for themselves. Grin was a mighty help, for his use of the dwarfish words could help fire to catch quickly despite the onslaught of the chill air.

When they and the horses had eaten some of the remaining stocks that Noth had given them, the southerner instinctively drew forth his musical instrument, but caught himself, and slowly tucked it away again. "Not here," he muttered to his spirit.

Authæn was dozing, and the gron was chewing on a piece of stone as though it were bread with his pearly teeth. Seeing that Gaba was watching him through tired eyes, the gron bared his teeth heartily, chuckling at the thought that this sight might cause the southerner some nightmares as Gaba presently also drifted into dreams.

The dawn was dim, and it caught the fireside empty and as warm as it could still be in such weather. The company which Lyn Ithæm had donned 'trine failure' had set out before the rising of the sun, for at this time of year, where all minds wandered to the feast of Sun's-ear, the days were dark and short. As the faraway grey, further barred by the rising fells afore, finally began to light their path, the moonstones in their keeping flickered and faded. At this the travellers cast them by side, and walked in the hues of climbing fog.

Though strange shadows hissed and whisked by distant trees, the company of trine failure did nothing to draw unnecessary attention, and were consequently left, as though they were just another three spectres in the misery of Darkholt.

Many more days passed like this, but they came and went like the frosting they now had to shake from their beards regularly (save Grin, who seemed to have no hair on all his body). Then they came to a place where a broad path, seemingly formed by weather and water, went by zigs and zags up into and over the great hills that stood between them and the wooden city.

"Here we come to the pass called Svænsfol," said Gaba. "This is where one of the sons of the king pushed another to fall into death's embrace."

"That is a story that sounds both dreadful, and as though one ought have heard it for the sake of caution," said Authæn.

"Err on caution's side, and you shall fall less often from hills," muttered Grin.

His companions looked at him with helpless sighs. He had not expected them to pay much heed to him. Quickly he popped another of his likenesses from out of himself, a likeness that immediately laughed and said: "Oh, Grin, you are so terribly funny! How do you think of these things! Oh, ha ha ha! I ought to follow you about, writing down all of your sayings and witticisms!"

"Yes, thank you, thank you Grin," said the first of the two gnomes. "You already do follow me around, but it is a poor state of affairs with your handwriting. You will have to pass it on orally. From one generation to the next, let your children's children never forget the great Grin! Great, because he eats his rocks every night, keeps the tooth-faeries away!"

Another Grin popped out of the second, who was silently marvelling at the first. Said the third: "Oh my, that is a wisdom for the bairns, how went it again?" And this third Grin produced a stone slab from a pouch in his tunic, beginning to scrawl something on its surface.

"Something like this, my good gnome, write this down: ..." began the first Grin, but he stopped himself, for he saw now — as did the two men nearby — that the Grin who scrawled on the tablet had actually begun carving two very life-like representations of Gaba and Authæn into the stone, and though their faces remained recognisable, their heads were the shapes of apples.

"No worries, brother!" said the third Grin. "I think I captured every word perfectly!"

"Now I begin to understand why the ghouls let your people go, Grin," muttered Gaba; Authæn had already begun the climb, leading up the horses and chuckling to his spirit about the strange little creature so aged and yet so child-like.

They went a ways up the pass of Svænsfol, eating as they went in order to make good progress. Then they came to a place where a thin, frozen fall of water filled a strangely cracked hollow in the stone. The crater in the stone before them was directly beneath the sheer rise of a cliff face, which must have climbed some hundred metres. Above this a rill must have once flowed from the melting snows, which now — along with the pool it had filled — were frozen.

"It seems the mountain fell asleep whilst mourning the king's lost son. Strange, I had heard that he was a dangerous fellow," said Gaba.

"You mean not so worth mourning? Hmm. This is where he fell then?" asked Authæn.

Gaba nodded, straining his eyes up to look to the height from where the man had been thrown.

"I would not have thought stone so soft to the bone-bag of a falling man," said Authæn bewonderedly.

"He was said to be ... I heard rumours amongst the close guards-folk of the Nornburg, when I dwelt there by the king's leave," began Gaba, then he seemed to think better of it.

"What did they say, uncle?"

The southerner's head went from one side to the next in a silent contest of whether-or-not. Finally: "I shall say. Let us catch our breath here a while, and I shall tell you what I heard: I heard that the sons of King Vinnytlas were a rather rowdy two."

"They were a rowdy three, if Ystrith was their sister," said Authæn.

"Ah, yes, this daughter. I believe she was much younger than they. She was only some seven years old when it all came to pass, this tragedy. I believe at that time her brothers were grown men that had done much violence, and their father had sent them, before young Ystrith had even been born, to the far fjords in the west. That is where the giants were said to have fled long ago. The brothers king's-son were meant to have been tempered by the relentless discipline of the harsh living there.

"Svæn, I have heard, grew wiser in the cold, less prone to impulse, and a little more attentive to what surrounded him, where before he had been nothing but a wild skald, playing crude music on

348

unlearned strings and working grotesque faces into wood by knife.

"Mathydras, the elder brother, had always been quieter than the younger, but he was a proud and angry man. His cold precision made of him an even wrothier danger in the north, for now he was less restrained, and all the more precise for what he had endured.

"It was because he was said to have despised his brother's slovenly manner that Mathydras cast Svæn from there above. But there was more to them still. The household of Imnir, my dear Authæn, is made up of skin-changers.

"If you have heard the legends that the kings of Imnir's house 'tame the bear', then it is because those that most directly partake of his blood are set upon by the desire to drink the blood of other men, and are transfigured into great, grey bears! It was to subdue this bloodlust that the sons of the king were sent to the giants — that is, they were sent to the half-giants, the offspring of the *gala* of old."

"Then this king of Glimwæth whom we go to meet ... How was his name?" asked the river-man.

"Vinnytlas. King Vinnytlas the Vain-winner."

"King Vinnytlas, then. He can change his skin to that of a bear?" pressed Authæn.

"No, no," said Gaba. "That is a good point you make. It is not Vinnytlas that descends directly from Imnir, but his wife and children. And she has not been an ordinary woman for as long as her sons have been dead. She now only heeds the word of her husband, bound to the form of a bear. And he? He sits tiredly in his chair. I suddenly hope that

349

Glimwæth still stands when we arrive there, for the sake of your village, and for the sake of finding these ghouls."

The two men looked down at the gron, who was testing his balance on the ice of the crater where Svæn was said to have fallen. Presently it broke, and he disappeared into the icy waters beneath. He re-emerged just a moment later, a sour look on his face, and climbed out bitterly. He seemed not to feel the cold.

"No, do continue, Hamathian. I would say that I listen with baited breath, but the breath has quite escaped me now."

The southerner smiled.

"How many years has it been since the fall of Svæn?" asked Authæn.

"Oh, I think some twenty or so? Twenty-and-a-half?" returned the southerner, and he began to guide his horse along the road again. "We best move on, or the gloom of this place shall overtake us.

"But the sun's only risen a couple hours ago, you rotten tomato!" complained the Grin.

"As it will tomorrow. I just want a hot bath, Grin. Let's move," returned the southerner.

A near four days they trekked that pass. It was tall, and long, and at the other end, they finally looked down into the highlands that roll southward and away beneath the high halls of Glimwæth. There stood the hill of Glimmer-mead, proudly upholding the Nornburg. The city still seemed to smoke with the fires of daily life, not yet those of ruin.

"By all that is grey and brittle," sighed the gnome in despair. "You call this masonry?"

"Perhaps the king would gladly take you on as his own house-mason, Grin. How does that sound?" laughed Gaba.

"Worse than working for the ghouls," said the gron.

Authæn only stared at the great city beneath them. To look down upon it from such a great height was to him what it must have been like to see through the eyes of a bird.

And then a vision flashed over his sight.

In the heavens above he saw the sudden, smiling beckoning of Lyn Ithæm — her finger curling and uncurling with her summons of him like the draw of a shepherd's crook. But it was as the crook of a shepherd that takes his lamb to be slaughtered.

Then he was falling; falling from a great height, through the clouds.

You do not know where you come from. You barely know your father.

Suddenly, Authæn plummeted through the clouds again, but after passing through hail, and shadow, and blinding lightning, he fell out into a vast, open darkness, a cavernous maw that seemed to have no end. He fell, and fell, and fell, and fell. It seemed forever, and he tried to catch on the air, if such a thing was at all possible. He tried to extend his cloak, and catch the wind, but there seemed to be no wind here, only stale air.

As he fell, the clouds above began to clear a little, and they began exposing a shape in the deep shadow beneath. He recognised far away grass-

351

lands, as though he were a raven flying at a great height, but then there seemed to be a mountain upon the plains; a glimmering hill. Only when the mountain arose, and took on the form of a horned man did Authæn recognise the etching he had seen on the black stone in the wilderness.

The Ibex looked darkly up at him, extending a black and metal talon towards the falling man. *Now our work begins, my son. The end of our beginning, as it were.*

Chapter Six-and-Twenty
Like Wrothy Nostrils

From the southern gate of the city, the highway led to a cliff that jutted from the hill like the shallow prow of a longboat. This was skirted by a broad stair, called the Styg ov Baugwera (the Climb of Kaupmen) up onto a courtyard of stone, housing the great oak of skalds. Above it all, the cliffs held high the Nornburg. Into those cliffs were hewn two great, arched passages that presently poured out smoke like raging nostrils, and from them echoed the ring and clamour of hammering iron.

A man with a mane of golden hair, and a newly washed cloak that furled rubine on the mountain winds, climbed the stair that led up to the court-yard. There he strode over the flagstones and by the great oak tree with sprightly step. He nodded to the guards gathered around the braziers on either end of the mountain's nostrils, then he entered the glowing red of the smith's workshop. This was the workplace of the Forge-bear of Glimwæth, the place where many a legendary weapon had been hammered into lethal shape by the Forge-bear's forebears.

The ringing of yellow-hot iron on the anvil pounded out a rhythm to which the stride of the Lion Pen-tooth matched itself as if by its own will, so mighty were the shudders that pushed through the air from the forge. After the tunnels that led in from the outside, the scrivener now lowered him-self by a broad, circular stair into a round chamber, the arching ceiling of which was still of stone un-cut. In the middle of the room, an octagonal pillar held up the roof, and about the bottom of this pillar were ringed shelves of all manner of tool and ore.

Tens of different hammers and tongs there were, as well as great spoons and shovels, pokers and crooks, clamps and drills, and much else. From the pillar, reaching into the other-most end of the workshop, went a long foundry, which in turn led to the smelter. To the right of the smelter was the forge, and alongside this stood the mightily renowned pounder of metals, grunting with every sparking stroke of his muse.

As though he were enraptured in the web of a wondrous dance, the Lion Pen-tooth stopped, and watched the master at his work. His broad figure was larger than any other man the scrivener had met before, and the mechanical ripple beneath the hairy coarseness of his besmirched skin was like the tensile tug of so many strings on a puppet. The smith was bare from head to waist, and about his waist he wore a fur loincloth over fur breaches. His feet stuck bare, black, and large, like those of a frog, onto the stone beneath. His beard was short and welded in places by stray fires past. His head was shaven, and all over he was shimmering with the gemstones of labour as they perspired on his hulking form.

His eyes did not look up as his rhythmic drum-ming of that iron firmament came momentarily to an end. He returned the raw head of a spear to the bright coals, then drawing forth a new, yet formless bar of metal with his tongs. On this he freshly went to work. First he hammered it arhythmically, and the Lion took another few steps towards him; but then the rhythm of before took the mighty machinery of his limbs, and the smith began to hum a low drone. As he then sang, the words which rumbled from his skaldic tongue made the walls melt away with memory of what he sang, and the Lion Pen-tooth felt himself drawn into the imagery of the Forge-bear's song like a fly is drawn in by the quick fingers of a spider.

Hear oh hear,
Father of the Forge-bear!
Bend thine ear
To the calling of the frozen.
In dark north,
Where the night-time draweth near,
Hail sunlight, pale sunlight;
From the south now wend your way!

In the dark
Of ages before daybreak,
Came the ring
Of the hammer-holding king.
He that wrought
In the shadows that were given
Bending midnight into starlight
Forged the sinews of an oak.

Yore-day tree,
Keeper of all mem'ry,
Singing sagas,
Of the roots beneath your crown.

And this crown,
Is the forge-work of the daylight.
Hail daylight, frail daylight!
Speed thy welder back this way.

Iron boughs,
Darkly looming above,
Need their fixing
By the fire of thine forge.
Bring the blue,
Not of night-time but of morrow
Take the sorrow; bleak, cold sorrow.
The long winter drive away.

The smith was about to sing another verse of the ancient song, when his eyes drifted up in the motion by which he swept the sweat from his brow. There the golden visage of the Lion Pen-tooth and that of the Forge-bear met in a momentary tension, both standing motionless. The silence on the thick air in this moment was alive with hesitation.

Finally the smith sighed in relief, his faraway mind having returned to this humble cavern to recognise the man that stood before him. Looking down, he saw that the spearhead was not bright enough to finish shaping, and so he returned it to the hot bed of coals behind him. Then he turned back to his visitor, wiping his hand in the fur of his loincloth, and smiling.

"To what mischief has my brother-in-law sent you now, Pen-tooth? Would you like to write the tale of my journeys to Steornufol?" asked the

Forge-bear. "You could write: 'Forsooth! 'twas cold in thither bleak and barren desert-land of snow and stone!' I think that is about all you would need for an honest account."

This cracked the face of the Lion into a smile. "No fighting with trolls then?" asked he.

"Oh!" said the Forge-bear. "Yes, that you could add, if you thought it captured the spirit of the venture somewhat better. That damned height is something like a troll to conquer, I tell you."

"It is strange how your close family seeks to draw away from the truth of their heroism, great metal-master," said the Lion. "I know that you did fight trolls there above. Why are you not proud of such a feat?"

The Forge-bear suddenly looked away from the scrivener, his face scowling at these words. Said he: "What for some may seem heroic has left my spirit scarred with silence, scrivener. Why have you come?"

"I have come to ask after a blade," said the other.

"I have let the word be proclaimed loud enough in the fore-burg: I shall not forge blades in this time where metal is needed for axes and spears! All must be armed when that ogre returns, not only the few! Besides which, you have a blade already. Has the rusty decay of age finally broken its bite?"

"No, the sword of Athilan is still as bitter as when I found it, my friend. I have not come to ask after the forging of a new blade, however. I have come to ask after a blade that bears your mark over its fuller, and a charge to one Ystrith king's-daughter."

The face of the smith waxed with astonishment, then it grew bright with delight, then it fell with concern. "You have found the blade?" whispered this hulk.

"Just so, strung to a young woman by leather thongs," said the other.

"Ystrith lives? Is she here?"

"She was living when last I saw her," said the Lion, "but listen to me, Forge-bear: she has run into Darkholt, fleeing from the hunter whom she sought out in the east. They were married a time, it seems, and then she departed from his tent to slay a river-dragon."

"She has slain one?" breathed the other in disbelief. "Then it was not idly she ran into the murky eaves."

"There is more, Forge-bear," said the Lion. "She was carrying two bones, as those that might have once been the leg bones of the dragon, and she also had a cloak full of its scales and teeth."

"Mighty deeds," said the smith, "but was there no flask nor bottle amongst her treasures? There was no vial holding a red liquid, perchance?"

The Lion frowned and cocked his head to one side. "No."

The other made for the exit, but stopped again, as the scrivener motioned that he still wished to speak with the Bear.

"What else?" said the Forge-bear irritably. "Can you not ask your questions on the wending way? I want to search these things that my niece has brought us myself!"

"I only want to know what your designs were," said the Lion.

"You fear for my brother-in-law, the king. I have no designs against him. You know that I love him well, scrivener. I only wished to learn better songs from the birds. They say that the blood of the river-dragons can grant a man the speech of birds, and what a skald I could be, were I to learn from the little masters of singing themselves! Imagine what rhymes lie hidden in their music!"

The Lion Pen-tooth laughed. "Now I understand better why you chose the forge, and not the throne, my friend; and for that I love you well."

"Good, good. Then let me rummage about in this horde that my niece has left you. If she has slain a dragon, I think not that her brother stands a chance against her," said the Forge-bear, then he sighed, lowering his face into his scarred hands. "The poor boy seemed so sensible after his return from the fjords. I cannot understand what happened between him and Mathydras."

"None of us can, my friend," said the Lion Pen-tooth sadly. "I doubt that even Mathydras himself could help us understand. Such things are too often the work of overpowering passions."

"Another song I would cringe to hear, yet my niece seeks it out as though it were the only song that mattered."

"I think she will not get very far before she realises that it is a vain song. At the most she will slay the ogre, and find herself the greater monster," said the Lion Pen-tooth.

The two friends of the king departed the warmth of the forge-works, bursting into the cold winds without as purposed and bold as true arrows. The Lion led the Forge-bear down to the stables, where the wagon of Jithron, on which Ystrith had slept, still held her treasures, hidden beneath the furs that had made her journey comfortable. Beside them, the steep houses smoked whilst silently regarding their descent. From the odd window, every so often, a curious face would peer out to observe them, pipe or friendly word in mouth. And then the houses climbed up behind the retaining wall that fell into the stabled tier behind the gates.

The master blacksmith was searching the bundled up cloak of the king's-daughter the moment the scrivener unveiled it to him. He marvelled at the scales. "I could make a coat of mail from these!" said he with a shine in his eyes. "And these leg bones, those would also serve well for an armour that even legends would return to life for, that they might bask a day in its glory."

At this, there was a commotion beyond the gate. Above, Gildolf made his way to see who had arrived, crying down onto the causeway: "Who wills to fare into our fore-burg? What is your business in the stead under Imnir's house?"

"One who, having endured much ridicule in the house of Imnir, now hopes that he has won double-glory in the eyes of Imnir's sons. I see my handiwork is strung up to the king's mead hall.

"By the ... By the things! By the things that
are!" cried Gildolf. He turned to where the
scrivener and the blacksmith looked up at him bemusedly.

"What is it, Gildolf?" asked the Lion.

"The ..." he pointed, but the words were fast in
his throat.

"Then open the gate, so we might see for
ourselves!" cried the Forge-bear. "If it is someone
that my brother-in-law has insulted, let me add the
salt of my black fingers to his wounds."

"Yea!" cried Gildolf, "but nay, Bear, harm not
the man. It is the Master Gaba. He bringeth with
him another of the *dokolvir*, and also a child, it
seems to mine eyes. Open the gates, you wardens!
Open the gates!"

At once there was a great shudder in the oak.
Two men at either gate lifted a great beam of wood
and laid it aside, then the *clinking* of vast chains
and tooth-wheels could be heard to draw back the
iron-bound wood. There, in the dying light of a
winter's day, stood three weathered figures against
whom the tugging winds were as proper as their
beards or garbs; two horses at their hind.

"The scrivener and the smith!" said Gaba at
once, raising his arms, and approaching them that
awaited the travellers in the entry court. He embraced one the friends of the king, one after the
other. Some folk had gathered above, on the stoops
of the public houses that looked into the stabled
tier. Behind Gaba, Authæn led in their horses, and
found a place for them to be tethered. He went to
work, unsaddling them, laying blankets over them,

361

to ward away the biting chill. Then he also went to where the Forge-bear was prodding the gnome with his hammer.

"And what do you know of artful craft, you ugly little wretch!" said the blacksmith, laughing. "If you had half a mind for art your face would be dressed daily with a mask."

"Oh, dearest, friendliest of fools," said the gron, barely any passion to his tone. He sounded as though he were speaking to an irritating child. "If you knew ought of artful craft you'd be careful with that hammer. I must admit you have a pretty face, but I can rearrange it until it looks even worse than mine. The journey to beauty from ugliness is a long one, and those that walk it have learned the lessons of beauty that the natural-born beauties could never ken. Should I teach you them?"

"Oh," uttered the Forge-bear, standing up straight. "I take my words, as hard as they were, and I shall put them in my pocket for now."

"May they burn a hole there," said the gron.

Gaba chuckled, and said, "I would have thought you to have learned your lesson by now, Forge-bear, insulting strangers at the gate like a fatherless street-wight looking for a beating."

"Oh, my black brother," said the blacksmith, "it is our way to test everything that meets us like the forge tests metal."

"Then I say as well, let your words burn a hole in your pocket," said Gaba.

"To you I am almost willing to listen, Master Gaba" said the Forge-bear. "For all your gentle manners, you have the mettle to break the helm of the Ibex. That is a frightful feat! But where is the twig with which you did it?"

"It is no more," said the southerner sadly. "It could not be helped."

"Well, if it could not be otherwise, then we shall have to find a new stick for you to scold children with, my friend," said the Forge-bear. "As they say: 'It is better to light a fire, than curse the dark'."

"I like that saying," said Authæn.

"My, you should follow this thick-skulled block of iron around, weird-eye; write down his profound wisdoms," said the gnome bitterly.

"I already serve that purpose to what degree it is needed, little fellow," said the scrivener. "And I am quite willing to retain it by blade."

"No need, I have no desire to become a chronicler. We are here to speak to your king, masters. We have come to return something that belonged to his daughter." As Authæn said this, he brought forth the manifold blade of Ystrith, and the eyes of the scrivener and the smith waxed with surprise.

"What have you done, Master Gaba!" cried the Forge-bear in sudden dismay.

"We only found it lying in new snows in the wood, Forge-bear," said Gaba. "We would not have taken it from the girl, and were we to have tried we may not have ended up standing before you, from what young Authæn has told me regarding her violence."

"That is a welcome relief, and yet … Do you always send dark elves to deliver the fruits of your great deeds, Master Gaba?" asked the Forge-bear then.

The southerner laughed, shaking his head. "No, Forge-bear. These river-folk, and particularly this river-man before you, have carried me on their shoulders as I travelled the east. Every step that I have taken forward was as though they led me blind by the hand. I have trusted them, and they have not betrayed me. That speaks more of their mercy, and of my folly, than it does of any great works I may have accidentally stumbled over in my blind tapping."

"Yes, the river-people that travelled with my company were also a greatly venerable people," said the Lion Pen-tooth, looking carefully at Authæn through his benighted eyeglasses.

"Some of my people are here in the city?" asked Authæn, looking at once to where he now recognised the wagons of his village alongside the stables. "Those are the wagons of Thænim!" said he.

"Then it is as I thought. You are the lost shepherd of your people. They have hoped for your arrival ardently, Authæn son of Thuineith. They will rejoice at your coming. As will our king, now that he can speak with one who answers properly for his kin. We are in need of as many violent hands as we can get. A shame that those of young Ystrith are not here to share in the glorious doom that awaits us."

Chapter Seven-and-Twenty
Hall of the Hill King

As the scrivener and the smith led their three new guests up the highway, a crowd began to gather along the sides of the road. Many of them cried out then, for they were villagers from Thænim, and they recognised their returned chieftain, who had sent them into this wooden city to wait for him. Upon seeing them, Authæn would nod and wave with a smile, acknowledging them, whilst indicating that he had urgent business to attend to with the king.

It was only when Wingilin suddenly burst through the crowds onto the street, that their procession stopped. She sped by a bewildered Forgebear, who sputtered out curses in the tongue of his fathers like an overcooked kettle; by the silently watchful Lion Pen-tooth; by the southerner that had rescued them from the fury of the Ibex. She nearly kicked over the gron, not having seen him, and slammed into the river-man at the end of the procession, squeezing him affectionately, and then letting him go, to say: "You smell like horse!"

Authæn laughed weakly, shaking his head in stunned gratitude. "I have never been more thankful for it, if it garners such a welcome," said he with a smile. Then he saw Huthram making his way by the people gathered along the road, joining his wife, and embracing his friend in the tired welcome that his slow recovery permitted him.

"Oh, it is good to see you again, my chieftain," said the captain of the scouts. "We have waited a long while for this day. You have been our chieftain in the making from the time you were a sapling."

"Then you cannot call me brother any longer?" said Authæn sadly.

"Only in words, brother."

"Oh, be less glum. Both of you!" Wingilin reprimanded them. "Today we may be glad that Authæn has returned to us, whether you call him chieftain or chief-tart."

"One sees that you were raised in a chieftain's tent, my heart," laughed Huthram. "I am glad. All of us are, my friend. Go now to the king. He has been desiring to speak with the true leader of our people with as much ardour as even your most devout followers." There was a spark in Huthram's eye as he said this, and a cunning smile.

"Huthram, where is Carbeth?" asked Authæn suddenly, his face grimming. He held up the bow that had been in his hand this past time, and the captain and his wife looked at one another, greatly concerned. Huthram took the bow, and looked at it a long and silent while.

"He was exiled, Authæn," said the scout captain at last. "Loangilin and Folgnuin as well. They spilled the waters of Wirthaumuin in a battle against imps in the woods. They saved themselves by doing so, but for that they had to be cast out, and Carbeth renounced himself to go with them."

"But the story goes deeper than that, my home," said Wingilin, looking from her husband to

366

her chieftain. "Ystrith was there, Authæn. She saw him and ran into the hills. He followed after, but he returned without her."

"It would appear that was not their most recent meeting," said Authæn. "We found not only Carbeth's bow, but also Ystrith's sword. It was unbloodied, if that is any consolation to us, but I shudder to think what has happened to them."

"Perhaps they are even now looking for their implements of war," said the gron. Huthram and Wingilin suddenly frighted, realising that this little creature stood listening to them, not having acknowledged it before.

"What in all riverbeds?!" gasped the captain of the scouts. The gnome chuckled like the rumbling earth at their surprise.

"Authæn!" said Gaba before he could introduce Grin to his friends, indicating that they had to away.

"We must be on our way," said the chieftain to his people.

"Farewell, Authæn. Honour us before the king," said Huthram.

Authæn nodded, and the procession was led by the hill's nostrils, up the winding stair that led to high Nornburg. Upon reaching the great doorway of the king's house, they saw the banner that had been planted by the goblin, flying black in the wind. In its middle, at times where its furling straightened out the cloth, this mark could be seen, as though it stood for the sigil of some house:

The guards stood aside, and the Forge-bear led them through the tall doors that presently groaned open, into the house of his fathers. There, tall and dark, the forlorn banners of a house fallen to despair limply licked at the smokes that curled upward from the long firepits at the middle of the hall. There, old and fast, rose great pillars stood on stone. There, at the farther end, a great and grizzly bear arose, and roared attention into those that stood in circles whispering to one another secrets of this ancient house.

The king arose. The father of his own trine failure raised his tattered hand, silencing the beast that had at one time been his wife. Of him, in this smokey place, a silhouette was cast by the pale lights that fell like dusty water from the high-set window behind him.

"*Kvath villtu, brothred mine?*" boomed his voice across that shadow place. "*Okvath thiz weros thigeftur?*"

"I bring upon thee, brother mine, the chieftain of those bearing Ibex-crown unto thy hall hereover," said the Forge-bear, walking on with his following, until he stood before his king. The smith then winked at the bear, which grumbled, shaking its head. "*Otu, systred?*" said he.

"Ah," sighed the king, collapsing into his high chair again. "You are the carpenter's son."

"My king, Vinnytlas," said Authæn, bowing, "I have come bearing you this gift, and bearing also many questions." At this the river-man drew the blade of Ystrith from where he had tucked it in his belt, so that it was raised with its tip toward the ceiling, and the flat of the rune-etched blade bare toward the throne. Catching the light, the blade began to sing like the high ringing of bells.

Then spake Gaba: "This blade is named Birdsong, great king. It is tempered in the blood of a river-dragon, which was slain by thy daughter at the behest of thine brother here standing. We found it a week or so ago, buried in snows not some days old. Alongside it was the bow of the man to whom she is married, but of them there was no sign, and there was no blood in the snow."

"Gabazi of the south!" cried the king then, and the bear roared again. "What a great breath of fresh air you are on my old and smoky spirit. You bring with you great hope to my hall, for we are embattled, but do not yet know how."

"Do you not see the sword of your daughter, king?" asked the Forge-bear.

"*Ik sær thath, brothred!*" growled the king wrothly. "I only was stunned by this southerner, because amidst the gloom he is me a light!"

"It is this hall, king. The windows are too small," said his brother-in-law.

The king sagged into himself with resignation. "Yes, brother mine, the hall is the problem. Not the ogre. Not the daughter. Not my firstborn traitor! I am the father of poisoned apples!"

"Ah, but these are good apples all, my king. Save perhaps the bespectacled wit-writer, you, and this brother of yours!" declared Grin of a sudden.

The Lion Pen-tooth cocked his head to one side as he looked down at the gnome.

The king sat tall in his chair with surprise.

"And what is this? A child with a man's bass?" said he.

"By wit alone, a child," muttered Gaba, shaking his head.

"Says a man so old in years that I should think him witless," the gron laughed coarsely.

"You have a keen tongue, witty child, but bitter words oft times evoke a returning strike. Have you the doughtiness to take a blow as well as you receive one?" the king wondered, tugging at his moustache.

"To strike at me is to strike at stone, Big-beard. It is folly, and hurts only the one who strikes," said the gron.

"Yet when *you* strike out the world bends to allow it?" said the king.

The gron: "The world bends whether I strike or speak, to hold the content of my works; for they are never for my own sake."

"What be you, then?" the king returned.

Grin stepped into the light beneath the blade which Authæn held aloft, so that he stood with it extended above his head. It seemed as though that spectacle were fashioned by an artful eye.

"I AM A GNOME, MIGHTY MAN!" boomed his voice, and the rafters above suddenly sweated sawdust, all the wood in that wooden house groaning loudly and, somewhere in its corners, snapped threateningly.

"By bleating dinner-tide!" shouted King Vinnytlas, rising to his feet again, and stooping to see the little creature better. "You are a mighty beast! Would you side with us against the ogre?"

"If you let me rebuild the damage that it wreaks on your city," said the gnome.

The pine-like eyebrows of the king went heavenward, and he raised his hands in silent exultation. Then said he: "So be it!"

This had taken the gron's companions by surprise, but now they smiled at the kindness of it.

"You yourself are quite a golden apple, Grin," muttered Authæn. The gron chuckled again.
The king then descended his throne, and led them through a side door behind that chair, saying: "Then come with me, my friends. Let me see this sword that you have built, blade-builder. Thank you, chieftain. Let me see now. Ah, you have left your signature upon it, and so led these brave souls here, just in time to save our home. It was a plan well-wrought, almost as well as this blade, and likely with less intention of its true consequence, brother."

"Such plans and schemes are for you and the courtly folk, my king. I am but a ringing iron on life's anvil. Strike me and I sing for you," returned the Forge-bear.

"Our courtly plans ..." began the king, looking knowingly in the direction of the Lion Pen-tooth. "They have never proven themselves so well-built."

They were led by a stair down to where a great cavern had been cloven away from the hill's north-

371

ward facing slope, so that they presently stood in a great hall of stone, without a northern wall, instead, sporting a balcony. Thereupon was a table of stone in the wintry dimness, and there they went, so that the king could lay down the blade, and look at it in the light of fading day.

"Here I go when the windows are too little for me, brother," said the king, and his brother-in-law laughed.

"You have lost your walking stick, brother Gaba!" said the king then. "You may take this blade in the meantime, for we shall have need of your war-crafty arm yet. A gift, for slaying our dread enemy in the east."

The southerner graciously took up the blade, swinging it once with a blurry heft. Then he held it upright again, and seemed to grow one with it in a way that the eye could not quite catch.

"I thank you, great king," said the southerner.

"Now, what questions have you?" said King Vinnytlas, stroking his beard impatiently.

"They are questions that involve your daughter in a manner, great king," said Authæn. "We found her blade and the bow of a loyal friend on a rise that looked down into the vale where a tall, dark tower rose up to capture the sun. Could it be that they were taken there? Is it a place to which we could venture and survive?"

At once the king and the smith looked at one another. The glance they shared was of great doubt.

"That is the spire of the ogre, chieftain," said the king.

"That is just where she wanted to go all those years hence," said the Forge-bear.

"Another question for which we come to you, good king," said Gaba then, "is the question after ghouls."

The king's head jerked up in the direction of the southerner, his eyes quickly narrowing. "Ghouls, you say? What mean you?"

"They are a swarthy people, oh king. They are said to dwell in mounds that burnt with forge-light once. These mounds are marked with trees that bear aloft seven branches bright, so as to lure the witless into the snares of lethal end."

"Ah," said the king. "I have seen such an ashen ruin once. It was a barrow of the dead, we thought at first. The skalds sing it in the songs of my father, Harrowbert the Held, in which he forged down into the belly of Imnir's Height. But that is no place for you, my southern friend. Your place, for now, is on the walls of this burg!"

"What war assails you, my king? The banner planted on your threshold was not beknown to me," said Gaba.

"The ogre himself, Master Gaba. He came into the fore-burg, as though he were a guest invited. There he marched with his loyal troop of forest hounds. The imps were at his heels, Master Gaba. Do you have imps in the south? Do you have such holts as we in the south? I thought not."

"We have goblins none the less; but a more desert brethren of these forest sprites."

"I see," said the king.

"Then you shall aid us in achieving the barrow-forge, if we aid you in achieving victory over the ogre and his horde?" the southerner proposed. The Forge-bear seemed to approve.

The king hesitated.

"There is something unsaid on your tongue, my king," said the Lion Pen-tooth.

"Yes, Lion, and you have a furball on yours!" spat the king angrily, but his scrivener seemed unmoved. After a moment King Vinnytlas sighed, righted himself, laid a hand on the shoulder of the Lion Pen-tooth in apology, and said, "I am not so certain that the two ends are far removed from one another, Master Gaba."

All waited quietly for an explanation to follow.

The king slid away from his trusty scrivener, moving out towards the rail of the balcony, staring at the snowy peaks onto which this hall looked.

"*Come to me strength and memory,*" said he to his spirit.

There over hills before us tall,
There yonder lies a height.
There lies a mountain that is brimming,
Steornufol is hight.
A mountain that with stars has warred,
And paid the price by bleeding ever after
With the waters that not shimmer aught,
Save when the black dwarfs laughter
Echoes through the caverns there-nether.

"This is how it goes in the song. These are the ghouls you speak of. When my son came here with his goblin hordes —"

"Your son?!" cried Gaba.

"Yes, Master Gaba," said the king, turning back to his guests. "The ogre of Darkholt is my son, Svæn. He revealed himself when he stood on my threshold. You are shocked, that soothes me. It was a blow to my soul like the blows of this brother mine against the anvil. Anyway, the ogre said this when he came, and it still hangs in my ear like the spiders in this hall's uppermost corners: 'The deeps return to claim the middle-earth again, as once when darkness fell, father mine. The under-earth is teaming now with youths as spry as wolves.'

"What am I to make of this, my friends? I hear in it the voice of vengeance. The king of the black dwarfs comes to undo the son, after the father delved into the deeps. My father perished after his great conquest into the south, paying with his own head for his hubris. I have held our people in peace for long a time, but even now the sins of the fathers wend a return to feast on us like crows and ravens. The blood that was spilled in the mountains shall wash through the dells and dales, clearing this land of all that once lived free, and it is for the theft that my father committed."

"What did he steal, brother?" asked the Forgebear.

There-nether, found that tyrant bold,
A blade of glass so black and old,

375

That by its very name alone
The world could sing in memory
Of a time when there had never been
The blighted dwarfs that lost their gleam.
And so, hearkening back to days,
When yore-ago there was no trace
Of this dark foe,
Harrowbert Held took up the blade as birthright
For inheriting a land which,
Long before the black dwarfs plied their hand,
Was that of Imnir.

"So goes the song. But my father had no right over the blade. He was a usurper, no direct son of Imnir; a mongrel from the east!"

"The sword of green fires was built by the black dwarfs?" asked the Forge-bear in disbelief.

"The sword of green fires? Your father wielded it, king?" said Gaba, his eyes ablaze with some sudden hungry lustre.

King Vinnytlas nodded wearily. The memory of these things was a clear burden on his spirit.

"*Lutûz*," muttered the southerner, turning away towards the inner darkness of the rough-hewn hall.

The gron suddenly shuddered, his eyes snapping onto the southerner with a heavy wariness.

"What was that, Hamathian? Why did you say that word?" demanded the little creature, but the threat of it could be felt like the trembling in the flooring.

"It is nothing, Grin. You know of what I speak as well as you know of what I seek," said the southerner.

376

"It is buried, south-man!" shouted the gron.

The southerner turned angrily on the gnome. "Stones have been moved before," said he.

"If you seek the sword of green fires, Master Gaba, I should advise you against it. What it cost my father was more than he could afford," said the king.

"I take your words to heart, king; but there has always been an Unthing in the tomb of Manutuz. I am sent to ensure that is the case again," said the former dragon hunter defiantly.

Again the gron cringed in ire, baring his teeth and growling at the southerner.

"SAY NOT THAT WORD!" roared the gnome, and there was shuddering in the stone all round.

"Check your pride, uncle, please," cried Authæn, "lest Grin bring down this place on our heads as the waterfall before it!"

The southerner did quiet, looking about with large eyes, holding his new boon at the ready.

"Be appeased with that sting for now, my black brother," said the Forge-bear. "It is a blade true enough. It has felled a dragon!"

At this Gaba laid his face into his left, nodding agreement.

"Forgive me," said he. "This is a quest that has taken so much from me. But, now I think on it, mayhap this blade will be enough to appease my countrymen. You speak truly when you say that it has slain a wyrm."

The gnome sighed, then smiled up at the southerner. Gaba, in turn, smiled back. The matter was settled for the moment.

"Then it is still for us to save this city, and to find those that conjured the Ibex of your guild's fellow founder, uncle," said Authæn.

"So it is, my son," said Gaba. "The last portion of my adventure begins. I feel hope again as I have not for a long while. Now I may be able to see my home again! My family! I might serve my queen once more! I thank you doubly, King Vinnytlas! This gift has solved a knot in my soul!"

And the king said: "May it aid you in solving a knot in mine!"

Chapter Eight-and-Twenty
Discernment Drear

It sat atop its tall, dark tower, long legs hanging from the edge. The gibbets were its company. Once held they this beast's meals. But the ogre, for all its appetite before, was weeping. It was fasting, and this not by choice. It could no longer savour manly flesh. The thought of it now made the monster sick; and all of this, because of that cursed sparrow so sweet, which now did much the same as he: she despaired in her bower; he, above it.

"Now why would she have said such things, brother," sobbed the beast. "Why would she have cleft so cruelly at my heart! I did not know, I had not thought … I had not thought that I would see upon our return so little a creature. She was so delicate a creature. She was swaddled, brother! Swaddled was she. She was swaddled in the arms of our dear mother, Yrsa.

"But I want not to remember!" bellowed the ogre then, swinging itself back onto the rooftop of the spire with an angry motion. "I cannot help but think these bitter, sick-like licks of thought! And they taste not well, but bitter! AAAAAARRRGH!"

The shout of the beast thundered across the vale in which the tower rose; but the monster was not even vaguely satisfied to see the toppling destruction wrought by an avalanche in the distant fells. That only made its wrath burn brighter, and the clouds that steamed beneath its flat nostrils became more rapid.

"I thought it was a fairly trade," muttered the monster through its tusks. "We told ourselves that it was wise at first. To sell the girl that we had not yet met into the hands of half-giants. Oh, such hands! They taught me the reverence of time and neatness! Hands that come like limbs of lightning, striking here and there without a better reason than to strike! Strike! STRIKE!"

The ogre lashed out against the metal orb in which the sunlight had once been captured, and a great dent was made where it struck. It struck again. Again. Again. One final time, and then that dark device was wrenched from its socket, flung into the air a moment, then falling away toward the frozen earth below.

There was a tremendous crash, and the shattering of well-ground lenses reached its tattered ears like music.

"Why did we sell her then? We had not even known our sister dear. She was so small and yet so formless; seemed so pure. Now she slurs her speak at us as though she were a strand-robber. She was so delicate a creature. She was swaddled, brother! Swaddled was she. She was swaddled in the arms of our dear mother, Yrsa."

It sat there a moment longer, and then it saw, distantly oncoming already, the dark and seething tides of its brother's return. The beast sighed. It watched on. They came like a dark liquid, clad in crudely hammered coverings; bolted leather; loosely tied with rugged strings.

It watched on.

They came, imps at first; little forest goblins. Their pale flesh was dun against the snow, their braided furs were like a hasty imitation of the men that claimed this land; they were like children handed weapons and then lied to that they were warriors.

It watched on.

Then came the thrum of sounding battle-horns. The trolls, of stone once cleft, that now dwelt high in bridges, over waters they so feared, were marching forth. These were the masons which the ghouls had called to do the work which once their faithful grons had done. With mason-hammers, newly fashioned for war, they pushed by the ancient, leafless dendrons, each of their bridge-families sounding a dreadful trumpet into the cold air, bringing a new kind of chill upon it. Their large ears were only ornaments for all the noise of their rocky work. Their large noses were like misshapen accidents that twisted downward from their brows. Their eyes glimmered red, as though a fire rested far beyond their lenses, and 'twas true that not much more than fury burnt their busy minds — busy with bitter hatreds. All their skin was the dark and leathery hide of behemoths, cracked and hard, so that no ordinary knife could cut it. Were they to stand amidst the crags, none would recognise the danger that they posed. They would see only another tall stone. That is how faraway Athilan fell. That is how Athiluz fell also: mistaking trolls for stones.

Then the seething masses parted, as their master rode afore. He rode upon the dire wolf, a werewolf once, but now a beast alone; what of it had been man, had long been driven into the deepest lockbox of the mind by the fell hand that now sat astraddle it.

There rode Mathydras the deathless, astride that dire varg, its nose ever out for the droplets that the sun and moon let fall into the middle-earth, its eyes like frosted pits of death. There rode Mathydras, who had cast his brother from the cliffs, because he had at last foregone what once he'd thought to be the only thing of consequence: discipline. And, with just the same discipline, which now was burnt like dry ice into his deathless form, the dark-haired draug reined in his beast, and brought it to a halt. He looked through thin and thawless angles upward, to where his brother watched on.

It watched on. Then the ogre arose, and threw itself from of that height with reckless abandon. It thundered into snowy depths, splashing far and wide the debris of its landing. Then it arose, and came angrily timid to meet the mounted dark-mane.

"Why so grim, brother mine?" asked Mathydras in a voice like breaking glass. The angles of his features made him all the more dreadful as he sat there proudly, clothed in all manners like a raven's giant cousin.

"I w-want that you not b-be h-he- … here, brother," stuttered the ogre, not looking down into those pale eyes, trying to withhold its wrath.

"Here I am," said the other. Mathydras tilted his head just then, and observed his brother as though for the first time. "You are not yourself.

382

When did you win something scared of losing? Did I not draw enough of stony sternness from you there in the mountain pass?"

At this the defiance was awakened in the ogre, and it looked with sickly yellow into it's brother's eyes. "*She* is here, brother," said it.

"Who is *she*?" said the elder.

"She is your sister," said the younger.

"What matters it? You will not embattle well the walls of Glimmer-mead, if you do not devour her. If you shall not, then I shall send her to the half-giants, where surely they shall honour us for keeping to our word."

It was in this moment as though something in the monster broke, and it snatched up its deathless brother in its hands, marching unto the tower he had built, to harness sunlight in his youth.

"What are you about, brother Svæn! Release me! What is this madness?" demanded Mathydras, but he was helpless against the mighty paw of the ogre. Though he dug his sharpened gauntlets into the beast's bare flesh, the monster did not flinch.

"I admit my crimes, brother. I have slain you in my carelessness," rumbled the ogre as it pushed by the dark entrance, descending into the low dungeon at the tower's heart. There the two river-folk frighted in their cage, having been attempting to pick the lock. But the ogre had no care for such things. It was not hungry. It was not in the mood for visitors, either; it was tired, for once, of the nets and lies in which it seemed spun tight.

The ogre of Darkholt held the biting and scratching menace of Mathydras in its hand above the melalith at the middle of the room, then it said: "but you deserve a tombstone, my brother, not a soul-stone. Too long have you been prisoner here. You need your discipline no more, for there is no flesh to beat upon your bones. Be at peace." And, with this, it touched the dark-maned draug against the circle-stone.

The stone lit up, displaying all manner of tales and adventures, all manner of memories and struggles, all manner of victories and defeats. There was all the tragic life of Mathydras king's-son spun out like a tapestry. Then the light of the stone faded, and the hand of the ogre held nothing more than dust. Outside, above, the hordes that had gathered around the tower had begun a massive up-roar. The tumult that was going on without was causing the very earth to tremble.

Carbeth and Loangilin only watched in fear and loathing, as the monster, which they feared more than they ought have, fell onto its knees with weary groans and sighs, and then flat on its face.

"Is it dead?" quivered the voice of Loangilin, shuffling to where Carbeth had rushed against the bars.

"It is sleeping, my ears tell me. It still breathes," said he.

"Is that what it intends to do with us, do you think? Turn us to dust by touching us to that stone?" asked she.

"Look! The beast is shrinking!" cried the hunter of a sudden.

"So it is! What can this mean? Its furs are also crawling back it seems, and shedding. How awful! What could this mean? What does this all mean?"

With the monster shrinking away into its shedding furs, the sounds above became far worse, and things began to drum against the tower's walls.

Then a tremor went through the earth that had not been there before. It was steady, and commanding, and was followed by the distant sounding of a horn, the bass of which could not be measured. Not long thereafter the tumult of the hordes above began to quiet, and another sound struck against the stones. A westerly wind, but mightier than those that were natural, was drumming on the eaves. This sound remained, but all others faded in a while. Carbeth and Loangilin fell again into the sought out comfort of embrace, whilst their eyes darted this way and that in deepest discomfort.

In her bower, the highest chamber of the tower, Ystrith rose and went to see what calamity had come upon the woods. She saw the last dregs of the horde, to which she had closed her ears, slither away beyond the bare branches. The ground was sodden where a thousand-thousand feet had trodden. The trees were rocking and swaying in the new gale that had been swept up. Even the tower seemed to bend a ways in this tremendous breath.

"The Horn of the West-wind has sung," she uttered to her spirit, "but what does it herald?"

It was then that something else caught her eye in the snowy clearing surrounding the ogre's hillock. A large wolf baring its fangs was trotting this way then that, salivating at the mouth. It had caught some scent, she thought. Then a sudden steep roof seemed to push itself up through the white, like a spear shedding water. In but a moment, a little, smoking house had arisen from the earth, eerily cheery in this bleak landscape. A figure emerged from its front door, seemingly colourless, even in contrast to the brightling snows. In his arms, Noth carried the lifeless form of Folgnuin.

At once the wolf's attention was upon those newly emerged, it growled, lowering its heavy form onto the ground. Noth stopped and turned to face it. He had been headed to the door of the spire. The beast pounced forth into a charge, bounding barking at its prey, its eyes lingering hungrily on the body of the river-daughter.

Noth said only a word, however, and the beast ground ploughing to a halt amidst the powdery floor. Another word caused it to cower back some, its furry bristles standing on end. A last word, and the beast fled. Then the colourless man entered the tower, as though there had never been a threat.

"A varg," muttered Ystrith to her spirit. "And now it has the scent of the children of the moon here held. I must find them!"

A fright took a hold of Ystrith's heart, for she thought now also to know what Noth planned with the girl. She ran to the door of her bower, and found it unlocked to her shaken surprise. Her boots hammered down the course stone stair, as she welled around and down its spiral. She reached the tall front door, but it was open, and the snowy tracks which the colourless man had left led down into the dungeon and the tower's heart.

She bolted after like a blur. The walls of the circular tower, curled away before her sight, and then she came upon a confusion of things that her eyes could not at first discern.

Only when Noth turned to her did she recognise her brother, lying in the shed furs of his shed monster's frame. He was a man again — still tall, hairy, and mighty — but peacefully asleep, and no longer a giant with tusks. In a barred off cell beyond, she saw movement then, and recognised Carbeth and Loangilin, freeing themselves with a key that Noth must have handed them. As for the girl, she lay lifeless still upon the black, round stone.

"Do not do this, Master Noth, I beg of you! Do you not know what this here stone has done to my brother? Oh, my brother! What have you done that he is man again?" And she fell to cradle his sleeping head in her lap. "He lives once more, sleeping soundly like the simpleton he ever was. How can this be?"

"Your other brother, Mathydras, has been set free of the bonds that tied him to this stone," said Noth. "Svæn was so shaken by your despair that the lies in which he had woven his monstrous self came undone, and he took Mathydras, touching his draug to the stone here.

"Many years ago, Svæn slew Mathydras, who had built this tower. It was when your eldest brother had finally learned of peace. It was when he finally regretted bringing forth that daughter of the sun, that Svæn came here, and slew him. Now even Svæn has found peace, for he has finally acknowledged the truth of his crimes, and has given in to the just demands. He will live knowing that he has failed; but he will continue, knowing that it is better to acknowledge failure than it is to smother it with lies. In the shadow of lies, failures are only fed and nurtured. He will not forget this easily again."

"But what of the girl, Master Noth?" Ystrith asked.

"I will not make a draug of her. That is ghoulish craft. These stones have been perverted by those once-dwarfs. But the time is coming in which they will be cleansed. In that moment, she shall be revived. For now, you must go to Glimwæth, for the city is still under threat. The hordes that were under the charge of your brothers have been called back to the master that twisted them into their present ire. They go back to the King of Ghouls, from there he shall lead them himself unto the wooden halls of your fathers, Ystrith king's-daughter. Your work here is done, and it was done well, for behold: your brother is healed. I shall take him into my house a while, so that he may recover his strength."

"I thank you, Master Noth," she sighed, and sagged a moment into the shed furs surrounding her.

"We thank you for delivering us from this foul prison, master," said Carbeth, finally opening the gate. He laid the key onto the stone, Loangilin close behind.

"It is what I promised," said Noth, smiling. "There are horses that I ordered to meet you by the entrance of my home. Take those, and be sure to check their saddlebags, laded as they are with food and drink. It should speed you well enough to reach the hill for which you now must make. Make haste, the time is short, and every crafty hand will be a boon to them that are in dire need."

The three thanked him again, and then the king's-daughter and the two river-people made for the horses, which they found grazing near the entrance to the House of Noth. The heavy winds still tore across that snowy place.

"In this moment, we are as those that dream, surely!" gasped Carbeth at the sight.

"It does feel so," said Ystrith.

She looked at him. He turned, finally to look at her, golden hair like banner in the wind. At first his glance was hard against her teary eyes. Then he softened, and tears welled on his sight also.

"What has become of us, my wife?" he whispered.

"What must," she returned. "Can we become what we must together from this point?"

"It has been my dream for many a year now," said he.

They embraced.

Loangilin went to check the saddlebags of the horses quietly. When she was satisfied with what she found, she mounted up onto a grey mare, and said, "Ystrith, your people await!"

The hunter and the king's-daughter came suddenly apart, as though they were brought from a

safe distance into the sudden urgency of the moment.

"Thank you, Loangilin," said the king's-daughter, and she and her husband also mounted up, onto
the remaining horses. She sat upon a mare as well,
white as the snow beneath its hooves. Carbeth sat
astride a black stallion, the largest of the three
mounts. From there they set off quickly, for their
heartbeats were like dread itself, knocking smiling
at the doorway to their souls. All the while the
West-wind warred with their passage, a herald of
mountain weather.

Chapter Nine-and-Twenty
The Halls of the Dead

Glimwæth was alive, like a glittering anthill. The many spears and arrows that the Forge-bear had crafted were handed to whatever burg-man could wield one in the face of what fiends from the wilds they awaited. Archers were trained, and they were shown their posts along the ancient wall that circled the wooden city. Armours of tough leather were readied, and now it was seldom seen for a man to wander the cobbled streets without some form of war-gear. The helms and axes of fathers' fathers were cleaned of filming rust, and made to shine again like in yore days; in war days.

Every day the circling wall was well-dressed with watchers. Row upon row of them, all the while singing the war songs of their people. When they were not singing, they were hearkening to the shouts of their overests. Proudest amongst these was Gildolf, who would again and again speak on how this city had never fallen to the hands of such evil wretches as they would face now any day. The hunters of the river-people stood amongst those on the wall, many of their scouts and other warlike members of their people were handed spears and shown how to strike at enemies, were they to flood through battered gates or down the wall's stair-ways.

There were companies stationed at the entrances to every tier, trained even to hold these, should the beasts reach them. These bulwarks of men were set as guards beneath the dark shale roofs, all the way up to the courtyard beneath the mountain's nostrils. Here the carpenters and crafters of both river-people and Imnir's children had builded great ballistas that could fire in all directions except north, for that is where the cliff to the Nornburg blocked their way.

Here in the courtyard where the skalds had often plied their lyres beneath the oak, now stood other bows than those strung with horsehair. Here stood the mighty longbowmen, who would shoot their great arrows all the way into the hordes they knew would gather beyond the walls. They had been sent, in their brown threads, from the other side of Murmur-mere as a gift to King Vinnytlas, establishing a bond between him and the sons of Imnir that had settled in those lands after the usurper Harrowbert had taken them by bloody force. Their arrival here was a great aid, both to the force of their arms, as well as to the morale of the indwellers of the burg.

It was on such a day that the king gathered the women and the children, leading them into the halls of the dead, together with Authæn and those close to both their councils. The halls of the dead were great chambers within the hill of Glimmermead, for the hill was hollow since before the time of Imnir.

Thus, those that would not partake of the fray with more than fervent prayer, were gathered like flocks of hesitant and well-cowed sheep, bumbling in chattering clusters towards the courtyard of the oak. It was a strange moment, to see those dressed

for war stand back with reverence for those that
were clad in simplest cloth, bearing no more lethal
arms than baskets and blankets, breads and bowls,
to make their stay within the womb of the mountain a more homely one. Those that were most dangerous, the men of the city, were utterly disarmed
by the realisation that now they would fight for
more than mere glory.

This meek flock was then led by a narrow passage, skirting along a hillside that departed from
the courtyard under the oak of skalds. This passage
led into a tunnel, which in turn led to the great,
open hall in the bottom of the king's house, in
which he had passed the blade Birdsong into the
hand of Gaba.

Through the hall they strode, entering the
darker recesses of it at its farther end. Here a great
door of oak had been opened. It would be closed
with the arrival of their foe. Past the door they
were led down a stair into the great hollow in the
hill. It was very round, a great alcoving chamber
that reached up from where they had entered, dom-
ing in white stone (mayhap marble) to meet a natural wall of stone, coloured black by contrast. In
this stone wall there had been hewn many passages
and stairs, which led to the various beds of the bygone kings, queens, and thanes of Glimwæth.

A hush fell over the gathering for standing on
such solemn ground. The torches in this place remained ever-lit, shimmering against the polished
black and white stone that surrounded them. The
king, who stood in the middle of the room, looked
up at the many pathways in the black stone before

them, he stretched out both arms, as though embracing the stale air of this place. Then he turned to face the weaponless of his city. Many of the *mith-aumuinan* would also remain in these halls henceforth.

"Good women, dear children, and steadfast menders of body and bone, this shall be where you reside until our war is won. This is the safest corner of our home, and you are the most prized of our members. If we do not guard you, it would be to leave open the heart for a lethal strike.

"For this you, menders of the broken, shall also remain here, so that, where of the fighters fall, they can be carried to you, out of the way of battle. Some of your fellow healers remain near the fray, but these you yourselves have elected, for they are the best of you. There is nothing to fear, for the enemy cannot enter here, save they slay all of us. That shall not happen. This burg has stood longer even than Imnir's children have belived it. It shall stand even longer than his children *can* belive it, and never will they let it fall into the hands of dour ghouls!"

His mien was stern, his words seemed to test and confirm the surrounding stone as strong and sturdy, scattering against it like water breaking over cliffs. Then he continued: "You are safe here, dear ones. And we shall be safe in our craft of warfare, for the trained arm at work in its field is better than the mighty arm, idle for fear. Where our idle limbs have shivered in times of peace, you have warmed us, you have heartened us, you have healed our spirits with your gentle ways. But now comes a time of great violence and dire carnage. Be strong in the way that you have ever been: be meek."

When the king was satisfied with what he saw mirrored in the faces of those there gathered, he nodded, smiled, and departed from their midst — they parting to make way for him to leave.

When he had gone, the many women with their children began to look about and see what they would need, to make this hollow seem more homely, or at least make of it a place liveable for the days to come. A comfortable chatter alit on the air.

Some of the king's thanes departed then as well, however some remained to hear the word amongst the women and children, or to learn about the craft of the *mith-aumuinan*. Authæn had remained as well. He presently looked at Wingilin, who was marvelling in bewonderment at this stone chamber, turning slowly about where she stood to take everything in with wide eyes.

Eventually, she found him watching her, his face righted towards her, but his eyes far from this dim place. His features were tired; cold. She smiled at him, drawing him back into the present. He blinked and smiled back, but then his smile split his face into teeth and laughter. A little bewildered, she shook her head, and began also to laugh.

When he had recovered himself, he crossed the distance between them, and said, "You look like a child in a house of honeyed bakery."

"Ah," said she, nodding. "Now I understand your laughter. But look at this place, Authæn! You were the son of a carpenter, do you not sometimes wonder what he would have made of such places?"

His eyes dulled with distance again, and he then looked around the hall, as though for the first time. The smile across his face tightened, then faded entirely. "Did I even know my father, I wonder at whiles? He was a great man, Wingilin. I do not doubt it; but I think, more and more, it was because of the evil that he had seen. He saw great and dark things bend their mighty limbs along the fringes of the world, before I even was. I never knew the woman that he loved. I do not want to know her ... and yet he loved her enough to care for her son. He never enforced great designs on me, as some fathers will. He sought to hand me into the hands of ... greater potters, perhaps."

Wingilin's smile had gone from the dancing laughter of the eyes to that smile that knows and recognises the subtleties in another. "You were *his* son as well, Authæn. Not only that of your mother. He was always a wise and funny man to me. And for that I will never forget or cease to love him. Just as I will never cease to love you."

Authæn looked into her eyes again. "Thank you, Wingilin. Thank you for teaching me what love is; for teaching me that it resides where life is spent wisely, rather than where life is clung to with the grasp of the eagle."

"It was you that taught me it, Authæn. If you learned it likewise, I am glad," said she.

"You are wise as our shepherd's wife was, Wingilin," said the chieftain. Wetness spilled suddenly from his eyes, and he did not try to hide it, nor did he wipe it away. It trickled from one curve in his grey face to another, and then beaded along his beard.

"I am sorry that you lost her, Authæn," said Wingilin. "Not only did you lose the only true mother you had ever known in her, you lost also your father. Orphaned to the world. A wight left to the gales like a tumbling weed. How you grew into the mighty oak that now stands before me, I cannot even begin to dream up."

The tears rolled and rolled, and Authæn sniffed. "I was shaped by crafty potters," he laughed then, wiping his nose. "I am not here on my own two feet, Wingilin. These boots of mine are cobbled of all those that carried me here. Not least of which are you."

She took him in her arms, and together they stood thus. After a long while, Huthram stood before them with an understanding smile.

"You carry a heavy weight, brother," said he.

"You say I am heavy, my home?" said Wingilin threateningly.

"Ha! you have said so, heart," said he.

She let go of Authæn, sliding into her husband's embrace, and said, "Well, if I am heavy, my husband, then it is because I carry your child."

Both Huthram and Authæn turned to her with raised brows and open mouths.

"That is wonderful, my heart!" cried Huthram, catching her up in his arms, and spinning her about. His strength was steadily returning to him. Then they came to rest again, eyes closed; her head in his bosom, his chin resting on her dark hair.

"I think that the world would be a better place, if all parents were like you," said their chieftain.

"They are, my chieftain, if I may say so. They are all only people," said Huthram.

"Not all," said Authæn, after a moment. Then he bowed to them and was away.

He returned to the courtyard before the Forgebear's forge-works by the tunnel and the pass. When he reached it, he lingered a moment, admiring the oak that stood in its middle. Then Authæn strode out to the edge from which one could look down into all of the southern burg.

Suddenly, an icy wind swept in from the west. Authæn thought it pleasant at first, and then it thundered forth, as though all of the mountain lungs were pumping out their breath against the open plains. Behind him, he saw as he stumbled to catch his stance again, the heavy west-wind caused the oak to bow again and again, whipping back and forth its many fingers, like a skeletal worshipper of the east.

A man drew up next to him then; his robes fluttering like madness in the gale. It was the merchant called Jithron, who had travelled together with his village for the last stretch of their journey. They looked at one another. Jithron nodded a greeting. The other responded in kind. Then they looked out again into the preparations below. The wind had caused slight havoc there.

"You know that they hang criminals on that tree," cried the merchant over the wind after a long while.

Authæn turned slowly to frown at the other.

"I saw you admiring it just a moment ago. It caused me to think, how strange that we can admire what we do not fully understand," explained Jithron.

"And you wished to rob me of my wonder?" said the river-man in steely wise.

"Not at all, my friend! Not at all!" cried Jithron. "In fact, I do pray your pardon if that is what I have done. The matter is only that the nerves have me in their hold just now, where I would want to have them in my hold; and I would speak with someone to forget about their shivering. The tree greatly disturbs my nerves, you see. I saw such a grim purpose fulfilled by its mighty boughs once. A criminal was hung from there."

"What had he done?" asked Authæn, softening towards this fidgety fellow.

"Oh, it was years ago, my friend," said the merchant. "In that time I had not yet mastered well the tongues of you northern folk. It has haunted me ever since, I must admit. It seemed to me, from what I caught of it here and there, as though the man that was hung took the place of his younger brother. The man for whom the king's doom-hammer felled the judgement was not guilty of the punishment. His younger brother was. And yet he stepped in for his brother."

"That is not a tale oft told," said Authæn.

"Even less is it heard," said Jithron. "And yet there it was for the eyes to be seen. A dreadful sight. But that was not the worst of it. The brother for whom the weregild was paid by another's life was not even present at the Thing here held. He was no-where to be seen, and still his brother stepped forward to free him."

"I wonder whether the guilty brother ever heard of his freedom," said Authæn.

Jithron twitched his collar in a shrug. Together they continued to stand there and stare out into the vastness of the world ahead. There, in not too long a time, they dreaded to expect the hordes of the ogre.

"Thank you, Jithron," said Authæn.

"Wherefore, my friend?" asked the other.

"You have made of my wonder a deeper wonderment. Where before I only admired a tree for its size and strength, I now admire it for the role it played in this tale you tell. How brave must a man be to go willingly into his end, only for the sake of an unworthy brother. I wonder at this, and there is something of folly about it; and yet, where life is spent wisely, there love abides."

Chapter Thirty
Beyond the Brink: Oblivion

*Seven days to Smith's-wend (that is Sun's-ear),
the New Moon*

It is, to the day, a week before the feast of Smith's-wend. It is the darkest night, with new moon to mark a new month for the people of my mother. As for the people of my father, they measure their months by the coming and going of the sun — the one who welds daily the heavenly branches, that they not fall upon our heads. But the day is quickly waning; the wintry night is gaining. The sun is far in the south, and he shall not heed our call until the feast has come around. I know not when our enemy intends to strike, but I sit here at my writing desk, and I am not so certain of my fate. I say it thus: I am afraid!

I do not understand the ogre's charge, for he has let the banner flutter on this ominous west-wind for far longer than is custom, and it makes me wonder: what manner of warfare has he devised? Is it after his mind to turn us brother against brother as he once turned upon his own? Is it to starve us out? The granaries are full this winter, and that would be a difficult task. And now descends on us this moonless night. Is this the night in which we shall finally feel the rumbling of the earth, the gathering of hordes that mass before our gates?

What hear I even now?

I think I hear the rumble of a great many feet. I hear the rhythms of war in drumbeat. I hear the horns of the bridge-dwelling trolls that have come down from the heights. Who shall save us from their coming? What machines do they roll out before them, so that they might overcome our walls?

Even with the heroes that stand at our side, we have a difficult battle ahead of us. But now the time is come for me to end this writ, and to stand alongside my battle-brothers on the brink. This may be the beginning of never-ending nightmare in the north. Might we all endure the falling of this dark night.

Written in mine own hand,
k.scr., the Lion Pen-tooth

***

White fire fell from nightly heaven, but it did not rain. This was a dry fury in the clouds, which were flying like the narrow wings of wyrms on winds that battered westerly. The sound of drums and horns could be heard distantly over the plains and in the mountains, but nowhere could the masses of the enemy be seen. All the while, a signal beacon burned atop the Shoulders of Imnir, to warn that enemies were on their way. Of a sudden one of the watchers on the wall cried out: "Someone nears the gate! Three! They are long-travelled! Two are women!"

"Open the gate!" cried Gildolf.

"Below, where the gate was being unbarred and pushed out, a large troop was gathered, holding ready their spears, should this be some trick of the enemy. A runner was sent to where the king was saddled proudly on the great bear Yrsa. They stood at the hind of a great ring of ballistas, aimed all away from the courtyard of the smithy's nostrils into the dark without the city walls.

The king met the runner, and heard what he had to say, and he reeled back in anger at the news. "She dares!" roared the king, and at once made his way down the stair to the highway, and down this toward the newcomers at the gate. The Forge-bear, who had taken up the post near his brother-in-law, was quick to hurry after, astride an ordinary brown bear of his own.

The king's-daughter, and her river-folk companions stepped glumly from their horses, all of them surrounded, in their hearts, by betrayers. Yet still the guardsmen that were near, recognised the king's-daughter after a whisper had scattered through their ranks, and they took from her and from her company, the horses that had brought them here.

At this moment the king flew down into the stabled tier once more, though this time not on horseback, but on bear. The horses reared and neighed at the sight of the bears, and threw those that tried to hold their reins, and they bolted from the gate, just before it shuddered shut. They went on their way, fleeing from the approaching doom, no doubt.

"How dare you, girl!" roared the king. But his mount seemed somehow dazed by the woman that now stood before it.

The Forge-bear sprang from his own great beast, and ran to embrace his weary niece. He heaved her up in the air, twirling her about, so that her bearskin cloak swung madly in the spin. Then the metal-master let her down again, and said, nearing tears: "My dearest niece! I thought that never I would see you again! How come you here? What has held you from us?"

"I come here by horseback, uncle," said she dryly, smiling wryly. Then she drew something forth that had hung about her neck. "Here is a gift for you, uncle. A return for all that you have done for me."

She laid the vial of river-dragon blood into his open palm, and he, with waxing eyes, rejoiced loudly, clasping it to his breast, and dancing about in a manner that was awkward for all to watch, save the king's-daughter. She laughed.

As the Forge-bear opened and downed what well-preserved liquid was in the bottle, the king dismounted, and drew nearer his daughter.

"I asked you how you dare, girl!" repeated he, angrily.

She turned to face him with a visage of stone, and said, "Would you not rather ask how I fare, father mine?"

The shudder of a shadow flickered across the king's wroth features. "You speak like your brother, the ogre. Where is he, then? If, for all of your uselessness as a daughter, you may tell me where he is, *then* I—" Yrsa growled, and nudged her husband disapprovingly with her snout. He sighed, then said, "Forgive me, daughter. I am in throes of sorrow, as though it were an inescapable death."

"Sorrow can be, father. But be at peace, your son is an ogre no more," said Ystrith.

The great grey bear's head jerked up.

"You lie! You had not even your blade with you! How could you have slain him?" There was more of sorrow in the king's pained mean than victory, hearing of the ogre's defeat.

Somewhat taken aback, Ystrith said, "I did not slay him father, but how is it you know that I have lost my sword?"

"It was retrieved by the chieftain of the river-people that now surround you," said the Forge-bear.

"Oh, Ystrith, I am sorry. I have given it to Master Gaba; he that slew the Ibex in the east. I thought never to see you again. You … cause me such bitterness," there was a strange sort of conflict warring in the spirit of the king as he said this. "I wish you did not!"

Ystrith was shocked again. "The Ibex is slain? The Ibex horned… My captor is fallen?" said she. Stumbling towards the nearby pillar of a stable, she sought to steady herself. Carbeth came to aid her with an arm.

"And *you*," growled the king, his eye finally having caught sight of this most hated river-man in his kingdom. "Of you I will make a quick end!"

Of a sickening sudden, King Vinnytlas lashed his long war hammer in the direction of the riverman's head. But Carbeth was a quicker hand than the old greybeard, and he sped his own goblin's mallet to save his pretty face. The steel of the hammer struck soundly against the stone, bouncing back a ways, but the mallet shattered like a goblet of glass.

Carbeth stumbled back with a roar of pain, his hands clutching his eyes. Ystrith lowered the arm which she had used to shield herself from the spray. The shaft of the shattered hammer clattered to the floor as a new tremor of thunder rolled over the night-time world. She ran quickly to her husband, hovering over his now kneeling form with deep folds of concern about her weathered eyes.

"Enough, my king!" growled a familiar voice. Striding out from among the numbers of the riverpeople, Authæn drew near, and a before unseen anger seethed from him like the steams of an overboiling pot. Behind him strode two of the chief *mith-aumuinan*. These quickly went to tend to the fallen friend of their chieftain, whilst he, their chieftain, drew close to the huffing beard of King Vinnytlas.

"My king!" growled the river-man. "This is not the time for division. This man that you have struck has betrayed me also, but he has been so loyal a friend that it was no betrayal to me. If I tell you that there is no better man for your daughter, and no better a man to have on your walls this night than he, will you not let your ire pass him by?"

"Authæn!" gasped the king's-daughter, having been pushed aside by the tidy *mith-aumuinan*. "It *is* you!" There was some manner of fear in her eyes that he had never seen there before.

"Ystrith," said he in acknowledgement, but there was no warmth to his tone.

"I see the sense in your words," said the king with a great effort. The wrath still burned in his eyes. There was another thing in his visage, however. He regarded the young chieftain before him with a dim amusement. "It is sense you speak, yes; save that now this man is wounded, and not so worthy of the wall. Have your healers pull him back into the hall of the dead. There they may ply their craft without worrying over the onslaught that we await so near the bulwark."

Authæn gave the command. Then he broke from the king, and embraced Loangilin, glad to see her alive. He led her to the hall of the dead, where she might wash and rest a while, where there was food and fresh clothing. She was not a woman made for warfare, she had often said, and as they walked she said so again. "I know, Loangilin. I know," said Authæn grimly. "You should rest. Your works have helped prepare the road to this night, and whatever the outcome, it has made of us all better folk. Wingilin awaits you whither I lead."

As for Ystrith, her uncle came to her again, and he said: "Come, my niece! I have a surprise for you, though it was tailored first for a man. Not for me, mind you! I am too large to squeeze into that tightly fitted framework. Come along now. No! No questions, girl, just come!"

She followed, shaking her head, permitting her uncle his insolence, for he was likely only giddy with his gift. How he had told her tale after tale of what he would do once he had this birdsong brandy in his gullet.

Atop the walls, Gaba and the gron had been watching. Beside them stood Huthram. He was strong again, but not near the strength he had once possessed. Around them were the spears and helms that shimmered red in the firelight. The chains of the linked mail sang with the many movements of their battle-brothers.

Then the Lion Pen-tooth made his slow way to join them.

"Many historic things have met in this city over the last month," said he.

"And now the month is new," muttered Huthram.

"Ugh," said the gron.

"What is this, Grin? Do your nerves clench you?" chuckled Gaba.

"No, Hamathian," said the gnome. "I simply do not want to think of the moon on the one night in which she is not in the heavens. Let her sleep. Her appearing has brought much horror for my people."

"You have been tight like this for much longer than only now," said the southerner.

"Yes," sighed the gron. "I have felt the shudder of their approach in the stone, and there is something about it that is not right. It feels …" The gron moved quickly to the battlements, clambering lithely into their embrasure.

Dry lightning again.

They listened a moment, all of them, for they had heard it also. The sounds of the approaching army were fading, growing muffled, and diminishing; and still they could not be seen.

"Could it be that they do not know where our city lies and have walked away instead of towards?" muttered Huthram.

"If that is true, we may desire to douse the torches. If they truly have no knowledge of our placement here on the hill, they shall not see us in the dark from so far away," said Gaba.

"I doubt that they have forgotten the city of the usurper," said the Lion.

Grin suddenly leapt down between them again, and scurried off along the wall. He descended the stair that led into the fore-burg. From there he hurried by the many moving warriors towards the nostrils of the mountain.

"Remarkable, how fast he moves for so small a one," said Huthram.

"Indeed, we should hurry to follow after! That creature knows our enemy better than we, I think," said Gaba.

"Douse the fires!" said the Lion of a sudden. He turned to the other two who had begun to move already, but had stopped now, surprise drawing together their miens. The Lion explained: "It is just a precaution. If what you say is true, Master Gaba, then we may have an advantage over them with this darkness in familiar land. They have known only mountain tunnels and river bridges. They shall now also learn fear of the dark which they've so long inhabited."

"If you think it wise, Master Pen-tooth," said Gaba. "Though your former thoughts seemed also sound to me."

As the three then sped after the gnome, the lights within the city faded one by one; like rings in a pool, the darkness fell on Glimmer-mead.

"They cannot take this city!" cried Gildolf from somewhere near the gate. "This is the wooden city of Imnir! This is the proud place of the bear, and both our king as well as his daughter still dwell in its lofty hall!"

The men roared their assent. Then a tense quiet fell, and utter shadow.

As the three behind the gnome came rushing up the stair into the courtyard beneath the nostrils of the smithy, the lightning fire lit again the world all round, and they shied a moment in surprise as a woman approached them, ebon-ivory in her attire.

She wore a scaled armour, a mail coat which fitted well, with bone as plates surrounding. The helm that dressed her brow just then was more fearful than the rest, for the Forge-bear had assembled the broken shards of the Ibex's skull-like visage, having cut short and filed down the heavy horns to nothing more than neutered stubs. One recognised Ystrith only by the golden locks of hair that still splayed over her shoulders like the mane of a willow.

Still, this was a frightening spectre in hither dark, and Gaba was reminded of the Watchers that he had so long ago left on their signal hill. He wondered even now — and now suddenly with dread — whether their lights still burned; alone, drawing undesired enmity. He spun about to seek that hillock to the east of the city.

Meanwhile, The Lion bowed before his king's-daughter, Huthram only staring stunned awe at the fearful work of smith-craft. All around the Long-bowmen of the south were nudging one another and whispering with quiet wonder. Even the king, who had returned to watch the battle from here above, was silent with regard.

"You look more frightful than any draug would ever dare, king's-daughter. I am without proper words," said the Lion.

"That from you, oh Pen-tooth, is the greatest of words. But now is not the time for warmth and welling of the eyes. Let us to war, my friends."

"My king's-daughter," said the Lion before she could depart, however, and the faceless visage that masked her fair countenance turned to bear down upon him. "I offer thee this, the blade of Athilan that fell. It will serve thee almost as well as that which thine uncle forged thee. If nothing more, let it be proof that I have more than just pens for teeth." And he unbuckled the scabbard from his waist, holding it out towards her with both hands.

"Ha! Perhaps there is a greater thing than speechlessness that you can offer, dear Pen-tooth. I would not have known to look for your kindness, but... it rivals even that of my uncle," said the king's-daughter, perhaps even welling tears behind her mask. She took the sword, bowed curtly, then departed, not glancing backwards even once.

411

The southerner returned to the other two, he had seen no light on the eastern horizon. The elderly couple that had so kindly taken him in, had likely taken to dousing their own fires at night since that time it had been done for them with a boulder.

"You give away your right arm, writer?" asked the southerner.

"I will find another among the racks below," said he. "I am skilled enough to recognise when a kingly gift is better than a clingy arm."

Suddenly a clamour arose from within the great nostrils ahead of them.

"There is no secret passage here, little goblin! This has been the forge of the Forge-bear for seven generations! It has gone from father to son, to son's son since it's very beginning!" issued the shout from within the blacksmith's workshop. The Forge-bear was not so pleased with the gron's visit, it seemed.

The three entered quickly, coming upon a dizzying scene. Nine gnomes were flying about the room on their fast-flitting little feet. They were tapping, listening, seeking for any sign of what must have been a doorway. "There must be some weakness in this place, there must be!" the many Grins were singing in a strange chorus of bewildering desperation. All the while, the Forge-bear tried to keep the little creatures from his most precious works and tools.

"What is this, Grin? What are you doing?" demanded Gaba angrily. "We brought you here to aid us, is that not what you promised the king? Why do you cause this uproar now? The enemy is nigh upon us!"

"They *are* nigh, south-man! They *are* nigh!" said the many little Grins.

"Then why are you doing this, has the battle-dread waylaid you?" asked the Lion, shaking his head in similar ire.

"No! No, no. No! You do not understand, gentlemen! You do not understand!"

"What is it we do not understand? How can we know without hearing what it is that you mean? How can we hear without your speaking?" said Gaba.

Suddenly the grons all stopped, looking up at the southerner.

"That was a good point," said one, looking at his neighbour. The neighbour-gron nodded in stunned agreement. From near the forge, beside a huffing Forge-bear, one of the Grins then said, "They dig now through the earth. They are moving by great tunnels on towards us. They shall emerge within the city, and we shall fall into their clutches like a wingless dove, falling into the open maw of a wolf! The mole-trolls are come, and they undermine this place we thought a bastion impregnable."

413

Chapter One-and-Thirty
Break Open Tides of Abyss

There was no time. Around them it seemed to have
been drained from the air, like a spider drains vam-
piric of its victims; like a drunkard drains his cup.
All the city had been righted for a war against the
outer walls, but now their fiendish foe would rise
upon them from beneath, tearing them down into
hidden depths. The city was dark as well, they had
only strengthened their enemy with all their 'cunning plans'.

The Lion Pen-tooth hurried to his king in the
courtyard. The west-wind drummed ever against
the tall oak that stood there.

"My king!" he cried against the gale.

The king turned to face him.

By the silver starlight, past the mottled clouds
above, a question was traced faintly on his brow.

Then a great crushing sound drowned out the
wind, and everything with ears and eyes was
pressed to spin its attention toward the noise. In the
fore-burg below, a great cloud of dust went up,
painting much of what could hardly have been seen
before with a thick grey fog. Only moments after, a
dreadful screaming, wailing, and then roaring issued forth, the earth shuddered, now and then, heralding the heaving works of mighty-limbed mole-
trolls from the deep.

"My king," the Lion repeated, now clear of
mind once more, for the worst was upon them, and

414

all that was left was to face it. "They have bur-
rowed through the earth, they are upon us!"

The king's face waxed with fear, then waned
and became as sweating stone in the night.

"Fire," said the king. "Light again the fires!
Aim downward the ballistas! We light up that below! Let the trolls shy in memory of the sun!
Winter is nigh upon us, and then the sun's return;
but he *shall* return to our heavens, and they shall
not forget it! *FIRE*!"

The longbowmen were already at work, seeking what of the embers still glowered in bitter defiance against the waters that had doused them. New
dried offcuts were added. A blaze of light took up
again the higher tiers of the city. Then, bound with
pitch, the bolts of the ballistas were set alight, and
in not all too long a time, these fired one volley
into the place from which they thought the burrow-
ing beasts must have emerged. The bolts went
forth, one after another in quick succession, so that
it was like fire raining from above into the murky
smokes below.

"There the enemy will be in their thickest
knots! Fire again!" commanded the king. "As for
you, my friends, with me; we go down to meet
them with our warcraft!" He had said this looking
at the company that had emerged from the nostrils
of the hill.

At once they joined him in his hurrying, descending to the place where the fires were being directed. They must have struck the correct place, for
the great bolts of the ballistas had been seemingly

swallowed up by darkness, their fires not spreading into the city.

As the rest of the city began now to follow the lead of the upper burg, fires began to flare to life again along the walls and in places where the now visibly teaming bodies of their enemy had not yet overwhelmed the forces of Glimwæth.

On their flight into the fore-burg, the king rallied those that were frightenedly scattering near the entrances that were in need of strong defence.

"Hold!" cried the man upon the bear, and the word went through the city, itself like the burning of dry twigs. "Hold! Do not go fading into darkness, like the dying breath of sparks! HOLD AGAINST THE DARKNESS! You are all the bulwark against the foe! Be fire! Burn brightly till the last!"

Suddenly, from out of corners before unknown, it seemed a great host of these sons of Imnir thronged about their king, descending as one into the murky dusts of war.

Then they were upon their enemy; imps with their crude weaponry and cruder still their chivalry. A terrible biting and scratching came upon the sons of Imnir, but their stout leathers, and here and there their mail hauberks, staved mostly bitter teeth away.

Spears plunged and stuck, and came away, and plunged again, and now would cut when drawing back. And then they were cast desperately into mounting ranks of heedless hordes beyond the front, replaced by brazen axes, bearded, broad of blade, or any other kind, to hew and heft away against the dying of the light.

There the blades and screams and spouts of blood, both black and golden-red, were the very draught of life; the giving of it like so many tireless sparks that grind away from grindstone into hay, and set ablaze those that had never known the heat of battle. The men did war against this dreadful foe that bit and hacked and hammered down on them with malice dark. All the while their king was in their midst, his mighty hammer never clearer than a blur of whirling steel and broken bones. It sent forth flying teeth like gravel stones; his mighty limbs, long shivering in idle hall above, now flung themselves with expert's ken of war and wrath against this horde of cruel creatures small.

Just then, the dusts were clearing, and the scale of the battle they had waged began to show itself, stretching all along all streets that met the eye. The highway, once of cobbles, now was cobbled new with the lifeless figures of the fallen. And this, all the more, drove those that looked upon their fallen brethren to war, and war, and war against that terribly tenebrous black maw which stood afore. A great hollow had broken away just behind the two inns at the entrance of the city. There some buildings and a portion of the highway had fallen into that dark hole, and it was like ten torn mouths, that had stilled their hunger whilst devouring one another.

Just then, as morale was at its zenith, a great many shadows, far larger than the imps, arose from the gaping hole, and drums of crooked war were hammered into the deep wells of beneath.

"What be these new devils that arise like mountains from there-nether?" cried Gildolf desperately.

"Those are the mole-trolls, gate-man!" returned the many voices of the gron, which spoke like scattered glass from amidst the fray. "They are those that tunnelled these deep roads, and now they come to swallow up your city by the earth! We must fall back, and catch them from clever hiding places, king of bears!"

The king heeded the gron, now taken with the clear note in the gnome's command. "Fall back! All fall back! Return to hold aright the gateways of the upper tiers. Do not let them enter there! Think of your women and your future heirs! This was all theirs to inherit, now it is fallen! Fall back! Return to the holding of the passageways!"

Again as one, but now with dread, the sons of Imnir scattered from amidst the fight — save here a one, or there a one, who had decided rather to be fading spark than spared. Along the way the scattering imps were hewn aside, even these dark creatures seemed to know to flee before the vast and lumbering beasts that now emerged behind them in the haze.

The clever engines up above were heard again to shower down upon the breach, and great roars as those of dire monsters were heard to moan the complaint of death too early found.

"Might those engineers of war never hear the end of songs sung to their glory!" cried the Forge-bear then. He himself wielding a great axe with both his hands, as he rode alongside his brother on his bear.

"Only let us survive this war first!" cried the scrivener, who was running near at hand.

"Why, when you say such things, Pen-tooth, it makes me want *at once* to sing!" bellowed the Forge-Bear. And just so he did, and the men cheered as his newly wetted whistle was sent forth to bound against the wooden houses of their home.

Hear oh hear,
Brothers of the fore-burg:
Bent were bows
That let rain down fire from heaven.
In dark north,
Where the winter draweth over,
Hail sunlight, brought by fire bright;
From above the ballistae!

Then the company surrounding the king was up above again, in the court of the skald's oak, and they looked down on what the city revealed to them. There the men were bravely holding back the waves of forest goblin that pounded against them like a foamy sea. Some of the mole-trolls that were slowly emerging from their self-made passage had been slain by the ballistas, but more were now arising than the machines could hold back in time.

In the halls of the dead, the women and the children had been quietly busied with thoughts of the

419

men on the walls and in the burg. The *mith-aumuinan* had been caring for the sick that could not battle. One such healer was tending to Carbeth. The hunter had fallen into the senselessness beyond pain, and slept.

Not far from where he had been brought to be attended, Loangilin sat, weeping into the shoulder of Authæn. Too many were the reasons for her tears, so that words could not help her now; her sorrows must be wrung dry by less wordy means. He only sat there, holding her, wondering what all she had suffered since he had seen her last, trying not to wonder where Folgnuin was.

That time so long ago, when last they had seen one another. It was a time in which the great opposing threat had been the Ibex. There they had had the mighty staff of Gaba on their side, but the staff was no more, and now they waited for war to break on them, in which only the skilled arms of ordinary men and a single gnome could save them. So it seemed: dire.

Suddenly a great shuddering brought dust to rain down from the ceiling of the cavern, and there was a great commotion among those gathered there. Someone screamed, but most were pressed quiet by the heavy hand of dread.

Authæn rose to his feet. The doors to this hall had not yet been closed. Then a distant hammering reached their ears, and children began desperately to cry.

Authæn made his way through the gate, stalking carefully through the passages and the dark hall, at the other end of which the great opening into the north lay. There the white of the mountains greeted his eyes, and the shimmering of stars betwixt scattering clouds. The hammering sounded again, now somewhat nearer, and he guilefully looked over the balcony's rail to see something out of a dream.

He slid down at once, his back to the rail. He shivered and felt much colder than only a moment before. There was wetness on his brow. His eyes were wide. Then he dared look again at the city wall below, and indeed, it had not been another of his dreams. There stood great figures on the wall; the smallest of which was the size of the great Ibex only recently recalled to mind.

The city had fallen into utter darkness, though presently the fires on the walls were rekindling, and Authæn wondered what all had happened since he had entered the hall of the dead. The fires burned only up to a point, leaving the northernmost parts in shadow. Cries of alarm could be faintly heard to trickle from the stations of the braziers. Then he saw that these great monsters, with ears like the wings of giant bats, and skins as creased as stone, had mounted and begun hammering down the ancient walls from above. They wielded hammers unlike any the river-man had seen before. There were dozens of them.

The bridge-trolls had come in from the north. Beyond the wall, Authæn now saw, there massed a great force of goblins as well. The assault had begun, but it had come to the weakest part of the city!

Quickly he rushed for the courtyard at which the king had stationed himself. The word had to reach King Vinnytlas as soon as was possible. He went by the secret door, and by the tunnel that led to the skirting passage. Thence he finally emerged to the heavy singing of both ballistas and bows, for both the engineers and the well-trained longbow-men were letting now their art into the burg below.

Like one lost in an unfamiliar land, the chief-tain stumbled nearer. From his right, the captain of the Longbowmen approached.

"Chieftain?" said he. "You are not a warrior, what do you seek here?"

The eyes of the river-man still sought what lay beyond the rim of this cliff, whence he and Jithron not so long ago had looked into a burg which was quite different then from what he now saw there below. Great clouds of smoke and dust, and the bit-ter desperation of battle moved there. The king and his brother-in-law were at the fore of the fray, astride their mighty war bears. Huthram fought with spear, then axe, as did all the other men about. The gron had split into all nine of his shapes, and they were doing pretty damage. The merchants were there as well, and the Lion Pen-tooth, but without his sword. Then Authæn even saw the an-cient blade, but wielded by a frightful lady garbed in ebon-ivory, whose golden locks betrayed her as the daughter of the king. From the walls, the arch-ers fired down into the fight; spears were hurled. All the while the longbowmen fired into the pit whence the goblins sprawled, whilst those man-ning the ballistas loaded another volley of bolts into their devastating engines.

Then a heavy hand recalled Authæn to where he stood, and a weathered face within a hood cast a shadow over his sight. Remembering the captain of the longbowmen, he said: "There are trolls along the northern wall, captain."

"Trolls along the northern wall? Have they breached it?" demanded the captain of the long-bowmen.

"They stand atop it, picking it apart with their great hammers," said Authæn.

"Men!" cried the captain at once. "We go to the northern walls! It is time to hunt renown by making pincushions of some bridge-trolls with our bows!"

The longbowmen cheered heartily, and then they gathered their things to do just this, leaving the ballista-men to explain their absence to the king. Authæn led them speedily along the way which he had taken to deliver his message, and they came again to the great, open-ended hall beneath the Nornburg that led to the halls of the dead. Thence they began to right themselves, establishing their great quivers for the task ahead. Below the trolls still hammered at the walls.

"Those are mighty fellows," said the captain. "They grow larger here in the north, it seems. Nock!"

The longbowmen nocked.

"Aim!"

The longbowmen took aim.

"Loose at will!" he cried, and took up his own longbow. A first volley was sent down against the brutes.

"Easy to hit for all the size to them, captain!" commented one of the longbowmen. The captain laughed, and loosed an arrow of his own.

Below, the trolls had begun to groan and flinch where the arrows struck them. Such mighty darts not even their thick hide could ward against; it was not as stony as that of their mole-troll cousins.

"They are not dying, captain!" cried another of his men.

"We have ever been there more to break rank than to slay, man. Pincushions, we said, pincushions; at least make them waken tomorrow with a stiffness to remember, if you cannot make a mortal end for them. For the Hills of Min! For our home!"

"For the Hills of Min!" cried the longbowmen.

It was then that one of the *mith-aumuinan* emerged from the halls of the dead, and approached his chieftain.

"Chieftain," said he. "What has happened? The gate is yet unbarred, the women and children are frantic. Nothing is as has been prepared!"

"They are upon us, brother," said Authæn. "We shall have to close the gate now, on our own. Return to the women and children. Tend to the sick. That is where you are needed. I will ask one of these fine men to aid me in shutting you in."

At this the nearest bowman said: "I will go with you, quickly now! I'd still try to strike one of these bridge-dwellers in the head, if I can catch the heavy wind correctly."

Authæn and he followed the healer to the oaken door. When the healer had entered, the bowman aided the chieftain in pushing the iron-bound shutters to. Then they raised a great sleeper to bar it from the outside. The way out was shut. Their hope was in the strength of their fighting men now.

Chapter Two-and-Thirty
Rendered Wordless

Aface of the mighty mole-trolls, the strength of the fighting men was failing fast. These beasts would cleave away both wood and stone as though they were of sand. Their mighty tine-like claws could crush three men at once, their rocky hide could not be split by aught, save the ballista bolts; and those were all but spent. Far too quickly, the entrances to the higher tiers of the city were falling into the grasp of the foes of Imnir.

From above, the king watched. The name of his father hung on his features, for he was harrowed then. Vinnytlas Harrowbert's-son he had once hight, and that name returned to him now as he looked on the vengeance which he thought was sent against his father's works. In part this may have been true.

The fore-burg was all but destroyed. Most of the horses had been slain, the wagons and carts rent asunder. The slopes leading to the Styg ov Baugwera were not much more than disordered heaps of rubble.

Then one strode out amidst the carnage, climbing up to mount the highest height below. Onto a hill of broken house that stood above the rest, a woman strode, clothed in death's dress. She was Ystrith king's-daughter — king's-dishonour — now perhaps returned in order to return what she had robbed her father of in years that lay long lost.

High she held the blade of Athilan, and it caught the red light of the flames surrounding, and a ring came off the metal as the high ringing of a bell. All eyes, both those of man and monster, were drawn to her at this. Then spake she, her voice carrying through the metal mask she bore, down towards the very edges of her city.

"Who dares stand against the Ibex reborn!" she challenged. The imps scattered from before her, fleeing back into the great chasm which the mole-trolls had wrought, relieving much of the fighting. It seemed that the Ibex had not only been a menace among men, but even among his own ilk.

The mole-trolls, however, were not wise enough for fear, and one that stood near lumbered aggressively towards the dread lady. It raised its talon high, growling out a massive scowl, then slung its arm towards her. She, however, was too fast, and not only ducked aside, but also severed whole the thick limb of the beast, so that is stumbled back, stunned, holding fast a stump of fore-arm with eyes larger and more sighty than those of any mole-troll had ever been before or would be after. It gurgled a confusion, and its brethren hesitated for the first time that night. No sword, they thought, would cut them — not to mention maim or kill.

She was fully with their thoughts, and desired only to grow them in their fear, and so Ystrith sprang upon the chest of the troll whose arm she'd lopped, looking deep into its horror-stricken gaze, and planted the legendary blade into its very middle with a final thrust. It fell back, and she re-

427

mained atop it with the balance of a cat. Up went the blackened sword of her, and the irons of all the men that watched. A shout of revival coursed through all of those that fought for Glimwæth.

"Dragon slayer! Troll slayer! Dragon slayer! Troll slayer!" went the call, and as it thundered on the heavy west-wind, the trolls began to cower at the drawing near of men, that until then had been no more than meaty ants to them.

In a desperate move, another mole-troll dashed against the forces of Glimwæth that were trying to press them back towards the grave which they had dug themselves. It charged near where Gaba stood, and he did not hesitate, seeing what power the blade of the king's-daughter had held, to trust the blade with which he'd been bestowed.

He charged right back at the beast, and its little eyes danced onto him with fury. It struck out, with its hand, but he merely gripped the hilt of Birdsong fast, and split its claw in twain. All the way to the elbow went the cut, and the creature roared in disappointment and in shame, falling at once to its knees with the fright of what had befallen it. Then its horned head was heft from its shoulders, dropping like a sack of bricks to the rubble beyond. And Gaba pounced towards the next victim of the blade he sought to test. In not too long a time the king was also in the fray, and the Forge-bear, and their bears were there as well. The spirit of the trolls was broken, and they fled now also into their deep birthplace to the bold cheers of men.

All hearts and hopes were high, the mighty arm of Imnir had proven itself again, after so long a time of warless shivering. The men were roaring, weeping, crying out their praise to the brave heroes and to themselves. They had won the battle, they had driven away the beasts!

But their cheering came too soon. Their haughty songs, which only just began to sing themselves, were soon to be put down; for then another sound issued from the crevasse around which they had gathered in their pride.

A scream, like that of the air itself tearing, rent through the blasting winds, and of a sudden these winds that had battered the north since the sounding of the West-wind's Horn ceased.

Crystal is a moment, when all that once was moving has suddenly grown still — immobile. So one might have thought this moment, were one to have looked upon it, were one to have been in it. The confident had ceased their chirping, the mountain air had ceased its sighing, the overjoyed had ceased their crying, for the world was holding its breath, anticipating the plunge. In that moment, all eyes were suddenly drawn to the great fissure in their midst.

Something black glittered in the darkness there below, something that, as it moved, unveiled itself to be a beast far larger than what nightmares would have conjured. They did not know that it was the many-legged Gruttin, the pet of the King of Ghouls himself. They did not know what it then did, for their minds were far too broken by the fear of it.

The Gruttin burst from the shadows with another rending scream, its smooth, scaled body swishing and swirling like an ocean unleashed on a gathering of wareless drunkards. Crushing tens upon tens, before it had even ceased to move. And only did it stop, when its eyes were fast on the daughter of the king that bore a helm known well to it.

There the Gruttin lowered itself, revealing that a figure — not too large — was roosting crookedly upon its back on a saddle made of unseemly leathers and black metals. This figure arose, striding over the sharp head of its spiny mount, until it stood just above the panting daughter of Imnir, poised along the ridge of the Gruttin's armoured nose. There it stood, a grim figure, garbed in black, armoured thus as well: black in the kind of the broken helm that fearful Ystrith now bore upon her head. There were no horns along the ridge of this stout creatures hooded crown, however. In it, all features seemed to try and melt downward in precise squares of rippling smithwork. No blade would find an easy purchase here, for this was armour shaped for glancing blows.

"I have slain wyrms before, dark dwarf, your beast shall share their fate!" cried Ystrith hoarsely.

It stared a long moment at her. Only the flames could be heard in the silence that followed, and the grumbling lungs of the Gruttin.

Said the black dwarf in a voice like wind through many mountain passes, in a tone just bare enough to hear across all that place, and yet reminiscent of a whisper from behind a beard; said the black dwarf slowly, as though each word that fell was with the most destructive of intention: *"This is no wyrm."*

The blade of Athilan clattered to the floor, where it had been held, somehow, in the hand of the dragon slayer but a moment before. She stepped back, as though losing her footing for an interval; yet the rocks beneath her armoured boots were sturdy as a foundation of stone.

The world had become a place of dread from a place of delight in the twinkling of an eye. How all can crumble, in a careless batting of the lids, was a lesson hard to learn, and yet who could bear the blame?

Ystrith shook herself, then, and took up the ancient sword again. Looking on it she remembered the great kindness of the Lion Pen-tooth; she remembered the wounds that her father had inflicted on her husband; she remembered the torment of her brothers, and the death of dear Folgnuin. She remembered *vengeance*!

"I will sheer you of that precious wool, dwarf! Then I shall wear it as my own!" she growled with lessening effort. The bear's blood was boiling in her, and she seemed at that moment to grow a match for the terror from the deeps. Had she not defied the laws of the world before? Could not what had been once be everlasting?

"*Pretty last words,*" said the black dwarf, then it leapt down from the snout of its pet, onto the pile of building beneath. It strode toward the battle-ready lady; but nearing her, she could not move her arms. The dwarf let its talons glide along the steel of the blade as it drew right near the daughter of the king. Again, the ringing of high bells scattered

431

from the sword, but no light was in it now; only a cold darkness.

"*Good metal,*" remarked the dwarf, and then it took her by the mail of her breast, and flung her to the floor. It raised its talon up, and there the men now saw that it was fiery aglow, as though the gauntlet had been brought forth from a forge only heartbeats before.

Then, in the least graceful and most careless motion, the dwarf dragged back the head of the girl by her hair, tearing the helm from her head, and casting it aside. There it revealed a tear-streaked and horror-bitten face. With the gauntlet that was not alight, the dwarf grabbed for her mouth, but she resisted. It took her by the midriff of her hauberk's scales, picked her one-handed up, and slammed her coughing against the stones there, then grasped again at her mouth. She resisted once more, and this time the dwarf simply forced the long tines of his metal glove between her teeth, until the muscles of her jaw were too worn out to ward against them. He let his brightly glowing glove reach cleanly down into her throat, to snip, then come away from screaming woman's maw, holding up for all to witness: a seared muscle in his hand. The tongue of Ystrith.

Suddenly, as though breaking from a waking dream, the king roared and charged astride his once-wife bear to do his vengeance for the only daughter he at last realised he could lose. The hammer came against the gauntlet of the dwarf, who threw the old man from his beast. The beast it simply grasped with its burning claw about the throat. It severed the gullet of it in one clean pinch of the talons, and it fell by-side, gurgling out a final growl.

"*The hammer of Imnir,*" said the black dwarf. "*Once, men called this the Maul of the Bear. I had planned for the ogre to receive it when he came into his rightful rule. But this sow, your daughter, woke him from the dreams that he was so very good in crafting for himself. Guilt she made him feel, little king. Do you feel guilt?*"

"What are you?" screamed King Vinnytlas, looking about him at the remnants of his family. "Svæn yet lives," he suddenly said to himself, nodding. "Svæn yet lives." Then a calm spread on his features like sleep. He breathed a sigh, and arose stiffly before the ghoul.

"*I am the King of Ghouls,*" said the black dwarf. "*Your reign is at an end.*"

Then King Vinnytlas Harrowbert's-son lowered his head, and the Maul of the Bear struck the life from him.

The hammer was cast aside, as though it were nothing more than a twig in a forest. Then the black dwarf took up the reforged helm of the Ibex in its hands. It chuckled, glancing a moment through black metal at the kneeling Forge-bear.

"*Crafty,*" said it. "*But I shall return it to its former glory.*" Then it looked at Gaba. "*And that is when you shall receive a crown, Gabazi kadonazd-Manutuz, to rule the south. For that is what you desire. Your queen shall be chained to your ankle, to be your lowest whims eternal slave; those that you once called brothers will be hounds to do your*

*beck and call. The secrets of the south shall all
flow into your lap, and finally the deserts of Olam
shall be conquered. You seek an Unthing forged by
ghouls to sit idly in the tomb of your fathers? I
think it better you wield an Unthing forged by
ghouls as you take up what rightfully is yours by
birth. You are the last son of Manutuz, you shall be
the first king since he has passed into ancient tales.
I look forward to our next meeting."*

The King of Ghouls mounted the Gruttin once
more, and then it slithered back into the deeps that
had unleashed it like a hungry tongue, moving
along atop its thousand-thousand clawed feet,
swinging up a sting like that of a gargantuan scor-
pion before being gone, and not the sound of it was
heard. Such horror had made of those brave souls
there gathered, hollow wreckages that now could
only hark and hear the groaning of their tongueless
king's-daughter, who once had spoken so bravely
to embolden them, and now would speak nevermore.

Part IIII:

of the   Brea
king

and   Welding

of Circles

Chapter Three-and-Thirty
See Not, Say Not

Red upon flickering red, and somewhere to the side what remained of a house fell away into a cloud of cast up ashes, silently. There was no sound made by all those empty spectres that now strayed by his sight. His hands that stared so vainly into smoky heaven, where once so many eyes would have looked back, but now were far too smirched with clouds of coughing white, were like two stones of forgotten hatred.

And all about the scene fell a gentle ash from those careless heavens; they the remains of what had been the fore-burg of Glimwæth; of home. There the husk, there the hollow, of what had once been the home of the Forge-bear; oh, dear Forge-bear now so drear! There, upon the threshold of madness knelt this Forge-bear, like a wight left to be a tumbling weed amidst the winds. But the winds had subsided, and his hearing began to return to him. The snapping and crackling of the hungry red upon flickering red.

The heavens were drowned in the heavy curls of sateless apathy, their many eyes closed to the quietly honest council of sorrow. Should he burn with his home? It was all that he had known and the last that he would know of a world that he had thought true and difficult and web-like, and yet homely. Here had been family! Here had been sister and sister-sons! Here had been brother-in-law and sister-daughter! Here had been memory.

Then stood up slouching, as though ten years older than his proper age, the Forge-bear of Glimwæth: naked to the world, waking to newness, born once more by trials of fire, or some madness set on by the coming of a beast and its rider — monsters too terrible to comprehend!

"Was it such monsters, brother, that taught you to sit so uncomfortably and yet so well upon your high chair?" muttered the Forge-bear, and he tottered slowly over to where the king lay dead beside the Hammer of Imnir, the Bear's Maul. The Forge-bear cast aside his own broad axe. He knelt down before the hammer, and took it like a swaddled child into his hands. Then his eyes were swept by dripping lashes to look at his beloved niece, writhing painfully on the ground not far from him. She clutched at her throat, the smell of burnt flesh now hanging about her.

Hooking the hammer into his belt, he strode over to her, taking her up gently in his arms as well, holding her tightly to his large, curly bosom, which rose and fell in shudders as his tears bedrizzled her slowly quieting form. She knew herself no longer to be alone, and so she pressed away her childish flailing, thinking only of how glad she was to be held tight.

It was she, the Bear now thought, who was an orphan in the ashes of a fallen home that would be nevermore the same. Nevermore: more terrifying a word could suddenly not bear down on the blacksmith's mournsome mind. He staggered by the other searching shadows that flittered flighty by his mighty, burdened frame.

He listened not to what they prayed, he saw not whither their eyes went, he had ears alone for the rasping breathing of the girl he held in arm. The woman, he must remind himself. How she had grown. And yet, in this state, she reminded him of that day on which her brothers had returned from the fjords to look upon their sister for the very first time. She had been swaddled in his sister's arms, swaddled in the dear embrace of Yrsa, who had long not been herself, and whom he would never-more see so in life before death.

"Nothing will harm you now, dear niece," he whispered between briny tears. "The foe is gone. They have left us to our defeat. They have left us to fear them evermore."

Suddenly he felt a hand lie firmly on his arm, and saw the bloodshot gaze of wounded Ystrith look that way with welling eyes. So the Forge-bear turned his head to look upon a grim Lion Pen-tooth, who held to her the sword of Athilan that fell. She smiled, almost, and then shook her head. He nodded, and then bound the blade again to his belt, where it had been before. Then said the Lion Pen-tooth: "For how you have returned to us this moonless night, dear daughter of our king, I shall be thine sword arm, until I have arms no more." And she wept in silent torment and joy.

"What now, Pen-tooth?" muttered the dull drone of the Forge-bear's voice. "What now?"

"Come, let us bring dear Ystrith to the healers of the river-folk, for they are mighty healers. I have seen their handiwork myself. To the halls of the dead with us, come."

This little purpose given was like the falling of heavy irons from the Forge-bear's back, and he straightened, marching after the scrivener that led them on their way through the desert of scattered wood and stone. Gaba also joined their company, then the gron did so as well. Huthram also came to meet them, limping and scowling, and weeping for all that had come to pass.

They climbed the stair, went by the heavy oak. They came into the hall beneath the burg, and there they stood still. For there was a scene of mighty horror which they had not foreseen.

"No!" screamed Huthram.

A vast bridge-troll lay dead in the hall, next to another of its kind. In the broken down entrance to the hall of the dead lay two more. They were like the pincushions of a thousand-thousand arrows. The river-man ran as fast as his legs would carry him; the limp suddenly forgotten by the fright, and pounced over these great creatures into the hall that lay beyond. Thither the others followed silently, wondering what further calamity could have befallen them in this dismal darkness oh so deep.

But it was no calamity. It was a small victory! Within the hall of the dead, where the trolls were piled like a little hill in the centre of the room, sat the longbowmen, drenched and panting in sweat of heavy labour. They all were still alive, not one of them had been lost.

"What has happened here? What are you men of the south that you sit here as though you have only finished ploughing a day's field? You have accomplished the impossible!" cried the Lion Pen-

442

tooth. The longbowmen laughed, but hadn't the wind for speaking yet.

"Where are the women and children?" asked Huthram.

"Where the healers?" growled the Bear.

"A man has taken them," gasped the captain of the longbowmen. "The trolls broke through, and we sought to stop them. We fought them, dropping them like catapults all the way from the wall. Even now you shall see a long line that leads to the northern wall; a line of dead trolls." The captain breathed a moment. Grin went out again, to look on the handiwork of these men.

Then the captain continued: "We held out with the flurry of arrows that we could muster, pushing them back at whiles after we managed to come between them and the folk gathered here in the hall. Finally we came into the hall itself, and we saw that there was a house standing in the middle of it. It seemed strange, but we had no further time to think on it, and the women, children — the healers and the healing — they all streamed into the house, no larger than a tent, as though it had plenty room within!

"The man that stood without the door, guiding them inside, was garbed in grey, methinks, and he said to us, as we battled with the trolls: 'You shall win this fight, take only my word for it, and do not falter in your hearts!' And just so —as you see the fruit for your very selves — it was. We have won against the trolls. The house, when all were in, save us, fell away into the earth, as though it had never been there!"

443

"Strange to believe, but we have also witnessed terrible strangeness this night. You have done work to win us something, even if all else was lost," said the Lion.

"How so?" asked the captain of the longbow-men.

"The war in the fore-burg was lost," said the Lion. "Go there, see if you can aid in any way. Show those that wish to see the work of your hands. It may inspire them to know that not everything is without reason for rejoicing."

"At your command, Pen-tooth," said the captain of the longbowmen, and they were about to depart, when Huthram called to them, asking: "Where is this man and his house now?"

"He said that he would return when the battle was done," said the captain.

Along the tiered descent, which Authæn had thought never to see again, the many that had been held within the halls of the dead now sat about in excited chatter. The chieftain of the river-people himself sat next to Carbeth and Loangilin. These two were silent and grim. Carbeth's pain had been relieved of him, but he wore a linen bandage about his head, covering his eyes.

"Loangilin, where is Folgnuin?" Authæn asked at last, and she looked up at him in surprise. Her mind had been adrift in dark and stormy seas. Not far away, Wingilin now also drew nearer again. She had been watching the quick fingers of the *mith-aumuinan*.

444

"She is in the tower of the ogre, Authæn," said Loangilin.

Authæn frowned.

"She is dead," rasped Carbeth coarsely. "But the master of this house promised to return her to life."

"Dead?" whispered Authæn, nodding to himself. That was as he had anticipated it, but he had hoped in his heart that things were otherwise. Then what the hunter had said to him of Noth's promise settled amidst his thoughts as well. He made to find the master.

"Authæn?" Wingilin called after him, her eyes were also wide with shock and confusion at this revelation. "Dear Folgnuin," she muttered to her spirit then, closing her arms about herself as though suddenly cold.

"He has saved us, Wingilin," said Loangilin, "Carbeth and I for not the first time. And this house itself is a strange secret to believe; yet here we are. He shall bring her back to life."

"Wait to see what happens to the longbowmen, dear Loangilin," uttered Carbeth hoarsely. "If his word holds true with them, then it may also be true for redeeming Ystrith."

"What do you mean, 'redeeming Ystrith'?" asked Wingilin, her brow furrowing.

"It was Ystrith that took the life of the girl," said Carbeth callously. "And now she strides out into the fray as though she will make all things right with her sword! Why can I only choose what is cruel?"

Wingilin spun to look in the direction in which Authæn had stormed. "He will not like this," said she. "He has never been well-befriended with the king's-daughter."

"He must know the truth, Loangilin. I know you fear his finding out, but I doubt that Master Noth shall keep it from him. If he cannot put aside his hatreds, he cannot lead our people into a city free of the burdens that our fathers cursed it with. That is the simple truth of it."

Authæn found Noth just beyond the door at the top of the tiered descent, opposite the entrance they had followed from the hall of the dead. There was a small, candle-lit room, along the walls of which were set narrow tables of bleached wood. The walls themselves held up diamond-shaped shelves of the same wood, all filled with scrolls upon scrolls of papyrus. There Noth was holding one such scroll near the light of a candle that had melted mostly across the table's rugged surface.

"You would like to know, I am certain, whether I scrape the wax from the table, before I replace the candle," said the colourless man. He looked up with so devoid a face and so bleak that Authæn almost regretted having had the thought for the briefest moment after entering.

"How?" asked the river-man in astonishment.

"You would like to know *how* I scrape it from the table?" returned Noth, almost in bewilderment.

"No!" said Authæn, not wanting to be misunderstood by the man that seemed to hold reins on fortune itself. "Not '*how* do you scrape away the

446

wax', master. *How* do you know these things? Who are you?"

"I am Noth," said the other simply, as though he was a little concerned about Authæn's memory.

The mien that the river-man bore would not re-lent, however. He demanded that the colourless traveller understand. He demanded with his golden eyes that this stranger answer, and become a little less strange. "I pray you, master!" said he.

Noth smiled with understanding, but that understanding soon gave way to anger. It was a deep anger — so deep that it needed not be drawn with lines onto the face; it glimmered in the recesses of his eyes. Then the walls, which had in the light of the candles been of a rich, brown hue, became a wan dun, all with the paling of the light. The bleached tables, having been grey, became white as bone. The candles of yellow, faded to look like sticks of ivory. The rich scrolls seemed to take on the quality of ash. All was drained from the room, and the light seemed alone to find a hold on the bright glow along the thread and twine of Noth. Suddenly his skin was olive, his hair was black, his robes were an assortment of hues, from the reddest of reds to the bluest of blues; and though it seemed a joyful thing in itself, it gravely frightened Authæn.

"*I am the End!*" said Noth, bearing the only colour remaining in the room.

Authæn cowered down into the corner near the door that had closed quietly behind him, this image of the man of all colours burning itself into his eyes, and the longer he stared, the brighter Noth's

447

own eyes seemed to glow with the gold that had once belonged to the eyes of the river-man.

Then Authæn blinked.

All was as it had been again. The earthen walls were the colour of fertility. The greys were grey, the candles yellow; the light itself seemed so warm, that a cold which had gripped the river-man's heart seemed to thaw after having momentarily frosted over.

Noth was squinting greyly at his scroll again.

"Would you like to know another thing, perhaps?" asked the master of the house then.

Authæn only shied back a little from the voice as it spoke. It seemed to speak both within and without him. "Many things, master!" said the river-man.

Noth turned to look at him, colourlessly.

"You have been set on the path, and you have nearly reached its intended mark. Do not stray," said Noth.

"How would I stray, when I do not even see a road?" asked the river-man desperately.

"The road will present itself. The question, rather than what road, is *how* you walk it, or if you even walk it at all. Staying seated on the ground there is a quick way to a shutting of the eyes, a folding of the hands, and a waking nevermore, dear Authæn," said Noth.

"Then I shall be rid of my many burdens," said Authæn, feeling himself slide deeper into his sitting posture on the ground.

Noth looked sternly down at him, then he laid aside the scroll, knelt before the river-man, and grasped his arm. In a sudden, jarring motion, the colourless man wrenched the river-person to his feet, so that he was thoroughly awake again.

Said Noth: "'The sleeper sleeps, and he is all', Authæn, save he that is a journeyman, whose hands are honed, who in employ, receiving that which him is owed, does labours with which none should toy. 'Let masterfully masters work their midnight craft; which is oft shirked'. Perhaps you are no master, Authæn; yet still you have been entrusted with the labours of a journeyman."

"To guide my people to the city of our fathers," said Authæn.

"A path with many needed steppingstones, no?" said Noth.

"Folgnuin is dead!" exclaimed Authæn suddenly. "Will you truly return her to life?"

"Have I not said so?"

"They have told me this, but I would hear it from you!" said Authæn.

"Are they not witnesses enough? Are they not witnesses true?" the colourless man looked with a strange calm of face onto the river-man.

"How did she die?" asked Authæn.

"Have they not said?" asked Noth.

Authæn shook his head.

"Then ask," Noth advised him, and the door behind Authæn opened again.

Slowly, the river-man walked out, back into the great circle where those were gathered that had fought in spirit for their dear ones in the battle for Glimwæth.

449

In the midst of the rubble that was the fallen city of Imnir; in the midst of despair and failure; out of the ashes of defeat, a shape began to push itself with the rising of the sun. Those that sat in idle worry, those that floundered about in the torrents of a world that they had once called their own with heedless certainty, those that looked for some sign from the walls above, and from the courtyard of the oak, began to come and gather about the steeple of a roof. A house seemed to be pushing itself through the remains of Glimwæth.

Someone on the wall made to run for the king, and then remembered bitterly that he lay dead, gathered beside the form of his faithful bear, and many others, beneath the oak of skalds. Still, somehow word reached the Forge-bear and those that held his company. When he stood afore the glowing window in the gable, the sweetly smoking chimney, still holding his sleeping niece against his chest, the door swung back, and Noth emerged, those that had been gathered from the hall of the dead stretching like yawning shadows from his house; their eyes large with horror at what they witnessed to have happened to their city.

After only a few brief moments, Authæn stormed by Noth, letting his searching eyes jump among those gathered to watch their safe return. Then his visage alit upon Ystrith, and there a lust for blood found flavour on his tooth-licking tongue.

"Ystrith!" he roared, and she frighted awake with a dreadful cough. "You will die for your robbery! How dare you rape the life of that girl with your singing sword! To think that I held it in my hand. It is my fate, it would seem, that those who are close as kin to me must gift me with the weapon that slew them after it is done! Now feel the sting of that which slew my father!"

And he charged the Forge-bear.

The great son of Imnir, who in stature was a mountain against this warless river-man, drew back with horror and fear mingled in his mien. He did nothing when Authæn grasped at the dragon-mail of the king's-daughter. He did nothing, when she was torn to the ground from where he had held her, save to fumble and let go. Only barely did he catch the glittering black knife that Authæn wielded, before it would have struck the painfully writhing form of his sister-daughter.

Then he would have become wroth, but he had seen in this strange dark elf's eyes something uncannily familiar. "You have the blood of the bear!" hissed the Forge-bear of Glimwæth, and all shied back some steps.

Suddenly, the Forge-bear held both the arms of Authæn in his hands, and he raised him into the air. "Who were your parents, boy!" roared the mammoth of a man.

"My father was Thuineith of Thænim, proudest and best of carpenters!" roared Authæn, seeming to have might enough in his struggling to cause beading on the Forge-bear's hide. "My mother is Lyn Ithæm, only named daughter of the moon!"

A shudder of voices rippled through the crowd. Then, suddenly, the river-man kicked the knees out from under the hulk that held him high, and they

451

both tumbled to the ground. The chieftain took up his father's killer again, and scrambled to where the killer of his friend coughed out blood and scab, but never a word in her defence.

Authæn held the dagger up. Then down went his hand, and … stopped.

A word had been spoken.

A word still hung in the air.

A word was now noticed which the colourless man had uttered whilst all others were too frightened by the cruel spectacle that unravelled now before their eyes to hear.

"That blade will only cut one more time, Authæn. It will cut your hand," he had said whilst none had listened.

Now Authæn was the one to bead with sweat, and the blade began to move itself, by the muscular machinery of his tired limbs, toward his hand that stretched out readily before it. He wrestled against the need to do what had been said. He wrestled with all powers at his command. He would not let himself do this thing, he cared little why not. He would resist. He did resist! He brought away his hand, uncut, and stumbled back some steps. Then he looked into the eyes of all those gathered. Lastly into those of Noth. They all looked on the riverman with fear, save the steady grey of the colourless man.

"Authæn," said Wingilin suddenly.

He looked to her.

"Your hair!"

At this, as though by her command, a lock fell from his head, where it had come free from the bun in which he had bound it, and it fell into his gaze. It was white as the snows beyond the walls. He tucked away his dagger, and unbound his hair, letting what of it could fall into his face. It was all of it white, as though with early ageing.

"You shall not harm her, Authæn. Not after you yourself have only just been saved from what would otherwise have been your end," said Noth of a sudden, and a great shame overcame the riverman.

"Then I will go to my wife," said Carbeth. "Ystrith? Beorn mine? Ertu thær? Ik kan ekni sær!" The hunter stumbled carefully, blindly from out of the threshold of the house of Noth. She reached for him, convulsing, then controlling herself again, then weeping silently with rasping breaths.

Then said sadly the Forge-bear, her trusty uncle: "She has lost her tongue, good hunter. It seems that she will have to be your eyes, and you will have to speak for her."

The blind man and his mute were led together then by the guiding hands of friends. One such hand was that of shamefaced Authæn. Then Carbeth and Ystrith lay there, holding one another, not aware for all their sorrow and all their likewise joy, that all eyes watched their reunion.

And, as all this dreadful spectacle came to a quiet end, a new boot struck the stair that led up from the House of Noth. It was a heavy foot that plied the wood, and a tall shadow that soon was seen. Then emerged a man as tall as was the Forge-bear, though not yet broad as he.

"My sister," said a rumbling voice, as one once full of cobwebs. "Is it you of whom they speak?"

Chapter Four-and-Thirty
Sheep Invited By Wolves

Soon after all were from his house, Noth departed again; his dwelling falling into the earth like so many loose planks. The bodies of the dead, with all the city gathered about the oak of skalds, were carried steadily into the nostrils of the mountain. There they were laid on the hot bed of coals, wrapped in their death-linens. There was both wailing and noiseless weeping. Songs for those that had remained behind were raised up, commemorating the dead, and how their sacrifice would now aid in shaping the metal of future generations. All the while fearful whispers wove among the people regarding the return of Svæn, this time not in the form of an ogre, but of the city's son.

When this ceremony was done, the fallen king and his bear were taken to the halls of the dead. There entered only the Forge-bear, Ystrith, and Svæn, who had emerged a sane man from the house of Noth. They laid the king and queen to rest in their own cavern, cleft from the black stone of the wall that faced the entrance. The bodies of the trolls still lay about, too wonderful a mark of heroic deeds to move aside just yet.

As those three stood beside the stony bed of their deceased, the Forge-bear turned to his returned nephew. He laid one of his heavy, blackened hands onto the other's shoulder and drew forth the Hammer of Imnir.

"This hammer was your father's, Svæn, and as he has spoken in seithing words, it shall now be yours for surviving him," said the blacksmith. "You are king by the words that your father wove when last you visited this city."

"Thank you, uncle. Were it only all otherwise! He should have remained king, only a little while longer. I would have joyed to see that," said Svæn with a grimace.

Ystrith, who had been attended by the *mithaumuinan* and now weakly stood again, said nothing. She only stared with riven cheeks.

When the kingly family departed the hall of the dead, they were met with a great crowd, and, seeing that Svæn now bore the Bear's Maul, all cheered (in trepidation and fear) the chant: "Hail Svæn King! Hail Svæn King! Hail Svæn King!"

They hailed him all the way into the courtyard beneath the nostrils of the mountain, where the fury of the dead still pumped like clouds of giant's breathing. There the Lion Pen-tooth met them, bowing.

Said the Lion: "My king, it is sudden after your long absence, and yet thy chair beckons, and thy people await. This is the command of your father. They are in need of wise an ear and discerning an eye to look on their dire need, and give them guidance further with a clearly speaking tongue."

Said the king: "Wouldst thou stand by me, Pentooth, as thou stoodst by my father? For thy ear and eye are weathered sharp by ageless wanderings through histories both far and near; thy tongue is honed and golden-red like the gold that glimmers

456

freshly forth, as pure as ever it could be, from fires of the past. Wouldst thou be me this kind of be-hoof?"

The Lion Pen-tooth looked a moment to the lady Ystrith, and she nodded, smiling wearily.

"As it is according to the mind of the lady whom I serve, I shall advise thee Svæn King," said the Lion.

"Thou art the truest friend of our house, scrivener. I name thee therefore kings own mayor!" returned the king, and they ascended to the high burg of Norn, led on by the rising cheers of their people.

Much of the daylight was spent distributing the foods for the week, ensuring that each family received their due, and that all was rationed well for the winter that stood at the gate; as threatening an enemy as any. Other matters were also discussed regarding the needs of the people, and how they would be sheltered. At this the gnome stood forth, and the people in the hall grew quiet with attention.

"King ogre," said the little creature, grinning brazenly as the hall erupted into disbelieving caco-phony. Then the gron said, with a voice that all felt in their bones: "Might I have this word?"

King Svæn raised his hand. The people there then saw that he was laughing himself into tears, and frightened silence fell again. Was he to be yet another mad king, as had been his grandfather?

"I do not know what you are, nor know I where you come from, little friend; but would you not hold a place forever in my court?" asked the king.

"Careful, good king," said Gaba from near the entrance. "That may encourage his strange humour!"

Some laughter began to stagger into the people now.

"Oh, we are long-suffering of bad humours, are we not? Still, you wanted a word, little friend: take as many words as you must," said the king.

"Your father I promised that I would rebuild what has been lost in this city. It is a joy to me to behold the waste at your door, not for all the death that has accompanied it — not for all the loss that has been suffered — but for all a builder's possibility that it presents to me. If you would have me, I should build for you a city of stone to rival even wherein dwelt those forgotten forest folk that indwelt this land, when wooded it was, before your fathers came to these shores. The men that dwell along the southern strands of Middle-mere shall journey with a thousand pilgrims to see the houses of Imnir's folk, stone upon stone, in the city of Glimwæth!"

"If your word you gave to my father," said the king. "I should not deny you the fulfilment of it. I should be glad to accept this offer, which humbles me more than your wondrous address of 'king ogre', ha! But tell me what you are, dear friend! Are you a dwarf, for of those I have but bitter memories."

"I am a gnome, king ogre. I am what once was servant to those that were once dwarfs," Grin explained.

458

"And what is foe to foe is friend, or no?" asked the king.

"Just so," said the gron with a grin.

Then the king let call forth Loangilin and Carb-eth, for he saw them in the crowd, and remembered the sad beauty of the river-woman with great shame.

"Dear dark elves," began the king, but he was red of face as never any here had seen, and he cringed before these simple folk; one blind, the other seemingly so very unremarkable. "This city was meant by my father as a bastion of peace, in which the old was reconciled with the new in the union of his marriage to the daughter of Imnir. He himself was the son of Harrowbert, a usurper and a man of violent conquest.

"I wish that you might live here, along with all your folk, in just such a peace. But I know that my rule here will rob you of it in nightmare and in memory; for it is not the first time that you shall have felt my tyranny. Therefore I offer this to you especially, but to all of your people. Might your chieftain step forth, I pray?"

Authæn obliged, stepping out next to these two friends from where he had been standing next to Huthram and Wingilin.

"I herewith offer any of the lands in league with the children of Imnir, lands that lie under the reach of their king, to your people, that thither you might move and make a home like never you have known before. What say you chieftain of dark elves?"

The chieftain: "I say that I would ask for only one land, great king; though I know not that you have the power to give it."

"What land be this?" asked the king.

"The Vale of Thrones," said Authæn, and a hush fell, even over the king.

Finally King Svæn said, "It is within the reach of the lands that were conquered by Harrowbert the usurper, but, as far as my knowledge goes, I know those lands have never been settled; not since they were abandoned by your fathers long ago. Therefore I shall pledge to you that I shall aid your people in reclaiming this, your birthright."

"I humbly thank you, my king," said the chieftain of the river-people.

At this, a runner burst into the hall, pushing past the people. King Svæn arose from his high chair, and climbed down to meet him where he ran. Said the king with wary eyes: "What news from the wall?"

"My king," said the runner, "there is a messenger! He is dour and rideth striding an varg!"

The King Svæn paled, his eyes grew distant. "Impossible," said he, and, "it cannot be! The varg must be that of Mathydras, I can think of no other that might find its way to this place. Here are children of the moonlight onto whose fine scent it's caught."

Fear rippled through the throng. Many did not know the tale of the Brothers in Darkholt, and were bewondered already at the return of their king's-son. Now they heard that it might be another such a long-lost king's-son, riding dour at their door.

All of the people of Glimwæth made their way to the walls, though these walls were not of much use, as the great hole still gaped at heaven from the earth in the fore-burg. Then they stood by twilight on the breach, and there all saw in both wonder and in fear this great beast — the werewolf that had lost its were. It was indeed the same one as that which Noth had chased from the tower, thought Ystrith silently.

Astride it sat no Mathydras, however. It was a ghoul; one of the black dwarfs. This one was also attired in black regalia, though its armour was of a different shape to the drooping square that had clad the King of Ghouls. It was more of the curves that cleave wind like a ship with speed.

When King Svæn stood above the gates of the city, the ghoul proclaimed, riding his varg from one side to another as he spoke, "*I have come to parley, king of Glimwæth! The ravens speak to us of thy return into thine own. Once thou wert among us, and now thou knowest of our kind and manner. Thou knowest that we are not dangerless. We offer thee terms of peace therefore!*"

"I will have no peace with you, ghoul! I have no peace with you in my heart, and you have struck out at these people through me, showing that you will have no peace, but oppression!" pronounced the king. "Beneath your twisting finger-work was rent asunder my family! Even now my sister stands as proof of — yes, your danger — but all the more of your *peacelessness*!"

"*Then thy city shall be consumed beneath the earth by greater feeders than the earthworms thou hast met so far!*" threatened the ghoul.

"Hear what they offer, king. So we might at the very least know against what it is we stand," counselled the Lion Pen-tooth.

The king sighed, nodded, and said, "What is the offer of your king, ghoul?"

"*Let me enter into your gate, and I shall parley with thee,*" said the ghoul upon the varg, bringing it to stand still.

The king scowled, and returned: "You have defiled this city well enough by breathing out so near its wall. Stay where you are, speak freely that these people hear how bent is your mind!"

"*Our mind is quite clear, and never has it been so bent as thine. But I shall speak and so be satisfied: The King of Ghouls seeks audience with two among your number. One from the south, a man who hunts dragons; another who is called chieftain of the children of the moon.*"

"Wherefore does your king seek audience with them, cur?" asked Svæn.

"*That is the business of the King of Ghouls; but they shall know in time. If they are let to go into his mountain home, along the whispering shores of Steornufol, no further war shall mark out thy city, great King Svæn. For wast it not thou that placed the banner of war? Was our purpose not that thou shouldst ascend to the throne which thou now besittest?*"

King Svæn turned to Gaba and Authæn, who both stood near, and had extricated themselves

462

from those surrounding to stand nearer the king and give their mind on the matter.

"What say you, my friends?" asked the king. "You are free here to go whither you will, but I know the minds of the ghouls to be bent only on cruelty and control, where they are not fallen into sloth and slumber."

"I, for one, am bound to go," said Gaba, "for it is a part of that which my banishment demands of me that I must know what I can about the Ibex which was wrought of our fallen kinsman, and I am bound to ensure that it happens never again."

"Then I shall go as well," said Authæn, "for I will not rest easy, knowing my people still live with the threat to loom over them of those that pulled our mothers from the heavens, and drove the Vale of Thrones into civil strife."

"If you do go, then know that I will send none with you. This will be your own quest to fulfil; your own danger to survive. If you do, you shall be heroes beyond compare, or villains without equal, for so clean is the line of dealing with these," said the king. "But if you remain, then we shall stand together against whatever tidal wave might dare to drown us."

"Then go with my people, king," said Authæn, "or send with them your forces, as you have promised, so that they might take back the Vale of Thrones. In my place, as it was before, Huthram shall be chieftain. Then they shall look for my return, whether it happens or not, but they shall — more certainly than my return — have a home at last. I will go into the mountain."

"I also am agreed," said Gaba. "The only thing I have to lose is this quest, and it leads into that heart of mountain, where the star once fell."

"Then you here have your answer, ghoul!" cried the king from the wall, but suddenly the varg threw down its rider, and the gathering gasped. The beast ran toward the gate as its dark rider rose again to stand upon his black-shod feet. He only stared through metal at the beast, waiting, wondering. It bounded and then came to a halt, so that it stood beneath the wall, staring up at Authæn as if expectantly. It was as though his decision had unlocked a secret in the beast's soul.

"*Ah,*" said the ghoul. "*It has found its master, truer master than I could be. Then the riddle as to how you have outlived our curse is finally resolved, son of moonlight. You were never the son of the carpenter to begin with! Who has played us so cleverly, I wonder? Who entrusted you into his loving arms? But these matters shall all clear up before the throne of my king.*"

Then the black dwarf drew a horn from his belt and sounded it thrice, loudly. After a time the earth near where he stood began to fall away, and a mole-troll arose. The ghoul climbed onto its back, to sit behind the horns that stuck like streaming lines over its head. Then the troll tunnelled down again, leaving behind a dreadful scar upon the land. The varg remained, poised on the movements of the river-man chieftain.

"What does this mean?" whispered Authæn to his spirit, and from far away the words returned to him: *You do not know where you come from. You*

barely know your father. And also the words of
Lyn Ithæm, which he had tried somehow to forget,
and yet had stuck in his mind ever since: *You are
Authæn, son of Thuineith the carpenter, according
to the law of Wirthaumuin*.

The law of Wirthaumuin demanded that
orphans be taken up into families that could sustain
them. He had thought her ignorant of such things,
but he had known better in the depth of his heart,
which had nagged at him ever since, sometimes
driving him to bitter ire; or had that been the bear's
blood in him?

"'Who are your parents, boy'?" muttered the
river-person to his spirit.

"You are the son of Mathydras," rumbled King
Svæn, who had until then only been able to stare
silently at this dark elf chieftain, now entirely another man in his own eyes. "You are the son of
Mathydras and the daughter of the moon that he
sought out so fervently by means of his dark
tower! You are my nephew! This varg was his familiar; his slave! Now it shall speed you hasty to
the end which you desire. It shall lead you directly
back to the dim hall of the King of Ghouls, whom
he and I both served a time."

465

Chapter Five-and-Thirty
Something of Folly

Stop moping, Authæn …

The chieftain of the river-people stood alone now over the gate. Only a moment before, Gildolf had still stood at his side, but now that the next watch had begun, and the evening was beginning to settle on this winter world, the watch-overest had bidden Authæn to hold the watch until his re-placement had come. The few that now still manned the walls were a mere outpost, whilst the rest of those who had survived the battle had been given temporary lodgings in the Nornburg itself. That is were the bulk of the fighting men kept up the guard.

Despite the chieftain's loneliness, a pair of frosting eyes were set, more shrewd a watch than his could ever be, far below. A silent werewolf sat there, waiting for its master.

"You are not another, are you, wolf," muttered Authæn, this time to the beast and not his spirit. "You are the quiet pool in which my soul is reflec-ted."

The vast wolf broke sight for a moment, look-ing back over the meadows whence it had come. But then it returned the silent gaze the river-man afforded it, and it sat itself down with dutifully ex-pectation.

You do not know where you come from …

The Even Star began to do its heralding work on the western horizon. Not far from it, a curved lunar bow was aimed to Authæn's right; into a sinister north. There the tall peaks stood like tombstones of mysteries that were slowly being turned to histories by the Pen-tooth's faithful labours. There the eyes of the river-man lingered a while, as the last of the dying light licked gingerly upon them.

You barely know your father.
Authæn remembered how Thuineith had chuckled, shaking his head. The chieftain could not remember his foster-father ever losing his cool; a temper as that of the blood of dragons, to be sure. They had spent so much time on the road together. Authæn had learned so much from him, and brought him his every fear and dream, and yet the kindly Thuineith had always seemed somehow unreachable.

It was, thought the chieftain presently, as though the carpenter had given himself entirely to this wayward son granted him by the shepherd's law, never once thinking of his own desires. Never looking back with reminiscence, always steady, always kind, and yet never undiscerning. So clear and wise had been the eyes of this father-man, that Authæn had never had the desire to protest against him — all the more because of how, in Thuineith alone, he seemed to have had a place in their village, and a healthy sort of attention from his peers.

For the longest time, it had been as though the carpenter had been the very web at the edges, where one thought the world must come to an end, and beyond which an everlasting, writhing, all-consuming nothing must abide. And then Authæn had been entrusted into the care of the shepherd of

his henge: Wirthaumuin and his wife. Authæn's
first mother. None better could have been.

*Keep that hunter close, Authæn. He is true.
And one day, you will know what that means.*

The way in which the shepherd's wife had
listened to him had always made him feel wiser
than any other, and her laughter at his foolish jests
was as the sun returning early, in the middle of a
winter's night. *She* had been true, he had thought.
She had been like a boulder, on which one could
rely. It could shelter, it could support. That is what
'Carbeth' meant: the set stone. Carbeth the Loyal,
however, had proven rather otherwise, Authæn
frowned to think. He had abandoned the entire village for the sake of one stray girl.

*I sense that finally understanding truth would
destroy me.*

Carbeth had nearly been destroyed in his blind
pursuit of the king's-daughter. Was that love? What
had Wingilin said to him those years ago of love?
'Where life is spent wisely, there love abides'.

For a moment, Authæn's eyes were involuntar-
ily drawn up to where the many fires in the skald's
court had coloured the bare oak a dancing yellow
in the twilight.

*Sometimes being destroyed is not the worst of
fates, but it depends on the reason for your destruction.*

"To be grass and water to the sheep," muttered
Authæn, and he looked back down to where the
varg was sitting. "It is a saying of the shepherds,
father. Nothing more. You speak in their language,
it seems."

The words returned to Authaen after what seemed an age. It had been mere months, and worlds had passed away. The callous hands of the river-man atop the wall went to his belt, and he un-fastened the dagger which had slain the carpenter whom he had long called father. It had been there, seeing the lifeless form of the greatly weakened river-person, laid atop the false stone of fathers, that something deep within this chieftain's heart had been awakened to wrath at injustice. It had been there that the many strands which he had held far off, had suddenly begun to tightly weave the understanding in his mind that he had never quite belonged anywhere — neither to the dust, nor to the moonlight.

To be sure, he had come from both, for a time. But now greater questions were asked of him, and he was certain that their answer was inevitable. Their answer was one. He tucked the black blade back into his belt again. It left a sudden itch on the palm of his right hand, however, and though he tried, he could not seem to scratch it.

Suddenly a familiar voice called out from be-hind, as though in jest: "Ho there! I come in peace! Would you speak with a weary wanderer?"

Authaen laughed aloud, throwing back his head in mirth.

"What would a weary wanderer want to speak about?" replied he.

"Oh," muttered Gaba, stepping up beside his friend, bringing forth a fresh-baked loaf of bread, and two skins of spiced wine as he let his eyes en-joy the last red of sundown. "Just such things as

469

the breaking of this bread. Perhaps the tide of what lies ahead. Such things, they cause me wakeful nights."

"Five still to come, I am sure," chuckled the river-man, gratefully taking a skin of the hot wine, breaking a large portion from the bread.

"I hope more than only five, my son," said the southerner, and they exchanged a tense glance.

"I drink to that, uncle!" the river-man burst out suddenly, and an unexpected smile alit on his features. His wayfarer's mane rippling to accommodate the friendly creases that now lined his once more youthful face. But the white of his hair and beard was one of the reasons Gaba could only smile weakly back, and then look down to frown at the varg that ever watched them. Its eyes presently darted from the one to the other.

Authaen broke a piece from his portion of bread, and let it fall to where the beast sat. It got up, to inspect the bit with its snout, quickly lashing it down with an awkward chomping. Then it returned to where it had sat, and its eyes to where they had settled.

"I see you are preparing not only your own spirit for the road ahead, but even that of your new pet," said Gaba. "Frightening creature."

"It is very familiar to me, but I do not understand how this can be," said Authaen.

"It was bound to the brother of the king. His blood flows in your veins. I do not envy you, Authaen. Yours is a difficult history, and a history of dreadful powers," said the southerner.

"And yet there is something in this history of mine, uncle, that lies not in the past, but in what is yet to come, and this something makes me content with it. Mathydras is my father, and that is in my footwork — a footwork that lets me stand here: beside you, uncle. This alone, is enough."

"Mathydras *was* your father," uttered another voice, suddenly. It was that of King Svæn himself as he came up by the stair that led to where the other two stood. "Would you let such a one as I stand beside such footwork, too, my nephew?"

"Such a one as is king of this whole reach?" asked the chieftain of the river-people with great irony. "You are a noble man, my king, as was your father before you."

The king bowed lightly, and said, smiling: "I would say neither of either; but to hear those thoughts from a tongue so heavy with loads that both I and my father have laded upon it is a kindness none could ever ask for, and is a gift that can never be returned. You are kind, Authaen. You have a heart."

"For what I did to your sister earlier this day, my king, I should cringe before you in shame. It is right that I now learn that she is my aunt, and to have you as my uncle, a man that has overcome the appetite of an ogre, is also an honour beyond compare."

"That is because it is no honour at all, and so cannot be compared," laughed the king.

"Not so!" cried Authaen, having no desire for his word to be so easily brushed aside. "There is truth in you, so mighty that it disarmed a lie more

dreadful than any tale I have ever heard told before!"

"It was not *my* truth, Authaen," returned the
king with a gentle smile. "It was compassion that
broke my spell. It suddenly fell over me from all
sides, it seemed. And in this compassion, I could
no longer do harm. It utterly ruined the taste of my
tongue, the strength of my arms, the will of my
heart, and the lustre of mine eyes, I tell you. And
then came your father, to benight the tower he had
built with a visit. He was riding this very varg."

The wolf barked up at the king of a sudden,
and jumped to stand readily on all fours.

"Tell me of him, my king," said Authaen, and
he sighed and looked into the west again, where
now a great sea of brightling jewellery was watching them right back.

"What is there to say, my friend. I was with
him all my life, and to the very end, I only knew
him through the eyes of regret, until I could lie no
more, and saw that I was part of what had twisted
and embittered him," said the king. "Who can truly
say: 'I am guiltless'?"

"Let this be a little chance to mourn a father
and a brother, my king; no matter who he was,"
said the river-man quietly.

The king looked a long while at his brother-
son, then he nodded to himself. Perhaps there was
something like a fright in the visage of that brutal
son of Imnir, but it was not dominant there.

Said the king of Glimwæth: "I shall begin by
saying words that could sound no emptier than
these; no less of meaning and worse in their appar-

ent dress of futile flattery. I will begin with this: He was a good man. I begin thus, because, really, no man is good, and neither was he."

"Has your appetite for bread been overcome, 'king ogre'?" the southerner suddenly interrupted, holding up what of the loaf he still had in hand.

"Hah! You have a keen wit. Let me have some of this bake! Thank you kindly, Master Gaba. But I will speak past mouthfuls, if you suffer me.

"We were children once, and in that time already, Mathydras showed that he was worthy of the throne. He had a mind for order and for action that could bring about the most reward for labour spent. I was different. In that time our grandfather still ruled this hill: Harrowbert. Harrowing indeed. That was a grim time. But neither of us ever learned what of it was so grim. I will likely never understand it all, for it was the world that raised me. But, in the gardens of Noth, much of the torment that I suffered then was shown to me as culture in my hands; for they grew suddenly more gentle for the pain which they had suffered.

"I think it was the same for him; for Mathydras, your father. He fell in love with a gentle creature: the lady of the moon. Her name was Lyn Ithæm, but it was in the time before her bondage and her bitterness. It was in a time before she understood the weightiness and heft that dust has on the soul. She did not know the passion that can burn on substance as fiery as heart.

"And when her curiosity — quite childlike, as is the nature of the daughters of the moon — had wandered to another thing, she faded. She faded seemingly from the face of all the earth.

"Nothing worse could have happened to my brother at a time more tender. At last, he builded his high home: the tower in Darkholt. He crafted it with the aid of the ghouls, which above all else worship the power of the moon. But it was not the moon which Mathydras captured in the spyglass of his spire. He began to look for any light, eventually, which would be caught within the glinting of that glass. And so he finally caught *her*. The red lady. A daughter of the daylight.

"In that time, I was an ogre. I had been, since my fall. It was the blood of the bear that transfigured me, that saved me from what should have been my death. Instead it became a doom far longer-drawn; far wilder. The lights and noises that would scatter through the eves would drive me mad with jealousy — a ghastly bile that had gathered in my belly many years. And I knew it somehow, in my bones, that Mathydras was the one who had built up that dark tower.

"And so I went to him. I made an end of him. So I thought.

"The ghouls came whilst I slept. They took his bones, as though they had known that this moment would come. They had bound his spirit to the black stone in the tower's base, you see. And so he could not die. Not until he were to touch the stone himself."

"And that is where the story that Carbeth has recounted meets that of which you tell, good king," concluded Gaba, when King Svæn seemed to falter in carrying on.

The king nodded slowly, then added: "And the story that the poor Lady Loangilin had to bear witness to."

They stood a long while atop the wall like this. Silent. The sounds of celebration echoed from the highest tiers. The southerner and the river-man took deep draughts from their wineskins, then Authaen handed his to the king to share in.

The king himself took a long draught, then returned it to his nephew. "That is a good brandy-wine!" growled he, well satisfied.

Then night had covered all the world, and the stars, a countless multitude of arbiters, bore witness to the three atop the wall: a king, a chieftain, and an outlaw stood there, looking west and north, to where a frightful voice had called two of them. And as they stood thus, in his heart, Authæn remembered words that once had been said to him, but now he heard them as if spoken by a voice which he had never heard in all his days; a voice as breaking glass.

Now our work begins, my son. The end of our beginning, as it were.

Chapter Six-and-Thirty
Hall of the Mountain King

One week later, the winds rushed by as hard against their faces as streams of water. It was difficult to breathe, if one did not press one's face against the fluttering furs of the varg. Upon its back the chieftain of Thænim and the outlawed dragon hunter now drew ever nearer the great mountains in the west. They drew nearer the broad Shoulders of Imnir, wherein lay the fabled pool of fallen stars. There the Forge-bear had fought trolls and harvested metal for kingly crafts. Thence had the steel of Gaba's Birdsong come, and thither now they flew like birds on the back of a werewolf.

Before them, trees and meads melted away like clouds that sun doth pierce through, and ever did they climb the rising fells and moors that clomb themselves towards the frosty peaks above. About the vast paws of the varg, the snow sprayed heavier and heavier, as it grew deeper and deeper; but never did they slow. And, as they rode, Authæn looked back in memory to his farewells from friends that had been lifelong. But now they fore into the very heart of darkness itself, going to confront the King of Ghouls, and that ancient pet of his, the Gruttin.

For a week they had prepared before departing, and now, upon the morn of Smith's-wend, the turning of the sun from its southward wade, they had departed Glimwæth with hope in their hearts. All

476

that time the dire wolf had waited beyond the gate for his new-chosen master to step forth.

In that time, Grin had with all nine of his forms begun to seal the breach in the earth. When he alone had not been enough, he had sent out signals in the stone to any of his ilk that dwelt nearby. Some three more had come to his aid, and together they had sped the work along marvellously.

There was hope in their hearts as they raced towards the Height of Imnir. There was keenness for adventure in their limbs as they neared the pools of Steornufol. They did not stop to eat or drink, and they did not have the stomach for it this day. They only stopped when the dark stones of the heights became more sheer and stark, and when there finally flattened before them a great basin in the height, where likely scree and course grass were padded by the snows that lay about. At the heart of the basin lay dark Steornufol, frosted over as though made of glass; and at the farther end of this great mere, there rose a dreadful architecture of black stone.

It shimmered in the gloss of frost that covered its dark surface, and here and there some of those crystal teeth of deepest cold had formed themselves to make of this black maw an even deadlier appearance. The wind howled moaning songs through that stone triangle, which stuck from the earth not dissimilarly to the House of Noth, thought Authæn then, but it was far, far larger.

The two adventurers dismounted from the varg, and now it seemed to follow them excitedly, with both wagging tongue and tail, towards the great entrance into the mountain. Posted at either end of the opening, the travellers soon saw, stood two ghoulish guards, both holding high halberds, which looked to be of the same make as their armour. Then they saw as well that there were written dwarfish runes over the threshold, like those that gron had shown them. These runes seemed somewhat faded, though, and did not do much with the stone; unless it was by them that the stone had been raised up into a gateway in the first place. Such seemed to be the power of the dwarfish words, after all.

"*You are awaited by the king*," droned the mountain voice of the nearer ghoul with their approach.

"I have one question for you, master ghoul, if it is permitted to learn regarding your ways whilst one is guest in your halls," said Authæn. To the surprise of the southerner, the river-man seemed strangely calm.

"*Ask, and we shall deem the worth of your question,*" said the other of the two ghouls.

"What say these runes here above? I know only the rune for moon in your mighty speech, but it is so wondrous how, by it, the very web of the world can be changed," said the river-man.

"*It is not changed, son of moonlight. It is described, and revealed. I shall show you the meaning of this simple password there above, for it is one that I have chosen to mark this door. Behold, you stand before the architects of this dread gate! My brother and I are Orochal and Aynavar!*" said the ghoul that had addressed them first.

478

Pointing with his halberd, having strode some steps back from the doorway into the mountain, the proud and ghoulish architect now pointed out which rune was what, and said, "*The sense of the phrase is as much as this: Swallowed up is the sun by stone. In our speech: Nifla izdin vevon. That central word 'izdin' is sun. That last word 'evon' is stone. This is the entrance into the westernmost mountains, guests of the king. This is where the sun strikes its head, bleeds out, and dies.*"

"*Izdin*," muttered Authæn to his spirit. "*Nifla izdin vevon*. I thank you, master ghoul. Would you lead us to your king?"

"*For that your hound is better than I, guest of the king,*" rumbled the ghastly voice of the black dwarf.

"Very well," said Authæn, and they strode by the crafters of this gate, entering the gloom that lay beyond.

They did not walk long, before the glittering, square passage caught the shine of pale moonstone lamps ahead, and indeed, as they rounded the corner into a stair, they came into a great entrance hall in which such moonstones stood atop pillars at regular intervals to mark out a walkway in the shallow pool that covered all the floor of that place.

"*Be washed, my guests, before you enter any further in,*" spoke a voice as though from out of the stone surrounding them.

"That is the voice of the King of Ghouls!" hissed Gaba, looking from side to side.

"Are you certain?" asked Authæn carefully.

479

The southerner turned to look at his companion with a stern aspect: "As long as I draw breath, and I hope only so long, I shall never forget this voice, Authæn."

"I believe you," said the white-haired riverman, and they strode along the path that had been laid out for them. Presently the varg that had brought them here splashed out ahead of them, and they followed its lead into the great darkness.

At the other end of the entrance hall, they clomb out of the waters, and stood at the lip of yet another descending stair; yet this one was broad, and led down toward a vast doorway. Here again stood two ghoulish guards that, with the approach of the king's guests, drew back the levers which sent to lively work the many cunning mechanisms by which the door would dwarfish open.

The two newcomers to these dark halls passed through the clockwork door, and strode into another pooling chamber of black and shimmering stone. Again there were pillars of moonstone, but they were somewhat smaller, somewhat drawn away from the walkway, and vastly overshadowed by the greatest of these glowing orbs that hung above the throne at the far end of the hall. It was a little sun to shed faint light over all the matters that were brought before its maker. A light that shone alone the colours that its masters sought to see.

There, in his tall throne, raised like a rotting tree from the waters, sat the King of Ghouls, still all attired in the armour of weeping squares. Behind the throne wrothe the vast form of the Gruttin, though it was so dark a figure, that mostly its endless pits of eyes were seen and not much more of it.

"*Approach, my guests,*" spake the voice of the Ghoul King again. "*I have only gifts for you.*"

"And we have not much more than questions to offer, great mountain king!" returned Authæn, his voice going far across the waters before it was swallowed up by the shadowy cavern.

"*Ask,*" said the King of Ghouls, "*and I shall deem the worth of your questions.*"

They drew nearer, until they finally stood before the frightful throne. The long cloak and the dark robes of the black dwarf splayed over the chair in a manner reminiscent of waters rolling from a hill.

"You are the father of our race, King of Ghouls, in that it was you that called forth the daughters of the moon in yore days. Why did you do this?" asked Authæn.

"*We sought to gain a power unto ourselves, child,*" said the voice like mountain passes through dark metal. "*By them we proved that we had mastery over the world-words; that we could carve out our own truth in this world, by describing it according to our desires. We carved women from water, where the moon shone on Murmur-mere. But the men that we had ensnared turned them against us. They misbegat your race. You were no more than a mistake. It is why we sought to drive you away, to undo your race by sending you into the wilds; fatherless, motherless, helpless. But there were those that aided you despite us.*"

"*Still, you posed no threat. You, we had heard, were a chosen race. You were elected by our foes to overthrow our kind, and so we feared you, but look at you. You are no more than dust. There is nothing of your mother's power in you. But you are not like your younger brethren. You are of the deathless race which you call shepherds. You are the one I had thought, until mere days hence, to be dead.*"

"Why would I be dead? Did you mistake me for the man whom you slew with this?" demanded Authæn, drawing forth the cruel dagger with which his father had been killed.

"*Ah,*" said the King of Ghouls. "*You return my blade to me. How kind. It was through your father that I sought to slay you with a curse. I cannot slay the deathless ones, the shepherds, with my own hand. I have a covenant with them. They are each bound to a soul-stone, which in turn is bound to the stone that shines above my head, and so they live eternal.*

"*I thought that you were such a one. I thought that you were misbegotten as were your shepherd fathers. But you are of a new race. Still born of moon and man, you look as did the shepherds once, but you are not of their history. You stand apart. The son of Mathydras and Lûn Ithâm. You are a riddle to me, child. And it makes me want to pry you open with these talons here.*"

The dwarf rubbed together the sharp tines of his gauntlets, so that sparks flew from them and they began to glow red hot.

"Back now, Authæn. It is now for *me* to pry open this dwarf with my own tongue — if not that of my mouth then that which rests in hand!" the southerner drew ringing Birdsong in that half-light, and it glittered grimly in the manufactured moon-bright.

"*You need not pry, I shall show you willingly my desire,*" said the King of Ghouls then, and a sudden processions of armoured ghouls arose from the waters all about that throne. One of them strode forth, holding the helm of the Ibex. It was remade to look just as it had before, and for a bitter moment Authæn thought that that giant, slain so long ago, was in the room again.

"*This is a gift for you, Gabazi kadonazd-Manutuz. The crown of the South. Your conquest begins today.*"

"You think that I would willingly take this?" scoffed the southerner. "It stands opposed to all that I desire! I desire to be a true dragon hunter, not some usurper! I desire to honour the lineage of my father, by protecting it, not by devouring it! You would make of all men ogres, only to see them finally destroyed, leaving a world in which only *your* whims are words of truth, whilst Truth itself is left forgotten!"

"*Then you shall take it unwillingly!*" boomed the voice of the king. At once the ghouls all made to grab at the southerner, but then they stopped again.

Something splashed to the floor.

Blood dripped into the pool at their all feet.

Weirdest of the weirds!

Authæn held up his right palm, in which, with the blade of the killer of his father, he had etched a single dwarfish word:

The King of Ghouls sat up in his high throne. The other ghouls all shied quickly away. Gaba turned to see what they had all been frighted by. He saw first the cruel dagger beneath the ripples of the water at their feet. Then, frowning, he followed the blood that dripped to the cut palm of Authæn's hand. His brow rose in surprise and confusion.

"What is this, Authæn?" asked the southerner.

"This is how my people are freed, uncle," said Authæn, "and this is how the henges are cleansed of the soul-stone influence. I will extinguish their source. In so doing, my people shall have a new beginning in the Vale of Thrones. A beginning free of these black dwarfs; a beginning free of wandering; save where the need takes them anew."

Behind the throne the Gruttin had vanished silently, and the varg presently also bounded splashing away, towards the entrance they had come through. Standing before that chair, the King of Ghouls now lowered his hood, and cast aside his helm to reveal a face as wan and colourless as that of Noth, but far less youthful. The thin whisps of his white hair and beard waved vaguely in the cool air of the cavern. His eyes were wide, but pale. Still, he seemed to see through them enough to understand what this all meant.

"*Impossible!*" said that gloomy king.

"What have you written on your hand, Au-thæn!?" demanded the southerner desperately.

"The dwarfish word for 'sun', uncle!" declared the other proudly.

Then a bright golden colour swallowed up the right hand of the river-man, on which he had written the word. The golden light crawled quickly up his arm, and into the clothes of his body, shining all throughout the other arm, all the way into Au-thæn's legs, then it lastly crawled along his neck, it made an ever more celestial of his hair, and lastly it took even his smiling eyes, which had regarded Gaba until the very end with pure victory.

One last word issued from that unbearable glow, as Authæn's voice spoke louder than ears should have to hear: "You wonder at this, uncle, and there is something of folly about it; and yet, where life is spent wisely, there love abides!"

In the Shoulders of Imnir dwelt a hardy mountain folk. They were descended of Imnir as well, being the descendants of one of Imnirs three sons. Their village looked out towards Glimwæth, and it stood mainly to signal a fire, if an enemy approached over the mountains. Their fires had been lit all night during the Battle for Glimwæth, and the brothers Revar and Ascar still had not recovered their proper sleeping patterns.

"It is because the winter is so dark!" said Re-var, who was the younger.

Said the elder: "It does not matter how dark the winter, brother. It is like father says: 'A man is only so strong as his mind, and the strength of his mind is how well he does what he plies his hand to.' And so we must become stronger of mind, brother! I thought, perhaps we could swim in lake Steornufol! That will make us stronger of mind!"

"I don't know, Ascar," said Revar. "I've heard strange tales about Steornufol. I'm frightened of trolls."

The two boys finally reached the edge of a steep rise. From here they could look down onto the lake. To the distant north-east a frozen river shimmered a line towards what looked like a bridge of some sort.

"Oh, it is frozen over, brother! I don't think the ice will be thin enough to break through. Can we not go home?" said Revar.

"Quiet, Revar!" said Ascar. "I think maybe that is a troll-bridge! Perhaps we can hunt some trolls! That will make us stronger of mind!"

"I... don't think that is a good idea, Ascar," said Revar, frowning to his spirit, and wondering whether his spirit could frown back.

"Wait! Down!" hissed Ascar of a sudden, and they both dropped into the snowy white at their feet, as though they had been struck by arrows.

"What is it, Ascar?" asked Revar.

"There are little black creatures there below!" whispered Ascar. "I saw them!"

"Were they trolls, Ascar?" asked Revar.

"I think so!" said the elder brother excitedly.

They crawled to the edge of the cliff on which they were, casting snow over the edge as stealthily as they could.

Below, one of the black dwarf architects — Orochal — turned to the other, and asked his companion: *"Should we slay those children, and feed them to the vargs?"*

But Ascar and Revar were still convinced of their concealment, and stared down at the dwarfs, thinking them to be troll-children.

"They are only little trolls, Revar. We can take them! If we bring back their heads to the village, we'll be famous, and then we will never have to hold our watch again!" exclaimed Ascar as quietly as he could.

Where before Revar had been nothing other than sceptical, his eyes suddenly lit up.

"No more watch?" asked he.

His elder brother looked at him with the smile that suggests it has a fish at the end of a line. "No more watch, Revar!"

"Then let us begin this war by throwing this rune stone that Rune made for me! She said that it would cause any that tried to harm me to burst at once into flames! You have the better arm, Ascar. You do it!"

Ascar took the rune stone reverently from his brother, thanking him for his sacrifice. Then he jumped up, shouting at the dwarfs: "Ha ha, you little trolls! Today you meet your end!" And he cast the stone as hard as he could in their direction.

The ghoulish architects that had been looking up at the boys heard this, looked at one another, and then shook their heads.

Then the rune stone struck one of them in the head, and they looked at each other again with a wholly different humour. It was now time to make feed for the vargs, they both decided speechlessly.

"It's not working, Revar! Quick, get the axes!" cried Ascar.

"We don't have any axes, Ascar!" said the younger brother desperately.

Then, all at once, a great wolf bounded out of the entrance to the mountain, at unthinkable speed, knocking over the dwarfs. It ran up, past the children, and then a great explosion erupted there. The ice shattered on Steornufol, and the waters were cast up into the air. Fire leapt dangerously from the mouth of the cavern, consuming the two ghoulish dwarfs, and roaring across the water towards the children.

The brothers looked one at the other, and then ran as fast as their little legs could carry them in the direction the wolf had run, which was away. The roaring fires seemed to tirelessly gain on them, and they soon felt very warm indeed in their winter clothes.

The wolf suddenly reappeared before them, and before they had the chance to scream, it picked them each up onto its back, and rode away towards their village. They clung to it with all their worth, and soon they were cold again; behind them only a rising cloud, bigger than any other in the sky that day.

"Maybe," stuttered Ascar, "maybe tell Rune not to make the stone so big next time, Revar."

Revar only stared at the cloud behind them with the biggest eyes he had ever made, and nodded.

Chapter Seven-and-Thirty
The Blind Witness

The feast of Smith's-wend was celebrated for a week. The light would return now to the north. The battle was over. The demands of the King of Ghouls had been met, and so the king allowed for his people to revel in the joys of being freed from dread. He, all the while, remained sober. The time as an ogre had left scars upon his spirit, upon which he had been commanded to reflect in the House of Noth as he had tended to the garden of the colourless man.

His people still feared him, for they had seen him in the shape of an ogre when last he had come to this city. The river-people seemed simple, and friendlier toward him than his own, for they had not seen him thus; save Carbeth and Loangilin.

Presently, as he stood on the balcony of the hall beneath the Nornburg, staring at the place where the walls had been picked at by the trolls, the king thought of her. He thought of Loangilin. He remembered, with tears in his eyes, the dread that had been carven on those finely angled features as he had taken her up, as he had callously cast her into the cage beneath the tricycle. He could remember everything that he had done, and he could understand exactly why he had done it. He had been a fool, but at the time, he had not known the hope within which he now lived, breathed, and walked as a king beneath the waking sun!

489

He heard a tread approach across the stone of the hall's floor, and turned to see who it might be. They did not announce themselves, for the one could not see that the king was looking at him and the other could not speak, for her tongue had been cut from her mouth. At this sight, the tears did slide from the steely eyes that had held them prisoner. The tears slid, free; they were tears of heartening at a sight so pure.

"My sister," said the king, and came to stand at the other end of the stone table where the blind man now had laid his hands to steady himself.

"My king," said Carbeth, his wife smiling at her brother. She looked somehow more gracious than ever she had before, the wisdom of pain cleft in crow's feet on her eyes.

"Carbeth, bravest of men!" said the king, and he rushed about the table to embrace the hunter. The hunter cried out in a fright, not having sought this. His legs also dangled now above the floor, and as only a recently blind man, this greatly disconcerted him. King Svæn was now some forty years of age. His sister, far, far younger, smiled deeply, also wetting her cheeks with joy at a sight so meek by a man so mighty.

"I hope you take it not as venom to your heart, my brother," sobbed the king, "but I hope that you and my dear sister are now so dependant on one another that you nevermore must chase, and she nevermore tries running!"

The hunter patted desperately on the great king's back, for he could not breathe in that bear-like embrace.

490

"Thank you, my king!" gasped the hunter, finally, when he was let down again. "Those words are kinder to me than to your own kin," said he.

"Oh, Ystrith may have the honour of knowing that it was her desperate search for me that broke my waking dream. In that you are much like one another. Both fools made wise by perseverant kindness," said the king.

"I have come to speak with you regarding another matter, my king," said Carbeth.

"Call me brother, please, so it ever was with our uncle the Forge-bear, and our father."

"Brother, then," said Carbeth hesitantly. "I would ask you that you speak with my dear friend, Loangilin. She, more than your sister and I, was gravely wounded in spirit by your ogreous misadventures."

"It has been on my mind lately, master hunter. I shall see to it at once," said the king.

"She is to be found on the wall, looking…" began Carbeth, trying to remember.

"North. I see her from here, my brother. I see her from here," said the king.

"Very well," said Carbeth, and his wife took his hand again. They departed then, leaving the king to ready himself. Then the king went also on his way, through the passage that was now no longer secret, leading to the courtyard in which stood the oak of skalds. Thence he went down the stair into the burg, where the rubble had already been cleared by the grons. Some halls had been erected, within which his people could now sleep

491

at night. It had been done in a single day by the quick hands of the grons.

He wound his way into the darker part of the city, below the northern shadow of Glimmer-mead's hill. Here some of the old buildings had re-mained, and for that, King Svæn thought it rather homely. He wound his way along the shadowy al-leys between the steep and snow-white shale roofs. Then he came to the stair of the northern city wall, and ascended, there to find the Lady Loangilin.

And small, but there upon the wall, the fairest maid, alone. Hers was to him the fairest and most regal form, that now than evermore before be-trayed the touch of tragedy. He looked on her, he could not move — could barely breathe. He looked on her, and saw that she was looking northward, to where he could hear the summons of a tower tall, a tower dark, with histories that his own bloodied hands had wrought, call on his name; the name of an ogre.

Finally, as though he spoke through cobwebs, not his beard, he hoarsely whispered on the wind: "Lady Loangilin?" The name felt foreign and so careful on his tongue, as though he might break it by his crude speech.

She turned then from her wondering, and for a moment their eyes met, hers high-borne, his those of a beggar. And then a thing more dreadful happened than Svæn had dared imagine: her eyes — they waxed with fear!

He fell to his knees, pressed his massive, hairy hands against the flagstones of the floor. "Please, do not fear me!" he whispered. "Do not fear me, I beg of thee, my lady!"

He durst not to look up at her, for he feared that she had gone, and in the pit of his innermost midst he knew that this is what she had done. For that is what women did: they ran. Men gave chase. That is how it had ever been. Men were hunters out for gamy meat. Was he not just the same? And for this he hated himself. He did not want to hunt. His time as an ogre had spilt blood enough over his rugged hands. How would he ever again whittle wood, without the product rising like a screaming face of victim up to him?

The winds still sung their cold winter melody, and he, this man so vast and powerful by name, by right, by rule, was crushed in memory by guilt for having been a fool. In his very heart, he hoped to turn just there to stone, and be looked on by all the generations that were still to come, as the fool bear king. The man that had forfeit all that he could have been, because he could no longer do what was demanded of a man. He could not let himself stand for himself, for he had seen the wicked cruelty of his own two hands.

But nothing happened for as long as he stayed like this, and when he was certain that she had run away, he dared raise his head.

And frighted with a gasp.

And small, but there upon the wall, the fairest maid, alone. She had sunken to sit on folded legs, staring with those black-and-golden eyes, like a wary cat that did not know whether he sought to help her or to exercise his violence.

He sat up also, then, upon his kneeling legs; and for a small eternity they stared simply into one another's eyes. Soft steel against hard gold. But, just as the gold would soften, a voice was heard against the outer wall.

"Is this not mountain stone, my spirit? Have I at last found the walling of a house?"

A moment longer, her eyes lingered in his, then she warily arose, and looked over the wall. There she gasped, her hand flying to her mouth. At this even the king arose, and he looked down to whom it was that she had seen there. A weirdness came upon the world then.

There stood a weathered man; he wore nothing more than tattered rags, his members bitten somewhat by the frost. He had a sprawling mane of mostly silver curls that covered all his face. It was a southerner.

"Is that the Master Gaba of the south?" cried the king from the wall.

The southerner frighted back a few steps, swinging his head wildly about. "It is I, it is I! Who speaks to me from heaven with such thunder?" asked the southerner.

"It is the king, King Svæn! What has the Ghoul King done with you, my friend? Where are your clothes, where is that leather cloak of yours?"

"I…" began the southerner, and faltered. "I am cold, my king!" cried he then, and his body was racked by the shivering of nearly giving up. He was so close now, and there were helping hands not far. "Have mercy on me, king!"

But King Svæn had already flung himself from
the wall into the snows below, some of his ogrish
spring seemed to have lingered in his step. At once
he wrapped the southerner in the furs that he had
broadly held over his own shoulders. Even his tunic, he now unfastened, and laid over the shivering
head of the southerner. Then he picked up the
weary man in his hairy limbs, and began to march
toward the nearest gate. He carried the southerner
all the way into the hall of kings, and up to where a
bath was warmed. Thereto were also brought the
mith-aumuinan, to tend his bitten limbs.

When Gaba was refreshed, and when he had
slept the long road somewhat from his battered
form, he was guided down to the firepits of the
Nornburg, where awaited him the friends of Authæn, to hear what had become of these two travellers after they had ascended the sheer mountains.

He was guided by his healers to a chair at the
head of the fire, seated at the right hand of the
king. He was clothed now richly by the tailors of
the Nornburg, and his mane had been bound into a
frizzy tail at the back of his head. Not far away sat
Loangilin, next to the blind hunter and the mute.

There were also Huthram chief, who was
without his knowledge now confirmed in this role,
and wonderful Wingilin. The gron, Grin, was there
as well, and about him stood the other gnomes that
he had summoned here to help. To the left of the
king sat his mayor with sharpened ears that he
might record all of that which the southerner now
told to them. The Forge-bear, who was friendlier
about his forge, had deigned to join as well, for he

had special softness for the son of his nephew, though he would never have admitted it.

For a long time, Gaba moved restlessly in his chair, as though he were seeking out some comfort that he could not find.

"He is dead then, Master Gaba?" asked Carbeth.

The southerner froze, then sighed, and sank into his chair, defeated. "He is dead."

Quiet mourning set into the faces of all that were gathered there.

"Worse than this, I do not understand his reasoning. How I have turned his words again and again in my mind, thinking that — hoping that — in them I might find solace," said Gaba.

"Noth can return him to life!" cried Loangilin, suddenly, the tears were streaming from her eyes. "All we need do is bring Authæn to a soul-stone!"

All looked at the southerner, not daring to hope unless he gave them leave.

"It was," began the ebon man, "about these soul-stones that his speaking went. I do not understand. Help me, please! This is a wound on my spirit. I cannot bear it! Help…"

"What did he say, Master Gaba? We shall partake in your wounds by hearing you. Such is our way," said Carbeth.

The southerner breathed deeply. Then he began to tell the story with a great calm: "We stood afore the dark throne of the King of Ghouls, behind him wrothe that Gruttin that bore him swift destruction into this very city. He (that is Authæn) had been speaking with that dour king, and had asked after the history of your people, only to be confirmed in the knowledge that he was not of the river-people. He was simply a drop of moonlight, given shape by the blood of the bear. This made of him a man like none that walked the earth before. Then the Ghoul King spoke of the soul-stones which you mention. One such was used to make a draug of the Ibex."

"One to make a draug of my brother," said King Svæn.

"But the King of Ghouls said something frightful then!" continued the southerner. "He said that all the shepherds of the north were bound in secret covenant to him, to a stone that was held glowing above his head, from which they drew their everlasting life by just such soul-stones!

"For a moment, he turned to me then, and he offered me just such a fate — the life as that which the Ibex had lived. I could not take it! That was all that I had come to put an end to. I seek to be redeemed, not to destroy all that I love and have betrayed!

"But then I heard the splashing of a heavy thing in water, and I turned to see, and Authæn — oh, Authæn! Why did you do this so hastily? Was there no better way? If life spent wisely is to abide in love, then do so wisely! Was this not the way of folly?"

The southerner fell from his chair onto his knees, raging with despair at the ceiling which he could not see. Then, tired, he slumped again into himself, sighing out despondency.

"What had he done, Master Gaba?" asked Wingilin with a quivering voice.

"He had cut into his hand. Was it not as Noth had prophesied?" said Gaba. "He had hewn therein a word of dwarfish runes; just as Grin had shown us to make moonstones with. But these were not the runes for moon."

"Where did he learn more of their words, south-man? I did not teach him!" cried Grin suddenly horrified.

"We found more words there, in their gateway," explained the southerner. "The guards who had awaited us showed him the meaning of these runes. How went it now again. It was this morning still like the mint of a coin against my brain. Ah yes, this is what stood above the gate that led into the deeps beyond: *Nifla Izdin Vevon*. Swallowed is the sun by stone."

"It cannot be!" cried Grin. "It could not have killed him, he was but a man! How could he have channelled the light of the sun?"

There was a stunned quiet around the fire, for not everyone had followed through to where the gron had led in thought.

"Then," said the Forge-bear slowly, and with feeling, "the stone may have swallowed the sun, but it was a bite too big?"

"Yes," sighed the southerner. He found his way back into his chair. "Authæn had written the dwarfish name of the sun on his palm with the blade of the dagger that had slain his foster-father. And so, for a short and glorious moment, he himself became the sun. In that light I saw all things laid bare unto the bone, and that was the last of which I saw. Or perhaps I saw aught else; I know not whether it was a dream or waking truth.

"It must have been a dream: I saw a figure, drawn together of light, stand in the place where Authæn had turned to light. It was no blinding light, either, but a soft, clean light; a light that shone no more than it must, to reveal this figure. And then the figure grew brighter, broader, bigger somehow! It grew into a great tree, that carried on growing, until it claimed all the world with its roots, and grasped all of heaven with its branches.

"Then I felt warm of a sudden. I felt as though the closest friend had laid a mantle over my shoulders, and had said to me that all was well, and that I needed not fear. It seemed as though the great tree were looking at me then with seven eyes, and in a frightening moment, I woke up to the bleak witness of blindness!"

"A dream, then," muttered Huthram, nodding to himself. "I thought I saw a stranger cloud than any I had ever seen above the mountains on the day of Sun's-ear."

"You still showed it to us, my home," said Wingilin, laying her tear-streaked head onto his shoulder.

Loangilin arose, and left the hall. It was all too much for her to bear. When all had followed her out with their eyes, and to the surprise of them all, their king suddenly leapt up and ran after her.

Chapter Eight-and-Thirty
The Return to the End

In the second month after Smith's-wend, the river-people and the troops of Glimwæth that had decided to venture to the Vale of Thrones, began the march to Urmingwey. From that haven on Murmur-mere, they would request longboats to fare them far across the sea, to where the tall houses of the forsaken city dressed themselves in mist by morning.

They marched horseless, for too many of the livestock that had been within the city wall had been slain by the trundling of the mole-trolls, and many of their otherwise belongings had been ruined, so that they had only what rations the king could spare them in his generosity. Most of their wagons had also been destroyed; those that remained having been traded to the king for more food and clothing.

At the head of their company marched Huthram. Alongside him strode the golden-haired Lion Pen-tooth, who had gone forth both as scrivener to record this history, as well as in the role of king's mayor, so that the king could stay behind in Glimwæth to manage affairs there. The merchants, Jithron and Qeremun, had also come along, seeking adventure and profits — or neither of the two, if they were not to be found in the Vale of Thrones. In truth, they had grown fond of the river-people, and desired to see from what place their people had long ago sprung.

"I am certain that the king wishes dearly that he could accompany you, Huthram chief," said the Lion Pen-tooth on the day in which they finally stood looking over the gentle fields that fell down to where wooden Urmingwey stood stilted on the muttering waters.

Huthram looked a question at the scrivener, and saw then that the Lion Pen-tooth was smiling, looking to where Loangilin was playing a game of rhymes with some children.

"Ah," said the new-chosen chieftain of Thænim, smiling likewise. "How is her mood to-wards him, though, I wonder?"

"I think the image of the ogre will take a long time to defeat. But if the persistence of his sister has found roots in him at very last, then perhaps he shall be the one to help her overcome it," said the scrivener.

"It would make a brighter tomorrow for today," muttered Huthram, looking to where his wife was speaking with the old wives of their village.

"It would bother the earls, I am certain. She is no daughter of Imnir," said the Lion.

The chieftain frowned at him. "Neither was your own mother, scrivener."

"Quite," said the scrivener. "And for it I have had to move mountains. It is the way of these snowmen, Huthram. They are just as tribal as your people, according to their own manner. It is a way in which they think to attain safety for themselves. Shall we be so rude and tear the bindings from their eyes? As the mayor, I certainly could not ad-vise it. Are we so different in the end?"

501

"Still, after the king of Imnir's children has been so long an ogre, they should be glad that their queen would be a woman at all," said Huthram.

"After so long a time with a bear in place of a queen, they should be," said the Lion, nodding. "We shall see how the web is woven in time. For now, our course takes us to eastern mountain vales, and to high houses bearing thrones of ancient men."

The earl of Urmingwey was glad to do as the king had bidden, seeking to rebind his friendship with the ogre who had returned to the realms of men. The river-people were taken in with an unexpected timidity on the part of the Urminwegians, who had not expected them to win their war against the King of Ghouls. Whilst they let themselves be cared for in the houses on the water, Huthram and the Lion Pen-tooth were called to the longhouse of the earl.

"I did not fight at Glimwæth for his father," said the earl when they stood before him in his hall. He sat on a stool beside the firepit, sombre of mood, and contemplative in tone. "And from what your runners have reported, and then from what my own have seen, it was a mistake for me not to trust in that old bear. I am sorry that he is gone; but here is to a friendship with his son, who is a man just like his blacksmith uncle, I have heard tell. Strong and true, they say he is. If it is so, then he shall be a force to reckon with, and I for one would reckon him to my side."

And so it came to pass that, under the leadership of Huthram, successor to the Shepherd of Thænim — the high-held Authæn, who had given all he was to offer them this freedom — a people were led into the land whence their fathers had long ago been cast out. It was in this land, between mountain and water, that there now dwelt a people that were of cursed blood.

To be certain all people, when they are burdened by the mistakes of their forefathers, regard themselves cursed; but these were burdened, not merely by the mistakes of their forefathers, but with their own nature. It was because of their nature that they had been driven out of the lands of their forebears, because they were the children of a bitter union: that of light and dust. They had been called by most "the river-people", because they would settle for a time alongside a river, where the ground was good, and then they would move, when the time came, to another part of the river. But those days had passed. Now they were called by most the "dark elves", and they dwelt in a city slowly rebuilding itself in the shadow of the mountains in the middle of the world.

As word of this people and this city spread, many more of their kin from all clans in the eastern steppe-lands, journeyed to join the rebuilding of the fallen home of their fathers, there to establish a long-sought permanence. It was through these newcomers to the city that word reached Huthram and his folk of the shepherds. They had all pilgrimed to the Mother-henge before Sun's-ear, came the tiding. The students of the henges had all

503

been sent back to their villages and told to hold open their ears for a voice that called them over the waters. The voice had called, and they had come; but the fate of the shepherds, none had yet dared venture to find out.

For a time, Gaba had also dwelt in the Vale of Thrones. He and Carbeth becoming fast friends in their shared blindness. They spoke much to one another, mostly about Authæn, their lost friend. Ystrith looked after them well, having cultured a garden of herbs, as well as having taken to the working of sourdough that she now remembered her mother long-lost to have baked so flavourfully.

So the home of Carbeth and Ystrith became a public kitchen very soon, and it was not the least populated house in the Vale of Thrones, nor the quietest. The many wagging tongues of friends and travellers wagged more than enough here to make up for her tonguelessness; though at her appearing, a kind of hush would fall — a hush of awe — for she had lost that boyish churlishness that once had dominated all her manner. Now she was regal with sobriety. Her eyes shone softly with the wisdom that needs no tongue to speak into the heart.

After many a happy memory in this city of restoration, Gaba decided that the time for his return to his own city of Manutuz had come. He was sent off with some of the *mith-aumuinan*. Jithron and Qeremun also joined him, having heard that the south sought to join in with the commerce of the north.

For many a year after that, news regarding whether he had been taken up again or not was scarce in the Vale of Thrones. Then, one day, the merchants landed on the docks of the city again, and entering the house of Huthram, they brought tidings that Gaba had indeed been taken up into the house of the queen, where he now played music for her at court, singing songs of a land of lights and shadows of things that are and want to be.

***

The dark timbers of the house cracked in the cool of morning. It was the day of Smith's-wend, and the sun had just arisen from where it would now weathered wend its way back north. In the light of a circular window, set in the gable of a steeply roofed house, there stood a colourless man. A weirdness settled over all that scene.

It was a strange place for a house to sprout — if that is what houses did — for it stood aface of a tall, dark spire. As the man waited there, he studied that tower's surface.

"Ah, dear Mathydras. How you were the least-known of the gentle souls that walked these wooded wolds," sighed he. "If only Lyn had come to you again. If only you had known how to entice her. Instead you brought red wrath down on your head, in all the shapes of cruelty that could have been thought up. But be at peace, dear Mathydras. Your son will do a thing now, that never you could have guessed when you built this tower on the stone to which you had sold your spirit. Weirdest of the weirds, they shall call him, and also never a weird. He was far more fateful."

505

The sun climbed higher along the southern branches of Day. When it had reached the mark of the third hour after noon, a flash that dimmed the world a moment went up in the mountains to the west. Then a cloud began to rise there; the shape of which was not like any cloud should ever be. Likewise, a flash suddenly erupted within the depths of the tower, shattering all of its leaden-glass windows, and causing its dark form to tremble ominously with veiled power.

The man still stood and waited, smiling sadly up at the cloud in the berg, when a little figure emerged yawning from the open door of the tower. She stretched her little limbs, rubbed her eyes, and then looked blearily at the colourless figure who seemed so serene to her then.

"Blueberry-man!" she cried happily, and ran to slam an embrace into his legs.

"Dear Folgnuin," chuckled Noth, and she began by habit to lead him down into his own house excitedly. "I have told you, they are grapes, not berries. I have some more grapes inside, if you are hungry, but you seem to know that."

"You can grow them on your table, Uncle Noth! Of course there are more!" she said, a little concerned about his memory.

"Yes, of course, I know that. I was just testing you. You have been sleeping quite some time, if you don't know. Let me see your hands a moment, my girl. Ah! You have deft fingers. I heard a bird sing about how you were watching and helping the brave *mith-aumuinan*! How clever. Would you want to learn how to tend a garden, dear Folgnuin?

It is much the same as the work of the healers, you know; Only, there is less blood and more thankfulness."

"The last pages are for you."

Dear Po,

thank you for taking the time to read my book! I hope it has brought you some value and fed you some thought that has been more enriching than bewildering.

May the Peace of
the annointed
King
find you!

Philip 2021

508

Printed by Amazon Italia Logistica S.r.l.
Torrazza Piemonte (TO), Italy

26291952R00295